Marduk's Tablet

Marduk's Tablet

What If the
Legend Is True?

T. L. HIGLEY

BARBOUR
PUBLISHING

Published in association with the literary agency of Janet Kobobel Grant, Books & Such, 4788 Carissa Ave., Santa Rosa, CA 94095.

Published by Barbour Publishing, Inc., P.O. Box 719, Uhrichsville, Ohio 44683, www.barbourbooks.com

Our mission is to publish and distribute inspirational products offering exceptional value and biblical encouragement to the masses.

Member of the
Evangelical Christian
Publishers Association

Printed in the United States of America.
5 4 3 2 1

To Ron,
greatest resource,
dearest treasure

Acknowledgments

My heartfelt thanks to all those who guided, encouraged, and challenged me through this project, and to those whose input improved it greatly.

Thanks to Professor Ed Hardesty at Philadelphia Biblical University for an up-close look into biblical archaeology, and to Randy Ingermanson, for always being available from the book's inception with great advice. Thanks to my first readers—Barb and Amy Frizzell, Michelle King, Karen DeVost, Bette Jo Smith, and Ron Higley, for all the great insights and suggestions; to Jeff Gerke, my hardworking editor, for continuing to push me to the next level; to my agent, Janet Kobobel Grant, for opening up new opportunities and guiding me through them.

Thanks to the Kings and the Taylors for encouragement and brainstorming. There's no lobster, but there is a crane!

Thank you, Rachel, Sarah, and Jacob, for giving me time and space to write and for always cheering me on through the process.

Ron, once again this book would not have happened without you. From start to finish you encouraged, advised, supported, and loved me. This book is another joint project!

Acknowledgments

My heartfelt thanks to all those who guided, encouraged, and challenged me through this project, and to those whose input improved it greatly.

Thanks to Professor Ed Hardesty at Philadelphia Biblical University for an up-close look into biblical archaeology, and to Randy Ingermanson, for always being available from the book's inception with great advice. Thanks to my first readers—Barb and Amy Frizzell, Michelle King, Karen DeVost, Bette Jo Smith, and Ron Higley, for all the great insights and suggestions; to Jeff Gerke, my hardworking editor, for continuing to push me to the next level; to my agent, Janet Kobobel Grant, for opening up new opportunities and guiding me through them.

Thanks to the Kings and the Taylors for encouragement and brainstorming. There's no lobster, but there is a crane!

Thank you, Rachel, Sarah, and Jacob, for giving me time and space to write and for always cheering me on through the process.

Ron, once again this book would not have happened without you. From start to finish you encouraged, advised, supported, and loved me. This book is another joint project!

Chapter 1

Emilie's study carrel was shrouded in the back corner of the university library, like a tiny tomb buried far from civilization. Walled in on three sides, Emilie hunched over her laptop with her back to the stacks. She stopped typing and checked her watch once more.

Twelve minutes. Her fingers sprinted over the keyboard. Twelve minutes to finish this paper, proofread, print, and get to her 8 P.M. class, or yet another assignment would be late.

She paused in her typing to pick up the glazed bowl from the desk in front of her. For the hundredth time in the past hour, she held the bowl to her body as she peered over her shoulder.

Someone's here. I can feel it.

Emilie hadn't relaxed since Dr. Horobin had pulled the ritual washing bowl from its glass case in the university museum three hours ago. It was a huge favor, letting his research assistant turn the thing around in her own hands as she finished the paper she was writing about it. There were people who would do anything to acquire this piece. If something happened to it, she'd never forgive herself. Or be forgiven.

9

She skimmed her fingers around the Akkadian writing on the rim. Over two thousand years ago, someone had lettered these symbols onto the bowl before sending it to a Babylonian temple for a god's purification ceremony. *The words connect me to him.* She felt part of a great, cosmic surge of humanity, directing its own destiny through the ages, with the words her link to an ancient stranger.

Emilie set the bowl in front of her computer and pounded out the concluding paragraph. As she scrolled to the top of the document to proof it, the floor creaked behind her.

"Who's there?" She craned her neck to sweep a glance behind her. No answer. She shivered against the dry chill of the library.

Only one other person knew she was here with the bowl, and Emilie was beginning to regret telling him. She shouldn't have trusted Charles. *I know better than to let anybody get close enough to scam me.*

The quick read-through of her paper revealed her as a babbling idiot. No time for improvement. She still needed to print it.

As she clicked on the Save icon, the compressed silence of the library shifted. Emilie sensed breathing a few feet away.

She jerked her head around. No one. Still, she had heard something. Confined by shelves 120.2 to 146.7, she could see little except the aisle tunneling away from her desk. The tight space closed in on her, its weight heavy on her chest.

She clicked her laptop shut and slipped it into her carrying case. She nestled the bowl in the bag's outer pocket, then hitched the strap over her left shoulder.

The stairwell door beside her granted a quick escape. She would trek down to the bottom floor, exit onto the street, and get the bowl back to the museum. She'd be a little late for class, but it was better than carting this thing around all evening.

Halfway down the second set of steps, she heard the door above her swish open again. She froze, her right foot hanging in midair above the next step. Two footfalls drifted down to her, then silence. No, not silence. The heavy breathing. Her fingers tight-ened around the metal handrail. She lowered her right foot as though the next step might be a landmine.

The footsteps above pounded downward. Feeling like the unpopular girl in a horror flick, murdered in the second scene, Emilie stumbled down to the next platform, her computer case banging against her hip. The footsteps echoed her own.

She couldn't lose the bowl. Where should she go? Could she find a security guard?

The blood beat a rhythm in her head as she fled down the last set of steps and shoved through the street exit door. The cold city night slammed against her. She regretted not detouring onto the bottom floor of the library. Now she was alone in the street.

Emilie hunted for a way to get out of sight. Across the street, a city park offered shrubs and statuary. Should she take her chances there? She'd eaten lunch there many times. In the dark, the stone figures morphed into the monstrous nighttime shadows on her childhood walls.

The door handle pushed into the small of her back, reminding her that her pursuer would be more dangerous than a hallucination.

A taxi cruised past. Emilie watched in fascination as the man and woman inside laughed, heads together, in the lighted backseat.

Which way? C'mon, Em. Make a decision! A subway entrance gaped at her from halfway down the street, inviting her to descend.

She ran to the entrance and took the steps two at a time down to the black-and-white-tiled slime of the underground tunnel. The tracks and the platforms were deserted at this hour. A train's dis-appearing lights warned that she would be alone for awhile.

Except for muggers. Emilie looked away from a shabby man leaning against a wall, looking like he could eat her for dinner. *Probably homeless. And harmless. Don't freak out.*

She couldn't stand there on the platform waiting for her pursuer, so she slid down the wall until she reached an alcove and tucked herself into it, breathing through her mouth and concentrating on the sounds around her. A fluorescent tube above her flickered and buzzed.

Who would chase her? It had to be someone after the bowl. She should have known Charles was too good to be true. Then again, at thirty-one, she had given up scrutinizing every guy who seemed to like her. Her stupidity had endangered the artifact and possibly her life. Once again, letting a man gain her trust had proved to be a fatal mistake.

He's still following. Heavy shoes fell on the steps she'd come down, pausing at the bottom. Emilie held her breath.

The shoes rasped against the concrete floor, coming closer.

Emilie closed her eyes in terror, her thoughts oddly focused on how long it would take someone to discover her body.

And then the footsteps receded. She waited as she heard him ascend the steps and let out her breath in inches.

An instant later, the ragged man from the platform rounded her corner. He slid across the space between them until she felt as though he had pinned her to the wall.

"Hello, little lady." His reeking breath issued from a broken-toothed smile.

Emilie leaned back, trying to press herself through the wall behind her. Beyond her alcove, she heard the scraping footsteps pause on the steps, then return in double-time.

Don't scream. Don't scream! You'll never graduate if he steals the bowl.

Fear blazed out from the center of her body to her fingertips. The man in front of her still grinned. She held her computer bag in front of her, sending out a vague prayer that the bowl wouldn't be damaged by using it as a shield. Or could she use her bag as a club? She stiffened her grip and prepared to slug him.

"Ms. Nazzaro?"

Emilie's heart skipped at the sound of her name. The decaying man in front of her turned toward the sound, too. She leaned around him, searching for a familiar face.

"Ms. Nazzaro, are you okay here?"

A boy, maybe eighteen or nineteen, in a dress shirt and khakis, stood on the platform.

Harmless-Homeless Man moved away, disappearing down the tunnel.

Emilie's shoulders dropped, tension seeping out through every pore of her body. "I'm sorry," she said, lowering her bag to her hip. "Do I know you?"

The boy blushed. "I'm in Dr. Horobin's Cultural Anthropology class."

"Of course." Emilie tried to cover. As his research assistant, she sometimes sat in on Dr. Horobin's undergrad classes, but the faces had never distinguished themselves in her mind.

"I–I wanted to ask you a question," he said.

"Were you following me?" Emilie asked. "From the library?"

He picked at some imaginary lint on his shirt. "I'm sorry. I didn't want to disturb you, but when I saw you leave—"

"What can I do for you?" Emilie wished he'd mentioned his name.

"I was wondering if, maybe, when you were free, we could get some coffee or something."

Emilie waited, unsure if this was the actual question. Apparently, it was. A date? She'd run down three flights of stairs and through the subway to get away from a kid with a crush? She was almost old enough to be this kid's—older sister.

She smiled. "That's sweet of you. I appreciate it. But I'm afraid it wouldn't be appropriate, you know?"

He dropped his head. "Yeah, I guess you're right."

"But I'm glad you were here," Emilie added, turning toward the stairs. "I think you may have saved me from some trouble back there."

He brightened. "Glad to help."

They walked together up the stairs, into the night air. Emilie stopped and took a deep breath to fight off the oppressive closeness of the subway.

Her companion paused beside her. "Can I walk you somewhere?"

"DuWalt."

Emilie's would-be suitor left her at the door to the DuWalt Building, and she stood for a moment inside the door, undecided. She hadn't printed her paper to turn in, and she was already late for class. And she hadn't returned the bowl. Which first?

She'd go to class, explain to the prof, and hope for the best.

The door was closed when she reached the classroom. As she reached for the doorknob, a fleshy hand closed around hers.

"Emilie Nazzaro?"

No way, not again. Do I have a bull's-eye painted on me tonight? Emilie looked up into an expansive brow hanging over a jaw heavy with teeth. *I think I found the Missing Link.* She pulled her hand away. "I'm sorry, I need to get to class. Can it wait?"

"You need to come with me."

"If this is about that project for Dr.—" She reached for the door again, but a paw clamped around her upper arm. "Excuse me," she said, twisting away and trying to push past him. She might as well have rammed a wall.

"It's important, Ms. Nazzaro. It's about your father."

Emilie drew back as though slapped. "What do you know about my father?"

Cro-Magnon Man said nothing.

Emilie watched his eyes, trying to read him. "I have a class, a paper due."

"Miss it."

She tried to edge around him again. Could she outrun him? Behind him, the hall was empty.

"Can I at least tell the professor I need to leave?" She grabbed at the doorknob.

"No need." His fingers fastened around her wrist and pried her hand from the knob. He dragged her several steps down the hall, then stopped and twitched his head like an animal surveying the terrain. Emilie peered over her shoulder through the window to the classroom, at the rows of younger graduate students who were always punctual, and wished that for once she'd been on time.

▲ ▲ ▲

The first stars of the night glittered in the Turkish sky above Pergamum. Jack flattened himself against the splinters of a doorway on the village's cobbled street. The adrenaline rush had kicked in a half hour ago, when he had followed Layna Sardos from the café to the crumbling rowhouse where she had disappeared, fifty yards from where he now stood.

Jack was certain Layna hadn't seen him follow, even though the two had finished a bottle of wine together only moments before they left. She had kissed him good-bye and called him "Mr. Cal-e-mon," her slurred Greek accent butchering "Cameron," the name Jack had chosen as this week's identity.

Jack's legs were cramping, but he didn't dare shift positions. How long until Layna and the others would leave the house? He could almost feel the weight of the statue in his hands. Only a little longer and it would be his.

The clatter of cart wheels on cobblestone reached him from the bottom of the street. An aging farmer in the traditional Turkish vest shuffled past, bearing his unpurchased olives home from the market. *"İyi akşamlar,"* the man said as he passed, nodding his gray head in Jack's direction.

Jack returned the nod. *"İyi akşamlar."* Good evening. *And keep walking, old man.*

In the yellow stone wall of the rowhouse Jack watched, a blue door opened. Laughter floated down the street, past the old man's tumbledown cart, to where Jack stood in the shadows.

The cart's wheels scraped the street again. Jack watched as Layna tossed her unveiled black hair over her shoulder and turned toward the old man. Jack slowed his breathing and froze, pushing further into the dark. He would wait for his moment.

Layna turned away from the cart of olives and continued up the street. She and her fat companion would be gone several hours, Jack knew. Long enough to drink another bottle of Ankara wine from local Turkish vineyards. Layna's laughter hadn't fooled him. He knew she looked for happiness in the bottom of a bottle.

Jack had planned his assault well, knowing that only one person remained in the house. A negligible defense for such a treasure.

Ahead, Layna and her escort turned a corner and disappeared from sight. Jack waited for several minutes, to be certain.

This is life, Jack thought, his eyes on the blue door and his heart pounding like a chisel on stone. *This is life at its best.* He had only to finish this job, bring the statue to Vitelli, and he would be lounging on the beaches in the south of France by the end of the week.

His time had come. Jack jogged across the street and turned his back to the row of homes. His careful slide to the blue door took only a minute. When he stood beside it, Jack inhaled the night air and reached for the knob. It turned in his hand. Another mistake by these would-be professionals.

Jack edged the door inward, and the hinges protested. He waited, but from inside he could hear the gentle snoring of a man already deep into his wine. *Fools.*

The interior of the village home was dark. He extended his hands to check for obstacles. Nothing. He closed the door behind him.

The snoring stopped.

Jack waited. The smell of tobacco and coffee loitered in the air. And something else. Layna's perfume. Strong. Too strong.

Years of experience screamed at him to back up, get out. *Something's not right.*

A match flared. An oil lamp faltered, then blazed.

"Men," Layna said, "meet Jack Cameron."

Two goons stared at him like stone bulls at a palace entrance. The fat one from the street he knew. The other, younger, Jack had never seen.

Who's the fool now?

Jack reached behind him for the door. The younger man anticipated him. He cracked a fist against Jack's forearm. Jack swung his left fist at the man's face. The contact knocked the man backward. Jack delivered a sharp kick to his chest. The man staggered back and fell to the floor. Layna screamed.

The fat man charged at Jack. He yanked open the door and raced into the street, empty-handed.

He ran toward the Temple of Aesculapius. It was his best chance to escape.

Down the main street, a quick turn to the left. Jack could feel his pursuers behind him. He flew past the recent additions of parking lot and ticket office, now closed. The colonnaded street ended in the ruined stone courtyard. At the far side of the courtyard, a stairway led to a large square.

Jack hurtled across the courtyard, up the steps, and into the square. A dozen columns, pools, and shrines provided ample places to hide.

Were all three of them following him? Did they leave the statue unguarded? He searched the square for the best refuge. *I've got to get back to that house somehow.* He didn't want to contemplate his fate if he returned to Vitelli without the statue.

Jack ran to the stairway entrance to the underground tunnel. The tunnel shot under the Asclepium, to the temple of Telephus, the previous god who had been buried when Aesculapius came to town. From that temple, Jack could head up to the surface and retrace his steps to the village.

He took the tunnel slowly, careful that his footsteps wouldn't echo up to the square. The ruins of this temple to the god of healing had started all this, when south stoa excavations had unearthed the golden cult image of the god. Jack hoped he had buried himself far enough underground now. His hand slid against the wall as he tunneled through the blackness. Two millennia of dust filtered through his fingers.

Slower, Jack. Slower. His feet scraped gravel and stone. Dust filled his throat. He clenched his teeth. *Don't cough.*

Moonlight trickled into the tunnel ahead. Jack trotted, anxious for fresh air.

He reached the paved outer road that circled the temple, bypassing the arched openings into the interior. He was now on the south side of the temple of Aesculapius. His three pursuers would be on the north side, where he had led them in.

You've done it again, Jack, old boy. He circled the outer Pantheon-like wall of the temple. He would run back down the same street where he had entered. Maybe he'd get lucky and the statue would still be in the house.

He was halfway to the street when a figure vaulted from the shadows. In the sliver of time before impact, Jack saw his opponent, outlined against white stone. Then the stars above him exploded in his head.

Chapter 2

The university's visitor parking lot huddled at the outskirts of campus parking. Emilie had plenty of time to ask herself what Cro-Magnon Man could possibly want with her before they got near the dark sedan. And what could he know about her father? She dug her heels in when her escort unlocked the passenger door and opened it for her. This was crazy.

"Get in," he said.

"No way. Where do you think you're going to take me?"

In response, he shoved her into the car and slammed the door.

She contemplated jumping out again, but he could probably outrun her in five seconds. Emilie had time to slide her bag onto the floor before he was in the car beside her. *Does he know I have the bowl?* Emilie tried a bluff. "If I'm not in class, someone will know—"

He started the car and backed out. "Ms. Nazzaro, you're not in danger. My employer wants to talk to you. He sent me to get you."

Emilie's fingers tightened around the door handle, just in case. "What employer?"

Her driver watched the road, barreling through a stop sign at the edge of the parking lot as though it were invisible. "Thomas Fitzwater."

Emilie sat back in her seat, a combination of relief, curiosity, and annoyance fighting for top spot in her emotions. *Fitzwater.* How many years since she had heard that name? Ten? Fifteen? But why contact her now? What could he tell her about her father? And why send a psycho to storm the campus and grab her like she were part of a bad movie?

Her driver didn't offer conversation during the forty-five-minute ride, and she didn't beg. She'd ask Fitzwater her questions. She tried not to think about how the missed class might affect her grade. Only one week remained of the spring semester. A few summer courses, and she'd be finished with her M.A. in Middle Eastern Studies. All she needed was to pass the comprehensive exam that would qualify her for the Ph.D. program, and she'd be one step away from realizing her goal. *A few years behind but no later than anything else in my life.*

When they pulled up to a wrought-iron gate, distant memories sparked. A swimming pool. Black-tied waiters serving drinks to her parents poolside. The gate swung open to reveal the circular drive in front of a grand estate, and Emilie felt a tiny thrill, reminiscent of childhood. Yellow light gleamed from dozens of windows like firelight flickering in a medieval castle. Her driver parked the car in front of the steps and led her into the house.

In the spacious foyer, more than a dozen pottery pieces and bronze statues rested on tables or in corners. Emilie touched a bronze bull on the hall table beside the door. *A reproduction. Good.* A butler-type approached, and she dropped her hand to her side.

"Mr. Fitzwater is expecting you. Follow me, miss."

Emilie left Cro-Magnon Man behind and followed the butler across the entry hall and up a winding staircase. Her feet sank into the red-carpeted steps, and another fragment of childhood memory surged and then melted away.

Emilie hadn't realized what she'd been expecting until the butler swung open a door to reveal a shriveled man behind a desk. Could this be Thomas Fitzwater? Had he always been so small?

Fitzwater stood. "Ah, Ms. Nazzaro. Come in, please. Sit, sit."

Emilie took three tentative steps into a massive study, lit only by a half dozen candles flickering around the room. Music played softly—some kind of flute warbling notes in no particular melody—and the sweet odor of incense hung in the air.

Fitzwater dismissed the butler. "Look at you, little Emilie. I'd not have known you." He tilted his head back and forth as if to inspect her from every angle. "Pretty, I think. Though I've never cared for the long, straight hair hanging about the face like that." He pulled on his bottom lip and nodded, as though deciding whether to purchase the collectible in spite of its flaws. "Still, attractive."

Emilie managed a smile at the underwhelming compliment.

"A bit too much of your father around the mouth, perhaps."

"Mr. Fitzwater, I don't appreciate being forced from my classes like this."

He dropped to his chair. "You're wondering about my little game. Cloak-and-dagger—very mysterious, no?" He grinned, revealing still-perfect teeth. "Please, sit down."

Emilie felt as though she floated through the murky room to a chair in front of the desk. "I'm not a child any longer, Mr. Fitzwater. Your—employee—said this was about my father?"

Fitzwater folded his leathery hands and placed them on the desk blotter. "Yes, yes. Quite right. About your father. Well, of a sort, I suppose. But then I had to get you here, didn't I?"

Emilie bristled. "Why am I here?"

"Yes, you're curious. I can see that. Right to it, then." He grabbed a remote control from his desk and pointed it to the flat-panel TV mounted behind him. An image burst onto the screen, and Emilie couldn't stifle her quick intake of breath.

"You recognize it?" Fitzwater nodded, smiling.

Emilie felt the air around her grow heavy and warm. "It's been years."

"But you remember, don't you, little Emilie?"

She remembered. The clay tablet's image was seared onto her brain forever. The tablet that had killed her father.

▲ ▲ ▲

The sparks behind Jack's eyelids sputtered and faded. He forced open his eyes.

"He's back."

Layna's voice bounced around inside his brain. He put a hand to his throbbing forehead. *Stupid, stupid, stupid Jack.* A quick glance told him all he needed to know. He lay on the floor in the house with the blue door, all three of his targets watching him. He sat up, wincing at the rockslide in his head.

Layna leaned over him. "So now it is my turn to ask questions." She spoke in English, though her Greek accent lay heavily on it.

The fat man laughed. "Is that all you will do, little Layna?"

"Shut up, Ozko." Layna dragged a chair until it scraped Jack's leg, then hiked up her long skirt and straddled the chair. "For whom are you working?"

Jack fumed at the cute way her lips pouted when she spoke. He had been an idiot for those lips. "Who do you work for?"

Layna leaned in and traced the scar along his jawline. "Do not make this difficult."

Jack pulled away, laughing. "That won't work anymore, my dear."

Layna put a hand on her hip. "My handsome Jack. So charming yesterday." She swung a leg over the chair and stood. "So hostile today."

"Must be having a bad day," Jack said.

She smiled down at him. "You were not honest with me, Mr. Cameron. All that sweet talk, the gifts, the wine."

Jack rubbed the back of his head. "At least I didn't clobber you."

Her smile faded. "Do you think you are better than we? You also would do anything to get the statue. Lie, steal, cheat." She tossed her hair and turned away. "You are no better than we."

Jack shrugged.

Ozko crossed the room. His heavy beard parted into a thick-lipped grimace, revealing several missing teeth. "Enough," he said. "Tell us who hired you to steal the statue."

Jack folded his arms.

Ozko nodded to the younger man. "Yazil."

Yazil crossed the room in one stride and backhanded Jack's face, slamming him shoulder-first into the floor.

Layna returned to lay a hand on Jack's arm as he stood. "He must be German. That blond hair." She squeezed Jack's upper arm. "And he is big."

Ozko nodded. "German, ja?"

"Ja," Jack said, nodding. *Whatever.*

Ozko smacked his hands together. "I knew it. That German pig has been sending fools to ambush us for months." He laughed. "He will not be so bold when he sees what we can do." Another nod to Yazil, who pulled out a small, jet-handled blade.

Ozko circled behind Jack, grabbed a handful of hair, and yanked his head backward. "Shall we give you another scar to match?" he asked, his face inches away from Jack's.

I don't think so, buddy.

Jack twisted in Ozko's grasp until he faced his opponent. He pulled his head back several inches, then jerked it forward. His forehead slammed into Ozko's. The man's grip released. Jack finished him with a right cut to the jaw.

Yazil would not be so easy. The two squared off. Jack kept his eyes on the blade. He lunged, going for the wrist. Yazil pulled back. Jack got his fingers around Yazil's arm and twisted. He ducked under Yazil's swinging free arm, his back to Yazil's chest. The younger man's fingers slackened around the knife handle. It clattered across the floor into the shadows.

Yazil jammed his arm against Jack's windpipe. He couldn't get a breath. He released the wrist and pulled away from Yazil and turned. Head lowered, he hammered Yazil's chest.

With an oomph, Yazil smacked into a table. The oil lamp teetered, then fell. Oil flooded across the table and poured over the edge. The flame followed.

The burning table distracted Jack's attention, and Yazil tried to drive a fist into Jack's stomach. Jack twisted away. Yazil stumbled. Jack clasped his fists and smashed them into the back of Yazil's neck. He fell without a word and lay still.

Where was Layna? The floor caught fire. The room was filling with smoke. Had she gone out the back? The flames blocked the back of the room. Wherever she was, did she have that knife?

There she is. Why was she on the floor? Had the smoke taken her out already? Or did one of them hit her without realizing it? Either way, she was no danger to him. He had to find the statue.

The room was dark in spite of the flames. The fire spread in all directions. Jack scanned the room, but it was already filling with smoke. *I've gotta get out.*

He opened the door. The rush of oxygen mushroomed the fire.

Get Layna. Jack groused at his inner voice, but complied. He ran back, wrapped his hands around Layna's upper arms, and dragged her into the street.

He left her across the street on the cobbled walkway, then ran to the next rowhouse beside the blue door.

"*Yangin!*" He pounded on the first door, then ran to another. "*Yangin!* Fire!"

As the first doors opened, Jack sprinted down the street into the darkness.

Two hours later Jack pounded on another door, this one in the Hotel Oba in İzmir, seventy miles south of Pergamum.

The door flew inward. A beefy hand grabbed his wrist and dragged him in. "You got it?"

Jack looked down into George's pasty complexion and exhaled. "I ran into some problems."

The other man shook his head, heavy jowls quivering. "Vitelli's called three times. You'd better call him."

Jack sighed. "He's not going to like what I have to say." He crossed to the phone and dialed the call. The connection was grainy, but sufficient.

"Jack?" Vitelli said. "What've we got?"

"I'm sorry, sir. There was some difficulty. I didn't get it."

A long silence followed, broken by Vitelli's cigar-smoke cough. "Where is it?"

"I'm not sure. It may have been in a burning house."

Vitelli swore. Jack cringed, waiting for more.

"Not good, Jack. Not good. I was counting on getting that statue."

Jack stared through the window at the night sky of İzmir. After tonight, he was supposed to head for the south of France. Something told him that wasn't going to happen.

"Jack?"

"Yes, sir?"

"Get yourself together. I've got a new job for you."

Jack nodded. A new job was better than what he had feared.

"But, Jack," Vitelli's voice lowered to a mutter, "no more failures. If you fail me again. . ."

Jack chose to ignore the threat. "Where am I going, sir?"

"Israel."

Emilie searched the onscreen image of the tablet for a long moment. The memory of it haunted her, though she hadn't seen it since childhood. The clay tablet was the size of a man's two palms and covered with Babylonian cuneiform. Emilie hated the sight of it.

"Can you read it?" Fitzwater asked.

Emilie stood and circled the desk to get a closer look. Many of the symbols were instantly recognizable to her—temple, grave, bull's blood. She followed the lines of text, skipping symbols she didn't know. It would take awhile to fully decipher the Akkadian-rooted inscription.

"My father never finished translating it."

Fitzwater's head bobbed. "Eighteen years ago. Your memory is good."

Emilie collapsed back into her chair. The incense in the room dizzied her. "I thought all the photos disappeared with him."

Fitzwater smiled. "This picture was taken three days ago."

Emilie's back stiffened. "You have the tablet?"

"I have—acquired it, yes."

"On the black market, you mean." Emilie felt her face grow warm. "I would have expected more from you. I thought you were interested in archaeology for the sake of knowledge."

Fitzwater smiled again. "Your principles are laudable, little Emilie. And yes, the tablet should never have been circulating for the past eighteen years. But let us remember how that happened in the first place."

Emilie closed her eyes. The memory of her father's betrayal still burned as though it had happened this morning. "What are you going to do with it?"

Fitzwater pressed the remote and the screen went black, leaving them in candlelight again. He laid the remote on the edge of the desk and laced his fingers together, pursing his lips. "I am sick, Emilie." He paused and gazed at the darkened window, then waved a hand around the room. "The candles, the music, the incense. It is all part of my holistic healing efforts. But my doctor tells me I don't have much longer."

"I'm sorry."

"I'm not ready to die. I need a miracle."

"And you still think the tablet has healing power?"

Fitzwater's eyes watered, and he nodded. "We have forgotten so much of our history, Emilie. The Industrial Revolution has left us reliant on science and technology; but when they fail us, we have nothing left. What has happened to faith? We have forgotten the days when our ancestors went to the gods for answers, for healing."

Fitzwater leaned back in his chair. "The Israel Antiquities Authority knows that I have acquired the tablet. Because it was originally uncovered in Israel, it technically belongs to the State of Israel. They threatened to pull the approval for my Ashkelon dig if I didn't donate it. I can't let the dig be closed down—the work there is my legacy. So the tablet belongs to them. But I've convinced them to give me the dig season to study the piece. I'll give it up after it's been translated. After I've had a chance to find my miracle."

Emilie exhaled. It was strange to think of the tablet behind glass in a museum. It had risen to almost mythic proportion in her mind. "Who's doing the translation work?" she asked. *Better be somebody good.*

"You are."

Emilie hoped her gasp wasn't audible. "I can't, Mr. Fitzwater. This is too important a find. I'm not qualified—"

"I know. But I trust you, Emilie. And trust is everything. The tablet will eventually be translated by an expert at Tel Aviv University, but I need someone to translate it while I can still use it. I know you will treat the tablet with reverence because I know how you felt about your father."

Yeah, my father was a lying thief with no principles. Emilie's stomach turned over, something she could always count on when her emotions surged.

Fitzwater leaned forward. "I know you would never betray me.

Who else can I say that about? And I believe you may be the only one who can channel the power."

"Me?"

"Let's not pretend, Emilie. Not with each other. Your father and Marduk Bel-Iddin were—connected, somehow. Many people believe psychic power is inherited, you know."

"I'm not psychic!"

Fitzwater breathed heavily and nodded. "I knew you would be reluctant." His eyes watered again. "Emilie, you are my last hope. My life is in your hands."

Emilie shifted in her seat. The request was ludicrous. There was no way she was qualified to decipher the tablet, and it would take her three times as long as it would take an expert. But if Fitzwater were willing to give her the opportunity, how could she refuse it? The archaeological value of the relic alone was worth doing the job. And if the tablet held the power that her father believed, it had the potential to change the world.

But would her father's fate be hers if she took on this project? Emilie's mother insisted it was guilt over betraying his family that had been the end of him, but Emilie had always felt there was more.

"I don't know," she said, twisting the belt from her jacket around one finger.

"The tablet must be kept safe while an epigrapher is decipher- ing it," he said. "I know you're as anxious as I am to find the answers your father pursued. And it's your chance to answer all the questions you must have about your father's death."

"Mr. Fitzwater, I'm not finished with my degree yet. I don't know—"

He waved away her concerns. "I still have contacts at the uni- versity. I've asked about you. I believe you can do the job." He leaned his head against the back of his chair. "And as I said, you're the only one I can trust."

Emilie considered the offer. Was Fitzwater really so paranoid about theft that he would settle for a student? Or did he really believe she had inherited some special connection to the tablet? She had not dismissed the possibility of this type of power in the world, but was there a chance that she had it?

"Where is the tablet now?" she asked.

"In Ashkelon, at the current dig. The IAA won't let me take it out of the country, of course. You'll have to go there to decipher it."

Emilie hadn't been on a dig site in years, and working with a valuable piece like this was the chance of a lifetime, a young epigrapher's dream job. She could make certain that it was handled properly and maybe make a name for herself at the same time. *If I don't fail totally.*

"I could go in August," she said. "After my summer courses are finished and I take my exams."

Fitzwater shook his head. "Not August. Next week."

She hid her disappointment. "I'm afraid that's impossible. I have two summer courses I have to finish if I'm going to get into the Ph.D. program in the fall."

"Perpetual student?"

Emilie stifled her annoyance. "I'm going to teach, eventually."

"Postpone your classes."

"That would mean postponing my degree. My life is already behind schedule, Mr. Fitzwater. I'm sorry, I can't do it." Emilie felt some relief at having made the decision. It was a crazy idea, anyway, and a project better left to experts.

Thomas Fitzwater dropped his head, frowning. "You disappoint me, Ms. Nazzaro. But I'm afraid I must insist."

Emilie bristled. "Mr. Fitz—"

"I've already spoken to Professor Krager."

"My advisor? How did you—"

"You'd be surprised how willing to accommodate they can be when dealing with one of their biggest donors."

"Still, you can't force me. . . ."

Fitzwater tapped a finger on his desk. "Professor Krager assures me that if you will work with me, they will work with you."

"And if I don't?"

"Pack your bags, Emilie. You're going to Israel."

▲ ▲ ▲

Twilight crept into the second-floor study where Thomas Fitzwater smoked his final cigarette of the day. He stretched backward in his leather chair, watching the sun dip below the line of juniper trees at the edge of his property. He'd reached his self-imposed limit on cigarettes early today, but he would respect his own ban. He had no intention of actually succumbing to the cancer diagnosis he had manufactured for Emilie Nazzaro.

His private phone line rang. Thomas stubbed out the cigarette and reached for the phone.

"Fitzwater?" The male voice boomed across the telephone wires.

Thomas sat straighter. "What can I do for you, Mr. Al-Mirabi?"

"We here are counting on the piece you promised, Fitzwater. How much more of a delay must we endure?" Al-Mirabi's impatience traveled along the overseas lines as if he were on the other side of Thomas's desk.

"There have been some complications." Thomas twisted a pen in his left hand. "The Israeli government learned that the relic was in my possession."

"I expect you are working to resolve the problem?" Al-Mirabi said.

"Yes, of course. The details are all set. I am only awaiting the execution of the plan. I assure you that the relic will be in your hands very soon."

"You can guarantee this?"

"I personally guarantee it."

"I have been convinced by others here that you are committed to our cause. I hope you will not disappoint."

"No, Mr. Al-Mirabi. It is only a matter of time. I realize that acquiring such pieces is crucial to your—to our—efforts."

"The fate of the world rests on what we do here, Fitzwater. You realize that?"

Thomas tapped the pen on his desk. Al-Mirabi's power trip was well known, but Thomas did agree that this covert, worldwide coalition held the power to turn governments on their heads. "I won't disappoint you, Mr. Al-Mirabi. As we speak I have someone moving into place to recover the tablet."

"And its disappearance will not be linked to you? We cannot have any hint of impropriety traced back to our organization."

"I understand. And I assure you, the blame for the tablet's disappearance will fall on one person alone. She is completely unaware of her purpose there. My employee on the inside will make certain she is in the right place at the right time."

"Good. You are only one stone in a grand, new building, Fitzwater; but each stone will be of utmost importance if we are to raise up our new world leader."

"All for peace, Mr. Al-Mirabi." Thomas offered the bywords of their organization as a farewell.

"All for peace, Mr. Fitzwater."

Thomas replaced the phone and reached into the top drawer of his desk for his cigarettes. Remembering his limit, he tossed them back in, closed the drawer, and settled for chewing the end of his pen instead. Al-Mirabi's call was troubling—not because Thomas doubted that the tablet would soon be in the coalition's possession, but because Al-Mirabi obviously doubted him.

He was a recent addition to the organization, eager to prove his worth. Eager to be an important part of the new government that would soon arise from the ancient dust of Babylon.

And although she would never know it, Emilie Nazzaro would play a crucial role.

Chapter 3

Emilie jammed one last pair of socks into her suitcase before pressing a knee into the top and yanking the zipper closed. Dr. Krager's face flashed before her as she gave the zipper another nasty tug and stood the suitcase on end. Her academic advisor had been a friend as well as mentor to her over the years, but there had been nothing of friendship when he called her into his office.

Vague promises, that's all he can give me. Meanwhile, my life gets put on hold again.

Emilie dragged her suitcase down the hall of her apartment and deposited it near the worn brocade couch her grandmother had handed down to her. She only had a few more minutes before she needed to leave for the airport. She glanced around and asked herself what else needed to be done before she left for seven weeks.

Seven weeks. A strange country, a team she'd never met. Emilie breathed deeply. Would they resent her late arrival or would they make her part of them? And what about the warnings Fitzwater had issued when she met with him again last night? Would there be tomb-raiding thieves around every corner, waiting for her to get careless with the tablet?

A knock at the door canceled her self-pity. She swung the door inward and smiled at Margo on the other side.

"You ready?" Margo asked.

"Almost. I really appreciate this, Margo." She stepped aside to let her friend in. "The dictionary should define 'friend' as the person who volunteers to drive you to the airport."

Margo laughed and breezed into the apartment. Her willowy body, perfectly accessorized, set off Emilie's T-shirt and jeans and what her grandmother had always called Emilie's "plain Jane" look. Emilie didn't mind. She knew where she belonged in the food chain. She was one of the "personality people," whose inner beauty makes them attractive.

Yeah, right. Not that any men have gotten close enough to see it lately. No grown men, anyway.

Margo lifted a double-ringed hand to smooth a few errant hairs. "I still can't believe they're forcing you into this." She hefted Emilie's suitcase and then dropped it with feigned astonishment at its weight.

Emilie smiled. "I'll get it. Just let me look around one more time." She took a quick inventory of the apartment. She yelled from her bedroom, "I just hope I do a good job." Satisfied that she'd not forgotten anything, she headed back to the living room.

"You'll be great, as always," Margo said.

Emilie frowned. "I get the feeling that if anything happens to that tablet, my career goes with it. Dr. Horobin nearly kicked me out of the program when I didn't return that bowl right away!" She hefted the suitcase. "Okay, let's go."

Margo dropped Emilie curbside at JFK Airport in New York. Her flight wasn't scheduled to leave for four hours, but El Al Airline's myriad of security procedures would fill up her time. She endured the luggage checks, where airline personnel searched her bags and interrogated her as though she were an international spy. The airline had the best security in the world, but there was a cost.

She finally found her seat onboard the 747 jet bound for Tel Aviv. Seat 23F required climbing over a couple in their fifties who looked dressed for a night out rather than an eleven-hour flight. Emilie smiled and nodded, but didn't make conversation.

As the plane crossed the Atlantic, Emilie tried to sleep, but her thoughts were too scattered to give her peace. She thought back to her conversation with Mr. Fitzwater last night. He had her father's journals in storage, he'd said. He would send them along to her in Ashkelon. Emilie didn't know whether to be angry that Fitzwater had kept the journals or to tell him to toss them into the trash. Sitting on the plane now, however, she wished she had the journals to read. Instead, she pulled out a couple of the reference books she'd brought to brush up on her Akkadian cuneiform.

I'm never going to be able to do this. She thought back to the brief conversation she'd had with her advisor, Professor Krager, just before leaving. He wasn't exactly subtle. *If I protect Fitzwater's interests, my academic placement will be guaranteed. Fail him, fail everything.*

The woman beside her leaned in. Heavy perfume drifted across Emilie's space. A pair of glasses hung from a gold chain around the woman's neck, lying against the stylish black dress. She lifted the glasses and studied Emilie's book. "That looks complicated. Is it Greek?"

Emilie closed the book slightly. "Akkadian."

"Ah." The woman nodded. Her accent was New England, Boston maybe. "You're on a tour to the Holy Land, too?"

"Not a tour, exactly. More like a research trip."

Emilie's seatmate nodded to the man beside her. "Harry, we're sitting with an adventurer."

Harry sat forward. His slightly rumpled suit and bad comb-over didn't seem to mesh with his wife's chic look. "Oh? Like Indiana Jones?"

Emilie laughed. "I'm afraid adventure's not very high on my priority list. I'll just be doing some academic work over there."

"Are you a teacher?" the woman asked.

"Leave her to her books, June," Harry said, going back to his magazine.

Emilie closed the book. "That's okay. It's a long flight. I have plenty of time to study." She smiled at June. "I plan to teach someday."

"Our daughter's a third-grade teacher in Charleston," June said.

Emilie shook her head. "I don't think I could handle third graders. I'd like to find a small university somewhere and tuck myself away there for a few decades."

June frowned. "Sounds lonely."

Emilie shrugged. "Or just safe. Most relationships aren't worth the risk anyway."

June patted Emilie's hand and several bracelets jangled. "You've been hurt." When Emilie didn't respond, June changed the subject. "We're so excited to finally see the Holy Land. Is it your first time?"

Emilie nodded.

"Imagine, walking where Jesus walked, seeing things the way He saw them."

"Actually, I'll be spending my time in Ashkelon. It's on the coast, in the southern part of Israel. I don't think Jesus ever got down that far. And it's a fairly modern city."

"Oh." June's excitement seemed to deflate. "But still," she brightened, "going to any part of Israel is like a spiritual quest, don't you think? You have to feel closer to God there."

Emilie opened her reference book again. "I'm afraid I gave up on trying to believe in God a long time ago."

"Hmm. Then you truly are alone."

"I'm doing okay by myself so far," Emilie said and flipped the book up to read.

June took the hint and found a magazine to read.

By the time the plane circled Ben Gurion International Airport, Emilie had decided there was no sense in whining about the forced trip. She'd get in, get the work done, and get back out. Perhaps she could even fit in a summer class.

It was midmorning in Tel Aviv, and the combination of flying all night and being thrust seven hours forward in time made Emilie ready for a hot shower and a bed. But Israel's airport security personnel had other plans. When Emilie had satisfied all of them that she was neither spy nor terrorist, she consulted the letter she had crushed into her purse before leaving home. One of the team members should be meeting her outside the airport soon. She threaded her way through the crowd toward the exit, hoping for a comfortable bench outside where she could park her exhausted self.

Ten yards from the exit, two figures closed in on either side of her, narrowing her vision. The man on her right pulled her suitcase from her grasp.

"Excuse me!" She stopped walking. They grabbed her elbows and kept moving.

"Come with us, Ms. Nazzaro," the other said. They pushed past the throngs of people.

"Can I help you?" Emilie glanced from one to the other. Were these the team members who were supposed to pick her up?

She watched the larger man signal his partner to open a narrow door leading off the waiting area. Her hope that they were from the dig site dissolved.

"In here." Before she had a chance to react, he shoved her forward. Emilie stumbled into a dimly-lit room. The two men pushed in behind her.

▲ ▲ ▲

Jack straightened up and shielded his eyes. The Ashkelon dig site was only a few hundred yards from the sea, but the glare on the white sand made it difficult to see. He scanned the beach for the tenth time that morning. Nothing. *Where is he?*

"Cabot!"

Jack dropped back to his knees in the dirt and turned his head. "Yeah?"

Victor Herrigan, the Ashkelon excavation director, stepped into Square 38 where Jack worked. When Jack didn't stand, Herrigan folded his arms over his chest and waited, as though commanding complete attention. Jack stood.

"I have a job for you, Cabot."

Jack ditched the pick he'd been using to hack away at the Middle Bronze Age. "Anything's better than this."

"We've got an addition to our staff coming in this morning. You need to do an airport pickup."

Jack glanced toward the beach once more. "Why me?"

"Because you're the only one rich enough to rent a car while you're here." Dr. Herrigan looked at his watch. "You have half an hour before you need to leave. Check with me then." He nudged the pick with his toe. "In the meantime, get back to work."

Jack gave Dr. Herrigan a mock salute before retrieving the pick. *Great. If Muwabi doesn't show in the next half hour. . .*

He'd been on the Ashkelon dig for two days, and already muscles he didn't know he had were yelling at him to quit. But after the disaster in Turkey, there was no way he would give up on this one.

Jack stretched again and watched the volunteers for a minute. Some squatted or kneeled, carefully brushing off the pieces of the past. Others, like him, dragged picks through the dirt, hoping to hit something amazing without damaging it. Nearly a hundred volunteers worked the grid. He could never check out all of them. He needed Muwabi. He checked his watch. *Twenty-six minutes. He'd better get here.*

The volunteer in the square beside him sat back on her heels and wiped her forehead with the back of her hand. She wore a white T-shirt and khaki shorts, but both were stained with mud. Her black hair was pulled into a ponytail, and sweat beaded on her neck. "So how's the new guy doing?"

"Feeling my age," he said, grinning. "I'm Jack Cabot, by the way."

She stood and swung her pick. "Jenn Reddington."

They worked in silence for a few minutes. Jack managed to search the beach only twice.

"Anything exciting turn up here yet?" Jack asked.

She laughed. "Are you kidding? I would have thought the whole world was talking about it, from the way Dr. Herrigan's been acting."

"So what's the big discovery?"

She leaned on her pick and shrugged. "Nothing we dug up, unfortunately. Something the guy with the money bought. Some kind of sorcerer's thing."

Jack tried to look uninterested. "Where is it now?"

Jenn went back to her work. "You got me. Nobody's answering questions. They have it under lock and key, I'm sure. Bringing in an expert to decipher the sorcery."

"Herrigan thinks someone's trying to steal it?"

"Who knows?"

Jack looked up. Across the dig site, a black figure stood on the beach, watching. Jack angled his pick into the dirt again and turned his back to Jenn. He heard her shovel dig into the sandy soil. A minute later he leaned his pick against the bulk wall between squares and strolled toward the beach.

Jack's sneakers sunk into the sand. His ankles twisted, slowing down his walk toward the African man. "Where've you been?"

"You want friendly conversation or information?" Muwabi said.

Jack nodded. "What do you have for me?"

The other man shook his head. "Not much. There doesn't seem to be much black market talk about the tablet. Too quiet, in fact. Makes me think someone else is involved, and no one's saying anything."

"Any guesses?"

Muwabi shrugged. "All I can tell you is that Leon Hightower is in Ashkelon."

Jack's gaze drifted back to the dig site. "It's gotta be him, then."

"I don't know. Word is, he's here for some other buy. Somebody's brought something in from Turkey. Some kind of healing god or something."

Jack whirled. "The statue of Aesculapius?"

The other man shrugged again. "I think so."

Jack clenched a fist. If the statue wasn't destroyed in Pergamum, there was a chance he could still retrieve it! *As long as I stay focused on the tablet at the same time.*

"Cabot!" Dr. Herrigan's voice competed with the breakers.

Jack waved a hand at the director.

Dr. Herrigan cupped his hands around his mouth and yelled, "Get to the airport!"

▲ ▲ ▲

Emilie's captors forced her through the door in the airport wall. She thrust a foot backward. One of the men yanked on the door. Her foot propped it open.

"Cooperate, Ms. Nazzaro." The little man pulled her back. "You are in no danger."

I'll be the judge of that. She tried to squeeze her body through the crack in the door her foot had preserved. He hauled her fully into the room and slammed the door. She was too tired for any heroics.

"Ms. Nazzaro!" The taller man was evidently in charge, leaving his colleague to do the suitcase-carrying and girl-holding.

"What do you want?" Emilie looked him in the face now, willing herself not to show her fear. The olive-skinned man definitely looked Jewish, and Emilie wondered if she were still under suspicion for some crime. He reached into his jacket. Emilie winced; but when his hand emerged, he held a business card. The other man dropped her arms, allowing her to take the offered card.

"I apologize for our rudeness in detaining you, Ms. Nazzaro. But I hope you will understand our need for discretion."

Emilie turned the card face-up in her hand and read the block lettering. "Amir Sudiwitz, Anti-Theft Unit, Israel Antiquities Authority." She fumed and looked up. "You're from the IAA?"

Mr. Sudiwitz gave a half-smile. "You are in Israel for research purposes, I understand?"

Emilie nodded. "The Thomas Fitzwater dig at Ashkelon."

"Yes." He pointed to the card. "Please keep that. You may need it later."

Emilie slid the card into her purse.

"We are aware of the work you will be doing in Ashkelon, Ms. Nazzaro. Relics such as this often gain undue attention. Rumors about ancient power still residing in artifacts can motivate undesirable people to take interest."

"I can assure you, Mr. Sudiwitz, the tablet is in no danger from me."

Sudiwitz held up a hand. "It's not you we're worried about. But certain—intelligence—has come to us that the tablet may be targeted for theft."

"Who wants it?"

Sudiwitz smiled. "If this tablet possesses healing power, Ms. Nazzaro, a good many people will want it. A find like this one is important to our country."

"Why are you telling me this?"

Sudiwitz nodded, as if glad to get down to business. "We've checked your background, Ms. Nazzaro. We want you to be our eyes and ears at the dig. Keep a close watch on your colleagues and on any outsiders who appear overly interested in the tablet. Contact us if you observe anything suspicious."

Emilie exhaled. This project kept getting more complicated. "Why me?"

"For one thing, because you are new. It was easy to intercept you rather than try to contact someone on the inside already. And

40

none of these people know you. They don't know what to expect from your behavior. You won't seem suspicious to them."

"I don't know."

Sudiwitz pointed to her purse. "You have my card. All we ask is that you make a simple phone call if you sense anything amiss. Can you do that for us? For Israel?"

When you put it like that. . . She nodded. "I'll call you if I see or hear anything."

"Thank you." He pressed her hand in his. "Thank you."

As the three emerged from the storage room, Emilie glanced around the airport self-consciously, but no one seemed to be paying attention. The Israeli agents melted into the crowd, and she was left alone again.

Outside in the heat, she scanned the sidewalk and street, not knowing what to look for.

"Hey, are you Emilie?" The American voice behind her materialized into a well-built, blond man wearing a black T-shirt, cut-off jeans, and heavy boots.

"Yes." She dropped her suitcase and extended a hand. "Emilie Nazzaro."

He thrust a hand toward hers, clamping his fingers around her own. "It's your lucky day, Emilie."

She smiled. "Why is that?"

" 'Cause you've got me for a driver!" He flashed a smile back at her. "Jack Cabot's the name."

Was this guy serious? He was more Ken Doll than human, with his surfer looks and huge smile. And an ego to match. "Are you part of the volunteer team, Jack?"

"Sure am." He snatched up her suitcase as though she'd packed only feather dusters. "Car's over here," he said, walking away. "We'll head straight to the dig site. I'll pawn you off on the director. I've got a beautiful girl waiting for me in Tel Aviv."

Emilie frowned at Ken Doll's back. "Don't let me inconvenience you."

"I'll deal with it," he said.

Emilie trotted to keep up with him, crossing her fingers that the rest of the team members didn't act like rich playboys on a holiday.

When they reached the car, a brand-new Mitsubishi Galant, he surprised her by opening her door. *Maybe he's not a total narcissist.*

Jack Cabot proved to have a gift for continuous talking. Emilie nearly fell asleep as they drove toward Ashkelon. The only useful bit of information she picked up was a warning about Dr. Victor Herrigan. According to Jack, he was a dictator, running the dig site more like an army sergeant than a university professor.

As they neared Ashkelon National Park, where the dig site was located, Emilie forced her eyes open to watch through the window. The city wove a spell around her immediately, with its eclectic mix of old and new battling for control.

"So you're here to work on the artifact, huh?" Jack asked. "You must be quite the expert."

If you only knew. "I'll do my best." She wondered if her work was common knowledge around the dig. She would have expected Fitzwater to be more discreet.

"I'd love to hear more about your work. Maybe we could get together sometime, get some dinner?" He smiled across the front seat, his right hand resting on the seat between them.

Emilie lowered her window. Did it suddenly get hotter? "Uh. . ." She tapped her fingers against her thigh as warning lights went off in her brain. Agent Sudiwitz's words replayed. ". . .a close watch on your colleagues. . .anyone overly interested. . ." *You're not here to make friends, Em.* She glanced over at that smile. *Or anything else.* "I'll be very busy, I think."

As they drove through the main entrance of the park, Emilie's stomach did flips in spite of her determination to keep things businesslike. She hated meeting new people. She assumed the rest of the team wouldn't be as arrogant as Jack. *They'd better not be. I don't think I can tolerate seven weeks as an outsider.*

They continued through the park until they neared the beach. Emilie sucked in her breath at the sight of the expedition. She'd been a child the last time she'd seen a dig site. She hadn't expected to be so awed today. Dozens of workers crawled over the grid, laid out in ten-meter squares. The remains of the oldest arched gate in the world, still standing two stories high, loomed over the laborers as they picked and brushed their way into the past.

Jack parked the car, jumped out, and circled to her side. Another car pulled up beside them. Emilie opened her door and the heat hit her once again, along with a wave of nostalgia that came with the long-forgotten yet familiar sound of the volunteers' picks striking hardened soil.

A man twice her age opened the car door beside her. Jack grabbed Emilie's elbow and hauled her out of the car.

"I have her, Dr. Herrigan." Jack pulled her around to face the older man. "I brought the sorceress."

Emilie looked from one man to the other. She'd been shoved around too much lately, and she was beginning to resent it. And what was this about a "sorceress"?

"You're sure this is her?" Dr. Herrigan was looking her up and down. He was well built for his age and much taller than Emilie, with a shock of hair the color of bleached sand.

Jack let go of her arm and raised his eyebrows at her. "She said so."

Dr. Herrigan pulled out a pair of black-rimmed glasses to inspect her more closely. "Let me see your identification, Ms. Nazzaro."

Emily fumbled in her purse. "Is there a problem?"

"Just being cautious. You understand."

Emilie thrust her passport at him. "Is that enough?"

He studied the picture, then her face. "Do you have anything else? A driver's license? Passports can be faked."

Emilie handed him the small card. "So can a driver's license."

Dr. Herrigan grunted, but handed her license back.

Emilie stuffed them into her purse again and turned to Jack. "Why did you call me the 'sorceress'?"

"Sorry," he said. "Wasn't thinking, I guess. Everyone's been talking about you."

Great. And I'll bet you've been doing most of it.

Dr. Herrigan reached into the front seat of his Ford Focus and pulled out a black case. "Ms. Nazzaro, follow me."

Not wasting any time, are we? As excited as she was to see the tablet, jet lag had turned her legs to rubber bands, and she wished Jack would have dumped her at her hotel instead. Emilie followed Herrigan's footsteps in the dirt across the dig site to a picnic table covered by an awning and glanced back at Jack's car. What would happen to her luggage if Jack headed off to Tel Aviv to meet his "beautiful girl"? But it looked like Jack wasn't going anywhere: He was still right behind her.

Dirt and sand had already wormed their way into her shoes by the time they reached the lean-to. Dr. Herrigan set the black case on the picnic table. Emilie sat on the bench.

For the first time today, she allowed herself to think about what was in that case. Her father had spent a lifetime searching for this tablet. What he had found had sucked the life from him, convincing him that he had a connection to the dark powers of Marduk Bel-Iddin—a connection that the passing of the ages could not destroy. Now here she was, about to unlock the secrets her father had given his life to uncover.

"Jack!"

Emilie jumped at Dr. Herrigan's sharp command. Jack Cabot shrugged and backed away from the table. He disappeared into the grid of volunteers bent over their tools.

Dr. Herrigan turned back to Emilie and licked his lips, his fingers rubbing the silver latches on the case. He remained standing, like an angry parent scolding a child. "Ms. Nazzaro, I assume you have been informed as to the delicate nature of this artifact. Discretion is vital as the work here progresses—"

"I assure you, Doctor, I will be very careful."

Dr. Herrigan clenched his jaw. "In the future, Ms. Nazzaro, you will not interrupt me when I speak. Is that clear?"

Emilie swallowed. "Yes, sir."

"You will work here at the dig site during the day. The public nature of the area should serve as a deterrent to would-be thieves. A guard has been hired and will remain nearby as you work."

Emilie nodded. Her eyes strayed back to the case. She was having difficulty focusing on his words. *Open it. Open the case.*

"Are you eager to see the tablet again?" Dr. Herrigan asked.

"It's been many years," Emilie said. "I was only a child."

"Yes, your father was instrumental in its recovery. However, as I'm sure he would tell you, it is an object of study, Ms. Nazzaro, not a sideshow freak to be gawked at."

Dr. Herrigan lowered himself to the bench across from her and set the case on the table between them. He twirled the numbers that locked the case, then flipped it open so that its lid obscured Emilie's view. Slowly, he slid the case in a semicircle until the tablet lay before her, cushioned in black foam padding.

It looked just as it had in Thomas Fitzwater's photo. But having it in front of her, close enough to touch, was. . .different.

She reached a hesitant hand toward the tablet, then pulled it back. A moment later, she reached in again, this time laying the tips of her fingers on the face of the orange-red clay.

Her fingers tingled for a moment. A rush of warmth filled her body. The sounds of the dig dropped away and a high-pitched singing filled her ears. Her eyes fluttered and closed.

Night. An ebony sky, close enough to dip her hands in and scoop out the stars. A hot wind rushing past her lips. The cloying smell of blood nearby and the taste of charred meat on her tongue. She stood on the edge of a platform, the ground hundreds of feet below her, where flickering torchlight mirrored the stars above. She swayed, lightheaded. A hand caught her arm. A hand that reached from a black robe, from a man with a shaved head and

45

empty eyes, who had once been so familiar. . . .

"Ms. Nazzaro!"

Dr. Herrigan's voice pierced her thoughts. Emilie shook her head. She blinked against the afternoon sun and pulled her hand from the tablet.

"Ms. Nazzaro, are you unwell?"

She shook her head again, clearing the haunting images from her mind. *No, not unwell. But perhaps. . .unwise.*

Chapter 4

Jack attempted to look busy with a pick. From the corner of his eye, he watched Emilie Nazzaro reach toward the black case. The tablet had to be in there.

He paused in his digging, fascinated by Emilie's reaction when she touched the tablet. He watched as her eyes closed and her body trembled like a reed in the wind. Then she seemed to shake herself out of it.

What's that about? Some kind of trance? Maybe she really was a sorceress. She didn't fit that image, though. She was too. . .ordinary.

Jack shook his head at his own thoughts. One of the reasons he was good at what he did was that he had accurate instincts about people, but occasionally he got caught up in seeing the world through other people's eyes, feeling their pain with them. He usually had to fight that connection with people. Unless he could use it to his advantage.

Dr. Herrigan seemed intensely interested in Emilie's arrival, and it was clear to Jack that he wasn't going to get anywhere near the tablet right now. Time to get to Amtza's. He tossed the pick into the dirt and strolled to his car, hoping Herrigan wouldn't turn around.

When he had cleared the dig site, Jack floored the accelerator, shooting through the park and into the street. He sped toward the Afridar district of Ashkelon, unconcerned about any speed limits. The police in Israel were too busy keeping people safe from terrorism to worry about highway patrol.

Traffic picked up as he neared the Afridar district, and Jack swerved and braked to avoid collisions. His heart was already pumping when he parked outside Amtza's, a sit-down falafel joint. The round-the-clock Israeli pop music blared from the restaurant's speakers.

Inside, Jack ordered a drink and sat at the bar. The late afternoon crowd was sparse. A blond-haired woman across the bar waved red-painted fingernails at him. He smiled but looked away. *Sorry, sweetheart. No time today.*

He could wait, but not long. He needed to get back to the team before he was missed. But he wasn't going to leave without the information he wanted if he could avoid it. *Who's selling the statue? Who's buying?* He planned to set himself up as a buyer. Then when he went to meet with the seller, he'd find a way to grab the statue.

Jack's mind wandered back to Emilie Nazzaro as his knuckles rapped against the bar in time with the beat. Since Muwabi hadn't been able to tell him anything on the beach about a hit on the tablet, he was back to watching everyone on the team, including Emilie. He had a feeling Vitelli was betting against him.

Could Emilie have more on her mind than translation? She seemed honest and sweet, even a bit naïve; but Jack had been suckered by too many women like that to be fooled again. Case in point: Layna Sardos in Turkey. And Emilie's odd behavior when she saw the tablet made him think this was more than a job for her.

A sudden rush of memory made Jack smack himself in the forehead. Emilie's luggage! It was still in his trunk. She'd probably be heading back to the hotel soon and wanting her things after the long flight from the States.

He glanced around the restaurant once more, then stood and threw a few bills on the bar. It didn't look like Muwabi had come through for him, and he'd better get that luggage back. *As though she doesn't already think you're an arrogant fool.* But that couldn't be helped. It was part of his cover persona this time around.

The blond stood when Jack did. He watched as she rounded the bar, her lips curving into a smile and her overstyled hair bouncing above her shoulders.

"Too hot out there to leave so soon," she said, sliding onto a barstool beside him. "Why don't you buy me a drink instead?"

"Wish I could," Jack said. "Duty calls."

She swung her legs under the bar and tapped a quick rhythm on it with the red nails. "Much hotter here than, say, Turkey?" She turned her face away from Jack. Her glance circled the room.

Jack dropped to the stool beside her. "You've been to Turkey?"

"Not recently. But I hear they have some beautiful artifacts there."

Jack waved down the bartender, then nodded to the woman to order a drink and ordered one himself. Muwabi hadn't let him down, after all, though the messenger wasn't what Jack had expected. She looked more like a vacant-eyed supermodel than an antiquities trader.

"Name's Jack," he said, extending a hand.

She rested a delicate hand inside his. "Tawny. Tawny Turner."

Is that your stage name, sweetheart? "What can you tell me about Turkish artifacts?" Jack asked. "Any for sale around here?"

She shrugged. "If you know the right people."

The bartender brought their drinks. Jack took a swig and then smacked his glass onto the bar. "Let's cut the double-talk, honey. I'm looking to make a purchase. If you can point me to the right item and the right people, I'll make it worthwhile."

She swiveled on her stool, her long fingers still wrapped around her drink. Jack took a moment to appreciate the look of hard steel behind the pretty face.

"Aesculapius," she said. "Is that what you're looking for?"

Jack folded his arms over his pounding chest. "Can you introduce me to the seller?"

She smiled. "We have mutual friends."

"Who is he?"

The woman sipped her drink, then licked her lips delicately. "Not he. She."

Jack squinted. "You?" He doubted even Muwabi could have set up a direct contact this fast.

She laughed. "Not me. Someone a little more exotic."

Jack relaxed. "Exotic how?" he asked, not caring about the answer.

"Greek, I think. Long, dark hair, even longer legs." She looked Jack up and down. "Your type, perhaps?"

A mental picture formed for Jack. *Coincidence? No way.* The blond had just perfectly described Layna Sardos.

▲ ▲ ▲

Emilie rubbed her tingling fingers against the splintered wood of the picnic table. Dr. Herrigan stepped away from her to answer a volunteer's question. Her fingers had grown cold in spite of the boiling afternoon sun.

Had Dr. Herrigan been able to sense what had happened? What had happened? Emilie reached for the tablet again, but when Herrigan turned back toward her, she changed her mind.

"Ms. Nazzaro, the team is finishing up for the day." He pulled the black case toward himself and snapped the lid closed. "You may go to the hotel with the others." He grabbed the case, turned away from her, and headed toward his parked car.

What did I see? Where was I? Was it some kind of out-of-body thing?

Emilie inhaled and stood. Her stomach churned as she followed Dr. Herrigan toward the parking lot. If she could get to the hotel and find some privacy, maybe she could understand all of this.

Emilie shuffled to Dr. Herrigan's car, but stopped when she saw his look of surprise.

"The buses that take the team to the hotel are over there, Ms. Nazzaro."

Emilie turned to see the volunteers climbing aboard four small buses. "Oh. I'm sorry."

Her heart was still hammering when she pulled herself onto the first bus. She was dismayed to see every seat occupied. Many of the volunteers sat in twos. Emilie lifted her chin and scanned the crowd, hoping someone would make eye contact and invite her to share a seat. The bus grew strangely quiet as she stood there, and all eyes seemed to focus elsewhere. Emilie's nausea intensified.

The driver got on behind her and leaned close. "You must sit," he said. When she didn't move, he said it again, this time with a shove against her back.

The push jolted her into the aisle, and she swung down into the first seat. The girl beside her gave a cold smile and looked out the window.

What am I doing here? The odor of burned flesh still lingered in her nose, and she tried not to think about it. As the bus bumped out of the national park and into the city of Ashkelon, newscasts of Israeli buses as bombing targets flashed in her mind and a new kind of fear gripped her.

Now you're overreacting to everything. She'd read enough guide books about Israel in the past week to know terrorist violence rarely occurred in this part of the country and that if every murder in the United States got as much press as every act of violence in Israel, she'd be more afraid to live in her own neighborhood than to live here.

The fear didn't leave. She knew the cause but tried to ignore it. A minute later, however, amidst the chatter that started up again on the bus, she was replaying the strange vision she'd seen in her head.

Am I going crazy? In a way, she hoped she was. It might be better than the alternative, finding that she was more like her father than she ever imagined. Or perhaps there was more to the mystical realm than she had let herself believe.

The bus hit a bump, and the girl beside her threw her shoulder into Emilie's upper arm.

"Sorry," she said and slid closer to the window.

The initial deciphering her father had done on the tablet had made the potential of the tablet clear. There was, allegedly, healing power for any person with connection to the gods. And a curse for anyone who scoffed at its power.

Would Marduk Bel-Iddin reach across time and seize her, too? Her father had unearthed other tablets farther north in Israel, which chronicled the sorcerer's extensive power in Babylon. In those, Tobias Nazzaro had found references to a tablet that contained the healing rituals that had given Marduk his power. Tobias had spent years searching for that tablet; and when he finally found it, his quest soon turned to obsession. He insisted that he was in contact with the ancient sorcerer, even channeling Marduk's words to a new generation. He would permit no one to see the tablet.

One day both he and the tablet disappeared. It was clearly an act of theft, though no one knew what he hoped to accomplish. Emilie had never seen him again. His body had been found on the beach in Gaza and his death determined to be an accidental drowning. The tablet was not in his possession.

Emilie pulled her thoughts from the past. She was not her father. But could her genetics have been the cause of what happened when she'd touched that tablet? Perhaps fatigue from the flight, anticipation of the project, and the mystery of the past had combined to cause an episode.

An "episode," yeah, that's a good name. Makes it sound like a disease, instead of just crazy.

Emilie's seatmate seemed to change her mind about conversation. "Who are you rooming with?"

"I don't think I—I mean, I'm not really sure, I guess." Emilie closed her eyes. Had she said one coherent sentence since she'd arrived? They were already calling her "sorceress." She didn't need to add "stupid" to her nickname.

A roommate? Terrific. She wouldn't even be alone with her thoughts in her hotel room. But at least she'd be able to take a hot shower and a quick nap. Then, if Dr. Herrigan didn't mind, she'd get started with the tablet and forget about this afternoon's "episode."

Several minutes later the bus pulled into the parking lot of the five-star Ashkelon Plaza Hotel. The white stone of the twelve-story hotel seemed to glow in the blinding afternoon sun. The line of palm trees between the circular drive and the glass-fronted hotel did little to shade the area.

Emilie piled out into the heat with the others but lingered outside as they entered the hotel.

Dr. Herrigan walked toward her. "Ms. Nazzaro, I'll take you to the front desk. They will give you your room key."

Emilie followed him through the double doors, received her key, and escaped into the elevator. Only when the doors had closed did she remember that Jack Cabot had her luggage.

Emilie looked again at her card key. *Room 576.* A hot shower and a nap were only five floors away.

Emilie could tell before she even stepped into the room that it would be a welcome retreat from the dig site every day. She pushed through the door and let it close behind her.

"Hello," a female voice called from inside the room.

Emilie walked into the room and peeked around a corner, toward the head of the two double beds.

A young woman sat on the edge of one bed, unlacing her muddy boots. She smiled at Emilie. "They told me I'd be getting a roommate. I figured it might be you."

Emilie took a deep breath. What did this girl already know about her? "I'm Emilie Nazzaro."

The other girl stood and extended a hand. "Jenn Reddington. Welcome to Ashkelon."

Emilie smiled in relief at the first real welcome she'd felt since she arrived. Jenn was thin and pale, with heavy circles under her eyes, but she seemed friendly. She wore a silver ring in her nose, and her dark hair was tied on top of her head in a silver hairclip. She seemed unlike anyone Emilie would expect to find on a dig.

Jenn returned to unlacing her boots. "You got lucky, coming in on a Friday."

"Lucky?"

"Shabbat—the Sabbath—doesn't begin until dusk, but we usually get the afternoon off anyway." Jenn set the boots aside and stood.

"I'm exhausted," Emilie said. "All I want to do is shower and sleep."

"Go ahead," Jenn said. "You can shower first."

"The guy who picked me up at the airport still has my luggage."

Jenn shrugged and turned toward the dresser. "You're about my size. You can wear something of mine. Hit the shower. I'll find something and toss it in."

"Thanks." Emilie smiled. Maybe fitting in here wouldn't be so hard.

The bathroom was as beautifully appointed as the rest of the room. Having Thomas Fitzwater finance a dig certainly raised the comfort level of the workers. At most dig sites, volunteers shared cottages in a kibbutz, a Jewish commune.

As the hot water pounded away the tension, Emilie's thoughts returned to the incident with the tablet. Would Dr. Herrigan allow her to work on it after she'd rested? The team would have the day off tomorrow since it was Shabbat. She would hate to wait until Sunday to get her hands on it again.

She could have stayed in the shower for half an hour, but she knew Jenn was waiting. When she stepped onto the bath mat, she found no clothes waiting for her. She wrapped herself in a fluffy towel and headed out into the room, wrapping another towel around her hair as she walked.

"Jenn? Did you find—" Emilie stopped in shock.

Jack Cabot stood in front of her, arms crossed like a club bouncer and eyebrows raised. "Sorry about taking off with your luggage," he said. "I brought it back as soon as I could get free." He pointed at her suitcase and computer bag, standing against the bed.

Jenn slid around from behind Jack to stand between the two of them. She circled a hand around Jack's bicep and smiled up at him. "I was just telling Jack that a bunch of us are heading into the historic district this afternoon to do some sightseeing. Tell him he must come with us, Emilie."

Jack never took his eyes from Emilie's face, and she felt herself redden.

"Excuse me," she said, clutching her towel while she reached for her suitcase. Jack seemed about to lift it for her, but then apparently changed his mind and let her take it. Emilie escaped back into the bathroom, closed the door, and leaned against it.

She could hear their voices outside the door, but she forced herself not to listen. *Remember why you're here.*

When she'd dressed and reentered the room, Jack was gone.

"I'm going to shower now," Jenn said. "You're coming downtown, though, right?"

Emilie chewed her lip. She needed to get back to the tablet, but she didn't want to chance it until she'd rested. Sightseeing didn't fit into that plan at all.

"I don't know. I'm totally exhausted."

Jenn shook her head. "You can't crash yet. Best way to get over the jet lag is to stay awake until bedtime."

Emilie exhaled. Turning down an invitation on her first day here didn't seem like a good idea.

"Okay, I'll come," she said.

"Great. I'll be out of the shower in ten minutes."

Emilie collapsed onto the bed for five minutes, but sleep didn't come. She got up, brushed her wet hair into a ponytail, and put on some makeup. When Jenn emerged from the steamy bathroom, Emilie was ready to go.

With eight other members of the dig team, Emilie boarded a bus outside the hotel. The drive to the Migdal district would only take a few minutes. She and Jenn sat together.

"Are you a student?" she asked Jenn as the bus lurched into the street.

Jenn shrugged. "I'm a student of life," she said. "I think the world is too large to be confined to a classroom and textbooks."

Emilie nodded. "And what does a student of life study?"

Jenn laughed. "Anything. Everything. I'm interested in learning where we've come from, where we're going. The past four hundred years of scientific 'progress' have skewed humankind's thinking, made us believe in the purely rational. And before that, Christianity interfered. I'm trying to connect with those who came before, those who knew that life exists on a higher plane. The ancients knew that the universe is power and energy, there for the taking."

When Emilie said nothing, Jenn continued. "You do agree, don't you? That's why you're here, too, isn't it? To find out what kind of power we've left behind in our search to dissect and categorize the cosmos."

"Yes, I'm a student of the past, I suppose."

"Exactly."

Emilie rubbed her fingers where the tablet had left such a strange sensation earlier. Perhaps it was time to ask herself some questions. This country seemed like a good place to find answers. But not right now. "What's with Dr. Herrigan?" she asked. "He's quite the tyrant, isn't he?"

Jenn laughed. "From what I hear, Fitzwater's getting rid of him after this dig season, and he's fuming over being out of a job."

"But the dig season is only in the summer," Emilie said. "He'll go back to teaching during the year, won't he?"

Jenn shook her head. "I heard he resigned his position for some reason. Guess that leaves him with nothing. Fitzwater's bringing in some young guy soon to learn the ropes and replace Herrigan next year. I've seen his picture. Definite improvement."

"Better than Jack Cabot? You guys seem pretty friendly."

"Jack? He hits on every woman here. I've even seen him flirting with Amanda Taylor, and she's married with kids!"

"So what's the story on him?" Emilie asked.

"Rich. Conceited. Bored with making money, so he thought he'd try this for awhile. He paid to be part of the dig."

"Are most of the team paying to be here?"

"Some. Unless they were specifically asked to volunteer, like you."

Emilie nodded. "So why'd you pick Ashkelon?"

Jenn shrugged. "It has such a rich history. It was originally one of the five main Philistine cities. Over the years it was conquered by a ton of different people—Assyria, Egypt, Babylon, Tyre. Eventually it came under Greek and Roman rule, and then it was conquered by the Crusaders in the twelfth century." She peered out the bus window. "Every invader left its remnants behind for archaeologists to dissect and explore."

"So when did it become part of Israel?"

"It was abandoned from the thirteenth century until 1948, when the new State of Israel began to rebuild it."

The bus stopped first at the scant remains of a sixth-century Byzantine church, and everyone unloaded. As they worked their way through the historic site, no one besides Jenn spoke a word to Emilie. She was glad, after all, that she'd gotten a roommate.

With a jolt, Emilie remembered her meeting with Agent Sudiwitz in the airport. She had been so busy trying to make friends, she'd forgotten that she was supposed to suspect everyone. As they surveyed the ruins, she looked at Jenn. She was strange, but Emilie couldn't picture her being an international antiquities smuggler.

An older woman stood on the other side of her. Emilie glanced at her, just as the woman looked her way, making eye contact.

"Isn't it fascinating?" the woman said, pointing to the mosaic floor.

Emilie nodded. "Beautiful."

"You came in just today, didn't you, hon?"

"Yes." Emilie smiled back at the woman, but did a quick look-over. *Could this woman be a suspect?* She looked about fifty, slightly overweight, with long, salt-and-pepper hair and a wide smile that made Emilie feel warmer. She wore several heavy rings on her fingers.

"I'm Margaret Lovell," the woman said, squeezing Emilie's arm. "What's your name?"

"Emilie Nazzaro."

"If you need any help getting settled, Emilie, you let me know."

Jenn pulled on her from the other side. "We're moving on."

Their next stop was the Painted Tomb in the Afridar district. Two other tourists stood inside the cool interior of the third-century Roman tomb. There was no guided tour here, and most of the team members spent only a few minutes inside. Jenn seemed fascinated by the painted ceiling, however, and lingered after their group had left. Emilie waited with her and studied the painting of the god Pan playing his pipes, along with various birds, stags, and antelopes.

After a moment, Emilie wandered over to the end wall of the tomb to look at a fresco of two nymphs resting beside a stream. A man in a business suit and tie stood near the wall, a cell phone to his ear. Emilie looked away, amused that someone would continue doing business while sightseeing.

"I don't care what he said," the man said into the phone.

Emilie noticed from the accent that he was American, too. She moved a few feet away.

"Tell him to transfer the funds into the other account tonight. Yes, tonight. We can't afford any bad publicity on this." He glanced up at Emilie, and she turned slightly to return his look. He turned his back to her, so she continued to watch his back. He seemed uptight, but she couldn't help noticing how attractive he was, though he was probably fifteen years older than she.

"Tell no one but Reynolds," he said. "I want this thing kept quiet." He snapped the phone shut and spun around toward Emilie again, catching her studying him. "What are you doing?"

"Excuse me?" Emilie glanced around. Jenn had left.

"Who are you?" The man approached her and crossed his arms. "Who do you work for?"

Emilie stepped away, searching the tomb for anyone else in her group. She was alone. "What are you talking about?"

"Do you think I'm an idiot?" He shoved the phone in his pocket. "I saw you at the church. I know you're following me, and I know you were listening to my conversation. Who sent you? Pioneer Corp.? Redegen?"

He took a step closer, and Emilie braced a shaking hand against the flaking wall of the tomb.

Chapter 5

Yacov's Bar was home to locals, mainly. The flaking paint, the weed-choked parking lot, and the sign with half its letters missing made it the kind of place that tourists rarely wandered into.

Victor Herrigan's car lurched into a narrow parking space behind the bar. He threw it into park, snatched the keys from the ignition, and grabbed his briefcase, cursing under his breath. He was late for his meeting with the mysterious Komodo.

The building had no windows. Inside, it could have been midnight. Victor searched the oily dive for the man he'd never met.

A small Asian man in the back inclined his head slightly in Victor's direction.

Victor squared his shoulders and threaded through tables and chairs to the booth in the back of the bar. "You Komodo?"

"Yeah. Sit."

Victor remained standing for another moment, choosing to look down at the little man. "I brought the photos."

"Good. Sit."

Komodo's voice had an edge to it that Victor didn't like. He slid into the booth, placing his briefcase beside him. He had no intention of letting the balance of control slide toward Komodo. "I hear you're the best."

"You get what you pay for." Komodo folded his hands on the table. His fingers were long and thin, Victor noticed. The hands of an artist. But he had the eyes of a criminal. Komodo's dark eyebrows drew together as he studied Victor.

Victor nodded. They still needed to agree on a price. He mentioned a number. "And I need it in one week—no later."

Komodo leaned back and folded his arms. "You'll have it in two weeks. And it'll cost you twice that."

Victor's jaw muscles tightened. He'd expected to negotiate, but Komodo was starting the bargaining too high. Victor was committed to his plan, but he had limited resources. He made another offer.

Komodo shook his head. "I don't haggle. That's the price."

Victor forced himself to look calm. How was he going to come up with that kind of money? Should he forget the whole thing? Still, wasn't it worth that much to make Fitzwater pay for what he'd done? Replacing him with someone younger was one thing, but without compensation? Victor was not going to be dismissed so easily, not after all these years of looking the other way. Victor intended to have his revenge. He'd get the money to pay Komodo somehow.

Komodo slapped the table with both hands. "Listen, Mr. Herrigan—"

"It's 'Doctor.' "

Komodo rose from his seat until he reached Victor's eye level. When he spoke, his words forced themselves through clenched teeth. "I don't care if it's 'President Herrigan.' If we're going to do this deal, we're going to do it for the money I say."

Victor equaled the stare for a moment. Komodo didn't flinch.

"Fine," Victor said. "I'll get the money. But I need it done in a week."

Komodo sat. "We'll see."

Victor exhaled. There was something else he needed to do—what was it? He recognized the tiny spark of panic as it began and fought it. *Think, Victor, think.*

Komodo held out his palms. "So are you going to give them to me?"

Give him what? *Oh, not now, not now!* Victor took off his glasses and pinched the bridge of his nose, a technique he found himself using more frequently to stall for time while his memory caught up with his reality.

"I don't have all day, Herrigan. Give me the photos."

"Of course!" Victor replaced his glasses and opened his brief-case. He pulled several color eight-by-tens out and slid them across the table.

Komodo studied the pictures, tracing the outline of the object with one finger. "Beautiful," he said, his voice reverent.

Victor almost smiled. With one word, Komodo had revealed himself as the artist he was reputed to be. Victor had no more doubts that Komodo could do the job. "Can you do it in a week?"

Komodo laid the photos on the table. "Maybe. The cuneiform is intricate. It won't be easy to duplicate. I need to see it in person at least once."

Victor nodded. "We can arrange that."

Komodo raised his eyebrows. "Isn't it locked up? Guarded?"

"Yes. But I hold the key."

Komodo smiled. "The fox guarding the henhouse, isn't that what they say?"

"Something like that."

"Just be sure there aren't any other foxes lurking around."

Victor shifted in his seat. "What have you heard?"

"Nothing. But an item like this. . . You can't be the only one with an interest."

Victor stood. "I'll call you to set up a time to see the tablet."

Komodo inclined his head. "Make sure you remember our price."

Victor grabbed his briefcase and navigated his way out of the bar. He checked his watch as he circled behind the building to his car. He needed to get back to the hotel for dinner with the team. He tried to relax the muscles in his jaw. Where would he get the money Komodo demanded? Would the job be done quickly enough?

But more than that, the thought that someone else might have his eye on the tablet, someone who would beat him to it, troubled him. His mind chewed on the problem as he drove back to the hotel. There must be something he could do to make the tablet less attractive to prospective thieves.

▲ ▲ ▲

Emilie stepped away from the angry tourist in the Painted Tomb. "I need to be going."

"Who sent you?" he asked again and grabbed her arm.

Emilie jerked her arm away and stepped back. "Take your hands off me," she said. "No one sent me. I'm a volunteer at the Ashkelon dig site."

His expression relaxed. "Oh."

Emilie rubbed her arm. "I'm not following you. We must be taking the same tour route. I was just looking at the fresco, and I happened to be standing next to you. I don't care about your phone conversation." She turned and trotted toward the exit.

"What did you hear?" the man called after her.

She ignored him.

Outside, the others were boarding the bus again. Emilie jumped on and breathed her relief when they pulled away. When she looked back at the Painted Tomb, the man in the suit stood outside, shading his eyes as he watched the bus kick up dust.

"Who was that guy?" Jenn asked.

"I have no idea. He practically attacked me, though!"

Emilie sleepwalked through the rest of the tour, wishing she had never agreed to come. When they boarded the bus for the last time, Emilie let her head drop against the back of the seat. She was surprised when Jenn shook her awake in the hotel parking lot.

The short nap helped, and Emilie decided she would join the team for dinner. She ran up to her room to splash cold water on her face and brush her hair.

The hall was empty when she emerged from her room. She hurried to the elevator and caught it just before the doors closed behind a couple stepping out. Emilie smiled at them and stepped into the elevator. She punched the ground floor button and the doors slid shut.

Involuntarily, she took a deep breath, as she nearly always did when closed into a tight space. At least it was only five floors.

Partway down, the elevator stopped. Emilie waited for the doors to open, for others to board. Nothing happened. She glanced at the numbers above the doors. None of them were lit. What floor was she on? Had she stopped between floors? Her breathing quickened. *Come on, move.*

She pushed the ground floor button again. And again. Nothing.

It's a nice hotel. The elevator must be in good shape. Nothing to panic about.

It suddenly seemed darker. The walls grew tight. She studied the ceiling and the walls. The polished metal reflected a pale face and large eyes. She pushed against the wall as if she could somehow expand the space.

She tapped a steady rhythm against the ground floor button with her thumb. Still nothing. Her breathing grew shallow, a precursor to the hyperventilation that might follow.

Breathe, breathe. Slower.

A small red button at the bottom of the panel said "emergency" in Hebrew and English. She was either going to scream or pass out if she didn't do something. She swallowed and pushed the button, and the elevator jolted into motion once more.

A moment later the doors opened on the ground floor, and Emilie tumbled out—into Jack Cabot's arms.

Jack laughed and put his hands on her shoulders. "Whoa, there, girl. We've only just met. You okay?"

Emilie inhaled deeply and nodded. "Sorry. Elevator got stuck."

Jack's eyebrows lifted in amusement.

Emilie inhaled again and shook her head. "Just panicked a little."

"You do that often?"

She walked toward the dining room and Jack followed. "Ever since I was a kid when I wandered into a cave at one of my father's dig sites at the end of the workday. I wanted to see the hieroglyphs on the walls in there. The team sealed the cave for the night with me inside that tiny, black, awful space. My father didn't miss me for hours."

Emilie glanced sideways at Jack, expecting a sarcastic reply. He was watching her, but said nothing.

Dinner was served buffet-style in a private dining room, and the team sat at round tables large enough for eight people. Jack was hailed by a table of college-age volunteers as soon as he entered, and he left Emilie at the food line. The crowd seemed small, and Emilie assumed that many of the volunteers were taking advantage of the weekend to get away. Margaret and Jenn sat at the same table, but there were no empty seats left. Emilie didn't know anyone she ate with, but she was in no mood for conversation. She searched the room for Dr. Herrigan as she ate.

Would he let her work on the tablet tonight? In spite of her exhaustion, she couldn't wait any longer to find out what had happened this afternoon. It was too early to go to bed. She wanted another chance with the tablet. Would it happen again? What if it did? Anticipation mixed with fear and left her stomach feeling like she'd been out to sea for the day.

When she had chewed and swallowed as much as her stomach would allow, Dr. Herrigan finally entered the room. She stood to speak to him, but he brushed past her and went to the front of the room to a podium with a microphone.

"Attention, everyone." He tapped the microphone and glared, waiting for the dinner chatter to cease. "There will be no lecture this evening since Shabbat has begun. For those of you who are interested, a film will be shown, beginning in thirty minutes." He paused as though he intended to say something more and took off his glasses. The crowd in the room watched as he pressed his fingers against the bridge of his nose, frowning. A moment later he stepped away from the microphone. The conversation around the tables resumed.

Emilie stopped him on his way out. "Dr. Herrigan? I was wondering if I could get started on the tablet this evening? I'm eager to see it again."

The muscles in his jaw worked silently. "The guard is gone for the day, Ms. Nazarro. Mr. Fitzwater was insistent that the tablet remains in the safe in my room unless the guard is present. I'm afraid you will have to wait until Sunday."

Emilie smiled as though they were coconspirators. "I promise not to tell Mr. Fitzwater," she said. "I'll bolt the door behind me and not let anyone in. I promise."

Dr. Herrigan took a step closer and looked down at her. "If there were a break-in—"

"No one will even know I'm there."

He nodded once. "Very well. What time?"

Emilie checked her watch. "It's already seven o'clock. If I don't start soon, I won't get much done. Thirty minutes?"

"Fine. Room 305."

"Thank you!" Emilie headed for the elevator—then decided on the stairs this time. She wanted to get a few books from her room before she started.

If she blacked out again, or whatever it was that had happened this afternoon, would she be able to do this job? And did it mean that she was crazy? Or did it mean that the Nazzaro blood that flowed through her veins was tinged with something worse than a love of archaeology?

▲ ▲ ▲

Victor sped up to his room after dinner. Emilie Nazzaro's dedication to her work had left him a half hour to make two crucial phone calls.

He steeled himself for the first call. He hadn't spoken to his brother in nearly a year. Would Don even come to the phone? He was Victor's only hope if this whole thing were going to work.

He hesitated, his hand on the receiver. It took a large dose of humility to ask his brother for money, and Victor wasn't sure he could do it. But what choice had Thomas Fitzwater given him?

"Victor, I can't be held responsible for your poor retirement planning," Fitzwater had said when they last spoke by phone a month ago. "Did you expect to dig in the dirt until you died?"

Victor had barely contained his rage. "Listen, Thomas, replacing me as dig director is one thing, but don't act as though you owe me nothing. I've kept silent for years about your growing collection of illegal antiquities. You've promised me that my discretion would be well compensated one day."

"Promised? Did we have a contract? I wasn't aware—"

"Don't be ridiculous. I intended to retire comfortably with that money. Do you expect me to live on my pension?"

Fitzwater's easy laugh infuriated Victor. "Perhaps you shouldn't have retired from teaching, then. Why did you retire, Victor?"

Victor clenched the phone. It had only been a year since his mind had started playing tricks on him, choosing when it would remember and when it wouldn't. He never gave a reason for his early retirement, never admitted it even to himself. He wouldn't name the illness that would be like a death sentence to a man who'd made his living with his intellect.

Fitzwater sighed. "Move somewhere warm, Victor. Write a book or two."

Victor had slammed the phone down. "My brain hasn't even left that as an option."

He had spent two consecutive days after that in a bar, drinking himself into a stupor. He'd lost his university position, his directorship of the Ashkelon dig, and the bonus from Fitzwater he'd been counting on. To top it off, he was losing his mind. What was left to live for?

A colleague had pried him out of the bar, sobered him up, and spent a day or two on suicide watch. Out of the fog of those few days, a chance comment by his friend had been the only thing to crystallize. Something about not getting mad, but getting even. That was when the plan began. The plan that brought him to this day, this phone call, this swallowing of his pride. He picked up the phone.

He found his brother at the auto shop he ran. After the initial awkwardness of reestablishing contact after so many months, Victor edged into his reason for calling.

"Are you kidding me, Vic?" Don laughed. "You're calling to borrow money from me? The high-and-mighty professor needs something from his blue-collar brother?"

"Give it a rest, Don. Can you help me or not?"

"What's it for? You haven't taken to gambling, have you?"

"Don, you know I don't have the slightest inclination toward your low-class vices. And it's none of your business."

"Whoa, boy. You came to me, remember? Begging for money!"

Victor clenched his teeth. "Don, you have no idea what the academic life is like. I have dedicated myself to the pursuit of knowledge and have contributed to mankind's understanding of himself. It has not paid extremely well, I'll admit. But I have accomplished more—"

"Save it, brother. We all know how much good Professor Herrigan has done in the world."

Victor was losing patience. "Will you loan me the money or not, Don?"

"Even if I wanted to, Vic, I don't have that kind of money. As you so often remind me, I chose the lesser road, remember?"

Victor rubbed at the muscles in his jaw. "You won't do it?"

"Won't. Can't. Sorry, brother."

They said terse good-byes, and Victor hung up. He checked the time. Only a few minutes before Eager Emilie would be rapping on his door. He'd worry about the money problem later. Right now he needed to set something up with Komodo.

He pulled his address book from his briefcase and dialed the number he found there.

"Yes, it's Dr. Herrigan," he said when Komodo answered. "Can you come to see the tablet tomorrow, during the Shabbat? No one will be working with it then."

"Yeah, I'll come tomorrow. And I want half the money up front, tomorrow."

Victor inhaled. "Fine. As long as you have it done quickly."

"Time will tell."

Victor replaced the phone and closed his eyes. His plan had seemed simple when he had constructed it in his comfortable townhouse in the States. Now that he was here, the reality was something different. He was haunted by the constant threat of someone else stealing the tablet first.

His mind jumped to Emilie Nazzaro. Why was she so eager to see the tablet here, without the guard he'd hired to protect it while she worked? Did she have plans of her own? And what about Jack Cabot, the unlikely rich boy playing volunteer, who seemed to be around every corner Victor turned?

69

Emilie intended to grab the books she needed and head to Herrigan's room, but Jenn stopped her inside their room. She sat cross-legged on the bed, the backs of her hands resting on her knees.

"Where are you going?" Jenn asked.

"Herrigan's letting me get started tonight."

"It's the weekend, Emilie."

"I know. I'm eager to start, though."

Jenn patted the bed beside her. "Sit down a minute. You've been running since you got here."

Emilie sat on the edge of the bed, her arms wrapped around her books.

"You need to relax, Emilie. Find your center. Do you know what I mean by that?"

"I think so. But I'm centered enough."

Jenn shook her head. "You're moving too fast to notice the beauty around you. You're not connected to the higher energy of the universe. You're going to run dry soon."

Emilie smiled. "Thanks for caring, Jenn. But I have to go."

On the third floor, Emilie searched for room 305, which was apparently at the far end of the long corridor. As Emilie passed room 315, the door opened.

"Hi, Emilie." Margaret Lovell's warm voice slowed Emilie's nervous rush to Herrigan's room.

"Hello."

Margaret frowned like a mother who's found her daughter with a skinned knee. "Jenn told me at dinner about that awful man who attacked you at the Painted Tomb. Are you okay?"

"It wasn't an attack, really. I'm fine."

"Are you sure?"

"I'm sorry, Margaret, I'm late for a meeting. Could we talk later?"

"Of course, hon. You come around my room whenever you feel like talking."

As Emilie continued her charge to room 305, she heard the elevator open behind her. Her arms ached from carrying the heavy books, and she hurried to the end of the hall and tapped on the door. Dr. Herrigan opened it immediately.

"Emilie, come in." He looked over her shoulder and his face darkened. "What can I do for you, Cabot?"

Emilie jerked her head around. She hadn't even heard Jack approach, but now he stood behind her, looking down on her with a scowl.

"Am I interrupting a private meeting, Dr. Herrigan?" he said.

"No. Come in."

The two entered the suite and Herrigan closed the door. He assumed an at-ease posture, his feet planted and his hands clasped behind his back.

"Ms. Nazzaro has just come to do some work here in my room. I am leaving her to it, of course. Did you need something, Cabot?" There was a challenge in his voice that Emilie didn't understand. A look passed between the two, something like two male lions circling each other, testing the other's strength.

Jack broke the moment. "I saw Emilie come up, and I was following her." He turned to Emilie. "A group of us are going out tonight." His voice changed, smoothed out. He smiled. "I figured you'd jump at the chance to go with us."

To go with you, you mean? This guy certainly was confident. But as Emilie watched Jack's eyes carefully, she sensed he was lying.

Dr. Herrigan straightened and coughed. "If you two will excuse me, I need to get something from the other room." He disappeared through a door.

"I'm sorry, Jack. I'm busy tonight."

He smiled, crossing his arms and leaning casually against the wall. "Are you starting work on the relic already? Here in Herrigan's room?"

"Where are all of you going tonight?" Emilie said.

Jack shrugged one shoulder. "I'm not sure. Tel Aviv, maybe."

The conversation stalled. Emilie sifted through things to say, but nothing sounded right.

"I guess I'll get going, then." Jack turned toward the door. "Thanks for the invitation. Maybe another time."

He waved, his back to her, and left the room.

Dr. Herrigan returned, the black case in his hand. "Has he left?" Emilie nodded.

"Good." He twirled the numbers and opened the case, laying it on the small table beside the window. Emilie winced as Dr. Herrigan brushed his fingers across the top of the tablet. But then he turned to her. "You must be very careful."

"Of course." Emilie laid her books beside the black case and pulled up a chair.

"I'll be back in about two hours. That will be enough time for tonight."

"That will be great. Thanks, Dr. Herrigan."

When Herrigan had left, Emilie turned back to the tablet. She almost felt like it was a living thing, waiting to devour her mind. She looked back at the door. Had it locked behind Herrigan? Hotel doors always locked automatically, didn't they? How easy was it to break into a room with key card entry? She crossed the room and locked the deadbolt.

The only person who knew she was here was Jack Cabot. He knew too much for Emilie's comfort, in fact. What was behind his following her here and his questions? She returned to the table, opened her zippered notebook, and took out Agent Sudiwitz's card. She'd be keeping her eye on Jack.

You've been keeping both eyes on him since you got here. Emilie shook her head, trying to ignore the truth. Jack Cabot was nothing she was looking for in a man, despite his fantastic looks. She wanted someone stable, hardworking, trustworthy. None of those adjectives seemed to fit the man who had just left. *Not to mention he's probably a thief.*

She faced the tablet again, knowing she'd put it off long enough. Pushing her books aside, she slid the case across the polished black table until it rested in front of her. Dr. Herrigan had touched it, and nothing had happened. This afternoon's "episode" had been jet lag and anticipation, nothing more.

With trembling fingers, Emilie reached inside the case toward the tablet.

Chapter 6

Down the hall from room 305, Jack waited in the glow of the soda machine, listening for doors opening. He had given Herrigan a few minutes to get out of the room before he returned to the third floor.

Jack padded up the hall until he reached Herrigan's door. Getting past the key card entry would be as simple as hotwiring a car. He could do it if he needed to, but was that the best idea? Was Emilie working in there, or was she packing up to leave with the tablet? He couldn't get any closer without Emilie knowing what he was doing. But she couldn't just pick it up and walk out with it, either. That would be far too obvious.

He watched the door for another five minutes. When Emilie didn't emerge, he assumed she was staying in there. Did that mean she was legit? Or was she waiting for a better opportunity? She'd have to work out something that didn't make her look guilty before she could walk away with it. Either way, standing outside the room wasn't going to accomplish anything. As long as Emilie was inside with the tablet, he had to assume it couldn't be stolen.

I could meet Tawny and be back in an hour. The blond from Amtza's who had told him about the statue had agreed to meet him again. If Layna Sardos were the seller, there was no way Jack could get close enough to the statue on his own. He needed inside help. Hopefully Tawny Turner would provide it.

He looked away from Herrigan's door to check his watch. If he were going to pull off these two jobs simultaneously, he'd need to do a little juggling. After one more glance at the closed door, he headed for the elevator.

▲ ▲ ▲

Inside Dr. Herrigan's room, Emilie reached for the tablet and laid her fingertips on its surface.

Nothing happened.

She waited, even closing her eyes for a moment. With a sigh of relief, she pulled her hand away. It had been a fluke, the vision she'd seen earlier. Just as she suspected, fatigue had played tricks with her mind.

She slid the case to one side and opened *An Akkadian Handbook: Paradigms, Helps, Logograms, and Sign Lists* to a page covered with symbols.

Emilie had questioned Thomas Fitzwater as to the method he'd prescribed for her work. She had offered to make a copy of the text and work from the copy so that the tablet could be donated earlier. Fitzwater had insisted she work from the original. "I've convinced them to let me keep it awhile," he'd said. "I want to have it on hand when you get it translated."

An hour later, Emilie was beginning to realize how challenging the job would be, taking apart every symbol and inferring its meaning. But she loved the work. It wasn't the archaeology that drew her to it. It was the words, always the words. To be able to understand a message from the past, with words the only way to connect with someone so distant, was a thrill. *And as long as I'm not going crazy, I don't care if it takes all summer.*

Soon, though, weariness set in. *Jenn was right; I'm running dry.* If she could sleep for a few minutes, like she had in the bus this afternoon, she'd make it through another hour of work. With a self-conscious glance toward the door, she pushed aside her books and the tablet case and dropped her head to her folded arms on the table. She stared at the black case, inches from her face, for a long minute. Her eyes grew heavy. Darkness surrounded her as she drifted into the mingled haze of wakefulness and sleep.

As thoughts and images tumbled through her mind, a growing awareness of the darkness intrigued, rather than frightened, her. She felt the dreaming begin before her consciousness left the hotel room, as though she walked into the dream, fully aware.

▲ ▲ ▲

From a dusky courtyard, she watched as men with bare chests and bare feet lit torches in the antechamber of a glowing temple. Past the slaves, through the antechamber, and into the oblong chapel behind it, this was where she would spend her life and give her soul.

The golden figure of Ishtar, regal yet unseeing, stood against the back wall, as it had stood for as long as she could remember, as long as she had been high priestess in this temple. She sighed, unwilling to enter, unwilling to make the sacrifice of her life, which Ishtar daily consumed as though never satisfied. Where was the fulfillment she had been promised?

A double clap and a familiar shout inside the temple drew her in. He would be waiting for her, she somehow knew. Waiting for her to assist him in the serving of the goddess's meal.

She was herself and yet not herself. Half dreamer, half participant, but wholly woven into the spell of the ancient night, with its smoking torches and chanting temple slaves.

She entered the chapel, pressing the back of her hand to her closed eyes and dropping to one knee before the goddess. Had she done this before? Had she always done this? Time and destiny and questions and the unknowable fused into deeds more automatic than understood. She knew only that she belonged here, for this was her home and her obligation.

She turned away from the goddess toward a voice, harsh and unyielding in its rebuke to the slaves. His back was to her. His black robe fell from broad shoulders; his clean-shaven head bespoke his authority in this temple as nothing else could. She waited, knowing he would turn to her. Knowing he would speak.

The slaves scuttled away to the temple kitchen. The shoulders flexed; the head tilted backward. He turned slowly. The pull of his deadening eyes was more than she could bear. She lowered her head. Would Qurdi-Marduk-lamur forever bring her heart to a standstill, as he had been doing since they first began to serve together in the temple of Ishtar?

"Where have you been, Warad-Sin?"

Where had she been? Her memory seemed to extend backward forever, yet she did not know where she had been the moment before. Vague and formless images of a black box and a clay tablet swirled before her. If she could reach out and pluck an image from the air, perhaps she would have an answer. She remained silent.

Qurdi shook his head. "It is of no consequence. It is time for the meal."

She was lost tonight, lost in the power of this place and in the fragments of memory. Together they drew the linen curtain around the statue and tables of food like courtiers ensuring their lady's privacy. Qurdi clapped, and slaves danced in with cymbals and drums, their twirling red robes floating into a scarlet haze as they spun. As they played, she performed the ritual fumigation for the goddess. Qurdi stood by and watched. After the meal, the curtain was opened and the tables removed. Water was placed before the goddess and the curtain drawn again so she could wash.

She performed these rituals as one who acted in her sleep, knowing and yet not knowing what her hands and her feet accomplished.

She watched in fascination, as though seeing for the first time, as Qurdi fell prostrate before the goddess.

"Great Goddess Ishtar, hear my prayer," he said, his voice a guttural moan. "Ishtar, grant my request. Grant me the power to overcome my enemies, who are your enemies also. Grant me answers to give to the king, answers to assure my place before him. When I am chief, then you also will rule."

She pitied him, she who was Warad-Sin and yet not Warad-Sin. He begged as she had seen him beg before, seeking answers and guidance and power for the life he wanted to lead, the life that had yet been denied. She pitied him and she loved him, though it was a love that went nowhere, that achieved nothing.

A sharp laugh behind her brought Qurdi to his feet. She turned, surprised.

"What do you want, Marduk Bel-Iddin?" Qurdi asked.

Their birth names shared allegiance to the same Marduk—chief god of Babylon—but there was little else in common between Qurdi-Marduk-lamur and the newcomer, Marduk Bel-Iddin.

Qurdi scowled. "You disrespect the evening meal by coming here."

"Your goddess is not mine, Qurdi," Marduk answered. "I care not."

Qurdi's lips curved downward farther. She watched a heavy fist clench against his robe.

She stepped between them. The powerful priest and the scholarly sorcerer. The two men she loved. But their quarrel was not about her.

She spoke boldly. "Why have you come, Marduk?"

His chin jutted forward. "With a warning. By the death of the moon god Sin this month, I will have disposed of the Jewish usurper. I will be made chief of magicians. You will do well to court my favor rather than my scorn, Qurdi."

She felt Qurdi rise up behind her, his breath hot on her neck as he spoke. "You are nothing, and your spells come to nothing. You will never be chief."

Marduk tilted his head. "The gods grant me the power to heal, Qurdi. They have dictated to me their sacred words. Incantations that will make my name great."

A knife blade gleamed in Qurdi's hand. She saw it beside her and reached for his arm. He twisted and shoved against her. She stumbled away. Desperate, she fell against Marduk.

"Stop this!" Her voice sounded shrill in her own ears. She covered Marduk's body with her own.

"I will kill him, Warad-Sin," Qurdi said.

She turned to face the knife, inches from her face.

"I will kill him," he said again. His empty eyes fell on Marduk as though to draw the life from his enemy through his gaze alone.

The knife thrust forward.

▲ ▲ ▲

Emilie jumped. She was back in Dr. Herrigan's room. She glanced wildly around her, but she was alone. The tablet lay safely in its case beside her on the table.

In the frightening chill that followed, her teeth began to chatter.

Chapter 7

The team started work Sunday morning well before dawn, reaching the dig site when the sun had risen enough to see only a few feet away. The break for Shabbat on Saturday had done little to pacify Emilie's concerns. She turned on a battery-operated lantern to start work at the table, while the rest of the team climbed into their squares to begin digging while it was still cool.

Each volunteer had an individual ten-meter square to dedicate his or her season to, with a one-meter barrier, the "bulk," running between each square to separate them. The grid was like a giant chessboard, with dirty, sweating chess pieces digging away in their squares. As the dirt was removed from the ground, volunteers took turns hauling it to the dump in wheelbarrows. Emilie worked under her canopy, her books spread before her and the tablet resting beside them.

At eight-thirty breakfast arrived, and they stopped to eat under canopies like hers. By lunchtime, they'd put in a full day's work; but after a meal at the hotel and time to rest, they headed back to the dig site for the most unpopular aspect of their work: pottery time. Emilie went back to her table, listening to the groans of a few team members.

Jenn walked by Emilie's table and wrinkled her nose at her. "Doesn't seem fair, you sitting in the shade while we're soaking and scrubbing and tagging every last jug handle out here."

"And don't you get to enjoy twice as much scrubbing today?" Emilie asked with a playful smile. "Since Friday's pottery time was put off for Shabbat?"

Jack approached them and Jenn crossed her arms. "She can tease," Jenn said to him. "She gets to sit in the shade."

Jack wrapped an arm around Jenn's shoulders and ignored Emilie. "But no one looks as good as you do when you're sweaty, Jenn."

Jenn tossed her head and laughed up at Jack. Emilie watched the two walk away.

Hours later, Emilie's stomach rumbled, alerting her that it was nearly dinnertime. The group began to gather tools, pottery, and artifacts to store in the corrugated metal Conex container before they left. Emilie watched them disappear into the dark storage shed, one by one, and rejoiced that she didn't have to go into that cramped space.

She glanced at the tablet, gratified to see that she had gotten further than she had expected today. There had been no more weirdness, but she had been careful not to touch the tablet at all. Or fall asleep.

Nearby, the Bedouin guard Fitzwater had hired to protect the tablet watched the proceedings around them. The man's dark skin and dark eyes contrasted sharply with his flowing white headgear and dress. Somewhere in the folds of those white robes, an AK-47 assault rifle was on call to protect Emilie from thieves. She wished the guard could protect her from her own mind.

The guard suddenly moved toward her, and Emilie stiffened. When he brought his rifle out, Emilie jumped up and followed his gaze.

A well-dressed man strode through the dirt toward her table.

The man from the Painted Tomb! By the time he reached Emilie, her guard had stepped in front of her. She closed the tablet case and locked it.

On the other side of the guard, the man laughed. "Stand down, soldier," he said. "I've only come to speak to the lady, not to pirate any of your treasures away."

"What do you want?" Emilie tucked a strand of hair behind her ear and remained standing. He wore a charcoal gray suit this afternoon and was still just as attractive, with wavy hair graying slightly at the temples.

He smiled and straightened his tie. "You must think I'm an ogre," he said. "The way I treated you a few days ago. I couldn't let it go. I had to find you and apologize."

"Apologize?" Emilie felt herself begin breathing again.

"My behavior was inexcusable. I was in the middle of some very delicate business dealings, and I'm afraid I let my paranoia get the best of me."

"You came out here to find me?"

"Please forgive my insulting behavior. I hope I didn't put an end to your sightseeing trip on Friday."

Emilie shrugged. "No, you didn't. It was no big deal."

The man took a few steps closer, skirting the guard, who hadn't relaxed. "My name is Sheldon Gold." He reached across the table to shake Emilie's hand.

"Emilie Nazzaro."

"Ms. Nazzaro, again, I am so very sorry for my rudeness. There was really no excuse for the way I treated you."

His smile seemed sincere. Emilie nodded. "Don't worry about it."

"Please," he said, "I was hoping you would allow me to repay you. Perhaps take you to see a few more sights and buy you dinner?"

In her peripheral vision, Emilie saw a man straighten from the dirt, watching Sheldon's back. *Jack Cabot.* She smiled at Sheldon Gold. "That would be nice, Mr. Gold. Thank you."

"Please call me Sheldon. Would you be free tonight?"

Jack still watched.

"Tonight would be wonderful." Emilie looked down at her T-shirt and cutoffs. "I'm nearly finished here—"

"Let me take you back to your hotel. I don't mind waiting while you get ready."

Emilie hesitated. "Uh, why don't I just meet you later? The Ashkelon Plaza?"

"Of course." Sheldon looked at his watch. "Will an hour be time enough?"

"An hour would be great."

Sheldon left, and Emilie could feel Jack approaching as she gathered her books and notes.

He stepped under the canopy. "Everything all right, Emilie?" He eyed Sheldon's car.

So now he's suddenly interested? "No problems." She handed the black case to the Bedouin, noting how Jack's eyes followed it. "Just making plans for tonight."

"Maybe you should check with Herrigan," Jack said. "He may expect you at the lecture tonight."

Emilie frowned. Jack was right. She should check.

She found Dr. Herrigan on the other side of the site.

He scowled at her request, but then nodded. "I suppose you must be free to keep your own schedule in the evenings, Emilie."

Jack was still standing under the canopy when she returned to retrieve her books. She gave him a small wave and walked toward the parking area where the other volunteers were boarding buses.

She had a moment of second thoughts. Had Sheldon Gold really come here to apologize, or had he come to check her alibi, making sure she wasn't some kind of business spy?

▲ ▲ ▲

Victor's position as excavation director came with only a few perks, but he appreciated the chance to sit in the shade occasionally and make a few notes. This afternoon he perched on one of the benches where the team usually ate breakfast, watching the volunteers finish up for the day. They would put away their finds and their tools and then head for the buses. Victor made a few notes in his daily ledger, but his thoughts were distracted.

He watched Emilie close up the case, hand it to the guard, and walk toward the buses. Jack Cabot wouldn't be riding the bus since he had a car of his own. Was having a car a necessary part of Cabot's plan to steal the tablet?

As if in answer to his thoughts, Jack dumped his gear in the corrugated metal Conex shed, waved to a teammate, and headed to his own car.

Victor swore. How could he keep an eye on both of them if they went off in separate directions?

His gaze drifted to the nearly empty grid where only a handful of volunteers still cleaned up. His mind was working on the problem of getting the second half of the money for Komodo. The only idea he'd had was a risky one. He'd agreed to Komodo's price, but he wouldn't have the money for him until after he'd sold the tablet. That meant convincing Komodo to give him the fake tablet before he was fully paid.

Komodo had come to the hotel yesterday to study the tablet. Once again he'd been noncommittal about how quickly he could finish it. Victor was desperate to get it done before Emilie had too much time to study it. The longer she studied it, the better the chances were that she'd recognize a fake. He would have preferred to wait until she'd finished to make the switch, but his buyer was anxious. The deal had to happen soon. And the sooner he made the switch, the less chance there was of someone else stealing it, though he'd had a few thoughts on how to prevent that, as well. As for Komodo, he had a plan to speed him up, too.

His attention focused on a volunteer who stood and strolled

toward him. *Margaret Lovell.* An interesting woman, as women went. Victor had never had much luck with them. This one had spoken with him several times, though he hadn't encouraged it.

"Certainly is hotter than I expected it to be," she said, sitting uncomfortably close on the bench. She fanned her face with her hand.

Victor edged away from her. "Can I do something for you, Mrs. Lovell?"

"Oh no, thanks, Victor. I just needed to sit a moment before I get on that stifling bus. Is that okay?"

Victor stood. "Mrs. Lovell, I prefer that the volunteers address me as 'Dr. Herrigan.' I realize that you are considerably older than most of them, but—"

She laughed. "A real sweet-talker, aren't you?"

He realized his mistake and fought to reclaim his dignity. "I only meant that most of them are students—"

"I know what you meant, Dr. Herrigan. I understand. You don't need to worry about me." She took a deep breath and stood beside him. "Better get going. What's on the schedule for tonight?"

"Tonight?" Victor paused, searching the elusive memory banks. "Tonight we will be, uh, having a—program—after dinner. . . ."

Margaret cocked her head. "You okay?" She raised her eyes to his, and he felt as though she had X-ray vision.

"I'm fine, yes." He stepped away. "I'll see you at dinner."

"I'm counting on it," she called as he walked toward his car.

Victor ignored the thought of Margaret's inquisitive smile as he prepared for his second phone call to Komodo. Once back in his room, he gave in to thoughts of Fitzwater's betrayal until he'd worked up enough anger to be convincing.

"Komodo?" he grunted when the man answered the phone.

"Yeah?"

"I need a commitment on a finish date for this thing."

"I told you—"

"I'm sick of your vague answers, Komodo. I want it done by Friday. I have friends here. Friends you don't want to meet. Don't force me to introduce you to them."

"Are you threatening me, Herrigan?"

"Have it done by Friday."

Victor hung up, angry that Komodo didn't sound worried, angry that he'd been forced into a bluff, angry that his life was spinning out of control. He should probably abandon the whole thing right now. But then he'd truly be left with nothing.

▲ ▲ ▲

Emilie showered and changed quickly, knowing the hour Sheldon had given her was disappearing. Would he leave if she wasn't in the lobby on time?

The flutter in her stomach surprised her. *Come on, Em. You just met the guy.* Her thoughts about the kind of man she was looking for—stable, hardworking—seemed prophetic. Aside from the initial conflict when they'd met at the Painted Tomb, Sheldon seemed like just her type of guy. *You also said trustworthy, and that remains to be seen. He's already shown with that phone conversation that he's got a temper. Go slow, Emilie.*

Despite the warnings in her head, as the elevator doors opened on the hotel lobby, Emilie's heart flipped. She stepped out and spotted Sheldon right away. Across the lobby, he was talking with an elderly woman, a hotel guest Emilie had seen shuffling through several times. Sheldon's head was bent to hers, his face lit by a smile. As Emilie watched, he threw back his head and laughed in apparent response. The woman placed frail fingers on his arm and laughed with him.

Emilie approached.

"Here she is," Sheldon said. His smile welcomed her into the conversation. The older woman turned.

"Hello," Emilie said, waiting for an introduction.

Sheldon took Emilie's arm and gestured to the older woman. "I was being entertained by this beautiful lady while I waited."

The woman shook her head, her eyes twinkling. "Don't let this one get away, dear," she said to Emilie, patting Sheldon's arm again.

Emilie smiled.

Sheldon turned to her. "You look beautiful. Shall we go?"

When she nodded, Sheldon returned his attention to the other woman, bending to kiss her translucent skin. "You be good," he whispered.

Emilie thought the woman might have actually blushed as she and Sheldon left the lobby.

Sheldon still held her arm. "I'm sorry I couldn't introduce you. We didn't exchange names."

"You just met her?"

"She was waiting for her husband while I waited for you."

Emilie settled back into the luxurious car. "Where are we going?"

"Gail Yahalom. Wonderful grilled fish. And then I want to show you the two Hellenic sarcophagi, since I think you missed it on your tour the other day. The one I ruined."

"You didn't ruin it," Emilie said, laughing. "You just dented it a little."

The restaurant, Gail Yahalom, sat in the town center on the main street of Sederot Ha Nassi. During the meal, Emilie asked Sheldon about his work.

"Finance." He shrugged. "Boring stuff to most people. But I'm not in Ashkelon on business, I'm vacationing for a few days between meetings."

"Then what was that phone call at the Painted Tomb—vacation plans?" Emilie laughed.

Sheldon smiled. "You got me there. I have a little trouble with the concept of downtime."

"I appreciate your taking time out tonight, then," Emilie said.

Sheldon reached across the table to lay his fingertips on her hand. "You're making 'time-out' much more attractive."

When she dropped her head, Sheldon leaned down slightly to catch her eyes again and pulled her gaze back to him. "I'm serious," he said, not letting her eyes go.

His fingers still lay across hers, and Emilie felt the spark travel up her arm. "Thank you," she said.

After the meal, Sheldon drove to the center of the Afridar district, where they walked past the sarcophagi. As they moved through the courtyard where the two mummified bodies were located, Emilie had the prickly feeling that someone was following them. She glanced over her shoulder several times, until Sheldon finally asked if she were looking for someone.

"No," she said. "It's nothing. Just a creepy feeling."

He pretended to be insulted. "And I was getting the impression you liked me."

Emilie laughed. "It's not you," she said, leaning into him slightly.

Sheldon wrapped an arm around her and squeezed. "Good."

Ashkelon was starting to swing into its nightlife when they arrived at a beachside café for dessert and coffee. They found a seat on the outdoor deck with a view of the Mediterranean. While Emilie sipped the hot brew, Sheldon excused himself and left the table.

Emilie looked around the café, tapping her foot to the pop music that blasted from the bar.

A familiar figure appeared in the doorway, lit from behind by the restaurant's lights.

"Jack?" Emilie squinted across the deck.

Jack stepped outside. "Hello, Emilie."

Another woman joined Jack on the deck, as thin as a fashion model, with chiseled cheekbones and flawless skin. She wrapped a red-fingernailed hand around Jack's arm and leaned her bleached-blond hair against him. "Our table's ready," she purred.

Jack barely acknowledged her. "What are you doing here?" he asked Emilie.

Her usual irritation with the man kindled. "I'm having coffee."

"Alone?"

"No. With a friend."

Jack nodded. "That guy I saw you talking to at the dig site? I didn't realize you knew anyone else in Ashkelon."

Emilie smiled. "I do now."

The girl with Jack seemed to have had enough of their conversation. "Jack, I'm hungry. Can we please sit down?" She tugged on his arm and threw a hostile look over at Emilie.

Jack touched Emilie's arm and searched her face. "Just be careful, okay? I–I wouldn't want you to get hurt."

Emilie bit her lip at the concern on Jack's face. She nodded once, unable to think of a reply.

Jack walked backward into the restaurant, his eyes still fixed on Emilie until other customers moved between them.

What was that all about? Emilie fought the churning feeling in her stomach. *Just when I think he's a total jerk, he turns all sincere and protective.* She shrugged, trying to dismiss the incident. *You're an idiot, Em. Concentrate on the guy you're with.*

Sheldon came back a minute later, and Emilie said nothing about meeting Jack.

During coffee and cake, Emilie learned that Sheldon was an antiquities lover as well. Although Ashkelon was rigorously promoting itself as a resort town, Sheldon had stopped here primarily for the archaeological interest. He'd chosen the Holiday Inn because it was near Sheikh Awad's tomb in the Barnea district.

When they had finished a second cup of coffee, Sheldon laid his hand on hers again, looking out at the moon tracing a path across the sea. "Would you like to walk on the beach?"

Emilie hesitated. Was it smart to walk alone with a man she'd just met? Probably not. She smiled. "I'd love to."

▲ ▲ ▲

Jack pulled out a chair for Tawny and then took the opposite seat so he could watch Emilie's table. When Emilie's companion returned, however, Jack found he couldn't get a good look at his face.

Was it the guy she'd been talking with at the dig? From the grid where he'd been digging, Jack had only seen the man's back and couldn't hear anything being said. Emilie hadn't actually admitted that's who she was with, but he knew it. The conviction aggravated him, like a pebble in his shoe, through his dessert.

He needed to concentrate on Tawny Turner and the chance of getting the statue after all. She was his only way to get around Layna. She wasn't the brainless beauty she seemed to be, and enlisting her inside help was the best idea he'd had so far.

"I don't know, Jack," Tawny said. "I'm not sure I can get that close to her without her suspecting something."

"You don't have to keep up the front for long," Jack said. "Just get me the information I need and you can walk away."

"How much information?"

"Where she's got the statue, who's watching it, what other buyers she has lined up."

"I don't know."

"Trust me, Tawny. It'll be worth it. A day or two of work, no danger, plenty of money. What more could you ask for?"

Tawny sighed and slid her hands across the table. Tucking her fingers into Jack's hands, she studied his face with raised eyebrows and a playful smile on her lips. "What more indeed?"

▲ ▲ ▲

Emilie and Sheldon left the café using the stairs off the deck.

Emilie was relieved not to have to see Jack again. They dropped their shoes in the car and started down the beach. Emilie was glad she had worn a light dress, and she laughed as Sheldon cuffed his pants above his ankles.

"What?" he said. "Aren't I stylish enough for you?"

An hour later, Emilie wondered how far they had walked. The moon had risen above their heads. Sheldon had taken her hand a long time ago, and they walked in comfortable familiarity. Sheldon asked probing questions about Emilie's life, and she found herself spilling out details of her childhood that she'd never told anyone.

"And that brings me up to the present," she said.

"I'm jealous," Sheldon said. "I'd love to be poring over some ancient relic every day, instead of my laptop."

"Maybe someday your laptop will be an ancient relic."

Sheldon laughed. "Tell me about this piece you're working with now."

"Actually, I'm not supposed to. The whole thing's a little secretive." Emilie hoped Sheldon wouldn't take offense.

"No problem. Something the tomb raiders would be after, is it?"

"You could say that."

Sheldon sighed. "It's a crime the way valuable pieces get plundered and traded without being studied properly in the places they were originally found."

"Exactly! People just don't understand that the provenance of a piece is just as important as the find itself. Once they've ripped it from its context, we can't learn nearly as much from it."

"Well, I hope you can trust the people you're working for." Sheldon slowed to a stop, glancing at his watch. "Perhaps we should turn around."

Emilie agreed, though she could have kept walking all night. "I have to be on the dig site by dawn tomorrow."

They turned back and walked in silence for a few minutes, until Emilie picked up the thread of conversation. "Why did you say you hoped I could trust the people I was working for?"

Sheldon shrugged. "I don't know. You hear stories. I'm sure you've heard them, too. About pieces being stolen from private collections, when the truth is that the collector has kept it for himself."

Emilie shook her head. "Thomas Fitzwater isn't a collector. He acquired this piece for—special reasons. He plans to donate it to Israel after I'm done working with it. I know he will."

Sheldon squeezed her hand as they walked. "I'm sorry I upset you. Forget I mentioned it. Let's talk about something else."

The tide lapped at their feet as Emilie and Sheldon drifted back toward the car, talking of antiquities and archaeology, but Emilie's thoughts ran as an undercurrent to the conversation. *This is the most interesting man I've met in years.*

The drive back to the Ashkelon Plaza Hotel took only a few minutes. Sheldon parked the car and escorted her into the hotel lobby.

"I'll leave you here, I suppose," he said, turning to face Emilie in front of the elevator.

She edged closer. "I enjoyed the evening very much, Sheldon. Thank you."

"So I've made up for my rudeness on Friday?"

Emilie laughed. "More than made up for it."

He smiled and took her hand in his. "I enjoyed myself, too." He paused, and Emilie's heartbeat sped up. "Perhaps we'll run into each other again sometime. Although I'm only in town for a few more days, so probably not."

Emilie smiled and waited.

"Good night, then," he said, releasing her hand.

"Good night."

Sheldon turned and walked through the lobby. Emilie waited. Would he turn around at the door? But when he reached it, he pushed the door open and disappeared into the night without looking back.

Emilie fought the lump in her throat as she ascended to the fifth floor.

Don't be surprised, Em. This is the way it always goes. One night of listening to your stories about Middle Eastern history and they all bail. But Sheldon had seemed different. They shared the same interests. What had she done wrong this time?

It didn't matter, since it had ended in the same way, with Emilie alone.

Chapter 8

The darkness shrouded her like a heavy mantle. A single candle flickered in the palace courtyard. She crossed the bricks on soft and silent feet, watching Marduk circle a flame over a large, shallow clay bowl in a hypnotically rhythmic pattern. She recognized him, even from a distance, with his back to her. His regal head, his heavy shoulders. The purple robe, woven with a golden moon and its attending golden stars.

She drew close and whispered his name.

Marduk turned slowly, as though not surprised by her visit, though it was late and the high priestess of Ishtar should rightly be bedded down in the temple by this hour.

"Warad-Sin. You have come." He turned back to the dish, to his study of the goat entrails.

She felt the confusion again, the bewilderment of belonging, yet not belonging. Of dreaming, yet knowing. Did she fit here?

"I am glad you came, Warad. Between us now we honor four gods. Your name honors the moon god, Sin; and your life is dedicated to Ishtar, goddess of fertility. And I honor Marduk, chief god of wisdom, and Bel, the sun god." He probed the entrails with bloody fingers. "Sun, moon, love, wisdom. We create a circle that the gods must honor with knowledge."

She shivered in the coolness of the desert night. The fires of the palace did not burn in the empty courtyard. "What knowledge do you seek, Marduk?"

Marduk resumed his flame circle over the entrails. "Divine direction. Knowledge to increase the king's domain."

"Nabu-kudurri-usur's domain encompasses nearly the world." The words tumbled easily from her lips, as though the name were a household one.

"The king rewards those who are loyal to his kingdom. The knowledge I seek may not increase the borders of Babylon, but it will bring fresh power."

"Power to heal?" She remembered his boast to Qurdi, as one remembers a distant dream. A boast of power granted by the gods. It was then she noticed the tablet lying on the table beside the dish of entrails.

He turned to face her again, his dark eyes reflecting the candle flame. Or were those eyes lit from within? "Yes, Warad. I have been loyal to the gods, have sacrificed in their names; and they have returned their favor by granting me healing power. Words that have never been spoken, words that summon the very gods themselves to do my bidding."

"What are these words?" She asked as one interested in the ancient language, in the patterns and rhythms long forgotten, as though she asked from a place far distant.

Marduk shook his head. "They are not to be spoken lightly. But I have written them down. All of it, the rituals and the story of how the gods have chosen me." He turned to the tablet. "And tonight I will consecrate the tablet to the gods, ensuring its eternal power."

The footsteps of a loincloth-girded slave whispered across the courtyard. Marduk signaled and the slave approached, eyes down toward the bricks. She watched the deference, somehow amazed to see that it extended to her as well.

"Remove the entrails," Marduk said. He wiped his hands on a

rag, then took her elbow and led her to the courtyard entrance, through the smaller garden court beyond, and to the front gate of the palace, with its vaulted archway. "You should not be here at this hour, Warad. Your loyalty will be questioned."

She wanted to be loyal, to live up to the dedication to Ishtar, but her heart was drawn to Marduk. She spoke of her reasons for coming, then. Reasons she had not known she had until she began to speak. "It is Qurdi. I have come to warn you."

"I need no warning about Qurdi."

She pressed her hand against his chest. "He will speak of you before the king."

Marduk frowned. "Speak of what?"

"He plans to tell the king that you have claimed to have healing power over every illness. He will influence the king to test you, to bring you someone who is surely ready to walk with the gods, and challenge you to heal him."

Marduk gazed at the night sky. His face was as one who looks upon the face of a friend. "Do not concern yourself for me, Warad. The gods will favor me when the season of my ascendance is at hand." He gave her a gentle push toward the gate. "Now, go. Before you are missed."

She studied his face for another moment, then melted into the shadows outside the palace walls.

The city streets were not as quiet as the palace. Babylon encouraged her inhabitants to slave for her during the day and revel in her excesses through the night.

She wandered through the streets, watching the carousing with the disinterested eye of one who walks in her sleep. And yet, some part of her wished to join the celebration.

A white-robed man ran past her with a flaming torch, a young woman chasing him and laughing. Had she felt such joy? Such abandon? She had given herself to the gods to find a higher calling beyond herself. Small fragments of joy had come to her, but only enough for her to taste and never be satisfied.

A small crowd enveloped her, chanting as they danced a cere-mony to Ishtar. She recognized the words, joined their dance, joined their chant.

"Emilie, Emilie, Emilie."

▲ ▲ ▲

Emilie sat up with a gasp, the darkness foreign around her. A hand squeezed her shoulder.

"Emilie! Emilie, are you okay?"

"What?" She swallowed and opened her eyes.

Jenn stood over her bed, surprise in her eyes. "You were saying something in your sleep. Like a chant or something. It kinda freaked me out."

"Sorry." Emilie took a deep breath.

Jenn returned to her bed, but sat on its edge. "Some dream, huh?"

"Yeah. Some dream."

"Want to talk about it?"

Emilie stood and went to the bathroom for a glass of water. She flipped the light on and stared at herself in the mirror. She looked the same as always, Emilie Nazzaro, drinking a glass of water. She went back to the bed. Jenn was waiting.

"I don't know, Jenn. It's a little weird."

Jenn propped her pillows against the headboard and settled back. "I like weird."

Emilie shrugged and sat on her own bed. "Like I told you, it's the second dream I've had like this." She told Jenn as much as she remembered of the most recent dream, trying to communicate the incredible sensory reality of the experiences. "It's as if I was really there." She ran her hands through her hair. "You know, I've stud-ied Babylon in depth. All of that stuff I already knew, of course. But it just never felt so real before."

Jenn was wide-eyed by the time she finished. "I'm so jealous."

Emilie laughed. "Of a couple of dreams?"

Jenn sat forward, her head shake intense. "They're not just dreams, Emilie. Don't you see? You've been given a vision of a past life."

"Come on. I told you, I've studied all that stuff. Combine that with your suggestion that I go back to the ancients and see what they believed before Christianity interfered with people's beliefs, and you've got the ingredients for a great dream."

"Are you sure? You sounded like it was more than a dream."

Emilie sat back against the bed. "I don't know. It was weird. But listen, Jenn. Take it from me. You don't want to go back to that. The ancients might have been religious, but all that stuff was pretty whacked out. Cutting up animals to study their guts for messages from the gods? And the gods they worshipped—the sun, the moon? You don't seriously think the sun is a god, do you? Science has come too far for that."

Jenn shook her head. "Not the sun, not the moon, no. But what they represent. The ancients were on a journey, a journey that is still continuing as we learn about our own divine nature. They worshipped what they could see of the universe, and they were right in doing so, for their place in history. But as time went on, humankind realized that the visible things of the universe were merely symbols. Symbols of the divinity of the whole universe, including humankind. We are all part of the divine. That's what the ancients can teach us."

Emilie exhaled. She thought about pulling out the journal she'd brought to write down some of her questions, but sleep was beckoning her again. "I don't know, Jenn. It makes sense, I guess. I just have to think about it more."

Emilie yawned as the bus pulled from the Ashkelon Plaza Hotel parking lot on Monday morning, heading for the dig site before first light. With her middle-of-the-night conversation with Jenn, the night had been too short. Now the warm darkness of the Israeli morning closed in around her, like an oppressive weight on her chest, reminding her of Babylon.

She had awakened an hour ago, vowing not to think about her dreams, or her evening with Sheldon, or about romance at all. She needed to focus on the work today. *At least Jack drives his own car to the dig site.* She was glad not to have to see him on the bus. He was starting to be a distraction, too.

Margaret Lovell squeezed in beside her. The seat's aging springs squeaked in protest. An elderly couple sat in front of them.

Margaret patted the woman on the shoulder. "Looking forward to another day, Ella?"

Ella turned and smiled. "Only a few days left for us. But that's all we could take, I think. Ben's not as young as he used to be."

"Hey!" Ella's husband frowned in mock indignation. "The years aren't going backwards for you, either."

Ella laughed. "I worry about this fellow every time he picks up a shovel." She nudged Ben with an elbow, and he rolled his eyes.

"It's the chance of a lifetime," Ben said. "We're glad we came."

Margaret nodded and leaned back in her seat. "Is everything okay this morning, Emilie?"

"Is my face that obvious?"

Margaret patted Emilie's leg. "Let's just say I have a sense about people. You seem sad this morning."

Emilie watched the sleeping city slip by outside the bus window. "A little, I guess. But it's no big deal."

"Are you homesick, hon? Missing somebody special at home?"

Emilie laughed. "No. There's nobody special."

Margaret patted her leg again, this time in understanding silence.

Emilie looked over at the older woman, once again struck by her kindness. "How about you, Margaret? Who's anxiously waiting for you to get home?"

Margaret's face clouded, but a moment later, she brightened again. "Oh, the other nurses on my floor are probably missing me. They're having to deal with all the cranky patients they usually foist on me."

Emilie laughed. "You're a nurse?"

"Cardiac unit." Margaret swept her graying hair behind her shoulder, and Emilie noticed a faded tattoo of a butterfly just above the neckline of Margaret's shirt.

"So, what are you doing on a dig site in Israel?"

"Killing myself, most likely." She shrugged. "It was a gift, believe it or not. I've always been interested in biblical archaeology, so a bunch of friends from my church got together and paid for this trip for my fiftieth birthday."

"How nice!"

Margaret's eyes twinkled. "I don't know. If the rest of the dig is as hard as these first couple of weeks, I'm going to start thinking they sent me here to kill me!"

Emilie laughed. "I'm sure you'll make it."

Margaret sighed. "I hope so. I'd hate to disappoint them. It was such a lovely gesture. That church has been my family the past few years." The cloudy look returned to Margaret's eyes.

Emilie searched for a way to delicately ask about Margaret's real family. She wasn't good at talking to people about their pain, perhaps because her own was always so close to the surface. "It's great you have that kind of support," she finally said.

Margaret half-turned to Emilie. "It's not just the people that are the support in tough times, though. It's the faith."

Emilie nodded without replying.

"How about you, Emilie? Do you have a faith that holds you up when life gets tough, that guides you through life?"

Emilie took a deep breath of the humid air. She could smell the sea and knew they must be nearing the national park where the dig site was. "No, I don't think I do." She grasped for words to define her hazy spiritual place. "I think I believe there's something out there, you know. But I don't feel connected to it at all. I wish I did, though." She faltered and stopped, wishing she'd made her beliefs sound stronger. Margaret was a sweet woman, but she was obviously very religious. That type of person usually looked down on the "pagans" who didn't agree with him or her.

But Margaret smiled across at her, nodding. "Then don't worry. If you're searching for a connection to something higher, you'll find it. It's a journey."

The bus hit a bump, jolting its passengers. Emilie and Margaret laughed.

"Hopefully your journey won't be this rough," Margaret said. "But there are some stops along the way. 'Signposts,' I call them. Places where I paused in my own spiritual journey to look around me, to understand a few things about my life."

"What kind of things?"

"Do you believe truth can be known, Emilie?"

Emilie shrugged and shook her head. "I think everyone makes their own choices about what is true for them. It's not right to impose my views on someone else."

"Well, I would never impose. But I do know that truth can be known. I can show it to you by showing you those discoveries I made. You let me know if and when you'd like to hear about them."

Emilie smiled. "I think I—" She stopped as the bus squealed to a halt in the middle of the street. The chatter on the bus grew ominously quiet. The driver swung the door open. An armed Israeli soldier climbed aboard and faced down the passengers as though they had violated a peace treaty.

Chapter 9

Emilie watched the soldier on the bus make eye contact with each passenger. "Look around you, please," he said in careful English. "Do you see any packages that do not belong to you? Please identify."

Emilie searched the floor with the rest of the team. One by one, heads popped back up to watch the soldier in silence.

"Is there anyone who finds something?" he asked.

When no one answered, he nodded and jumped off the bus. A moment later, the bus rumbled down the street once again.

Margaret put a hand over her chest. "What did I tell you? I think I'm going to meet my Maker over here, one way or another."

Emilie laughed. "I don't think it's anything to worry about. They're just very careful here."

"Careful is good." Margaret took a deep breath and blew it out.

It was nearly dawn when the team tumbled out of their buses at the dig site. Enough light to dig through the dirt but not enough to study the tablet, Emilie discovered. She turned on her battery-operated lantern and placed it on the table beside her books. She heard someone approach and turned, expecting Dr. Herrigan with the tablet.

Jack Cabot leaned against the table. "Good morning, Emilie."

"Jack."

"Did you and your friend have an enjoyable evening last night?"

"Yes, thank you."

"You sure have plenty of friends in this town for a sorceress, don't you?"

Emilie bristled. What kind of question was that? She smiled sweetly. "You can never have enough of them, right?"

Dr. Herrigan arrived, chasing Jack away and handing the case to Emilie. A chill shot through her as she reached for it, even though she'd had no more "episodes" when she touched it. Still, the dreams were continuing. She never felt completely safe when she was working on it.

"Ready to work, Emilie?" Dr. Herrigan asked.

"More than ready, sir." Emilie laid the case on the table, squaring it up beside her neat stack of books. She opened her notebook to where she'd stopped taking notes yesterday and retrieved two freshly sharpened pencils, rolling them together and lining them up with the side of her notebook. Thoughts of Sheldon and Jack would have to take a hike.

As Emilie sat down at the table, she realized that she could see almost nothing beyond her work area under the canopy. The Bedouin guard stood at the edge of her pool of light, his face as stonelike as usual; but beyond that, everything else in the early dawn lay in shadow.

They can all see me, though. Sitting here next to this spotlight. The thought made her chest pound with self-consciousness. She felt vulnerable, like those dreams where everyone is watching you do something incredibly stupid. She straightened the sheets of paper in her notebook, tucked her hair behind her ears, and lowered her head to the work. *Concentrate on the tablet.*

She studied the symbols covering the clay tablet. What secrets would she find today? Although she didn't feel safe with it, in a strange way she was beginning to form an attachment to this tablet. Almost like it was growing to be part of her. Was that natural? She thought of Margaret's words on the bus. It's a journey to find your connection to something higher. Was the tablet part of her journey? She felt a surge of something akin to affection for the piece of clay; and in an act of defiance against her rational mind, she laid both her hands across it.

No visions, no dreams. Only the roughness of ancient clay beneath her fingers and a strange serenity in her heart.

▲ ▲ ▲

Jack took a break from his tedious digging to stretch his sore muscles and swipe at the sweat running down his temples. The noonday sun beat down without mercy, and Jack had soaked through his T-shirt hours ago. He laid his pick on the bulk between his square and Jenn's and looked over at Emilie once again.

He watched as she pushed back the long hair that fell across her books, a habit he had seen countless times over the past six hours. She hadn't taken a break, even when the others had stopped to eat breakfast. From Jack's vantage point, she seemed to be working feverishly on deciphering that tablet. It was nearly lunchtime now, and Jack planned to spend the lunch hour accomplishing his other objective: retrieving the Aesculapius statue. He found himself wishing he could eat lunch with Emilie instead.

Jenn's voice cut into his thoughts. "She's still in the same place she's been every time you've looked, rich boy."

Jack turned and lifted his pick again, giving Jenn a guilty smile. *Yeah, go ahead and think I'm watching Emilie. Better you don't know it's the tablet I'm keeping my eye on.* But even as he said it to himself, he knew it wasn't entirely true. The guard on duty made the tablet difficult to snatch. It wasn't the tablet that kept drawing his eye.

Jenn laughed. "You sure you want to get involved with her?"

Jack studied the top of Jenn's head as she dug. "Why? What have you heard?"

"She's okay, I guess. But that thing she's working on. People are saying it's cursed."

"Who's saying that?"

Jenn leaned on a shovel. "I don't know. Everybody."

The group began to clean up the digging equipment. They'd be back after lunch to scrub pottery. Jack wandered over to Emilie's table. The Bedouin beside the canopy-covered table kept to his post like a guard at Buckingham Palace. *Does this guy ever take a break?* When was the tablet unprotected?

As he approached the guard, Emilie looked up. Jack flashed one of his charming smiles, though from the amused look on her face, she wasn't buying today. He loitered near the guard. "Digging's hot work," he said to the man. "But I think I'd rather dig than stand in one place all day."

The guard stared ahead, as though Jack were nothing more than a buzzing insect.

"They don't give you a break, do they?"

Again, his question was met with silence. Jack wondered if the man understood English. He could try Arabic, but Emilie was within earshot, and being multilingual didn't fit the cover he was using here.

One of the volunteers in his square called him over to help with equipment. With another glance at the guard, he walked away. He'd gotten nowhere, but one thing was certain. After the screwup in Turkey, he wasn't going to walk away from this one the loser.

Emilie dragged herself onto the bus, overjoyed that the morning was over. She'd skipped breakfast, not wanting to stop her work, and now her head floated somewhere above her shoulders, definitely not attached. After lunch at the hotel, she'd have a couple of hours to sleep before heading back to the dig site for several more hours of work.

The meal and the nap were a just reward for the seven lines of text she'd deciphered this morning. Actually, getting seven lines deciphered was reward enough in and of itself. With every symbol she translated, Emilie felt a closer connection to the world of the past. It was as if Marduk Bel-Iddin were there beside her, connecting with her through his written words. She loved every word etched into the clay.

She was already leaning her head against the window, eyes closed, when someone else dropped into the seat beside her. "Jack!"

"Okay if I sit with the prettiest girl on the bus?"

"You can sit anywhere you want." The line came out colder than she'd intended. Jack nodded and frowned. "Where's your car?"

Jack shrugged. "Just felt like riding with the team today."

Neither spoke for several minutes. The bus seats were small, and Emilie felt the heat radiating from Jack's sweaty upper body. She tried not to notice the way his clinging T-shirt defined the muscles across his chest and arms.

Jack cleared his throat. "That guard you have seems very dedicated."

"They pay him well. Better than he'd get herding sheep. He doesn't want to risk losing his job."

"The artifact's well protected, then. You never worry about its safety?"

"No." Emilie looked out the window. Everything about this guy sent mixed signals. His body language seemed to say he was interested in her, but all he talked about was the tablet. Maybe she was misinterpreting his interest in her, but there was no mistaking his interest in the tablet.

What did you expect? A guy like that doesn't go for your type. Remember his date last night? The thought was disturbing because if Jack weren't interested in her, his repeated conversations with her could mean only one thing: He was trying to steal the tablet. *It's too soon to be sure. But I'd better watch him carefully.* She smiled at her own thoughts, knowing she'd been watching him carefully since they'd met.

Jack leaned in close. "Sorry for that crack about your being a sorceress." He laughed and bumped his shoulder against hers. "A prize like you—who's gonna care what you do in your off hours?"

Emilie turned to him. "Why do you do that?"

Jack's smile faded. "Do what?"

"Act like you're some kind of plastic Hollywood invention, dropping lines on women all the time."

Jack stared at her.

"It's like you're afraid to be a real person, afraid people won't like the real Jack Cabot."

He looked away. "You don't pull any punches, do you, Emilie?"

Emilie touched his arm. "I'm sorry." Was there a real person under there, after all?

Jack focused on the road in front of the bus. "Don't worry about it."

"You know, you don't have to be like that for women to—"

"I said, don't worry about it." Jack looked out the opposite side of the bus. "Should've taken my car."

Emilie said nothing for the rest of the bus ride.

The air-conditioned hotel lobby felt like heaven. The heat had sapped her energy this morning as much as the work had. Across the lobby, two men talked animatedly. When one of them turned toward Emilie, her heart skipped. *Sheldon!* She watched as he broke away from the conversation and approached her. He held a small package in his hand.

"I wondered if I might run into you here. I needed to meet a client for lunch."

Emilie smoothed her damp hair. "It's nice to see you." When Sheldon didn't respond, Emilie pointed to the wrapped parcel. "What's in the package?"

He held it up. "Oh, it's a small gift for a friend who's staying at the Crowne Gardens Hotel near Delilah Beach."

"My roommate, Jenn, has been talking about going over to Delilah Beach sometime."

"Really? Do you think you could deliver this to him? I'm leaving town this afternoon and I don't know if I'll get a chance to run it over there."

Emilie's hopes crashed at the reminder of his departure. "I'd be glad to take it. I'm sorry to hear you're still leaving, though."

"Are you?" He smiled, his eyebrows raised. "Because I'll be back in a few days." He held up the package. "My friend may have left by then. But you'll still be here."

Emilie smiled. "Yes, I will."

Sheldon pulled a Day-Timer from his jacket pocket and tore two sheets of blank paper from it. "Let me just slip a note into the package, explaining to Lee why I'm having you deliver it," he said, scribbling on the top sheet. A minute later, he lifted a corner of the sealing tape and slipped it in.

"I'll write down his name for you." He wrote on the second sheet, then folded it and handed it to her. "I put my cell phone number on there as well, in case you need to reach me. May I call you in a few days when I get back into town?"

"I'd love that." Emilie put the slip of paper into her notebook.

"Good." Sheldon reached over and tucked a strand of her hair behind her ear. "I hope to see you soon."

Emilie was still staring out into the parking lot when Jenn approached.

"Who was that?" she asked.

"Sheldon Gold."

Jenn squeezed Emilie's arm. "I told you good things would come if you projected your desire out there." Emilie smiled at her roommate, who had commiserated with her last night when she'd returned from her moonlit stroll with Sheldon and advised her to "tell the universe what she wanted."

"When are you going to see him again?" Jenn asked.

"He'll be back in Ashkelon in a few days. He said he'd call."

Jenn shook her head. "You've got to take more control, Emilie. Stand up for what you want. The days are gone when women sit around waiting for men to summon them."

Emilie crossed her arms. She knew she should be more forceful, more aggressive. Why did she always end up retreating instead? She wanted everyone to like her, but pleasing everyone seemed impossible. "I guess you're right. He did give me his cell phone number." She pulled out the slip of paper from her notebook.

Jenn nodded. "There you go. You know what to do." Jenn's attention moved to the parking lot outside the front doors, and her smile faded.

Emilie followed her look. "What is it?"

"Nothing. Just Jack Cabot driving away. I wonder where he's going in the middle of the day."

Emilie eyed her roommate. Was her question more than idle curiosity? Did Jenn have her sights set on Jack? She wouldn't be the first. Emilie couldn't help noticing that every other single woman on the team competed for his attention, too.

But you've got Sheldon. So forget about Jack Cabot.

▲ ▲ ▲

Thomas Fitzwater cradled the figurine of the god Shamash in his left hand. He'd dimmed the lights in his private collection room, and the shelves of ancient pieces seemed to glow with the glory of centuries long past. His gaze traveled around four walls, breathing in the scent of aged pottery and crumbling idols. He loved this room with an intensity born of years of careful collecting and a belief that every piece here held special power for the person chosen to channel it.

"Shamash." He whispered the name of the piece in his hand and held it aloft. Just as the sun disperses darkness, so the all-seeing eye of Shamash supposedly brought wrong and injustice to light. "Shamash, hear my request. Grant success to my endeavors." The light seemed to flicker as if in response. He held his pose for another moment, then placed the figurine on the shelf.

A straight-backed chair in the corner of the room was the only furniture. Thomas lowered himself to it, his eyes still on the figurine, waiting for the calm that would assure him his prayer had been heard.

Thomas had been praying to the old gods since his mother first taught him their names as a child. Over the years he'd become convinced of one thing: The old gods desired the world to be united again, as it had been in the days of the ancient, mighty kingdoms. Not long ago, his government contacts had led him to an organization that believed as he did.

"One strong leader, both king and savior," they insisted. "The only way to save the world from devouring itself." The search for that leader had taken many years and much money, but now his kingdom was upon them. It only remained to raise him up.

And that was where Thomas could have his impact. More funding, massive funding, was needed to establish the new kingdom. More than that, it would take a depth of spiritual power such as no government had ever harnessed to bring the dream to pass. Thomas's contacts were limited, but he knew that all over the world others such as himself were collecting pieces of power, relics that could be used to channel authority into the new kingdom.

His cell phone rang, disturbing the peace of the room. He chided himself for not turning it off. "Yes?"

"It's me."

"Have you got it?"

"Not yet. But I'm moving into position. It won't be long. Just wanted to make sure you were ready."

"Call me the moment you have it. I'll be ready on this end."

Thomas disconnected and smiled. It had been foreordained that he'd left his phone on. The gods wished to reward his prayers even as he waited for the answer. He moved to the center of the vaultlike room and bowed his head in Shamash's direction.

"I am your humble servant."

▲ ▲ ▲

Jack signaled the bartender at Amtza's and got out his wallet. Beside him, Tawny finished her drink and swiveled to face him. She brushed blond bangs away from her eyes and tilted her head. "You sure we can do this?"

"Easy as a stroll along the Mediterranean," Jack said. "As long as you don't goof it up."

Tawny leaned her shoulders toward him and pretended to pout. "Do you doubt my ability to distract one idiot guard?"

Jack looked away. "Pull this off, and you'll be worth the price you're extorting from me." *And Vitelli will be extremely pleased.*

Tawny glanced at a slim gold watch on her wrist. "We'd better move. Layna's supposed to meet with her potential buyer at seven-thirty. If Leon Hightower's interested in seeing the statue, she may not be out of her room for long."

Jack remembered his African contact's comment on the beach. Muwabi had said that Leon Hightower was in town for something from Turkey. If Hightower had come for the statue, Jack didn't have much time.

"I'll bet that Hightower's connected," Tawny said. She lowered her voice. "The Mafia buys these things as a way to launder money, you know."

Jack merely raised his eyebrows without committing to a comment.

Forty minutes later, Jack checked his reflection in the mirrored wall as he climbed the lobby steps of the Crowne Gardens Hotel. He would set the Turkey fiasco right today, then give the tablet his full attention. He straightened the red velvet porter's cap he'd "borrowed" and smoothed the uniform where it pulled a little too tightly across his chest.

The only thing standing between him and the statue now was a small room safe, and Jack had the tools and the know-how to jump that hurdle easily.

Suite 109 was only a few doors from the top of the wide staircase. Jack eyed the hallway in both directions before he slid closer to the door. Keeping watch on the stairs, he popped the lock in under seven seconds and pushed against the door.

The suite was dimly lit, with heavy drapes blocking the afternoon sun. Jack slipped inside, holding the door behind him until it clicked shut. He waited, his senses alert to any sound within the room. Convinced he was alone, he padded across the thick carpet searching for the safe Tawny had told him he'd find.

He moved through the outer sitting room and into the bedroom. He didn't see anything resembling a safe. Was it disguised? Hidden? He reentered the sitting room and opened a closet.

There. In the corner, below a wealth of hanging clothes he assumed belonged to Layna. Jack bent to his work, pulling his instruments from his pants pocket.

The sound of laughter drifted in from the hallway. Jack froze, waiting for it to pass by, to continue down the hall. But a woman's voice, high and excited, penetrated the door. A hand fumbled at the knob.

Jack stood. He pocketed his tools and shut the closet. He turned, adjusted his valet's cap, plastered a smile on his face, and watched the door to the suite swing open.

Tawny stumbled through first, laughing as though she were

drunk, blond hair swinging in front of her face. Her beefy companion grabbed her from behind and kicked his foot backward to shut the door. Tawny looked up through her hair and met Jack's stare. The look told him all he needed to know.

"Quit it, Paulos!" She laughed, pointing at Jack. "We've got company!"

Paulos jerked his head up and stepped from behind Tawny. "Whatta you think you're doing?" His voice rumbled deep in his chest.

Jack anchored his smile in place. "I'm sorry, sir. Didn't mean to disturb you and your lovely wife. I was just checking for some lost luggage. Perhaps you've had a piece delivered here mistakenly?"

"We got nothing that don't belong to us." Paulos took another step toward Jack.

"Hmm." Jack shook his head. "Poor Mrs. Wentworth in 209. Can't imagine what happened to her valise." He pursed his lips and tapped a forefinger on his cheek. "Do you know I've been all the way up to 609, then down to 509, 409. . . ? Well, you get the idea. I just can't think what could have happened to it."

"It ain't here."

"Hmm. Yes. Well. Perhaps you could check the other room? It could have been delivered while you and your wife were out."

Paulos stared him down, but Jack didn't blink. When Paulos stomped into the other room, Jack glared at Tawny.

She whispered angrily. "I couldn't help it! He said Layna was coming back early and he had to be here!"

Jack shushed her with a quick shake of his head as Paulos returned.

"Nothing," he said. "Now get out."

"Yes, of course, sir. Sorry to have bothered you."

Paulos grabbed his arm. "Wait a second."

Jack kept his eyes fixed on the door.

"Watch him, Tawny." Paulos released Jack and went to the closet. When Jack turned to see what he was doing, Paulos thrust a chubby finger at him. "Turn around!"

Jack turned. He listened as Paulos spun the dial on the safe, swung the door open, and banged it closed again. There was no doubt the statue was in there. All Jack needed was a way to get it.

"Is there a problem, sir?" Jack asked.

"Don't know. I don't like nobody snooping around the room when I ain't here."

Jack turned, holding his hands out in apology. "No, of course not, but poor Mrs. Wentworth, you see. . ."

"Yeah, whatever. Take a seat, pal. You're waiting 'til my boss gets back. She won't be long." He folded his arms. "Maybe she seen your suitcase."

Yeah, like you really believe that.

Jack smiled, his mind racing. *If Layna shows up—game over. She'll recognize me in a heartbeat.*

▲ ▲ ▲

Emilie picked up a book from the table in her room, along with the package Sheldon had given her.

Jenn entered the room a moment later. "Didn't see you at lunch."

"I wasn't hungry. I need a nap."

Jenn pointed to the package on the table. "What's that?" she said, taking off her boots.

"Something Sheldon asked me to deliver since he's going out of town."

"Deliver?"

"To a friend staying at the Crowne Gardens Hotel. I told him we were thinking of going over to that part of town." Emilie took her shoes off.

"What's inside?"

Emilie stretched out on the bed. "I don't know."

"Hmm."

"What's that mean?" Emilie asked, propping herself up on one elbow and watching as Jenn lay across her own bed.

"Nothing." Jenn shrugged. "It's just that you don't really know this guy. That package could have anything in it. You said he was into antiquities. Maybe it's some kind of black market thing. Or drugs. Or a cash payoff. Maybe he can't get too close to the guy, so he's asking you to make the drop."

"Make the drop? You sound like a professional criminal."

Jenn laughed. "I'm just saying. . ."

Emilie flopped back onto the bed, staring at the ceiling. "So what should I do?"

"Hey, I'm just here to make you nervous, not to give good advice." Jenn rolled over on her bed, closing her eyes.

Emilie tried to sleep, but the intrigue of the package had chased away her drowsiness. Her usual pattern of relationship sabotage dictated opening the package, but she really wanted to trust Sheldon. She turned her mind toward to her conversation with Margaret on the bus, trying to fit it into the unnerving dreams she had experienced.

She sat up a few minutes later. "Jenn, what do you think about faith?"

Jenn opened her eyes. "I think 'faith' is just another word for connecting to the divine source of energy. There's more out there. We just have to find our place in it and remember where we've been already."

"Where we've been?"

Jenn nodded, sitting up to face Emilie. "Our souls are meant for more than just this one life, Emilie. We've been here before and we'll be here again. Each of us has a purpose for being here, a reason we chose this life, chose our parents. We need to discover that purpose, and then we'll be able to take the next step in our spiritual evolution."

"Spiritual evolution? Like a journey?" Emilie remembered Margaret's term.

"Something like that, yes."

"And have you gotten to the end of the journey?"

Jenn laughed. "No way. You never really get to the end. You just keep evolving."

"Until what?"

"Until you've raised your energy level so high that you don't really belong to this world anymore. You've entered what some people call 'heaven.' "

Emilie nodded, trying to fit it all together with what Margaret had said and what her dreams were telling her. Had her soul existed in ancient Babylon? Was she remembering a past life each time her mind went there? She pulled out her journal to do some writing, but it only made her think of her father's journals. When would they arrive from the States? Would the journals contain answers for her? Had Mr. Fitzwater even sent them yet?

"Emilie, you've got to get some sleep."

"I know. I'm too keyed up for some reason."

Jenn crossed her legs. "Lay on your back and follow my instructions." Emilie smirked, but Jenn insisted. "You'll see; it will help you find your center."

She laid back and listened to Jenn's gentle chant, low and soft. She didn't think she'd found her center, but she did fall asleep.

▲ ▲ ▲

Jenn focused on one particular ceiling tile for several minutes, allowing the thoughts and anxieties of the day to fall away from her, feeling herself being lifted to another place. The "center" she had spoken of to Emilie was a longed-for state of being that she could sometimes grasp if other thoughts didn't interfere. She tried to let them go now.

Her chanting slowed and stopped. Emilie was asleep. And anyway it was only a means to reaching that higher dimension where her thoughts would become clearer. Today was magical. She felt her consciousness hurtling through space, past stars, past galaxies and planets, toward the place where all consciousness had once dwelt together.

Fragments of images floated past. Pictures from childhood history books—or were they memories of past lives? She glimpsed a woman brushing long hair in a gilt-edged mirror, her high-necked pink Victorian gown embellished with creamy lace.

Another image, this one of a Roman soldier fastening a buckle around his ankle. A hand reached for him. Was it her own? It touched his shoulder, and he looked up. A smile lit his face.

Back further and further still. A tent, a shepherd beside his grazing flocks. She felt at home here but wasn't sure if she belonged with the shepherd or with the sheep.

A cave, a fire. Her body stiffened as a knife lunged toward her. The image faded.

She was back among the stars now. Circling her lives, remembering.

The key was remembering. She must remember why she chose to be born this time, what she had intended to accomplish when she left the universe and entered time and space again. If she could bring that vision into her consciousness, she could begin to live out her purpose.

She must remember. Remember why she had chosen to be born to Douglas and Christina Reddington, a couple who were much like rotted eggs—smooth and white and perfect on the outside—something altogether different on the inside. Why would she have chosen such a place to be born? Where instead of good-night kisses from Mother, she was told, "Get out of my sight; you disgust me." At least Mother paid attention to her. Her father barely acknowledged her.

Jenn fought to hold on to her higher level of consciousness as the memories threatened to sink her back to earth like a weighted corpse. She must remember, yet not let it drag her down.

A flicker of something bright beckoned from the edges of her mental vision. She hesitated, fearful, yet curious. This was a being she had met before. A spirit guide, perhaps. Another soul searching for a birth vision, maybe. It did not matter. The entity encouraged her to focus, to leave the confusion behind and rise above it. Sometimes Jenn felt that it asked to be part of her, but she still resisted that merging of their identities.

"You have come so far," the flickering light whispered. "Don't turn back now."

"How can I know if I am on the right path?" she asked. "There are so many."

"You are always on the right path. There is no wrong path as long as you never exclude others from the journey."

She understood what the light being meant. She had tried the one wrong path for a short time as a child. Sunday school, Bible memorization contests, church picnics—she had done it all with her friend Ashley and Ashley's parents. It had done nothing to make things better. The one thing she remembered was that everyone there insisted that their way was the only way. She knew that wasn't true. There is no wrong way as long as you never exclude others from the journey.

Jenn had begun her journey ten years ago, at fifteen. She woke up one morning, looked around her interior-decorator bedroom, and decided that none of it was worth it. That morning's silent breakfast with her parents was the last time she'd ever seen them. Had they even searched for her? She never knew. But the journey had brought her this far, to Israel, to a job more exciting than she'd imagined.

Jenn reached out to touch a star, but her hand floated through it as if it were mist. She felt comforted rather than disappointed. All of this was too wonderful to be physical. She wished she could share it with someone else.

Emilie's shallow breathing, coming from nearby, told her that her roommate did not share her philosophy, but she didn't care. There was only one person who mattered to her, and she was certain that, given time, they would explore the universe together. Perhaps at long last there would be someone to love Jennifer Reddington.

Chapter 10

Jack weighed his options. Layna could show up at any moment. Jack was closer to the door than Paulos, but the difference wasn't that great and Paulos probably had a hundred pounds on him. Still, the black T-shirt stretched to its limit across Paulos's gut didn't appear to be hiding anything other than a cell phone. Jack had speed on his side, and Paulos had brute strength. Should he take his chances?

"Paulos."

Tawny sidestepped Jack and crossed the room to lay her fingertips across Paulos's chest. "You promised we'd have a little time to ourselves before she got here." Tawny's lips formed a pretty pout as she looked back at Jack. "I don't want to baby-sit this silly bellhop until then."

Paulos's shoulders dropped as he looked down at Tawny. He squinted at Jack and back at Tawny.

"All right, get outta here," he said and crushed Tawny in a one-armed embrace.

Jack nodded, smiled, and tipped his cap. Three steps backward and he was out the door.

He was halfway down the stairs when he spotted Layna coming up. She was on the arm of Leon Hightower. Evidently they'd become quite chummy.

Jack shot a quick glance at them before ducking his head and fiddling with his cap. He turned to look out over the banister as they passed each other. His arm brushed against Layna's.

She slowed and looked behind her. "Excuse me," she said.

He lifted a hand and took the last few steps two at a time.

Outside, Jack hailed a cab and gave the address of the Ashkelon Plaza.

Once again he hadn't gotten the statue. And from the looks of it, Leon Hightower was about to walk away with the prize.

▲ ▲ ▲

The nap had refreshed Emilie. Now, as she followed the volunteers into the dig site, she hoped the afternoon would be as profitable as the morning had been. Dr. Herrigan was there already, sitting at Emilie's table and making notes on a small notepad.

Ella and Ben, the older couple she'd met on the bus, worked nearby. "Hey, Dr. Herrigan," Ben said. "When do I get a turn sitting in the shade like Emilie, studying some worthless old piece of clay?"

Dr. Herrigan frowned. "We each have our tasks."

An hour later, after struggling through a particularly tough section of the cuneiform, Emilie stretched her muscles and looked out over the grid. She saw Jenn and Jack working in adjacent squares and wondered how much they interacted.

She saw Ben stand up and take several deep breaths. Even from her place under the canopy, Emilie could see that he was sweating profusely. He was already a frail man, reminding her of Thomas Fitzwater. Could he withstand this kind of exertion?

Emilie looked down at the tablet. How long did Fitzwater have? She'd never asked for details about his cancer. Would he live long enough to see her decipher the tablet? And if so, would the incantation actually possess the power to heal him? Two weeks ago she would not have believed it, but much had happened since then. Anything was possible.

A commotion across the dig site caught her attention. Ben lay across the sandbagged bulk wall. Ella stood over him, calling for help. Emilie jumped up and ran. A crowd gathered around their square.

"He's not breathing!" someone called, and Emilie heard Ella's anguished sob.

"Get him out of the sun!"

The crowd parted, and Emilie saw two men carrying Ben toward her. She backed up, motioning toward her table. "Bring him over here."

She ran ahead and grabbed the tablet, which she put away in the black case. The men shoved her books aside to clear a space for Ben.

Emilie set the case on the ground and glanced at the Bedouin guard. He was watching the case. This had better not be a ploy to get the tablet. One look at Ben's gray face assured her that he was not acting.

Ella hovered over her husband. "Did I tell him he was doing too much? Did he listen?" She twisted her fingers together, her eyes darting from one volunteer to another.

Margaret barreled her way through the crowd around the table.

Dr. Herrigan trotted up beside her. "An ambulance is on the way."

Emilie glanced at the case again. It had not moved.

Margaret leaned over Ben and laid two fingers on his neck. "He may not make it until then. Give me some room."

Ella grabbed at Margaret's arm. "Can you do CPR?"

Margaret nodded and glanced around at the crowd that circled the table. "Give us some room, please. Everyone, please clear out." She stepped onto the picnic table bench, then kneeled on the table. Her knee bumped against one of Emilie's books. She leaned over Ben.

"Here," Emilie said, rushing to the other side of the table. "Let me get rid of this junk." She snatched her books and then reached for a pencil that rolled off the edge of one of them. Her fingers brushed Ben's arm as she picked up the pencil.

Immediately, Ben's chest surged with a deep intake of air and his eyes popped open. A collective gasp came from the crowd. Margaret had already tilted Ben's head backward and was about to pinch his nose and begin. She leaned backward and nearly fell off the table.

Ben's eyes darted around like a cornered animal, taking in his position and the dozen people watching him. "What's going on?" he said, sitting upright on the table.

"Ben!" Ella surged forward, knocking Ben backwards with her embrace.

"Ella, what the devil—?" Ben peeled her arms from around his neck and swung his legs off the table. "What happened?"

Margaret stepped away from the table and shook her head. "We thought you'd had a heart attack. Apparently not. Just a fainting spell, I guess."

"It's the curse," someone said.

The crowd fell silent.

Emilie searched the group for the person who had said those words. "What curse?"

A student she hadn't met called out from the back. "That thing you're working on. It's supposed to curse anyone who makes fun of it."

Ella gasped. "Ben had just called it a worthless piece of clay!"

"That's ridiculous." Emilie glanced at the case, moved closer to it.

By the time the ambulance arrived, Ben and Ella were in Dr. Herrigan's car, headed back to the hotel.

As the ambulance pulled away, Emilie sat at the table staring at her books but seeing nothing. The tablet was safely on the table in front of her again, but she couldn't begin to focus on it right now. Apparently no one had noticed that she had touched Ben just before he'd revived. But she had noticed.

I could understand if he had touched the tablet. But touching me? What's going on? She shook her head resolutely. Ben had fainted. That was all.

Yet, when the dinner hour finally arrived, Emilie had accomplished next to nothing. Every time she tried to concentrate, Ben's ashen face intruded into her thoughts. *He was gone. I saw him, and he was gone. But then he came back—right when I touched him.*

She was one of the first to board the bus. When Margaret appeared on the top step, Emilie motioned for her to share a seat. Several people pushed down the aisle ahead of Margaret, but Emilie knew there was no chance any of them would sit with her. Everyone else was convinced she was the "sorceress."

Margaret lowered herself carefully to the seat. "I'm aching today, Emilie. I have to admit to a little jealousy, watching you sitting in the shade all day."

"Are you okay?" Emilie asked, squeezing toward the window to give Margaret more room.

"I'll be fine. I just hope Ben's okay."

Emilie nodded. "I didn't know if he would make it."

"I was sure he was gone, Emilie. I've seen it a thousand times before." Margaret shook her head. "Very strange." Then she took a deep breath. "I feel bad for scaring Ella the way I did."

"Don't be silly, Margaret. Everyone was glad you were there, including Ella."

They rode in silence for several minutes.

"Do you think he went somewhere?" Emilie asked. "Do you think some part of him left his body for that short time?"

Margaret pursed her lips. "I don't claim to have answers about these 'near-death experiences.' But one thing I do know—there's more to us than just our physical bodies. You know it every time you go to a funeral. The person's body hasn't gone anywhere. But what's missing is more than just a pumping heart and breathing lungs. The body's an empty shell. The person that lived inside of it has moved on."

"Moved on? So you believe that our souls begin again, start a new life after this one?"

Margaret gave her a half-smile. "This episode with Ben has got you thinking, hasn't it, hon?"

Emilie shrugged. "That and other things. I just thought, since you're a church person, you'd have some answers about all of it." She suddenly felt childish, as though she were asking the endless "why" questions of a five-year-old.

Margaret squeezed her arm. "I told you earlier that everyone is on a spiritual journey. You've already made the first discovery on your own. That there is a spiritual side to life, not just a physical."

"Was that your first 'signpost'?"

"You guessed it." The bus hit a bump, and Margaret grabbed the seat in front of them. "Hey, I'm planning a little side trip after dinner, to Beth-Shemesh. Would you like to come?"

"I'd love to," Emilie said. "I have an errand to run first, though. A friend asked me to deliver something for him."

Margaret left Emilie to her thoughts. Why did the woman's "signposts" intrigue her so much? Was it because Margaret didn't fit what Emilie expected from a "church person"? She was loving instead of judgmental; understanding instead of intolerant. A person like that had the right to be heard, and Emilie suspected she could learn much from her. Her delivery for Sheldon should be simple, as long as his friend, Lee, didn't expect her to socialize.

▲ ▲ ▲

Jack sat with his fellow volunteers around the dinner table at the

125

hotel. Most were college-aged. He laughed at one of their jokes and slapped the young jokester on the back. But his attention quickly shifted to the table across the room, where Emilie was finishing her roast beef.

She had him completely bewildered.

When Ben had gone down at the dig site that afternoon and been carried to Emilie's table, Jack had been among the first to arrive. He'd watched Emilie as though she were a magician, whose sleight of hand might make the tablet disappear at any moment. He believed Ben's attack had been genuine, but he'd thought Emilie might take advantage of the situation.

Emilie, however, had appeared to be watching the tablet as closely as Jack had been watching her. Did she fear a con, too? But Ben had obviously been very ill.

Jack had seen what no one else did: When Emilie had brushed her fingers against Ben's arm, he had revived instantly. Coincidence? Probably. But it had clearly freaked Emilie.

"Jack," the college boy beside him said, "tell everyone that story you told me earlier, about the guys in your frat house!"

Jack turned away from Emilie and smiled. "C'mon, Ed. You don't want me to ruin my reputation, do you?"

The crowd laughed, but Jack's eyes strayed back to Emilie. He entertained the group with another anecdote, as he did at most meals, but his attention never left the other side of the room.

Emilie's comment on the bus earlier tickled the edge of his consciousness as he talked. *It's like you're afraid to be a real person, afraid people won't like the real Jack Cabot.* How had she seen into him as though he were made of glass? No one had ever made such a perceptive comment about him. Certainly not any of the women he'd had relationships with in the past.

And how many of them even knew your real name? Most of the time he spent with women was fake, using them only to get what he needed from them. His honest relationships had been few. Those women had turned out to be untrustworthy, too. Could

Emilie be the first truly honest and real woman he'd met? Or was she just a better actor than most?

The attention at the table shifted to a young woman, and Jack finished his dinner, sensing that Emilie would be leaving soon. Should he follow her? His head told him to follow through with the new plan he'd constructed to get the statue out of Layna's room before she sold it to Hightower or someone else. But right now he wasn't listening to his head.

The tablet was locked in Dr. Herrigan's safe. That shouldn't be a problem. He gulped the last of his water and turned back to Emilie. She was leaving! Jack stood, and his napkin dropped to the floor. The conversation around the table stopped as though he'd thrown a switch.

"Sorry, folks. Gotta run."

"Hot date, Jack?" the jokester asked. The others laughed.

"Wouldn't you like to know!" Jack squeezed the boy's neck and then waved at the group. "See you guys in the dirt."

Emilie was entering the lobby when Jack left the dining room. He could catch her before she got to the elevator if he hurried.

"There you are, Jack!" It was Dr. Herrigan, hustling up from the direction of the lobby. "Can I have a word with you about that dish you unearthed yesterday?"

"Uh. . .sure."

Jack answered the professor's questions and then darted into the lobby, but Emilie was already gone. He punched the elevator button, slapping his thigh as it began its descent from the fifth floor, Emilie's floor.

On the way up, he manufactured a reason to be on her floor. He didn't need it. When the doors opened on the fifth floor, there was Emilie waiting for the elevator.

Her face registered surprise to see him. Instead of stepping off, Jack stepped aside to make room for her, hoping she hadn't noticed that he'd ridden the elevator up and was now riding it back down.

She nodded politely and stepped into the elevator.

Jack noticed the paper-wrapped package Emilie clutched in front of her. Jack's stomach tightened at the way she held it: as though it contained buried treasure.

Chapter 11

Emilie clutched the package for Sheldon's friend as she stepped onto the elevator with Jack. She hoped he wouldn't ask what it was. She was reluctant to speak to him about Sheldon for some reason.

Neither spoke for a moment, then both began speaking at once.

"Go ahead," Emilie said, nodding.

"Are you planning to attend the lecture tonight?" Jack asked.

"I have some other things to do."

"I see."

The elevator doors opened before Emilie could make any more small talk. They stepped out together. "Have a good evening, Jack."

She strode toward the front entrance, then looked over her shoulder. Jack was standing there in front of the elevator, looking lost. She felt a surge of compassion for him. He wasn't the confident life-of-the-party guy he pretended to be. She knew it. *But what is he?*

Emilie's thoughts swirled as she rode in the taxi to the Crowne Gardens Hotel, where Sheldon had told her she'd find Lee.

You've got to stop thinking about Jack Cabot. There were plenty of other things to occupy her mind. Like deciphering the tablet, figuring out why she kept ending up in Babylon, why heart attack victims regained consciousness when she touched them, and how her own search for a spiritual connection to something outside herself fit into everything Margaret and Jenn had been telling her. She sensed that an understanding of true spirituality was the key to unlocking the events that were unfolding around her.

Dusk was falling as the taxi wound through the streets of Ashkelon, and Emilie watched the night life crowd begin to awake and crawl out into the city. Most of them would head north to Tel Aviv, where the "real action" could be found. Is that what Emilie was looking for?

She knew it wasn't. Since her father's death, Emilie had been searching for something else, something deeper. A connection that would heal the pain of the past, would show her how to live. A connection that would make her feel loved and accepted.

Maybe Margaret had the answers. Or maybe Jenn did. *Maybe there are no answers.* Did she have a past life like Jenn suggested? What would it mean to this life if she did?

When the taxi pulled up to the Crowne Gardens Hotel, Emilie's thoughts were as muddy as ever. She paid the driver, climbed out of the cab, and entered the hotel.

It was an even more luxurious hotel than the Ashkelon Plaza, and Emilie wondered what kind of business Lee was in to be able to afford to stay here. At the front desk, she laid the package on the counter and pulled from her purse the slip of paper that Sheldon had given her.

"Can I help you, miss?"

Emilie always appreciated being called "miss" rather than "ma'am," so she gave the desk clerk a smile. "I'm here to see this man." She handed him the paper.

The clerk nodded. "I'll see if he's in." He punched at a keyboard, then picked up a phone.

Emilie surveyed the lobby while she waited. Potted plants and trees framed discreet seating areas scattered through the room, and several couples lounged in leather-upholstered chairs. Emilie tapped her finger against the desk. The desk clerk replaced the phone. "I'm sorry, miss. He's not answering. I assume he's not in." He smiled sympathetically. "Would you like to leave a message?"

"I'd like to leave this package for him, if I could."

"Certainly. I'll put it in the hotel safe and inform him when he comes in."

▲ ▲ ▲

Jack watched from the other side of the lobby as Emilie left the package at the front desk and escaped into the night. He formulated his hundredth possible reason why she might be delivering a tablet-sized package to someone. Was it for the guy at the café, whom Jack had never seen from the front?

Several minutes later, he sauntered up to the front desk.

"Can I help you, sir?"

"I'm supposed to meet my wife," Jack said, leaning a forearm on the desk and surveying the lobby. "We're here to meet a friend staying in the hotel. Has she been here yet? She's about five feet, long dark hair."

"Oh yes, she was just here, sir."

Jack nodded, pulling away. "She must have gone up to his room, then."

"No, sir. I rang Mr. Hightower's room for her, but he's not in. She left a package for him and then left the hotel."

Jack's mind raced, but he kept his face impassive and shook his head. "That girl. She can never remember details. She shouldn't have left the package, though. Why don't I take it?"

The desk clerk frowned. "I don't think I should, sir. She gave it into my keeping. I don't feel comfortable letting it go."

Jack waved a hand as if the matter were inconsequential. "That's fine. We'll catch up with him later."

He trotted from the hotel, cursing himself for watching Emilie deliver the tablet to Leon Hightower, whose black market antiquities collection rivaled the finest in the world.

▲ ▲ ▲

Emilie returned from the hotel wondering if Margaret was still planning to go to Beth-Shemesh. She stopped in her own room first.

Jenn sat at the window reading. She looked up as Emilie entered. "So, did you meet the mystery guy?"

Emilie shook her head. "He wasn't there. I left the package at the front desk."

Jenn frowned. "Are you sure Sheldon didn't want you to meet him personally?"

"I can't be running over there constantly, hoping to catch this guy. Sheldon will understand."

Jenn's frown remained, but she went back to reading.

Emilie crossed the room and dialed Margaret's room number.

The older woman picked up on the first ring. "Yes, I'm going," she said. "I'm so glad you want to join me."

"I'll be there in a few minutes."

Jenn was watching her as she replaced the phone. "You're certainly popular tonight."

"It's just Margaret Lovell. We started a conversation on the bus earlier about her spiritual journey, and she wanted to talk more about it."

The frown was back. "Emilie, I've heard she's a Christian."

"So?"

"So, all they're interested in is reducing spirituality to a series of rules to be followed. They've completely removed the mystery from life. You're not going to find any answers there."

Emilie tucked her hair behind her ear and leaned against the bed. "I don't know, Jenn. She doesn't seem like that type."

"They all are, trust me. Don't go down there. Call her and tell her you're not feeling well or something."

"She's such a nice lady, though. I don't want to hurt her feelings."

"You never want to hurt anyone's feelings, do you? Sometimes you need to stand up for yourself, though."

Emilie stood. "Then I'm doing it now. I want to hear what she has to say. If you're so sure she's like that, why don't you come with me and hear it for yourself? We're going to drive over to Beth-Shemesh. It'll be fun."

Jenn hesitated, but then threw the book on the table. "Fine. You'll see."

A few minutes later, Margaret opened the door to the two of them. Emilie was quick to explain. "I hope it's okay that I brought Jenn. She has so many thoughts about spirituality; I wanted to hear your opinion about them."

"Of course." Margaret smiled and widened the opening into the room. "Come in, both of you." She gave Emilie a brief hug as she entered, but when she reached for Jenn, she was rebuffed.

"Sorry," Jenn said. "I don't really do the hugging thing."

Margaret grinned and took a step backward. "Then I'll just love you from over here."

The three left the hotel and hailed one of the taxis loitering in front. They got into the backseat, with Margaret in the middle. Margaret argued with the driver over the fare. After a minute, he threw his hands in the air and pulled away from the curb. Margaret sat back and winked at Emilie.

"So you decided to skip Dr. Herrigan's lecture?" Emilie said to Margaret.

"I was afraid I'd fall asleep if I tried that," she said. "I'll track him down later. See if I can talk with him."

"I hope you're not thinking of quitting," Emilie said.

Margaret shook her head. "Not a chance. No, I just wanted to chat with the professor. I think he's got a lot on his mind."

Jenn laughed. "Sounds like Herrigan's in for a therapy session." She raised her eyebrows. "Or is it something more than that?"

"Jenn!" Emilie leaned forward until she could see Jenn on the other side of Margaret. She was embarrassed at Jenn's implication. But she couldn't help noticing Margaret's mischievous smile. "How far are we from Beth-Shemesh?" Emilie asked.

"Less than thirty miles," Margaret said. "We won't have long to look around before it gets dark, but I'm not sure how much there is to see."

"Aren't they digging there this season?" Jenn asked.

"I believe they're still excavating the Iron Age village they found," Margaret said. "You know, Beth-Shemesh was home to Samson, the Old Testament judge. They're finding once again that the biblical record is reliable."

Emilie reverted to the topic she wanted to hear about most. "You were telling me about the spiritual journey you took."

Jenn interrupted, eyebrows raised at Margaret. "So you've arrived at the end of your journey?"

"I know the destination beyond doubt, if that's what you mean, hon."

Emilie watched Jenn from the corner of her eye as she seemed to sprout thistles over being called "hon." She remembered her conversation with Jenn about spiritual journeys. Jenn had insisted that you never reached the end, you only kept evolving. *Which is true?*

Margaret turned to face Jenn fully. "Why are you so angry, Jenn?"

The question threw Jenn back in her seat. "Who said I was angry?"

"Everything about you says it. I think someone hurt you, maybe very badly. And you're angry at everyone."

Jenn snorted, looking over at Emilie. "Okay, I'll admit she's not your usual fundamentalist, but still—are you buying the psychobabble?"

Emilie said nothing.

"I'm not talking about psychology, Jenn," Margaret said. "I'm talking about your heart. About anger in response to pain, anger rooted so deeply in your heart it affects everything you do. Anger you won't let go of."

Jenn looked away.

The cab snaked through the evening traffic and away from Ashkelon, heading east toward Beth-Shemesh. Behind them, the sun hung low in the sky, streaming through the rear window and warming their backs.

Jenn turned back, a challenge in her eyes. "Emilie told me you were talking about 'signposts.' Sounds like some kind of cult phrase to me."

Margaret laughed. "Oh, that's just my silly term for the different things I came to understand about my place in the universe. I've thought about them a lot, and I'd say there were seven of them. Seven signposts along the way that pointed me to the answers."

"See, there she goes, Emilie," Jenn said. "Claiming to have the answers. It's the church that has suppressed the answers all these years. They've been afraid to put spirituality in the hands of the people. The church leaders have wanted to keep all the authority for themselves."

Margaret shook her head. "You're not seeing the full picture, Jenn. But we're getting ahead of ourselves. That was the second understanding that came to me. The first signpost was something different."

Emilie shifted in her seat, trying to get a better look at Margaret beside her. "You said the first signpost was realizing that there is a spiritual side to life."

Margaret nodded. "That may not be so hard for you girls to accept, but in my growing-up years, people focused more on the rational, physical side of things. Admitting any kind of spirituality labeled you a 'religious nut.' It took awhile for me to get to the place where I knew there was more to me than just this over-weight, aging shell I'm living in."

Emilie remembered Ben's gray face when she had thought he was gone, remembered every funeral she'd suffered through, and thought of the recent dreams that had convinced her that something else existed out there.

Jenn shrugged in reluctant agreement. "I guess we're not so far apart on your first signpost," she said. "But I have a feeling it gets weird from here."

Margaret laughed. "Then we'd better move on. Do you want to hear about the second signpost on my journey?"

Jenn crossed her arms. "Whatever."

"As you said, Jenn, the church has not always had the best rep-utation. There have been times in history where it's been down-right barbaric. That had always bothered me. So I needed to take a look at history, to see the big picture of people's spiritual search in the past."

Jenn cut in. "I'll show you the big picture. In the Middle Ages, people realized that the church leaders who had controlled their salvation were corrupt. The only thing Martin Luther did right when he protested was to set people free to seek their own answers. But instead of evolving spiritually, they got stuck in a scientific quest to master the earth that's lasted four hundred years. But we're breaking free of that now. We're ready to take the next step in our spiritual evolution."

Margaret cocked her head and studied Jenn for a moment. To Emilie, the look on Margaret's face almost resembled pity.

"That's a very narrow view of history, Jenn. It only encom-passes the past one thousand years, for one thing. What about all the time that came before that?"

"Right—before that people knew better than to seek answers in the church or in science!"

Emilie felt the tension rising in the cab again and sought to defuse it. "I'm sure everyone sees something different when they look at history."

Margaret studied the landscape through the window. They had left the coastal plain behind and now crossed the gently sloping Shephelah, the grassy lowland transition into the hills of Judah. She smiled.

"I don't see history as a testament to our spiritual evolution," she said. "There hasn't been any advancement. There have only been people rightfully rejecting a series of failed attempts to reach God. As one theory fails, we discard it and try another, only to move on yet again when that theory proves faulty."

She leaned forward in her seat. "Jenn's right. In the Middle Ages, people rejected the falsehood that the church had embraced, the false piety that stood in the place of true salvation. Martin Luther insisted that salvation was not found in keeping the church's rules. But although a great spiritual understanding followed his protest, for the most part man couldn't humble himself enough to admit that he couldn't earn his own salvation. So he made up a new way to reach God—through science.

"We've spent centuries trying to conquer God that way. It hasn't worked. It's left us feeling empty and unconnected. The past few decades have seen us beginning to reject that failed attempt to reach God. Now we're trying something else. But it's not a spiritual evolution, moving to something better. It's trial and error, and we haven't gotten it right yet."

Margaret sat back in her seat, as if exhausted by her passionate speech. Jenn seemed unmoved, but she was quiet at least.

They seemed to be the only ones on the road, speeding across the valley. Emilie watched the green hills slip past and thought about what she knew of ancient Babylon. In many ways, that culture was similar to the developing spirituality of the twenty-first century. It was twenty-six hundred years ago, but not much had changed. *Perhaps we've only cycled back again.* "I don't know," she said. "It's definitely a different spin on things."

Margaret smiled and patted Emilie's hand. "Jenn said it gets weird from here. You'll have to wait to find out just how weird," Margaret said, "because that's enough about my journey for tonight. I want to hear all about you now."

Jenn shook her head and glanced at Emilie. "She sounds like a mother, doesn't she?"

Emilie started to agree, until she saw Margaret's face. The loving warmth fell away, leaving a shroud of pain behind. Emilie hurried to tell her life history, then nodded to Jenn to share her story. Emilie noticed that the details of Jenn's life seemed nearly as sketchy as her own. Some stories were better left untold. They asked Margaret for more details of her life.

"Nothing exciting," she said. "College, the Peace Corps for awhile. Then into nursing full-time. Married a man fifteen years older whom I'd met at the hospital. He went into international banking eventually. He passed away five years ago."

Jenn whistled. "Bet you guys were rolling in it."

Margaret smiled and looked out the window. "I've got a lot of money, if that's what you mean. But money doesn't keep you company during a long evening alone."

The sun was brushing the horizon when they reached Beth-Shemesh. The city had served as a border town between Israel and the Philistines and was the site where the Ark of the Covenant had been returned to the Israelites.

Margaret tipped the cab driver heavily and asked him to wait. "Follow me," she said to the other two. They climbed the tell, the seven-acre mound that marked the location of the old city.

The three wandered around the ruins, stepping over chalky white foundation stones that marked the walls of the ancient buildings and peering into the darkened, crumbling caverns where volunteers had already scraped away centuries of accumulated rubble. Emilie ran her fingers along the entrance of a rock-cut tomb and leaned inside, once again amazed by the endurance of the past.

They circled the site and inspected a long series of steps. Emilie shivered in the cool breeze.

Margaret pointed. "These steps lead down into an underground chamber. The entry to the chamber was blocked up with hundreds of pounds of rocks and dirt. It's a massive underground water cistern they used to sustain the city during attacks."

No one but the three of them seemed to be around. Emilie watched over her shoulder, uncomfortable in the twilight solitude. "Shouldn't we be heading back? It's getting dark."

Margaret walked past the steps, farther into the ruin. "I just want to see a little more." The wind picked up her voice and carried it the other direction. Jenn followed her. A sound behind Emilie hurried her on.

Margaret turned as Emilie jogged up to them. "Everything okay?"

"It's creepy here. I feel like there are people in the shadows, watching us. Let's go."

Chapter 12

Emilie arrived at the dig site in the predawn shadows the next morning. The disquieting feelings from last night's trip to Beth-Shemesh still lingered, but Emilie refused to yield to groundless fear as she had the night before. She found Jack loitering around her worktable.

"Good morning," he said, flashing his Ken Doll grin at her.

She nodded, trying to keep it all business, trying to ignore how he forced her to step around him to get to the table and the way he leaned toward her as she did. He was flirting, and they both knew it.

She turned on the lantern on her table. *There. Now we're under the spotlight together.* That ought to make him think twice. About what, she didn't know.

The guard brought the black case to her, placing it on the table beside her books, then retreated into the darkness beyond her canopy. Jack leaned against the table, his arms folded.

"Can I help you with anything, Jack?"

"Just soaking in your sunshine this morning, Emilie."

Please. The guy could turn on the charm with the best of them, but she'd given up thinking it reflected any real interest in her. "I'm afraid I don't have time to shine on you," she said. "But the real sun will be up soon."

"I guess I'll have to hold out 'til then."

Emilie sat, and Dr. Herrigan approached them.

"Can I help you, Jack?" he asked.

"No, sir. Just seeing if I can sneak a glance at the 'artifact of evil.'" He laughed. "People are really going for this stupid 'curse' thing, you know?"

"There's nothing here that concerns you, Cabot." Dr. Herrigan folded his arms.

"Right," he said. When Emilie raised her eyebrows, Jack finally began to move away. She felt his eyes on her when she snapped open the lid of the black case and laid it flat on the table. "Thanks for the sunshine," he said.

She nodded. *How lame.*

In spite of her sarcasm, Jack's interest in the tablet was beginning to concern her. If Jack attempted to steal it, could she stop him? How reliable were the measures they'd adopted—the Bedouin guard and Dr. Herrigan's room safe? Could Jack still get to the tablet? Would he just bribe the guard and walk off with it? She should probably contact the agents she'd met in the airport. She was angry about the prospect of losing such a valuable piece— and the possibility that she might be proven right about Jack.

She studied the surface of the orange-red clay, forcing her thoughts away from the places it seemed to take her. She needed to get some work done. *And Jack Cabot's enough of a distraction.*

In spite of her resolve to work hard, she longed to escape into that other world again. What new experiences would she encounter? She scribbled in her notebook and studied the tablet. She'd worked out the first few lines of text that detailed the power for anyone who knew the ritual and a curse on anyone who scoffed. Today she would delve further into the unknown parts of the ritual and hope to get a glimpse of Marduk Bel-Iddin's healing power.

Eventually her fingers edged closer to the tablet, and she closed her eyes.

A yell from the grid caused her eyes to snap open again. *Not again. Who's had a heart attack now?* She stayed with the tablet this time, not even attempting to get closer. Whoever it was, others would help. She couldn't risk the tablet's safety.

Emilie squinted into the darkness outside her pool of light. The crowd was dispersing already. Must not have been too serious. One figure approached her, his gait uneven. As he neared, she realized it was Jack.

She closed the tablet case and twirled the numbers. Jack hopped the last few feet, then lurched onto the bench on the opposite side of her table.

"Are you okay?" Emilie asked. She wasn't convinced yet that his injury wasn't a ploy.

Jack leaned over to rub his ankle. "Yeah, I will be."

"What happened?"

"I don't know. I came down with my foot on the shovel I'd just gotten from storage and the thing collapsed on me. I fell on my tail like a circus clown."

Emilie suppressed a laugh, but the smile showed up on her face anyway. Jack saw it. She covered her mouth with her hand.

He laughed. "It's okay, you have permission to make fun of me."

"Do you think it's broken?"

He shook his head. "I've had broken. This is just a sprain."

"Can I get you anything? Some ice, maybe?"

Jack smiled, one of the first genuine smiles she'd ever seen on his face.

Careful, Em.

"Some ice would be great."

Emilie glanced at the black case, then at her Bedouin guard. His dark eyes were fixed on the case. She hesitated, but then jogged over to another canopy where water jugs were kept. The jugs began the day almost entirely full of ice, which always melted to tepid water before lunch. Emilie glanced around for something to use as an icepack, but didn't see anything. After a moment, she pulled off the red bandanna she'd tied over her hair this morning, scooped some ice into it, and tied the corners together.

"Hey, Jack," someone called. "Looks like the curse has got you, too. Spending too much time with the sorceress!"

Emilie ignored the volunteer's stare, but she felt Jack's eyes on her as she returned to the canopy. He'd stripped off his boot and sock and rested his ankle on the opposite thigh.

"Sorry about the icepack," Emilie said as she approached. "It was all I could think of."

"My own Florence Nightingale. Think you can heal me the way you did Ben?"

"Y—you saw that?"

"I watch your every move, Emilie."

She felt her face redden. Then she waved his comment away. "That was a coincidence. The doctors said he had a 'coronary episode' or something. He came back on his own." She sat beside him on the bench and handed him the ice-filled bandanna. Their fingers touched as he reached for it. She half-expected him to claim his ankle was suddenly healed.

Emilie looked up into his eyes. She wasn't prepared for the expression she saw there.

▲ ▲ ▲

Emilie's touch sent electricity surging through Jack's arm and into the rest of his body. He took the icepack, his eyes never leaving hers.

"I need to get back to work," Emilie said. "I'm glad you're feeling better."

"Maybe I will just sit here for a few minutes, if I won't disturb you too much."

Emilie shook her head, as though her thoughts had drifted somewhere else. "Whatever."

Jack forced himself not to stare at her as she returned to work. The past twelve hours had completely befuddled him. Last night he had been certain that he'd seen Emilie steal the tablet and deliver it to Leon Hightower. This morning she had shown up with it again; and from the protective way she'd treated it when he'd approached, he knew she didn't think it was a fake. But then why contact Hightower? What had she delivered to him? Information?

Last night he had gone to bed furious with himself for trusting her, for thinking about her in any way other than business, when she was so obviously after the tablet. But now, with the tablet on the table behind him and Emilie's touch still tingling in his fingers, Jack didn't know what to think.

And what about all this talk about "the curse"? He remembered the claim that the tablet would curse anyone who didn't believe in its power. Could his comment about there being a "stupid curse" on this "artifact of evil" this morning actually be connected to his injury?

This was supposed to be a routine job. Not some crazy sorcerer's mumbo jumbo. Jack had never placed much value in talk about God or the supernatural. If others believed ancient pieces had power, so be it. That kind of thinking only made the pieces more valuable. But he didn't want to have anything to do with it. And then this tablet showed up that was supposed to have some kind of power, and it seemed to be true.

And if it were true, just what was Emilie's involvement in all of this?

▲ ▲ ▲

Tuesday evening after dinner, Emilie went to her room. She pulled a small, white card from her purse and read the name there. "Amir Sudiwitz, Anti-Theft Unit, Israel Antiquities Authority." She picked up the phone and dialed.

"Yes?"

"Uh, I'm trying to reach Agent Sudiwitz?"

"Ms. Nazzaro?"

"Yes, it's Emilie Nazzaro."

"What can I do for you?"

"You said to call if. . .I'm not sure about someone here. He seems a little too interested. . . ."

"His name, please?"

"Jack Cabot. He's a volunteer on the dig site."

"Jack Cabot. He has tried to steal the tablet?"

"No, nothing like that. He just seems. . .interested."

"I see. Ms. Nazzaro, we do appreciate your help, but there is no need to call at someone's first sign of interest. Do let us know if anyone makes an attempt to take the tablet."

"Sure. Okay. Sorry to bother you."

"No bother. We will check up on Mr. Cabot and let you know if there is a cause for concern."

"Thanks." Emilie hung up, feeling like a second-grader who'd just tattled on the class clown.

She grabbed a light jacket and headed out of the hotel. She needed to shop for a few personal items. Walking through Ashkelon would be a pleasant way to spend the evening.

"Going out, Emilie?"

Emilie turned to find Jack exiting the hotel right behind her. Big surprise. "A little shopping," she said.

"I was just going into town myself. Mind if I walk with you?"

Emilie shrugged. "Whatever."

Two minutes later, Emilie slowed to a stop, breathing hard. "Are you in a hurry to get somewhere, Jack?"

"Sorry. Everyone tells me I walk too fast."

"Too much energy, if you ask me," Emilie said.

Jack shook his head, smiling. "Too much excitement, so little time."

"I thought your ankle was injured."

"Feels better. Maybe you healed it, after all."

Emilie waved the idea away. "You're probably just a quick healer." She looked around Sederot Ha Nassi, a quiet street with a few shops and restaurants. "What's exciting around here?"

"You can find thrills anywhere if you know how to look."

"I guess that's my problem. I'm not looking." Emilie watched as a boy pedaled by on a bicycle.

"Maybe I'll make it my business to change all that," Jack said.

"And why would you do that?"

Jack laughed. "There's got to be a bit of an adventurer under there somewhere," he said. "Or you wouldn't be in Israel."

They wandered through the city streets. Emilie drank in the sights and sounds of Ashkelon and stopped to peek into every shop they passed.

At a falafel stand, Jack bought them both pita bread stuffed with spicy hummus filling.

"I don't know," Emilie said, looking at the sandwich.

"Come on. You've got to try it. It's part of the experience."

The sandwich was better than she expected. They drifted from the food stand and along the street again.

Emilie slowed beside a street vendor with racks of colorful scarves fluttering in the evening breeze. A few steps ahead, several local children dressed in dirty, ill-fitting clothes surrounded Jack. Emilie glanced through the scarves, watching Jack out of the corner of her eye. He pulled something from his pocket and handed it out. The children ran off, smiling.

The scarf vendor held up some orange-and-red fabric. "You like?" he said. "Seven."

Emilie shook her head and escaped before he could begin bartering.

She rejoined Jack as he took a hefty bite of his sandwich and started walking.

"What was that about?" Emilie asked.

"What?"

"Those kids."

Jack shrugged. "They must've thought I was a movie star or something." He took another bite. "This is good stuff, isn't it?" he said around the mouthful.

Emilie shook her head. "You're doing it again."

"Doing what?"

"Pretending."

"No, I'm not. I love falafel."

Emilie laughed. "I mean about those kids. You act like you're such a tough guy. So what was that back there? And now you're trying to change the subject before I say what a sweet thing you did."

Jack chewed, but smiled. "Sweet, huh? You think I'm sweet?"

Emilie snorted. "Don't get too full of yourself. I said you did a sweet thing." She tapped his chest with one hand. "Why won't you just admit there's a caring person inside there?"

Jack's smile disappeared. He grabbed her hand before she could pull it away.

Emilie stopped and faced him.

"I care." He said it softly. "I care. Okay?"

"Okay." She nodded. He let go of her hand.

They walked in silence for a few minutes until Emilie saw a pharmacy. "I'm going to stop in this store. Can I meet you somewhere or should we just get back to the hotel on our own?"

"Why don't we meet at the clock tower in Main Square? I want to see those sarcophagi. Is half an hour enough time?"

Emilie nodded. "I'll meet you there in thirty minutes."

When she'd gotten everything she needed at the store, Emilie wandered toward the clock tower. Jack hadn't arrived yet, so she sat on a nearby bench to people-watch.

Several minutes later, a familiar face appeared, but not Jack's.

"Sheldon!" Emilie waved, trying to get his attention. For a moment, he appeared to be looking straight toward her, but then he turned away. He was walking past the clock tower, talking to another man.

"Sheldon!" She stood and took a few steps toward him, until he turned again and looked at her. She waved enthusiastically.

Sheldon seemed to force a smile as he crossed Main Square to reach her spot at the bench. His companion followed. "Hello, Emilie."

"I'm so glad you're back in town already! I thought you'd be gone for several days!"

Sheldon nodded and glanced at the man with him. "I finished early."

Emilie looked toward his friend, waiting for an introduction, but Sheldon didn't oblige. Instead, he turned to the other man and apologized. "This will only take a minute," he said. "It's nice to see you, Emilie."

"Sheldon, is everything all right?" Emilie caught his sleeve.

"Everything's fine. I'm just surprised to see you." He frowned. "Why didn't you deliver the package to my friend?"

"I'm sorry—I did take it to the hotel, but your friend wasn't there. I didn't want him to leave—"

Sheldon waved a hand. "It doesn't matter." He glanced back at his companion. "But I really do need to go."

"Okay. I'll see you around." *That was lame, Emilie.* She waved a hand toward him as he and his friend walked away. Again, he hadn't said they would see each other again. She watched Sheldon's back until someone closed in behind her and touched her elbow.

"Was that the same guy from before?" Jack asked.

Emilie watched Sheldon's back. Why had he seemed so distant? As if he didn't want her to meet the other man. "It was no one."

"It had to be someone—you seem upset. When am I going to actually meet this guy?"

"Just forget it, Jack. It doesn't concern you." Emilie regretted the words instantly. "I'm sorry—"

"No, you're right. None of my business."

Now Jack seemed hurt, and Emilie felt doubly rotten. Jack had apparently forgotten his desire to see the sarcophagi. They walked back to the hotel in silence and parted in the lobby.

▲ ▲ ▲

Upstairs, Emilie found Jenn in sweats and a T-shirt, sitting cross-legged on the bed and munching on popcorn. Emilie fell onto the bed with a sigh.

"What's with you?" Jenn asked.

"Nothing." She rolled over and propped her head on her hand, facing Jenn, who waited for more. "I ran into Sheldon in town."

Jenn's face registered surprise. "Where?"

"Doesn't matter. I don't think he's that interested."

"What do you mean?"

"He acted like I was some kind of criminal just because I didn't deliver his stupid package in person."

Jenn shook her head. "There's something not right about that guy."

Emilie flopped onto her back again.

"First, he acts like he doesn't care if he sees you again," Jenn said. "Then he's your best friend, wanting you to deliver that package. Now he treats you like this. He's definitely weird."

Chapter 13

Emilie made it through Wednesday with no visions, no healings, and a forced effort not to think about Sheldon's coldness the day before. Just a good day's work of deciphering the tablet, focusing on the words and their incredible power to connect her to that other world, Marduk's world. The tablet's other potential power was what made her uneasy today.

She showered and changed for dinner, read a chapter in a book on Israeli history, then picked up her journal to record some of the thoughts of the past few days. She tried to focus, but her thoughts kept drifting to Sheldon.

Stop it, Em. You've already made too much of one evening with this guy. Where was her usual cautiousness? She was crazy. From Sheldon's attitude yesterday, the relationship clearly did not have the same weight with him. She went back to her journal.

Jenn finished getting ready soon after and sat on the bed across from Emilie. "Didn't you tell me that Fitzwater was sending you a package? Your father's journals, right? Did you get them yet?"

Emilie set her own journal aside. "Not yet. I'm eager to read about his work, but in a way I'm beginning to dread seeing them, too."

"Bad memories?"

Emilie shrugged one shoulder and looked out the window.

"You've got to let the past go, Emilie."

"How am I supposed to do that?"

Jenn leaned forward and crossed her arms. "It's just part of your history, something that makes you who you are. It's not a wrong to be avenged or held as a grudge."

Emilie wrinkled her nose. "You don't even know what happened."

"All I need to know is that you're a hypocrite."

"Excuse me?" Emilie felt the heat rise in her neck.

Jenn sat back. "Think about it, Emilie. You spout all the right words. You say that everyone has to find their own truth, that no one should impose their beliefs on anyone else, right?"

"What's your point?"

"Just that you don't follow through with that thinking. If there's no objective truth that can be known and applied to everyone, then there's no good or evil. There are only choices made by people who may or may not be doing what's best for themselves. If there are no wrong actions for you to take, then no one else's actions toward you have been wrong, either."

"But, you don't know what he—"

"It doesn't matter. You have to follow the philosophy through to its logical conclusion, Emilie. You can't say with one breath that there's no right or wrong and then turn around and call yourself a victim of someone else's wrongdoing."

Emilie exhaled. "Did I say there's no right or wrong?"

"Sure you did. The minute you agreed with me that there's no objective basis for truth."

"So is that how you look at your past?" Emilie asked. "No one's wronged you?"

Jenn's mouth turned up in a half-smile, and she looked away.

"And what about all the wrong things you said that Christians have done in the past? They must not have been wrong, either, right?"

"It's not that simple."

Emilie closed her eyes. "I'm hungry. Let's go eat."

Jenn shrugged and stood; but before they could leave, the phone jangled beside Emilie. She answered it.

"Emilie? It's Sheldon."

"Sheldon?" She covered the receiver with one hand. "Go ahead, Jenn. I'll be right down."

Jenn nodded and left.

"Emilie, I wanted to apologize for yesterday. I may have been rude."

"That's okay," Emilie said. "I'm sorry I didn't deliver your package personally."

"Don't worry about it. My business finished early. I hoped the three of us could get together."

"Three? Oh, you mean your friend?"

"Yes, Lee."

"That would be great."

"How about tomorrow? We can have dinner and get you two together after all."

"I'd like that." Emilie hoped Sheldon couldn't hear her smiling through her words.

"We'll have dinner with Lee, but then we'll get rid of him and enjoy a more—private—evening after that. Perhaps a concert in Tel Aviv?"

"Sounds wonderful."

"I'll come for you at six o'clock."

"I could meet you at your hotel, if that's easier for you."

"No, there's no sense in that, since we'll be traveling farther north. See you at six?"

"Six o'clock."

Emilie replaced the phone and grinned, pulling her knees up and wrapping her arms around her legs. Maybe she wasn't crazy after all.

▲ ▲ ▲

Sheldon Gold punched the disconnect button, stood, and crossed the room to the windows, the phone still in his hands.

He dialed another number. "Room 112, please." The phone rang twice before someone answered. "It's Sheldon. How are you this evening?"

"I got the piece you sent but didn't meet any girl."

"Sorry about that, Lee. A little mix-up. Can we do dinner with her tomorrow, though? In Tel Aviv?"

Lee grunted. "Is there a reason it'll be worth my time?"

Sheldon laughed. Civility was not Lee's best quality. "Trust me. You'll be pleased you came."

▲ ▲ ▲

Downstairs in the dining room, Emilie loaded her plate and pulled Jenn toward the table where Margaret sat alone.

Jenn shook her head as they walked. "I don't get your interest in this lady. She wants to tie you up in her religious straightjacket until you can't think for yourself."

Emilie frowned. "I thought you were supposed to be the open-minded one, Jenn. You're sounding judgmental. Besides, Margaret strikes me as a woman who's done a lot of thinking for herself. I would think you would respect that. Plus, if there's no right and wrong, then how is Margaret's view wrong?"

Jenn raised her eyebrows in disgust and looked away.

Emilie smiled at Margaret. "Room for two?"

"I'd be delighted," Margaret said.

Emilie placed her tray on the table and frowned at Jenn until the other girl dropped into the next chair. "Jenn's wanting to hear about more of your signposts, Margaret."

Jenn sniffed. "I'm only here to protect you from whatever she's selling." She picked up a fork and attacked her roast beef.

153

Margaret laughed.

"Besides," Jenn said, "you don't need to hear any of this, Emilie. You already know the answers." Jenn turned to Margaret. "Emilie's figured out that she had a past life as a high priestess in Babylon."

Margaret's eyebrows arched. "Is that right?"

Emilie shrugged. "It's a long story. I hope we didn't upset you with our questions last night, Margaret."

"Of course not, hon. I love all those questions. And God loves them, too!"

Emilie sipped her water. "I didn't mean the questions. You seemed sad last night when we left, Margaret. Was everything okay?"

Margaret's smile faded, and she glanced down at her food. "Sometimes the old pain comes back to bite you when you least expect it, Emilie. You probably wouldn't know anything of that yet. But when you're my age, you may have much to look back on and regret."

"What do you regret, Margaret?"

The older woman smiled. "Many things. But last night I was thinking about. . ." She stopped and looked away. "I was thinking about my daughter."

"You've never mentioned you have a daughter." Emilie watched in concern as tears spilled onto Margaret's cheeks.

"She isn't living anymore," Margaret said. She wiped her eyes and looked up.

Emilie wished she could rewind the conversation and head down another path. "I didn't mean to bring up painful memories, Margaret. I'm sorry."

"You can't help it, I'm afraid," Margaret said. She retrieved her purse from its spot beside her chair. From inside she pulled out a wallet-size photo and handed it to Emilie.

Emilie's heart fell. "I look a lot like her, don't I, Margaret?" She handed the photo to Jenn.

"Wow. That's amazing." Jenn gave the photo back to Margaret, who replaced it in her purse.

"Every time I look at you I see her," Margaret said. "Don't feel bad, Emilie. The memories are bittersweet. Perhaps that's why I've sought you out, why I've been so interested in you. Although you are a lovely girl yourself, and I've enjoyed getting to know you."

Emilie smiled. "If you don't want to talk about it, we don't have to."

Margaret nodded. "Maybe I'll tell you about her someday. The memories are difficult." She paused. "You know, it's funny. You look so much like her, Emilie." Margaret turned toward Jenn. "But it's your heart, Jenn, your opinions, that remind me of her. You and she would have had much in common." Margaret's voice cracked midsentence.

"Tell us more about your journey, Margaret," Emilie said, eager to change the subject. "We're ready for the third signpost!"

Margaret laughed, wiping away the remaining tears. "You're kind to an old woman, not making fun of my silly analogy."

"You're not old or silly, Margaret," Emilie said. "I keep thinking about what you said. How you needed to stop along your spiritual journey, to look around and understand where you were. It makes sense."

"How many of these signposts are there, again?" Jenn asked.

"I suppose there are seven. That's the way I've grouped them, at least. The best is yet to come."

Emilie picked at her salad and waited for Margaret to continue.

"Once I'd decided that there was more to life than the merely physical—the way that four hundred years of scientific progress had taught us to think—I knew there had to be something spiritual. When I looked at the bigger picture of history, I saw that humans have always been searching for it. We've always been reaching for God.

"That's when the third understanding began to percolate. We're more than physical beings. We're spiritual, too. And we want to connect with our Source. We want to know if we existed before we inhabited these bodies and where we're going after we no longer live in them. We want to find the higher purpose and calling for our lives."

Emilie was surprised to see Jenn nodding. "Exactly. The universal energy. We're all trying to connect with it."

Margaret smiled. "We agree, Jenn, but we don't agree. Our definition of 'the universal energy' is quite different, I believe. And so is our method to connect with it." She pushed her half-empty plate away from her and folded her hands on the table.

"So how are you two different, then?" Emilie asked.

"Now you're pushing ahead again," Margaret laughed. "That answer comes next. Before I was ready to understand what it took to connect to my Source, I had to see that I was trying to use many other things to fill up that longing for connection."

"Like what?"

Margaret shook her head, eyes closed, as if lost in the past. "It was the sixties. We were all trying to find something outside ourselves, rejecting the traditions our parents had given us. We did many things to break free of that authority and experience something new. Things I'm not proud of."

Jenn leaned across the table. "You were a hippie?" Emilie heard something new in her voice. Admiration?

Margaret smiled and raised two fingers in a V. "Peace."

"Cool."

"No, Jenn, it wasn't cool. I was empty and unhappy, and all I did was add to my guilt, not get rid of it."

"You must not have understood the movement," Jenn said.

Margaret's face grew serious, almost annoyed. Emilie bit her lip.

"I think I understood it pretty well, Jenn. Perhaps it's you who don't understand."

Jenn clinked her fork onto her plate. "I think I've heard enough for one night. I'm heading upstairs. You coming, Emilie?"

"I'll be there soon."

Jenn looked back and forth between the two women and then shrugged. "Whatever."

When she had left, Margaret turned back to Emilie. "She's a very confused and hurting girl, Emilie."

Aren't we all?

"I'm glad that you're still searching for truth," Margaret said. "And God's not afraid of tests. But be careful. Evaluate what everyone tells you. I've seen what Jenn's philosophy can lead to, and it can be dangerous." Her voice caught.

"What happened to your daughter, Margaret?" Emilie asked, squeezing Margaret's hand where it lay on the table.

"She was desperate to open herself to any kind of power, any supernatural force that might be out there. Unfortunately, not all supernatural power is what you'd call good. There is power in this world that does not seek our best interests. She began to connect to some of that power. It pulled her in until it controlled her."

Margaret stopped. Silence seemed to fall across the entire room. When Margaret spoke again, her words were whispered. "Be very careful, Emilie." She looked into Emilie's eyes. "There is power out there that will find its way into your head, if it can. And then it will destroy you."

Chapter 14

Jack felt like Sean Connery in an early James Bond movie, but hiding behind a newspaper was still the best way to remain unnoticed in a hotel lobby. An overnight bag rested at his feet. Occasionally he lowered the paper enough to check the wide staircase where he'd brushed elbows with Layna two days ago. He was counting on seeing her again tonight. And hopefully she wouldn't see him.

His mind went back to the one subject that seemed to preoccupy it lately. He should have gone with Emilie to see the sarcophagi last night. He'd been distracted by the mystery guy who kept disappearing before he got a good look at him. Emilie wasn't forthcoming with information, either, which made him more suspicious. Who was he? Did they exchange some kind of information about the tablet? His mind still puzzled over that package Emilie had delivered to Hightower. Somehow he fit into all of this, too. Jack tried to construct a scenario in which Emilie was an unwilling pawn in a grab for the tablet. Every part of him resisted admitting that she was dishonest. But he couldn't make it fit.

And why do I care so much about her integrity? I'm not exactly an up-front guy myself.

He lowered the paper once more and was rewarded with a glimpse of Layna descending the stairs. He waited two minutes after she'd gotten into a cab outside the hotel, then folded the newspaper, laid it on the table beside him, and picked up his overnight bag. *Time for Plan B.*

He crossed the lobby in long strides and picked up a courtesy phone along the wall. Punching the number for room service, he coughed and assumed his gruffest voice.

A young woman answered.

"Yeah, I wanna get some food," he said. "A steak and some potatoes."

"Room number, please?"

"109."

"And you'd like to order steak and a baked potato?"

Jack coughed. "Baked, fried, whatever. Just make it big." He resisted the urge to smile. Sometimes this job was too much fun.

"And how would you like your steak cooked, sir?"

"Rare. Bloody rare—you got that?" Bloody meat disgusted Jack, but it seemed fitting for the animal upstairs.

"We'll bring that right up, sir, in just a few minutes."

"You'd better make it quick. I'm half-starved."

Jack disconnected, picked up his bag, and headed for the men's room. He emerged several minutes later, minus the overnight bag and back in his porter's uniform.

Upstairs, he loitered around the elevator for ten minutes, tapping his fingers against his thigh and watching the numbers above the elevator rise and fall. Finally, a chime rang out and the doors slid open. A linen-covered cart entered the hallway, followed by a restaurant employee.

Jack stepped forward. "That the cart for 109?"

The waiter looked up in surprise. "Yes, 109."

"I'll take it." When the waiter hesitated, Jack shook his head. "Guy's a paranoid nutcase. But he seems to have taken a liking to me. Doesn't want anybody bringing his food in but me."

The waiter snorted. "Yes, Rachel took his order. She warned me." Jack slapped him on the shoulder. "Takes all kinds, right?"

"Are you new to the Crowne Plaza?"

"Just started. Got lucky with this guy." He checked the boy's name badge. "Don't worry, Saul, I'll bring your tip down."

"Thank you." Saul pushed the cart toward Jack and punched the elevator button. The doors opened immediately and he jumped in, giving Jack a small nod as the doors closed.

Jack waited until the elevator closed completely, then sped the cart three doors down. He pulled a tiny plastic bag from his pocket, removed the domed lid from the dinner plate, and sprinkled the contents of the bag onto the steak. A moment later the powder disappeared. He replaced the lid, wheeled the cart back to the door to room 109, and backpedaled halfway down the hallway to the house phone. Here was where it got tricky.

Layna's goon, Paulos, would never fall for the porter he'd found searching for Mrs. Wentworth's luggage bringing him steak he had not ordered. Jack had a plan, but he wasn't sure it would fall into place.

It has to. He sensed his second chances were running out with this statue. Maybe Layna had already sold it to Hightower. Jack dialed the room service number once more.

"Yes, I'm delivering luggage to a suite on the first floor, and I see a room service cart here in the hallway. Looks like it hasn't been delivered yet. Outside room 109. Okay. Yes. You're welcome."

Jack walked the length of the hallway, passed the staircase, and continued down the hall. When he felt he was far enough away, he leaned against the wall to watch and wait.

A minute later, Saul reappeared in the hallway. Jack pressed himself against the wall as Saul glanced at the cart, then looked down the hall in both directions. Shrugging, the kid knocked on the door to room 109.

So far, so good.

"Room service," Jack heard him call out. Saul waited, obviously listening.

"Are you certain, sir? I have a meal here for you."

The door swung open, and Jack could see Paulos's gut pushing into the hallway. "Whatcha got there?"

Saul lifted the lid. "It looks like steak and a potato, sir."

"Yeah, that's mine, I guess." Paulos stepped aside to let Saul wheel in the cart.

Mission accomplished.

Five minutes later, Jack was standing outside room 109 when he heard glass and metal collide and a loud thump on the floor. He smiled. *The bigger they come, the harder they fall.*

He was inside in seconds. Paulos was sprawled on the floor beside the cart, face down with a fork still clutched in his fist. Jack stepped around him and opened the closet door. Once again, he knelt and removed his tools from his pocket.

It took longer than he'd expected to open the safe. Was he getting rusty? By the time he finally swung the door on its hinges, his palms were sweating and he'd half-convinced himself that the statue wouldn't be there.

But it was. It was Jack's first look at it; and even though this kind of thing didn't really excite him, he had to admit it was striking. Only about ten inches tall and as thick around as his forearm, the gold looked like it had been cast yesterday. He picked it up, appreciating the weight.

And then, as though the whole scene were a repeat of two days ago, he heard a woman's voice outside the door.

A moment of indecision followed. He thrust the statue back in the safe and shut the metal door. He jumped to his feet, slid the closet door across. One look at Paulos on the floor and he knew he couldn't bluff his way out of this one.

He retreated into the bedroom. The outer door swung inward. Jack searched the room for a half-second. He slipped noiselessly into the bathroom, stepped into the shower, and closed the glass door.

The outer door clicked shut. Jack heard two women in midconversation. He recognized Layna's Greek accent. Tawny's voice was a surprise. After his first attempt to grab the statue from the safe had failed, he'd told her she could part company with Layna. Why was she still hanging around? Their conversation stopped abruptly.

"What the—?"

Jack breathed slowly. Layna yelled at Paulos. Jack raised his eyebrows at the string of expletives from the other room. Apparently Layna could curse bilingually.

He recognized the sound of the closet door opening. She'd be checking for the statue. He had second thoughts about leaving it. He might have gotten out of here with it. Now he'd have to wait and hope to get out unseen. He couldn't take a chance on Layna knowing that he had the statue. Not while he needed to stay in Ashkelon for the tablet.

"What are you doing?" Tawny asked.

Jack heard a popping sound, like a briefcase opening.

"I'm leaving," Layna said.

"What about our deal?"

"I'm not doing anything right now. Not until I find out what's going on here. I'll contact you when I've relocated."

A lid snapped shut. The conversation ended. The outer door opened, then closed again.

Jack waited five minutes, then stepped out of the shower. He walked out into the sitting room and opened the safe again, just to be thorough. It was empty.

Strike three, old boy.

▲ ▲ ▲

Jenn Reddington sat outside the Ashkelon Plaza Hotel, on a bench under the stars. The night was clear, the breeze laden with flower scents, and music drifted from the restaurant bar on the main floor of the hotel. It was a perfect night.

Jenn cursed herself for letting things get out of control with Margaret. That woman made her so angry. She couldn't figure out why. She tried to rise above the anger, but it needled her like a wound she couldn't ignore.

There had been another Margaret-type in her life. Back in her Sunday school days. Of course, this woman had been more the respectable churchgoing image, not an aging flower child who'd betrayed the ideals of her youth. But their talk had been the same. Jesus this, Jesus that. Jesus is the only way.

Jenn battled the hatred that seemed to boil under the surface. She should be increasing in love toward all people, increasing her energy by tapping into the divine source of the universe. Hatred toward another person made you lose power, not gain it. *You think you're controlling them by your hate, but it always ends up controlling you.* She needed to lay it all aside and concentrate on connecting to the universe for her energy.

So why wasn't it working? Why wasn't she loving Margaret, trying to help her rise above her own mistaken beliefs? Jenn shifted on the bench and studied the stars. Answers. She needed answers.

Perhaps she resisted Margaret so strongly because Margaret was not a searcher. Instead, she claimed to have found all the answers. She embodied the fear that people had of reaching their true potential. If Margaret stood for the fear, it would be best to avoid her, not to engage her in higher thinking. Any contact with Margaret would only serve to pull Jenn's energy level down.

She would just have to work harder to resist.

▲ ▲ ▲

Victor Herrigan turned off the light on his way out of the hotel meeting room, hoping Margaret wouldn't be waiting around the corner, ready to pounce on him after his lecture.

He had no doubt that either Jack or Emilie or both of them were after the tablet. He couldn't keep track of either of them, the way they kept to themselves and were always leaving the hotel at odd hours. He even wondered if they could be in on it together. More than once he'd seen them talking quietly apart from everyone else.

But Ben's heart attack, or fainting spell, or whatever it was had given him an idea. The team was convinced that the tablet's "curse" had caused the incident. He had begun to think that perhaps a curse was just what was needed to keep people at a distance from the tablet. Sabotaging Jack's shovel to cause his ankle injury had been a simple matter.

Victor wondered if he were growing paranoid, but he had even begun to suspect Margaret Lovell. If it weren't so preposterous, he could almost believe she was a thief, too. It would explain her bizarre behavior. Everywhere he turned, there was Margaret. Chatting with him, forcing him to sit with her at meals, prying him open and dragging out the details of his life. What would possess a woman to act that way? He wasn't immune to her smile and her warm laugh, but he was suspicious. He was glad she hadn't come to his lecture tonight, either. He would have found her presence too—distracting.

The hall outside the lecture room was empty. Victor headed for the elevator. When he reached his floor, he fought the ridiculous urge to knock on Margaret's door. But as he passed room 315, the door swung open.

"Victor!"

"Hello, Margaret." Victor slowed to a stop. How had they fallen into using first names?

"I was just going down to the coffee shop. Why don't you join me?"

"No, thank you. I'm very tired."

Margaret let the door close behind her. It pushed her against him. He leaned backward. She linked her arm through his.

"Then you definitely need coffee," she said. "I won't take no for an answer."

And so Victor found himself across the table from her again. Why did this woman seem able to control him? It was a new and not altogether unpleasant experience.

They ordered dessert and coffee; and before they had finished, Victor had told Margaret more than he ever intended. Somewhere along the way, she had guessed at his memory problems.

She touched his arm. "What does the doctor say, Victor?"

"Haven't seen one. It's not necessary."

"Of course it is! Your memory loss could be caused by any number of things. It may be treatable!"

Victor pulled his arm away. "I don't want to talk about it."

"I'll tell you something else, Victor. Your anger toward Thomas Fitzwater isn't helping your physical condition any."

Victor reached for his wallet. "I don't need a diagnosis, Margaret. Physical or psychological. You can keep your opinions to yourself." He stood, throwing a few bills on the table.

"You're angry?" she said, looking up at him.

"I don't need to be angry. Your opinion has no effect on how I feel."

Margaret smiled that knowing smile he'd already grown to hate and love.

"Good night, Margaret."

"Walk me to my room, Victor. I know you're gentleman enough for that."

Victor clenched his jaw, but waited for her to join him. They walked to the elevator and rode up three floors in silence.

At Margaret's door, Victor felt the need to say something further. "I think we should limit our association to the dig site, Mrs. Lovell. I think that would be best for all concerned."

Margaret replied by standing on tiptoe and kissing his cheek. "Good night, Victor."

A moment later, Victor stood at his own door, fumbling with

his keycard. He couldn't seem to make the stupid thing work. He glanced down the hall toward Margaret's room.

The moment he stepped into the darkness of his room, he knew something was wrong.

"Good evening, Mr. Herrigan," a voice said from the dark.

"Who's there?" He flipped the light switch. A man he'd never seen before sat in the chair across the room. He was thin, but the intensity of his black eyes frightened Victor.

"What are you doing in my room? How did you get in here?"

The man stood. He wore long sleeves and black gloves.

"I have a message for you," he said. "From Mr. Komodo."

"Yes?"

"Mr. Komodo says that he will not be threatened. That he, too, has powerful friends. And we are committed to protecting Mr. Komodo's interests." He took a step closer, pushing the gloves further between his fingers. "Is that clear?"

Victor tried in vain to stand taller than his visitor. The tension in his jaw felt too tight to ever unwind. "It's clear."

It wasn't until the man had left and Victor had sunk into the chair, rubbing his jaw, that he finally faced the truth. He had completely lost control of his life.

▲ ▲ ▲

After she returned to her room from dinner, Emilie read a book about Henry Rawlinson, one of epigraphy's most distinguished scholars, until her eyes grew heavy. She resisted sleep tonight, knowing that it could mean the return of her dreams. The more she tried to avoid the confusing thoughts of what her dreams might mean, the more her mind continued its subconscious search for answers. Was she remembering a past life in Babylon? Were the things she dreamed about Marduk factual or an elaborate combination of study and fancy?

Eventually, she laid the book aside, no longer able to fight the fatigue. Jenn returned and fell into bed without speaking. Emilie snuggled down into the bed, trying to think of anything other than Babylon, trying to enter her sleep world without thoughts of Marduk Bel-Iddin intruding.

It was not to be. Sleep brought darkness, and with the darkness came the smell of burning, a smell she recognized from her first visit to this place.

The stars were close here, the city far below. The platform atop the highest tower of Babylon, the central location for the city's worship. Etemenanki. Platform of Heaven and Earth. A dais raised to heaven, torch lit and consecrated for the gods.

Tonight she felt a stronger connection to the person she also was, the person who was not Warad-Sin, though she performed her duties at the sacrifice as one accustomed to the practice. She held the lamb's head still on the altar. Marduk slit the throat expertly and caught the spurting blood in a gold cup. She watched Marduk's eyes as he performed his oblations to the gods, his distant look, enraptured by something beyond, something she could not see.

"Do you feel it, Warad-Sin?" he asked. "Do you feel the power?"

She did. The night air shifted around them, a whispering presence surrounding them. She reached for it, trying to connect to it.

The power of the universe, someone had told her. *Connect to it; draw your power from it. It is the universe, and you are the universe.* She reached for it.

Marduk's hands were lifted into the night, his head thrown back. His purple robe fell away from his arms. The sacrificial blood dripped downward from his fingers. She looked away, uneasy with the blood tonight.

"Great gods of the night! Hear my cry!"

Marduk's shout startled her. She took a step backward, toward the dizzying edge of the platform.

"Hear my cry! I consecrate myself to your power and ask only that you work your healing power through me!"

She glanced around her. The torches blazed wildly as if a sudden wind had blown up from the desert. And then they extinguished, doused by a great, unseen hand. The two were left in inky darkness.

She felt Marduk's hand on her own, felt the sticky warmth of the lamb's blood. He brought his face close to hers, until she could see his expression in the moonlight. His lips were drawn back from his teeth in a hideously feral smile. His eyes glowed with an unnatural yellowish light. The smell of smoke burned her nostrils.

"The power is inconceivable, Warad-Sin. The power to control the gods."

She looked at his face. "The gods, Marduk? Or the demons?"

He laughed, a guttural laugh from deep in his chest. "Does it matter?" he said. "Is there a difference?"

She felt the power, then. Yes, there was power in the universe. Was it personal, as Marduk believed? Was it the universe as a whole, including her?

And more importantly, was it good?

She blinked; and in the impossible movement of dreams, she was in the palace again, this time in the king's throne room. She knew it well. The bright blue walls ornate with yellow and red lions. White columns supported the towering ceiling. Nabu-kudurri-usur resided on his throne, raised above his attendants on a platform. His long, bare legs extended beyond the throne. Wide, gold bracelets circled the dark skin of his wrists and ankles.

"You would be chief of magicians?" the king said.

She followed his gaze to where Marduk stood to the side of the crowded throne room. Over his robe he wore a pouch of animal skin on a strap around his neck. Qurdi stood close behind.

"O King, live forever," Marduk said. "I wish only to serve the king and his gods in whatever place the king so chooses."

The king nodded, his lips pursed. "And what of Belteshazzar

and his One God? Has he not shown that his God of Israel has given him wisdom?"

Marduk bent in a slight bow toward a smallish man near her. He was about her own age, with dark features, but not Persian. He wore a simple tunic rather than the ornately embroidered purple and gold of the other diviners. But it was his face that held the most contrast. Peaceful was the only word that came to mind. She studied him, noting the difference but not understanding it.

"Belteshazzar is certainly a favored one, O King. I only request that you do not anger the gods of Babylon by giving your loyalty to another."

"Hmm." Nabu-kudurri-usur waved toward a slave at the edge of the crowd. The young man, whose bare chest and shoulders gleamed with oil, disappeared from the throne room.

"You make great boasts, I hear, Marduk Bel-Iddin," the king said. "Perhaps it is time to test your abilities."

She who was Warad-Sin did not miss the small smile on Qurdi's face. A moment later the slave returned, joined by another identical to him. Between them they carried a litter with a naked man stretched upon it. Whitish lesions had erupted all over his skin.

Leprosy, a distant part of her mind told her. Incurable in this place, this time.

The king flitted a hand toward Marduk. "Entertain us, Marduk Bel-Iddin."

Marduk brought his hands in front of him. She saw that he held a small, jewel-encrusted gold container. A bluish smoke rose in undulating wisps from the openings in the top of the container. *Incense.* He stepped to the naked man and signaled the slaves to place him on the ground and move away. He waved the incense over the man once, twice, three times. Marduk passed the incense to a nearby slave and opened the pouch he wore. The crowd shifted to get a better look. She moved to the side until she could see Marduk's face. His eyes held the glow she had seen on Etemenanki. From the pouch he brought a clay tablet. His lips moved silently.

She looked at the king. His expression held only amusement, as if this were a show engineered for his pleasure. Behind Marduk, Qurdi's pleasure was also evident, but it was the gloat of one who is about to be vindicated.

On the stretcher below Marduk, the man stirred and groaned. Marduk continued his silent chant, his body swaying now above the sick man.

And then the man shot up from the stretcher as though burned. The crowd gasped and moved backward as one. The dying man's gaze darted around the room, the look of a man waking from a nightmare and still fearful of its horrors. His lesions had disappeared.

The king stood and looked down from his platform. "Are you well, man?" he asked.

The naked man looked up at the king, then fell to his knees before him. "O King, live forever! The gods have restored me to life!"

The king clapped for a slave, and a robe was brought to cover the man. He was led out, weeping and grasping at the hands outstretched to him by the wondering crowd.

And then they were alone. She and Marduk, still in the throne room, with the echoes of the departing crowd still singing through the outer courtyard.

"Do you now see, Warad-Sin?" Marduk said.

"I see. You are very powerful."

"Not I. The gods. But I can use their power."

"Do you use their power? Or are they using you?"

A flicker of doubt crossed Marduk's face, and he turned away.

Now she was in another place. The temple of Ishtar. Qurdi stood nearby, his back to her.

"You must, Warad-Sin. Marduk is becoming too powerful. The king will choose him to replace the young Jew Belteshazzar soon if we do not do something. I must be chosen!"

"What you ask, no high priestess may do."

Qurdi whirled on her. "You enter the Akitu House every year

with the king, to represent Ishtar in the sacred marriage. You ask the temple prostitutes under your direction here in the temple to do their duty every feast day. Why can you not do the same?"

She shuddered, that distant part of her revolted at his words. "Because he is the king's diviner. His position, my position, does not allow it."

Qurdi loomed over her, his dead eyes seeming to swallow her. "Exactly. When word of it reaches the king, Marduk will be disgraced."

"And what of me, Qurdi?"

He waved away her concern. "You exist to serve the goddess. Beyond that, what use have you?"

"Perhaps I belong to the universe as much as you, Qurdi. I deserve to connect to the power beyond the symbols of the gods."

Qurdi whirled, his black robe flying. He was laughing. "And why would the universe care about you, Warad-Sin?"

He was gone a moment later, leaving her to think. She did not know how to please the gods, only that she wanted to. But would their pleasure rest in her helping Qurdi to destroy Marduk? Or would they desire for her to help Marduk bring down Qurdi?

Despite Marduk's entrails and Qurdi's prayers to the stars, a part of her suspected there was no way to really know the mind of the gods.

Chapter 15

Emilie stepped out of the shower Thursday afternoon satisfied with the day's work and excited about the evening ahead—dinner and a concert in Tel Aviv with Sheldon. Her dream of the night before had faded, and what details remained she avoided thinking about. As she dressed, she wondered what Sheldon's friend Lee would be like. It was the after-dinner part of the evening she most anticipated, though.

With her makeup perfect and her hair swirled into a French knot on top of her head, Emilie still had forty-five minutes before Sheldon would arrive. She stood in front of the mirror and smoothed a crease in her red silk dress. *If I sit that long in this dress, it'll be nothing but wrinkles.*

The door to the room opened, and Jenn sailed in. "Wow, you look great."

"Are you sure this dress isn't too much?" Emilie bit her lip, then remembered her lipstick.

Jenn shook her head. "It sets off your hair. It's great." She flopped onto the bed. "When is he coming?"

Emilie made a quick decision. "I'm going to leave now. Meet him at his hotel. It'll save time and give me something to do instead of getting nervous."

Jenn sat straighter. "I don't think that's a good idea."

"Why not?"

"I don't know—it's not you. Too bold."

Emilie laughed. "You're the one who's always saying I have to quit waiting around for men, right? Jenn, I'm thirty-one. It's time to get a little bold." She grabbed her purse. "Don't wait up." One more great comment came to her mind, but when she turned, Jenn was dialing the phone, so she decided to save it for later.

During the cab ride to Sheldon's hotel, Emilie's thoughts strayed to her latest dream. The enforced temple prostitution of the Neo-Babylonians and so many other cultures was a stain on human history. Too bad for those women that no women's rights movement had yet sprung up to save them from being victimized.

But then Jenn's words came back to her. "You've got to follow through. If there's no absolute truth, then there's no right or wrong."

How do you reconcile someone's freedom being upheld at the cost of someone else's freedom being curtailed? She wanted to say that temple prostitution wasn't right. But according to Jenn there was no right. And even claiming to be right was wrong. But there was no wrong, either.

Wait just a minute. If the only truly wrong thing is to insist that I am right, isn't that saying that I know what is wrong? And if I know what is wrong, then I must know what is right. Doesn't that mean there really is right and wrong?

She shook her head to clear away the ridiculous puzzle.

The Holiday Inn Ashkelon was perched atop a pristine cliff on the city's northern Mediterranean shore. The hotel, a favorite of traveling executives, was built like two large domes, with all guest rooms facing the sea.

Stepping from the taxi in front of the hotel, Emilie took a deep breath of pleasure. Inside, the hotel's air-conditioned lobby was decorated in a classical style, in shades of sand and blue that blended with the outdoor landscape as though the entire scene were part of an artist's painting. Emilie approached the gleaming mahogany front desk and waited, smiling, while two elegantly dressed women with gold name badges conversed. She ran a finger across the marble inlay at the edge of the desk.

"Can I help you?" the younger of the two asked, turning to face Emilie with a professional smile. The woman looked as though she'd stepped from a salon, and Emilie suddenly felt tacky in her cardinal red dress.

"I'm here to meet a friend," Emilie said. "Sheldon Gold. Could you ring his room for me?"

"One moment, please."

Emilie drummed red fingernails on the counter as the woman tapped her keyboard.

"What was the last name?" she asked.

"Gold. Sheldon Gold."

"Hmm." The woman pursed her lips. "Goldstein, Goldfarb. Eli Gold?"

"No, Sheldon."

She nodded. "Just a moment, please."

"Emilie?"

She swung her head at her name being called from across the lobby. Sheldon strode toward her, buttoning his suit jacket.

Emilie smiled. "Hello, Sheldon."

"What are you doing here, Emilie?" Sheldon smiled and smoothed his hair back. "I thought we agreed that I would pick you up?" He cradled her elbow and guided her away from the front desk.

"I know. But I was ready early, so I decided to come here." She squirmed while Sheldon searched her face. "I'm sorry," she said. "Did I cause you a problem?"

Sheldon smiled again and shook his head. "No, it's fine. It's good to see you." He leaned in for a quick peck on the cheek. "Shall we go?"

The forty-five-minute drive up the coast to Tel Aviv flew by in easy conversation. Emilie laughed at Sheldon's stories of foreign business deals gone wrong. They arrived at Shle'ykes Restaurant by six-thirty. Sheldon led her to the bar to wait for Lee.

"You'll love the ribs here, Emilie. This place is famous for them."

Emilie looked down at her dress. *Not exactly my rib-eating wardrobe.*

The restaurant was intimate and romantic. Emilie wished that she and Sheldon would be dining alone. But at six forty-five, their dinner companion arrived.

Lee towered over both of them. He was a rugged type whom Emilie guessed was in his forties until she got a closer look at the lines around his mouth and eyes. Despite his lumberjack size, he exuded a quiet elegance. He wore an expensive suit and heavy gold rings on his fingers.

Sheldon stood and shook Lee's hand, then circled Emilie's waist with his free arm. "Leon Hightower, this is Emilie Nazzaro."

Emilie extended a hand. "I'm sorry about the confusion with Sheldon's package."

He smiled. "Call me Lee. Oh, don't be sorry about that. It worked out for the best, since I can now enjoy your company for an entire meal."

"Shall we sit?" Sheldon asked. He nodded to a hostess, who led them to a shaded balcony surrounded with greenery. She seated them near the low wall, where they could look down over Hayarkon Street. Sheldon sat in the shadow of a potted tree, giving Lee and Emilie the seats with the best view.

At Sheldon's insistence, Emilie ordered the house specialty—three double spare ribs in a special sauce. Before the main course, they each enjoyed wild mushrooms in cream sauce. Emilie savored each bite. Finally, the conversation turned toward artifacts.

"Emilie, I thought you'd enjoy meeting Lee," Sheldon said. "He's a big antiquities collector."

"Is that right?" Emilie wiped rib sauce from her fingers carefully, not meeting Lee's eyes. Could she change the subject gracefully? She replaced her napkin and bit into a rib.

"Are you beginning to collect pieces yourself, Emilie?" Lee asked.

Emilie chewed slowly, the conflict-avoiding side of her personality fighting with her principles. "No," she said. "I wouldn't want to contribute to the problem of unprovenanced pieces on the market."

Lee smiled. "Ah, one of the 'serious scholars.' I understand." He sipped from his water glass. "It's too bad that none of you have come up with a decent solution to the problem yourselves. You'd rather see pieces rotting in the ground or crumbling to dust in an overcrowded storeroom than appreciated by the public."

Emilie felt the heat rise in her face. She looked up at Lee. "That's not true. If there were no collectors, the looting would stop. Sites would not continue to be plundered, and the finds from them would stop being scattered without any scientific study at all. Most of the pieces that end up in collectors' homes have never been studied in situ. They've been ripped from their original locations without any photographs, any data recorded. Nearly all the pieces on the market are unprovenanced. The only way to stop the destruction is to stop the collectors from giving looters a reason to destroy history."

Emilie took a deep breath. She'd gone too far. Sheldon had already said that Lee was a big collector, and here she was accusing his type of sacrificing knowledge for their egos. Great way to make a good impression. She twisted the napkin in her lap and studied her ribs.

Lee laughed and glanced at Sheldon. "She's got an opinion, I'll say that much. But Emilie, while your solution seems sensible, it isn't plausible. There is no way to stop collectors from collecting, and all your efforts to vilify them only serve to drive the market underground, where no scholars can profit from seeing the pieces."

Emilie took several swallows of water. He was right, of course. As passionate as she felt about pieces being dug up and sold without proper study, her profession had not solved the problem. "So what would you suggest?"

Lee shrugged. "It's simple. Artifacts dug up by archaeologists produce no money. After they're studied, most of them end up in storerooms. Those same artifacts dug up by looters produce money. Most 'looters' are actually impoverished locals trying to feed their families. The only way to stop it is for serious archaeological digs to produce money. Let them excavate the site properly, record their data, take their photos, and then sell the pieces to pay for the excavation. Get the locals to do the labor, and pay them. Let museums and institutions have first chance to purchase the pieces."

Emilie nodded. "Maybe. But wouldn't the sudden availability of legal antiquities make collecting them much less attractive?" She met Lee's glance. "Perhaps the lure of collecting these pieces lies in the accumulation of something forbidden, rather than a pure love of history."

Lee tilted his head and gave a slight nod, smiling as though Emilie had scored the victory. She had surprised herself, debating to the point of accusation. Most of the time she'd rather back down than argue. *Oh well, some things are worth arguing over.*

Lee crumpled his napkin and tossed it onto the table. "It's been great fun debating with you, Emilie, but I must get going."

Sheldon leaned forward. "Off to purchase some highly illegal artifact, Lee?"

Emilie smiled, appreciating Sheldon's attempt to lighten the mood. *Although he could have stepped in earlier and saved me from myself. And why is he leaning way back like that? He's almost sitting in the potted plant.*

"No," Lee said. "Just a boring, ordinary overseas business call." He stood, extending his hand to Emilie. "I enjoyed our talk. Perhaps we can continue it some other time."

Emilie took his hand and returned the strong grip. "I'd like that," she said, surprised that she meant it.

When Lee had left, Emilie wilted against the back of her chair. "I don't think that meal lived up to your expectations, Sheldon." She studied his face. "I'm sorry."

Sheldon laughed and took her hand. "I wanted you two to meet. That's all. I'm glad you both found it interesting."

Emilie nodded, relieved that Sheldon wasn't annoyed with her.

"Let's order dessert," Sheldon said.

The night was sultry, with ocean breezes drifting through the greenery around the balcony. They talked about Emilie's days on the dig site and about her future plans.

By the time the warm strudel with fresh whipped cream arrived, Emilie had forgotten about Leon Hightower. Sheldon leaned toward her, his fingers brushing hers on the table as she took her first bite.

"Do you like it?"

"It's wonderful." Emilie smiled. *Couldn't we just stay here all night?*

A young man appeared beside their table, camera in hand. He held it up, as if in a question, and said something in Hebrew.

"No, thank you." Sheldon shook his head and raised a hand.

The boy smiled as if he didn't understand Sheldon's gesture and lifted the lens to his eye.

"No," Sheldon said again.

"It's okay, Sheldon." Emilie smiled and nodded at the boy. "Just let him take our picture. We don't have to buy it."

Sheldon erased his frown for an instant, until the camera flashed, then waved the boy away.

He shrugged when Emilie lifted her eyebrows at him. "I don't know, I'm camera-shy, I guess. I've never liked being photographed."

"I don't usually like how I look, either," Emilie said. *But I like how you look, and I wish I could buy that picture.* She wouldn't, though. Something told her Sheldon would not be pleased.

"You look beautiful tonight, Emilie." Sheldon was smiling again, his hand returning to its place on hers, as though it had settled into its home.

"Thanks." Emilie felt a blush of pleasure creep up her neck. She looked down to her strudel. *This night is too good to be true.*

When they'd finished dessert, they returned to Sheldon's car and drove to the Mann Auditorium. The Israeli Philharmonic Orchestra would play the opening bars of Stravinsky at eight-thirty sharp.

Emilie and Sheldon stopped on the way into the auditorium to study a blackened iron sculpture. Three connected circles towered over them, like a snowman with all his body parts of equal size. But the circles tilted at an impossible angle, leaning far enough to amaze the spectator that the whole thing didn't topple. Emilie felt off-balance studying the looming sculpture—a delicately balanced enigma, ready to crash at her feet with a little persuasion.

"That's Menashe Kadishman's work," Sheldon said. "He was a maverick Israeli sculptor back in the sixties."

They entered the sweeping entrance of the auditorium. Emilie expected a décor steeped in history and was surprised by the modern style. She commented on it to Sheldon.

"What is it they say?" Sheldon asked. " 'Come to Jerusalem to pray, come to Tel Aviv to play.' This city is a different animal than Jerusalem. They call it the 'Miami of Israel.' You're more likely to find rock music than holy rocks."

Emilie laughed. "But it's not rock music tonight?"

"No." Sheldon smiled and led her toward the stairs. "The orchestra is a little more highbrow than that."

Twenty minutes later, when guest conductor Yoel Levi raised the baton, Sheldon stretched his arm around Emilie's shoulders and left it there. Emilie settled back into her seat, contentment spreading through her like warmth from a fire after a long chill. A thirty-one-year-long chill.

Schumann's Fourth Symphony and Stravinsky's "Rite of Spring" flowed effortlessly from the orchestra, but Emilie enjoyed the walk from the auditorium to the car, with her hand tucked into Sheldon's, just as much.

"Coffee?" he asked as they pulled out of the parking lot.

Emilie smiled and nodded. *Anything*. Her inner voice had other things to say, more cautionary than eager, but she chose to ignore it.

They found a small table in a smoky coffeehouse, where a guitarist played Israeli music from a small stage.

"This Fitzwater," Sheldon said over the music. "Why did he choose you to help him decipher the relic?"

Emilie paused. She'd been careful not to give Sheldon any details about the tablet, not even mentioning what type of relic she worked on. How could she answer this question without seeming evasive?

"He had a connection with my father," she said. "And he had kept up with my training. He trusts me."

Sheldon nodded, frowning.

"What?"

He shrugged. "I don't know. It just sounds a little strange to me." He grabbed Emilie's hand. "No offense, of course, but it seems like he would have gotten a professional."

Emilie smiled. "I tried to talk him into that, but he insisted."

Sheldon's gaze wandered to the musician, and Emilie felt a knot in her stomach at the way his forehead creased. "What are you thinking?"

His attention returned to her. "Are you certain he plans to donate it when you are finished?"

"That's what he told me. Why?"

"I'm just thinking out loud, of course. But maybe he thinks you'll be easier to fool than an expert. Maybe he's planning some kind of switch, and then he'll have it smuggled out of the country."

Emilie remembered the grilling and search she'd undergone with airport security. "I don't know how he would do that. Or why."

"There are ways to get things out, if one wants to. If he took it out of Haifa, he could probably sell it for a hefty profit."

Emilie shook her head. "I don't think so," she said. "Besides, he's—" She had almost said "he's sick," wanting to explain Thomas Fitzwater's reasons for wanting the tablet deciphered, but that was too much information. "I don't think so," she said again.

"Still, I know how you'd hate to see it on the underground market!" Sheldon smiled.

Emilie frowned. Thomas Fitzwater's incense-laden office floated through her memory. The idea that he might have other plans for the tablet seemed unlikely.

"There is a way to be sure, though," Sheldon said. "Have you heard of ISIS?"

"The Egyptian goddess?"

Sheldon laughed. "No. It stands for 'Intrinsic Signature Identification System.' It's a system that registers digital micro-images of objects. The images are like a fingerprint, identifying one particular object, protecting it against fraud."

"I haven't heard the name 'ISIS,' but I do know the university uses something like it. The idea is to know if your piece had been switched or to identify it positively if it's stolen, right?"

"Right. They take magnified pictures of a certain area of the object. The same area of a duplicate object, magnified to a super-high level of detail, would look radically different." Sheldon folded his hands together, pressing his fingertips to his lips. "You might want to think about it. I might be able to connect you with some-one here who uses the system."

To Emilie's relief, Sheldon dropped the subject and moved on to more personal conversation. She didn't want to say more than she should. As the music played, they leaned their heads together and exchanged details of their lives. The night grew late, and they drove back to Emilie's hotel. At the door to her room, she turned to face Sheldon. He had left only a fraction of space between their bodies.

"Good night, Emilie." Sheldon rested his hands lightly on her shoulders, then skimmed her bare arms until he clasped her wrists.

"Good night." She looked into his eyes, wondering for the hundredth time if this could be the relationship she'd been searching for.

Sheldon leaned in, and his lips barely brushed hers, but then returned with intensity. He pulled away a moment later. She felt his eyes looking into her soul. "Dinner tomorrow night?"

"I'd love it."

He took a step backward. "Take care of that relic."

She smiled, and he turned and strode down the hall toward the elevator.

Emilie touched a finger to her lips, leaning her head against the door. Nights like tonight shouldn't be allowed to end.

Chapter 16

Jack drummed his fingers on the bedside table in his room at the Ashkelon Plaza Hotel. Layna had checked out of her hotel, and the statue was once more out of his grasp—unless Muwabi, his African contact, could give him a crucial bit of information. His phone rang. "Cabot."

"You are going to like this, my friend."

"Just give it to me, Muwabi."

"Layna is staying at the Ashkelon Plaza Hotel, room 612."

Jack exhaled and clenched a fist. Four floors up and two doors down from his own room! Not good. "Thanks, man." He hung up and sat back against the headboard of the bed.

In the past twenty-four hours, Jack had gone from anger at himself to anger at Tawny, who had obviously double-crossed him, to anger at Layna. Now he was just plain mad. He didn't know what Tawny's game was. She couldn't have the kind of money it would take to buy the statue from Layna. Was she planning to steal it herself? Either way, between Tawny and Hightower, Jack knew his chances for the statue were slim. And the split focus was making the tablet job look shakier every minute. It had to end. He was going to get that statue tonight.

It didn't help matters that Layna had moved to his hotel. They could run into each other at any time, in the elevator, in the lobby. His cover at the dig site could be blown. The whole thing was about to implode. Jack was fed up, sick of games, and certain he was headed for disaster. Tonight had to be the end of it.

He thought for a few seconds, then picked up the phone before he changed his mind. He punched 6-1-2 and waited.

"Hello?"

"Layna. Jack Cameron. How ya doin'?"

A pause. "Mr. Cameron. This is a surprise."

"I don't see why. I'm still interested in our little objet d'art. Only now I'm ready for the more traditional approach."

Layna laughed, a low, humorless murmur. "You are anything but traditional, Mr. Cameron."

"It's Jack, please. Can't we be a little friendlier? After all, I did pull you from a burning building."

"True. And I thank you for that. But I'm afraid the statue is quite spoken for."

"I'll pay more."

"You do not even know—"

"I don't care. Whatever it is, I'll pay more. My employer is very interested in acquiring this specific piece."

"Did you drug my guard, Jack?"

"What?"

"You heard me."

"Layna, I told you: I'm ready to pay. Whatever you ask. Are you going to say no to easy money? It looks like you've already rid yourself of your two sidekicks from Turkey. No one to split the money with. This job will make you richer than you'd dreamed."

The silence lengthened on the other end. Jack tightened his jaw.

"All right, Jack. I will meet you. But if this is some kind of trick—"

"Layna, Layna. Haven't I earned your trust by now?"

"Ha!"

They arranged to meet in the lobby of the hotel in thirty minutes. Jack didn't mention that he was calling from four floors below her. He spent the thirty minutes getting ready for the next part of his hastily laid plan—changing his clothes and hiding a necessary part of the strategy under them. By the time the half hour had elapsed, he'd fueled his plan with a bitter supply of rage at the way the whole thing had gone wrong.

Two minutes after he was supposed to have met Layna downstairs, Jack knocked on the door of room 612. He felt, rather than saw, Paulos loom up behind the peephole.

"Yeah?"

Jack straightened the cap he wore and smiled pleasantly. "Hello again, sir." He held up a small suitcase. "Here it is."

"What's that?"

Jack allowed a confused expression to cross his face. "Why, it's the luggage you left behind at the Crowne Gardens Hotel. I promised her I'd bring it over directly."

The door opened. "What luggage?"

Jack tugged at his uniform and smiled again. "Don't you remember me, sir?"

"Yeah, I remember. The lost luggage guy."

"That's right, sir. And I have yours here."

Paulos reached out an arm to swipe the suitcase from Jack's hand. Jack pulled away. "Do let me set it inside for you, sir. I just wouldn't feel I'd done my job completely."

Paulos shrugged. "Suit yourself."

Jack stepped inside the door and pulled the small stun gun from his waist in one movement. When he turned back to Paulos, the man never saw the Taser. Jack squeezed the stun gun's trigger. One short burst and Paulos lay at his feet.

Jack tucked the Taser away, dropped the suitcase, and went to work. The safe was easy to find, easy to break open. The statue lay inside. Jack grabbed it, jammed it into the suitcase, stepped over Paulos, and left the room. Four minutes later, he was back in his own room, and the statue was in his own safe.

Layna would be returning to her room anytime now. She'd have no doubts about who had taken the statue. It had been a last resort. Now he could only hope it hadn't been his last job.

▲ ▲ ▲

The team bus bumped along the Ashkelon streets, southward toward their dig site at Ashkelon National Park on Friday morning. From her dusty bus window, Emilie could see the sea, glinting like blue sapphire in the morning sun.

Today would be a short day, since Shabbat began at dusk, and Emilie was glad. She'd have plenty of time to relax and get cleaned up for dinner tonight with Sheldon. *I still can't believe he's really interested in me.*

She had coaxed more secrets from the tablet the day before and was eager to begin again. *It's growing on me, in spite of the weird dreams. Or is it because of them?* The conversations with Jenn and Margaret seemed to be coming together because of the tablet. *What am I going to do when it's behind glass in a museum?*

The thought reminded her of the uneasy conversation with Sheldon last night. Could Thomas Fitzwater be having the same thoughts? Would he resort to theft to make the tablet his own permanently? He had detailed photos of the tablet. Could he manage a forgery and a switch? How?

Jack Cabot. If anyone were waiting for a chance to steal the tablet, it had to be Jack. His interest in it was too pronounced for a rich boy, and his indifference toward the archaeological process made no sense for a volunteer. Emilie didn't trust him. Then again, knowing whom to trust was not exactly one of her strengths. Now she wasn't trusting Mr. Fitzwater. Was she merely paranoid?

Still, the tablet was such a gift to the field and, if it possessed true power, to the whole world. If it were stolen out from under her, she'd never forgive herself.

"You're pretty quiet this morning." Jenn poked Emilie's ribs from her adjoining spot on the bus seat.

"Am I? Thinking, I guess."

"About?"

Emilie shrugged. "Just this thing I'm working on. Sheldon got me thinking last night that someone might try to switch it with a copy."

Jenn looked out the window into the city street. "Sounds like you and Sheldon are getting pretty tight."

Emilie studied Jenn and said nothing. Her roommate almost sounded jealous.

Jenn turned back to Emilie. "Anyway, you'd recognize a fake, wouldn't you?"

"I think so."

Jenn shrugged. "Don't worry about it. It's not your job to keep it safe."

Emilie remembered Agent Sudiwitz and the IAA. *I wish.*

"Maybe there's a way to mark the original somehow," Jenn suggested. "So you'd know."

Emilie nodded, deciding to drop the subject. Altering the tablet in any way would be heretical, but there was a way. . . . *Sheldon's ID method.*

By the time she'd reached her table under the canopy, Emilie had decided to call Sheldon at lunch to get more information about ISIS. She popped the black case open, sat on the bench, and got to work.

Some time later, a muffled shout roused her from her books. She looked around, searching for the source. Her Bedouin guard stared at the Conex container.

Emilie locked the tablet in its case and handed it to the guard. Several other volunteers were moving toward the storage shed as well.

Emilie reached it first. It was dark inside, compared to the brightness of the morning. Emilie took a deep breath, not sure she could go in. She squinted into the darkness.

"Hello? Is someone here?"

A moan near the floor forced her inside. She moved through hesitantly, her hands in front of her. When her feet bumped something, she knelt, feeling with her hands. Her eyes focused in the dim light, and she noticed two other volunteers coming up behind her.

"It's Dr. Herrigan!" one of them said.

Emilie reached for him. "Are you okay?"

He moaned again. "My head."

Emilie reached for his shoulders to pull him upright. But then his eyes opened, and he held out his hands, as if to protect himself from her.

"Don't touch me!"

Emilie pulled back as though burned.

"You and that curse!" he said. "Are you trying to kill me?"

Emilie pushed her hair behind her ears and backed away. Someone pushed past her and knelt beside Dr. Herrigan. "Do you need a doctor, sir?"

He moaned once more and sat up. "I don't think so." He looked up, rubbing the back of his head, and pointed to a Philistine-era jug on the floor. "That thing fell off the shelf and clobbered me on the head."

Behind her, Emilie heard a whispered comment. "Wasn't Herrigan joking about the curse this morning?"

So the tablet claims another victim.

"Dr. Herrigan, that jug is huge!" the volunteer said. "You could have been killed. Are you sure you're all right?"

"I'll be fine." He looked at Emilie, accusation in his eyes.

Emilie stumbled back to her table. She saw Jack staring at her from Square 56, his shovel hanging from loose fingers. Emilie forced her constricted throat to swallow.

Jack dropped the shovel and climbed out of the square, his eyes still fixed on her. It took him only a few seconds to cross the distance between them. "Are you okay, Emilie?" He rested his fingers on the table and leaned across it.

"I'm fine." The words caught, rasping as if she'd grown hoarse from screaming. She stood again and retrieved the case from the Bedouin.

Jack touched the case, then glanced back at her. "I don't like what this thing is doing to you."

Emilie gathered her hair and tossed it behind her shoulders. "There's no problem here, Jack. Thanks for your concern."

Jack shook his head and returned to his square as though Emilie were a stubborn child insisting on playing with sharp sticks. But Emilie hadn't missed the way his hand had drifted to the tablet's case when he was supposedly concerned for her. She wouldn't call Agent Sudiwitz again yet, but she remembered her resolve to call Sheldon about ISIS. She couldn't let anything happen to her tablet.

Chapter 17

The giddy atmosphere in the dining room during lunch on Friday resembled a fourth-grade classroom just before the final bell. The team had been officially released from duty for Shabbat by Dr. Herrigan, and the weekend frame of mind had turned the meal into a celebration.

Emilie's thoughts were subdued. She grew more agitated as she waited in the buffet line, until finally she returned her plate to the stack at the head of the table and retreated to her room upstairs.

She found the slip of paper in her purse, the one with Sheldon's cell phone number scrawled on it. She dialed the number and sat on the bed.

"This is Sheldon."

"Hi. It's Emilie."

A slight pause. "What can I do for you, Emilie?"

She rubbed her forehead. "Am I interrupting something important?"

"No. I'm glad you called."

"Sheldon, I've been thinking about our conversation last night, about that identification method you mentioned."

"Yes?"

"I think it might be a good idea."

"I agree, Emilie. We'll talk more tonight, okay? I'm about to head into a meeting here at the hotel."

"Oh, I'm sorry."

"Quite all right. I'll see you tonight."

Emilie hung up. The oppressive feeling she'd had all morning lifted slightly, even though nothing had been accomplished yet. But tonight she would find out how she could get the tablet registered. Somehow she'd figure out how to do it without Herrigan or Fitzwater finding out.

Suddenly hungry, Emilie returned downstairs to the dining room. Jenn sat at a table alone. Emilie ladled some beef in gravy onto her plate and grabbed a salad.

Jack slipped into line behind her. "Hey, beautiful. Care to find a cozy little table for two somewhere?"

"Not today, Jack. Thanks." Emilie put her food on a tray and went to the bucket of bottled water.

"Oh, come on, Emilie. You can't resist an invitation from me, can you?"

She stared him down. "Jack, I know you're used to controlling everyone with your charm, but I'm just not up for it today, okay?"

She left him standing there open-mouthed and went to sit beside Jenn. "Mind sitting with the sorceress?"

Jenn lifted an eyebrow. "You know that kind of thing doesn't bother me." She shifted her tray to make room for Emilie. "Besides, you're the high priestess, remember?"

"Very funny."

"Who's joking?" Jenn speared a green bean. "Any good dreams lately?"

"Actually, I did have another. And I've got a question for you." She took a bite of salad and chewed while she put her thoughts together. "I've been thinking about this 'connecting to the universe' thing. Do you think that's where we go when we die?"

Jenn shrugged. "If we've achieved a high enough level of energy. Otherwise, we come back and do it again."

"So if we get it right and we don't have to come back, then what?"

"We become one with the universal consciousness, the divine energy."

"So my ultimate goal is to be completely absorbed, a total obliteration of my uniqueness?"

Jenn frowned. "That makes it sound negative."

"No kidding! See, I don't get it. We're always telling each other how special and unique we are, but then we're saying we're all part of the same thing, trying to become one big, undifferentiated glob of energy. It doesn't add up."

"Well—"

Emilie put down her fork. "And that's not the only thing. You're saying that if we do this life thing the right way, then we don't have to come back and do it again. But then you're also telling me there is no right way. If there's no right or wrong, no absolute truth, then the whole 'karma' idea makes no sense. How can we do it right when there is no right?"

Jenn folded her arms. "But we have to love each other, accept each other. That's the only right—"

"So there is a right thing to do?"

"Just that one thing."

Emilie shook her head. It was all starting to unravel in her mind. "You don't get it, Jenn. If there's one right thing, then there really is right and wrong, after all. And if there really is right and wrong, your whole philosophy falls apart."

Emilie turned at a movement behind her. Margaret stood there, holding a tray and smiling.

Jenn glared at her. "I guess you have something to say?"

Margaret's smile widened. "Emilie, it only works in the classroom. Don't try to transfer that line of thinking to reality."

Jenn pushed her tray away in disgust. "You two talk Bible stuff if you like. I'm going out for the afternoon."

But Margaret didn't talk "Bible stuff." She sat beside Emilie and asked about her work, which Emilie enjoyed explaining. She asked about her family, and Emilie changed the subject. Margaret mentioned Jack, which surprised Emilie. "I'm just noticing things, that's all," Margaret said. "Never mind."

When they'd finished, Emilie left Margaret in the hotel lobby. "I'm not sure what I'm going to do today," Emilie said. "But first, I think I'll take a nap!"

▲ ▲ ▲

Emilie welcomed the dreaming today, eager for more, wanting to find answers. As the hotel room drifted hazily away, a large, wooden door sharpened into focus before her. She knocked.

Someone yanked the door open. The room beyond was dark. A hand pulled her into the room.

Marduk Bel-Iddin leaned his head into the hallway, searching both directions, then closed the door heavily. "What are you doing here, Warad?" His voice was hushed, as if speaking would betray her presence.

She said nothing.

Marduk strode to the other side of the room. "I don't care what they think. I am glad you've come. I must have someone to talk with, someone who understands."

She moved toward him, concerned by the wildness in his eyes, the way his hands never stopped moving when he spoke. "What is it, Marduk?"

He stopped and looked at her. "Can you not see what they've done to me?"

She studied his face. It was thin and hollow, like a shadow of when she had last seen him. His shoulders slumped; his skin had a grayish cast. "Who has done this?"

Marduk looked through the window of his private quarters, through the tiny square that allowed him access to the gods of the night. He whispered and pointed upward. "They have."

Her heart pounded at his blasphemy. To accuse the gods of bestowing misfortune was to invite more catastrophe upon oneself. She wished she had time for a cleansing omen.

Marduk faced her again. "You were right, Warad. You were right. They let me believe that I was able to summon their power at my discretion. They came when I called; they did what I asked. But it was a deceit. They waited until I had given myself, and then they showed me that I was the one controlled, not they."

"Marduk, you mustn't—"

He twisted his hands together, then pulled them apart and tore at his hair. "Mustn't I? Why not? What more can they do?"

"Marduk—"

"Will they take my life, Warad? Will they? Then they will have one less slave to do their bidding." He raised a fist at the tiny window. "One less slave!" The words died in a choking cough. Marduk doubled over and backed away from the window.

She went to him, bent to search his face. When he turned to her, she backed away in fright. His face was a twisted mask of anger and hate.

"Why have you come here, Warad-Sin?" he asked. His voice was deeper, rasping.

She stood straighter. She knew why she had come. In obedience to Qurdi. In loyalty to the goddess. She was here to compromise Marduk's position.

"Get away from me!" he said, as if he knew her mind.

She backed away from his wrath, retreating until she bumped a table behind her. She turned to steady it and her hand fell upon the clay tablet she had seen earlier. The clay was still soft under her fingers. She studied the tablet, the distant part of her recognizing the symbols she had spent so many hours poring over. "This is it," she said. "The healing ritual the gods gave you."

Marduk cackled. "The gods gave me. Yes, yes, the gods gave me!"

She ran her fingertips over the symbols, the words that would one day form connections from this distant place to a more distant future. "Why do they torture you, Marduk?"

"Why indeed? When they have me so thoroughly?" He smashed a fist against the wall of his chamber, then smashed it again and again, until it was bloody. "Because I resist."

"Resist what?"

"Resist their bidding."

"But Marduk, mustn't we always do what the gods ask of us?"

He wrapped his bloody fist in the edge of his robe. "Even if it is not right, what they ask?"

"There is no right, Marduk. There is only what the gods want."

He nodded. "They want me to kill the young Jew, Belteshazzar."

She gasped. "But he is favored by the gods and by the king. Killing him would mean your certain death!"

Marduk laughed again. "So now you see, Warad. They care nothing for me. They do not do my bidding. They only seek to control and destroy, then they will toss me aside for someone else."

"Will you do it, Marduk?"

"Will I give the king reason to execute me?" His eyes took on the wild look again. "I—will—NOT!"

At the final word, his body began to twitch and writhe as though in agony, in the final throes of death. She watched in horror. He kept his balance while the upper half of his body trembled. His robe fluttered in a cold wind that whipped through the chamber. Flecks of white appeared at the corners of his mouth.

And then he was still. She thought at first that he was dead, still standing. But his eyes opened. He looked at her as though she were not there, then pushed past her. Just before he reached the door, he snatched an obsidian-handled knife from a table. Then he tossed the door open and strode into the hallway.

She followed, knowing the purpose for which Qurdi sent her

would not be fulfilled tonight but needing to know where Marduk was going, what he would do.

Through the halls of the palace, past the chambers of the royal wives and concubines, past servants' quarters and eunuchs' chambers, she followed.

Finally, he stopped before a door. She knew the place. Belteshazzar would be inside. Marduk breathed deeply.

She squeezed his arm. "Don't do this," she said. "You do not want to do this."

He yanked his arm from her grasp and said nothing. He pushed the door open without knocking.

The hour was late. Belteshazzar lay upon his bed, already asleep. The door did not awaken him. Marduk moved silently to his bedside. She followed, knowing she sealed her own fate, but unable to leave.

Belteshazzar's chambers were opulent, with rich tapestries and embroidered bed coverings. An oil lamp flickered on a table at the side of the room, casting a yellow glow over the sleeping man. Barely a man. Still almost a boy.

Marduk raised the knife in one hand over Belteshazzar. He paused and wrapped the other hand around the lifted knife.

Belteshazzar opened his eyes. He stared at Marduk.

Marduk faltered, hesitating above Belteshazzar.

"No."

It was a simple word, spoken quietly by the younger man. It seemed to strike with more force than a knife ever could. Marduk's arms lowered, then rose again in determination.

Belteshazzar had not moved. "By the Most High God, I command you to drop the knife."

Marduk stepped away as though struck. He turned to her, confusion twisting his face. She closed the door behind them and moved closer to Marduk, until she also stood beside the bed. Belteshazzar's eyes rested briefly on her, then returned to Marduk.

The eerie calm of the room suddenly exploded. Marduk

screamed and dropped the knife. He clutched the sides of his head, bent forward, and retched. "Stop—stop—stop!" His screams echoed off the chamber walls until she began to cry. Why did no one come? Marduk fell to the floor, rolling and screaming.

And then he was silent. For the second time, she thought him dead—until she saw his gray hand reach from beneath his robes, saw the fingers wrap around the hilt of the knife once more.

Belteshazzar raised himself on the bed. He swung his legs over the side and stood.

Marduk stood also, then rushed at Belteshazzar, the knife raised to his shoulder and aimed for the chief of magicians.

She watched in astonishment as Belteshazzar again said simply, "No," and Marduk staggered backward and fell as though he had run headlong into a stone wall. He lay on the floor, panting, staring at Belteshazzar.

She looked back and forth between the two, watching as the expressions of each gradually changed. Marduk's anger fell away, replaced by fear, even desperation. Belteshazzar's determined courage gave way to compassion.

Marduk coughed and whispered from the floor. "Please—make—them—stop."

Belteshazzar moved to him and knelt. He laid a hand on Marduk's forehead, his lips moving in silent prayer. Marduk shuddered, then lay still, his chest rising and falling in the manner of one sleeping in peace.

Belteshazzar turned to her. "Your gods are impotent against the One True God."

She backed away, opened the door behind her, and fled into the shadows of the palace. She heard the door close behind her.

Emilie woke up panting. The afternoon light shone in the room.

Jenn stood by the door as though she had just closed it. "You okay?"

"Yeah. Yeah, fine."

"What are you doing on your afternoon off? Not napping all day, I hope."

"No." Emilie stood and ran her hands through her hair. "I don't know. I'm going out with Sheldon tonight."

"Not 'til tonight? Why not go early? Surprise him."

"He was in a meeting earlier."

"So, he's gotta be done by now. Go ahead, be spontaneous for a change."

"The last time I was spontaneous, you said I was being too bold."

"So I learned my lesson."

Emilie smiled. The dream had been a frightening one this time. She could use a little fun to change the atmosphere in her brain. Maybe she would go see Sheldon. But still. . .

"I don't know, Jenn," she said. "You're as on and off as Sheldon."

"What's that supposed to mean?"

"First you tell me women shouldn't sit around and wait for men to come calling. Then, when I decide to do just that, you tell me not to. Now you're telling me to be spontaneous again. Are you sure you're not on some medication you're not telling me about?"

Jenn dropped onto the bed with a laugh. "Call me moody."

▲ ▲ ▲

Emilie had second thoughts on the way to the Holiday Inn Ashkelon. Would Sheldon want to see her? Would he be finished with the meeting he'd been about to start when she called earlier? What other business would she be pulling him away from this afternoon?

As the taxi turned into the hotel parking lot, Emilie wondered why she'd even come. It was Jenn's suggestion, but at the time Emilie had felt it would help. Now she suspected that she was doing exactly what Margaret had said—using a romance with Sheldon to fill up the holes in her life. The dreams had begun to reveal some kind of hole. She felt desperate to connect to something higher, something better. Something different than another mere mortal.

She paid the driver and pushed through the front door of the hotel. The coolness of the lobby washed over her as it had last night, reminding her of the fairy-tale evening she'd spent with Sheldon. *I'll just say hello, tell him I'm out sightseeing for the afternoon. If he's busy, I won't even disturb him.*

The classic beauty behind the front desk today was not the same woman whom Emilie had spoken to last night. She asked again for Sheldon's room phone number. If he wasn't there, she'd leave a message and find something else to do for the afternoon.

"I'm sorry, miss," the woman said. "There's no one by that name registered here."

Emilie shook her head with a patient smile. "Sheldon Gold," she said. "Could you check again, please?"

"Perhaps he's checked out?" the clerk asked. "I'll search previous guests." A moment later, she smiled up from her keyboard. "No, I'm sorry. We have no record of a Sheldon Gold ever staying at this hotel."

Emilie frowned, unwilling to ask her to check again. "I. . .must have gotten the hotel wrong." She backed away. "I'm sorry."

"Have a nice day, miss." The young woman flashed her perfect smile again, unaware that her answer had turned Emilie's heart to stone.

Emilie lay stretched out on her bed in the Ashkelon Plaza Hotel, her eyes closed but her mind racing. Jenn must have gone sightseeing. The silence of the room did nothing to calm the roaring in Emilie's brain.

She didn't have the wrong hotel. Sheldon had met her in the lobby of that hotel last night. Why would he lie?

She reviewed every moment they had spent together. Was it possible that it was all a sham? Did he care for her at all, or had everything been faked? Why? All for the tablet?

Confusion and suspicion gave way to anger. She'd been so careful, walked on eggshells ever since she'd met him in the Painted Tomb. She hadn't let herself admit that he had an unreasonable temper. Instead, she'd played the fragile female, eager to please. And she'd fallen for every line he'd handed her. Stupid girl. *You're so busy worrying about offending people, you don't see what's right in front of you.* Once again, her bad judgment had cost her dearly. She'd believed in the wrong person and found betrayal at the end of her trust.

The phone rang. Emilie ignored the first two rings, but then slapped at it, eyes still closed. "Hello?" She didn't care if she sounded like she was in the middle of a raging hangover.

"Emilie? It's Sheldon."

Emilie shot up, heat pounding into her arms and legs. "Yes?"

"Did I wake you up?"

"No." Emilie pulled the receiver away from her mouth and took several deep breaths, willing her heart to slow down.

Sheldon cleared his throat. "I wanted to let you know, I talked to that friend of mine, the one who has the ISIS system. He says we can do it."

"Where are you, Sheldon?"

"Excuse me?"

"Where are you? Did you finish your meeting?"

Sheldon was silent for a moment. "Yes, yes, we finished a few minutes ago. I'm still here at the hotel, back in my room."

"At the Holiday Inn?"

"Yes. Did you hear what I said about my friend, Emilie?"

Emilie closed her eyes. "I heard." Images of Sheldon kissing her last night mocked her. It had all been an act. From the walk on the beach to the final bars of Stravinsky, it had been a calculated sham. There was no real Sheldon Gold.

Emilie popped her eyes open again. Unless. . . ! What if Sheldon had used a different name to check into the hotel? He might have some legitimate business reason to use another name. Should she come right out and ask him? She didn't want him to think she was prying.

"Emilie? Are you listening?"

"What? Yes."

"I was saying that my friend says we can do the authentication tonight. Can you meet me in Main Square at six o'clock?"

"All right." Emilie searched frantically for a way to ask about the name he'd used. She felt like a drowning woman clutching at a fraying rope.

"Oh, and Emilie?" Sheldon said. "Bring the tablet with you."

She'd never told him the relic she was working on was a tablet.

Her rope broke.

Chapter 18

Sheldon Gold disconnected and smiled. Everything was going perfectly. Emilie Nazzaro had no idea what was waiting for her tonight, but she was falling right into his scheme. He lifted a finger from the phone and waited for the dial tone to buzz in his ear before he dialed again.

"Yes?" The voice on the other end sounded as close as the next room.

Sheldon sat a little straighter. "It's all set up."

"Good. You're sure she doesn't suspect the truth?"

"The girl's as gullible as they come." Sheldon picked off a stray piece of lint on the sleeve of his shirt. "Don't worry. We'll get it."

"If this goes wrong, you'll never work for me again."

Sheldon nodded to the unseen voice. "Nothing will go wrong." He would make sure of that.

"I expect you to do whatever it takes to get the job done."

"Whatever it takes." Sheldon repeated the words. What did that mean, exactly? Sheldon knew he was many things, but a killer wasn't one of them. Sure, he'd sacrificed a few ethics along the way, but he couldn't hurt anyone physically, could he?

"Good. Call me when it's done."

"You got it."

▲ ▲ ▲

Emilie paced her hotel room, trying to put the pieces together into something that resembled more than a blurry image of herself as an idiot.

What had she missed? Sheldon had seemed too good to be true, and yet she had believed him. When her inner voice was telling her to be suspicious, she had ignored it as her usual relationship-sabotaging ritual. She had forced herself to trust him. She should have known better. Nobody had ever proven trustworthy in her life. Why should a stranger in a foreign country be any different? Sheldon had tricked her and used her. He'd known about the tablet from the beginning, and had tried to manipulate her into handing it to him.

Emilie grabbed her purse and dug through the accumulated junk in the dark recesses of the white leather bag. Perhaps Sheldon thought he'd strung her along like a puppy chasing a doggie treat. Well, she had a little surprise for him.

The purse yielded what she had been searching for: Agent Amir Sudiwitz's business card. Emilie slid her finger along the sharpness of the card's edge and nodded once. Yes, she'd have a surprise for Sheldon.

She dialed the number, fighting to hang onto the anger which was quickly being displaced by misery.

"Sudiwitz."

"Yes, hello again, Mr.—Agent Sudiwitz." Emilie rolled her eyes at her juvenile beginning. "This is Emilie Nazzaro."

"Do you have something more for us, Ms. Nazzaro?"

"Yes. Well, sort of. I've been—approached—by someone."

"Someone has assaulted you?"

"No, not assaulted. It's someone I've been spending time with. You see. . ." Emilie took a deep breath. "There's a man. Sheldon Gold. He and I have been seeing each other since I arrived in Ashkelon. But I believe he may be trying to steal the tablet."

"I see. When will you see this Mr. Gold again?"

"I'm supposed to meet him in Main Square at six o'clock. With the tablet."

"Ms. Nazzaro, you did the right thing." Emilie heard a click and then the hollow sound of someone on a speaker phone. "Please tell us the entire story."

Emilie took a deep breath and tried to explain her relationship with Sheldon. She left out a few details she didn't see the need to repeat, like the tingling feeling of Sheldon's hands on her shoulders, and the way the moon had seemed to smile on them as it climbed over the Mediterranean Sea when they'd walked on the beach that first night.

"Sounds like this guy's a professional." Sudiwitz's voice was muffled, as though he was speaking to someone other than her.

"Can you arrest him or something?" Emilie asked.

"Not without your help."

Emilie sighed. "I was afraid of that."

"I assure you, you'll be in no danger."

Emilie shook her head. "I'm not afraid of him. I just don't want to ever see him again."

"I regret that will not be possible. You must meet him at six tonight as he has requested."

"Won't he suspect something when he sees I don't have the tablet?"

"Certainly. You'll have to bring it."

Emilie glanced across the room, through the window. "Bring it to Sheldon?"

"We'll be watching. But he's not the one we want. We'll follow him to his buyer and make the arrest when the transaction occurs. It is the only way."

Emilie exhaled. "Can't I just bring some other package, wrapped up to look like the tablet?"

Sudiwitz cleared his throat. "That would be too risky. If he is alerted, he'll be gone, and we'll have nothing. And if he takes a fake, we don't have him selling the real antiquity."

"But—"

"Ms. Nazzaro, I suggest you leave the plans to us. Get some rest. Pick up the tablet. Tell no one of the situation, we don't know who is involved. We'll call you at five-thirty and tell you where to meet us."

"Meet you?" Emilie's mind sifted through information as though she were lost in fog.

"So we can give you final instructions." She heard him pick up the receiver, heard his voice loudly in her ear. "Are you going to be able to do this, Ms. Nazzaro?"

"What? Yes. Yes, I can do it." Emilie focused on her mental picture of Sheldon's charming smile, his smooth-as-butter flatteries. Oh yes, she could do it.

Sudiwitz disconnected and Emilie studied the digital clock as if it held answers to the mysteries of life. Four-thirty. She had an hour to get the tablet and be back in this room before Sudiwitz called. Just long enough to get herself good and panicked. She'd told the Israel Antiquities Agency people that she wasn't afraid of Sheldon. But the moments of intensity she'd witnessed in him came flooding back. Was he capable of hurting her? What if he figured out he was being watched? That she knew what he was up to?

Emilie sat on the bed. She looked at the ceiling. It was as good a time as any to talk to this God that Margaret was so certain of. The thought of addressing Him personally almost made her laugh. But Margaret's challenge echoed in her mind. "Try Him," she'd said. "He's not afraid of tests."

"Okay, God," Emilie began, her eyes still lifted toward the ceiling. "I guess I'll give this a try. I'm in some trouble here. Of course, I probably don't have to tell You all about it, right? But I need some help. I don't know how to pull this off. I'm afraid that when I see this jerk I'm going to wreck the whole thing by kicking him or something." She slowed, breathing deeply and dropping her eyes. "And I'm just afraid, too. Afraid of getting caught in the crossfire. Literally."

Emilie waited. Waited for a feeling of peace, of comfort. Waited for some kind of answer to appear in her mind, some reassurance. But she felt nothing. She heard nothing. Just as she'd suspected: There was nothing there.

She shook off the foolishness. It was time to get down to business. Where would Herrigan be on his Friday afternoon off? What if she couldn't track him down, then convince him to let her back at the tablet, unguarded?

▲ ▲ ▲

Victor Herrigan was just finishing his chicken and wild rice in the private dining room at the Ashkelon Plaza Hotel when his cell phone rang. He patted his lips with the burgundy linen napkin and slid the phone from his suit jacket pocket. "Yes?"

"It's done. Meet me now with the rest of the money."

Victor swept a gaze around the room. "How did you get this number? I told you to only call me on my room phone."

"Do you want the fake or not?"

Victor clenched his jaw. "Keep your voice down!"

"No one can hear me where I am, Herrigan. Now are we going to do this or what?"

Victor's mind raced through details. "I can meet you in about ninety minutes."

"Yacov's Bar again. Bring the money."

"Fine." Victor pocketed the phone and signaled the waitress for the check.

Since his last meeting with Komodo, Victor had managed to set up a buyer for the tablet. His plan had fallen into place better than he'd expected. All that remained was to take the real tablet to the buyer, collect his money, and pay Komodo a fraction of it to give him the fake. It would all be over in a few hours.

Victor signed for the bill, took a last sip of water, then stood. He'd call his buyer from his room, where there was privacy. Victor headed across the lobby toward the elevator.

"Dr. Herrigan!"

He slowed. Daniel Kritzner, one of the younger volunteers, jogged toward him. He was an overweight university student whose hair was prematurely thinning, and seemed to feel he had to work twice as hard as the others to overcome his handicaps. Victor cringed inwardly at the overeager expression on Daniel's face. The boy stopped beside him, panting from the exertion of his jog across the lobby.

"Yes, Daniel?"

"Do you have a few minutes? I wanted to talk to you about that jug handle I found this morning."

"No, Daniel, I'm sorry. I'm in quite a rush at the moment."

"Okay, I'll just take one minute, then."

Victor sighed.

"I was just wondering, I mean I know you said it was probably Byzantine, but the more I looked at it, I really thought it could be older than that. Maybe even Philistine." Daniel juggled a book he carried until it fell open. "Do you see this picture? Don't you think. . ."

Victor's mind fogged over then. The boy was still talking, he knew. He could see his lips forming the words, his chin bobbing. But there was nothing that made any sense finding its way to Victor's brain.

"Yes, yes," he said, interrupting the boy's excited babbling. "We'll have to take a closer look at that. I really must go."

"Okay, Dr. Herrigan. Thanks." Daniel looked as though he might actually bow, but then he caught himself and merely waved, the large book tucked under one arm.

Victor escaped into the elevator and pushed the button for the third floor. He rubbed at the tension in his jaw. It was disturbing, having things blur like that, even if it were only a rambling student. Especially when he needed to stay focused, stay alert, so that he could. . .

What? What was it he needed to run off to do? Victor cursed loudly and pounded the inside of the elevator door. It opened.

He stepped off, working backward in his mind through his previous actions. Before Daniel Kritzner stopped him, he had been eating dinner in the dining room. He'd left quickly because. . .

Victor wandered toward his room, still foggy. He was barely surprised when Margaret's door opened. She seemed to have a sixth sense, able to pick up when he was walking past her room.

"Well, you're just in time," she said, giving him one of her toothy smiles.

"Am I?"

"I was trying to decide what to do this afternoon. I'd like to see a little of the country, but I just hate to take one of those tour buses. What I need is a personal tour guide."

"Margaret, I'm sorry, I have something. . ." He tried to walk past her, but she slid one step sideways and blocked his path.

"Come on, Victor. All work and no play? Even you have to take a break sometimes, don't you?" She tilted her head and smiled again. "Take me on a tour."

He tried to step around her again. When she made a move to block him, he pushed her the other direction. "Excuse me, Margaret! I said I have things to do!" He brushed past her, but then turned. "I have repeatedly asked you to keep our relationship professional, Margaret. You overstep your bounds in a most unattractive way.

I have not asked for a friend, nor do I want one!"

Margaret wide smile faded to a thoughtful, almost pitying amusement. "Ah, Victor. That right there is your problem."

For lack of a better response, Victor snorted.

Margaret stepped toward him and touched his arm. "Let me know when you realize what's important." She turned and disappeared into her room again.

Victor stepped into his room and the fog in his mind cleared. He needed to call his buyer and set up a meeting as soon as possible. Perhaps his little scene with Margaret had helped get his brain pumping again. If so, that was the only good that could come of the incident.

Victor checked his watch. Five o'clock. He had already wasted fifteen minutes chatting with inconsequential people. He only had until seven o'clock to meet Komodo with the money.

He pulled out his wallet and slipped a small, white card from it. A number was scrawled on the back. He dialed, then loosened his tie and sat on the edge of the bed.

"It's Victor Herrigan. I'm ready to make the deal. It needs to be now."

The male voice on the other end came back immediately. "Can't do it now. In a few hours, maybe, but not now."

"You don't understand. This whole deal is about timing. I told you to be ready."

"Herrigan, I've said before that you're in over your head here. Every time I turn around you're blustering about with threats and superiority. You don't even know who you're dealing with. We deal when we're ready to deal, and I'm telling you, I'll meet you tonight. Eight o'clock."

"Fine." Victor slammed the phone down and glanced at the safe. He'd have to meet Komodo without the money, convince him to wait until later tonight for payment.

Should he take the tablet with him anyway, to compare the two versions? He could go directly to his meeting with the buyer after he met Komodo. *No, better to leave it here.*

Someone knocked on the door.

▲ ▲ ▲

Emilie took the elevator to the third floor, hoping to find Dr. Herrigan in his room. She was a little annoyed with herself for her ridiculous "encounter with God." It had only been Margaret's signposts that had driven her to it. But her principles were nonsense, and her God didn't exist. The elevator chimed and the doors slid open to reveal Margaret standing in the hallway, facing the elevator.

"Hello, Emilie."

Emilie stepped past her and held her hand against the door to keep it from closing.

"Don't worry about that," Margaret waved a hand toward the elevator. "I'll catch the next one."

Emilie shrugged and pulled her hand away. "I was just headed to Dr. Herrigan's room to do some work."

Margaret nodded. "I'm going to do a little sightseeing." The lines around her eyes deepened. "You okay, Emilie?"

"Yeah, I'm fine."

"You look upset. Anything I can do?"

Emilie shrugged. "I don't think so. Your God must be on a break, Margaret, because He doesn't seem to have a clue about what's going on in my life. Or maybe He just doesn't care. Either way, it's a little hard for me to swallow that He's there at all." Emilie sighed at the expression of surprise on Margaret's face. "Ignore me, Margaret. I'm sorry. Rough day."

"I won't ignore you. And neither will God."

"I just don't think it's possible to be so sure of the truth."

Margaret tilted her head and studied Emilie. "It's interesting to me, Emilie, that your life is centered around discovering the truths of the past when you don't believe there are any truths of the present."

Emilie studied the carpet.

"But what would life be like without truth, Emilie? No laws of nature, no laws of physics." She glanced behind her. "You can't even walk down the hallway without basing your life on the truth of gravity and direction."

Emilie glanced at her watch. Nearly five o'clock. "Listen, Margaret. I've got to go." She took a couple of steps down the hall.

"Emilie, there's a reason you don't feel any connection to God when you talk to Him."

Emilie turned, willing to give the older woman a few more seconds.

"You're blocked from connecting with Him, Emilie. Too much junk in between that can't be ignored."

Emilie stared at the floor. "That's the fourth signpost, isn't it?"

"Now you're catching on." Margaret moved toward her until she was an arm's reach away. "All that junk blocking you from a connection with God has made you look elsewhere. It makes everyone look elsewhere. Some people decide just to be their own god."

Emilie nodded. "Some of us think we'd do a better job of it." She waited again for a look of shock on Margaret's face, but was greeted only with a warm smile.

"You go do what you have to do now, Emilie. God's not giving up on you, and neither am I." Margaret retreated and pressed the elevator button.

Emilie turned and walked toward Room 305.

Dr. Herrigan yanked the door open after her first knock. "Yes, Emilie? What is it?" He seemed out of breath.

"I was hoping to do a little extra work tonight. I reached a crucial section today and just ran short of time. I hate to have to wait until Sunday." Emilie hoped she sounded casual.

"Tonight?" Herrigan looked back over his shoulder into the room, and then faced her again. "I have to go out right now."

"That's fine. I didn't want to intrude on your privacy anyway."

Herrigan nodded. "Right." He seemed to be debating. "Fine. Just give me a minute." The door closed in her face.

Emilie checked the time again. She'd have twenty minutes to get back to her room with the tablet so she'd be there for Agent Sudiwitz's call—as long as Herrigan left right away. She couldn't believe it had gone as smoothly as it had.

The door opened and Herrigan stepped out carrying a briefcase. "I opened the safe," he said. "Just be certain to lock the door behind me, and when you leave, replace the tablet in the safe and turn the dial."

"Thanks, Dr. Herrigan." Hopefully the man wouldn't open the safe again until after the whole thing was over. She didn't know how she'd get the tablet back in there, but maybe by then she'd be a hero, and the whole story could come out.

He left, and she threw the deadbolt. Emilie entered the room, pulled the case from the safe, and placed it on the small table beside the window where she'd worked the last time she was here. She closed the door on the safe and turned the dial, then sat in the chair beside the table and checked her watch. She'd give Dr. Herrigan five minutes to be safely away, and then she'd return to her room with the tablet.

▲ ▲ ▲

Emilie tapped her fingernail on the table in her own room, a replica of the table in Herrigan's room. Beside her sat the case. She watched the phone, feeling the second hand on her wristwatch sweep across the numbers in slow motion.

The phone rang. Emilie jumped. She grabbed the table edge to steady herself, then crossed the room. "Hello?"

"Ms. Nazzaro, meet us in Room 117. Bring everything with you. You'll leave from here once we've given you instructions."

"I'll be right there."

Emilie disconnected and took a deep breath. This was it. She looked down at herself. Her T-shirt and denim shorts didn't seem like the right outfit for a sting operation.

T-shirt and shorts! With all the confusion today, she'd never thought about what she was wearing. Under normal circumstances, she'd never go out for an evening with Sheldon looking like this! He'd know something was wrong if she didn't change.

Emilie ran to the closet and yanked out a lemon-yellow silk shirt and white dress pants. The pants had a slight crease in them from the hanger, but she'd have to live with it. She ripped off her T-shirt and shorts, washed up quickly at the bathroom sink, and changed into the silk shirt and pants. She allowed herself a quick glance in the mirror, then grabbed a hairbrush and slashed at her dark hair a few times, until it fell smoothly below her shoulders. She tossed the brush to the counter and picked up her lipstick.

"What am I doing?" she said, dropping the tube onto the counter beside the brush. "Who cares?"

She raced back into the room, grabbed the case and her purse, and jogged into the hallway. The door closed behind her with a heavy thunk that echoed down the carpeted silence of the long hall. Emilie suddenly felt exposed, vulnerable. Was she as isolated as it seemed? There was nothing between the tablet and a thief except her.

And the IAA agents waiting for me. Emilie shook off her fear and trotted to the elevator, hoping Dr. Herrigan wouldn't be on the other side of the door when it opened.

The elevator was empty. Emilie pushed the button for the first floor and concentrated on breathing normally. The elevator chinged to a stop and the doors slid open onto another empty hallway. She found Room 117 and knocked twice on the door. It fell open before her third knock, leaving her hand swinging forward in midair.

Agent Sudiwitz stood before her. "Come in." He wrapped fingers around her wrist and pulled her into the room.

The shades were drawn and only one small lamp turned on in the room. Emilie blinked and looked around. Agent Sudiwitz's shorter, rougher sidekick stood near the lamp. He nodded in recognition, a quick, businesslike nod that made Emilie feel like a back-alley informant in a bad movie. A woman she'd never met stood beside him.

"You've met Agent Washko," Sudiwitz said. "This is Agent Zacharia." Emilie tried to smile. "They'll be on surveillance when you meet with Gold."

Emilie looked at the intense woman, who stood at least five inches taller than her. Her black hair was pulled back from her face in a tight, sleek ponytail. She didn't smile.

"Okay," Emilie said, tightening her hold on the case in her hand.

Sudiwitz pulled her farther into the room. "Agents Washko and Zacharia will be watching you at all times." The two nodded. "We'll be watching for Gold and follow you both if he takes you somewhere."

Emilie set the case on the floor but kept her eyes on Sudiwitz. "Do you really think he'll go directly to his buyer? With me in the car?"

"It's doubtful," Sudiwitz said. "He'll probably think of some way to get rid of you—"

"Get rid of me?"

"Don't worry. We'll be all around you. Stay in Main Square if possible, and at least in a public place. If you feel you're in danger at any moment, you can signal us."

"How do I signal you?"

Sudiwitz glanced around the room, as though searching for an idea.

Emilie watched their faces. "How about an ear-piercing scream of terror?" she said. No one smiled.

"Ms. Nazzaro, we're putting a lot of stock in your ability to remain calm and do this job."

Emilie inhaled. "Don't worry. I'll be fine."

"Good. If you feel you're in any danger, pretend to see a friend in the distance and wave. We'll be at your side in seconds."

Emilie leaned over to pick up the case. "With friends like you, who needs. . ."

"Excuse me?"

"Nothing. What happens after you catch him selling the tablet?"

"Don't concern yourself with details, Ms. Nazzaro. We'll take care of everything. After Gold leaves you, please return to your hotel room. We'll contact you there, and return the tablet to your keeping."

Sudiwitz looked at his watch. "You've got fifteen minutes until Gold meets you. You'd better go."

"Where will you be?"

"We've got it covered. You head to the lobby. Don't speak with anyone unnecessarily. Don't make yourself conspicuous in any way."

Right. With the black market after me and a stolen treasure in my hands. Emilie nodded.

Sudiwitz extended his arm toward the door. Emilie tightened her hold on the case and left the room.

Once again, she stood alone in a silent hallway. The agents in the room behind her comforted her only slightly. She strolled toward the lobby as though headed toward nothing more than a casual dinner date, though she wondered if those who passed her could read the terror on her face. When would the agents emerge from the room to follow her as closely as they'd promised?

The lobby held only a few hotel guests in quiet conversations at seating areas. Emilie strolled through the front doors and into the hot evening sun. She hailed one of the cabs lined up at the curb lying in wait for tourists. She opened the back door and had just pushed the black case onto the back seat when she heard her name called. She turned toward the sound, relieved that the IAA was checking in with her once more.

But it was Jack Cabot jogging toward her. "Haven't seen much of you today."

Emilie closed the cab door partway, hoping Jack wouldn't spot the case inside. "Yeah." Emilie's mind went blank trying to think of something more to say.

"Going into town?"

"Uh, yes. For dinner. I'm running late, though. See you soon?"

Jack nodded. "Maybe we could go back to Main Square tomorrow. I never did get you to show me those sarcophagi."

"Right. Okay. I'll see you."

Emilie hopped into the cab and shut the door before Jack could speak again.

The cab pulled away from the hotel. Emilie turned in her seat to watch through the back window. Was it a coincidence that Jack was flagging down a cab right behind her?

Chapter 19

Jack had a bad feeling. It was the feeling he got when a job was about to go south. When Emilie's cab pulled away from the hotel, Jack backed up a few steps, then found a cab of his own and instructed the driver to follow her.

Something wasn't right. Emilie was leaving in a cab alone. She'd acted strangely. Seemed to be hiding something inside the cab. Jack swore under his breath. If he'd been on his game he would've been outside two steps earlier and he would've seen what she'd been carrying. He'd let himself get too casual about watching her lately. If she'd stolen the tablet from under his nose, he was in serious trouble.

Vehicles clogged the streets heading toward the center of town. Jack sat on the edge of the back seat. "Don't lose her! Can't you drive any faster?"

His driver shrugged. "Why must everyone be rushing?"

Jack growled. "It's important, buddy. Step on it."

The man sighed deeply, but edged around a small bus and accelerated. Jack squinted, trying to catch a glimpse of Emilie in the back of the cab they followed. She was too far away.

Several minutes later, the cab pulled into the parking lot of the Crowne Gardens Hotel. Jack swore under his breath. "Hightower's hotel. I knew it." He leaned toward the front seat. "Pull up behind that cab and let me out there." He scrounged in his wallet for a few bills and tossed them over the backseat. He was opening the back door before the cab had completely stopped.

Jack was beside the other cab in several long strides. He yanked the back door open and bent over to haul Emilie out.

Inside, a small, white-haired woman stared back at him, eyes wide.

Jack swore again. "Sorry. Thought you were someone else." He slammed the car door and searched the parking lot, knowing the effort was useless. She was long gone. Had she seen him and dodged him? If so, she was definitely guilty.

Ten minutes later, Jack was knocking on Herrigan's door, his safe-cracking tools inside his jacket. When no one came to the door he pulled a special card from his pocket, slid it into the door and pulled it out. The green light blinked and Jack opened the door.

It took five minutes to open Herrigan's room safe. The metal door swung open, confirming Jack's fears. The safe was empty.

Jack sat back on his heels and took a deep breath. *That conniving...* He pulled out a cell phone, shaking his head. He should have known. He hadn't met a woman yet he could trust. All Emilie's quiet insights into his psyche and her deep laugh and her love of history had lulled him into a half-sleep until he couldn't see what was right in front of him. Now his job was as good as dead. He punched a few numbers into the phone. A female voice answered on the second ring. "Get me Vitelli."

Vitelli answered a moment later.

"It's Jack. The piece has walked."

"Talk to me, Jack."

"Emilie Nazzaro. Supposed epigrapher. I think she just left with it in a cab heading toward downtown Ashkelon."

The silence on the other end rubbed Jack's nerves raw.

"I'll call in local authorities to help," Vitelli finally said. "I'll expect you to be in the area when they intercept."

"Yes, sir."

"Jack, let's hope you can pull this one out of the garbage like you did the Turkey thing. You've been doing well in Israel, Jack. But you have to get this tablet. The IAA won't be as forgiving as the Turkish government was. They take their antiquities pretty seriously."

"Sir, I—"

"Save it, Jack. But if you blow this one you'll want to start thinking about other work. Agents who can't get the job done have no business being part of Interpol."

▲ ▲ ▲

When Emilie saw Jack jump into the cab behind her, she instinctively hugged the black case to her chest.

"Main Square," she said to the driver, "but someone is following me. Can you take an indirect route and try to lose him?"

Her driver grinned. "Like an American movie, yes?"

She half-smiled. "Right."

He must have spent half his life in a movie theater. Long after Emilie was certain that Jack was gone, the cab kept screeching around corners and shooting down narrow alleys. Emilie felt nauseated when they finally arrived at Main Square.

The square was crowded with tourists when Emilie entered. Her fingernails dug into her palm where she held the tablet case. It was crazy, walking around with this valuable piece, trusting it and herself to IAA agents she couldn't even see.

Sheldon had not arrived yet, so Emilie found a bench near the clock tower and sat down. She placed the black case beside her on the bench and wrapped an arm around it, hugging it to her body. She leaned back against the bench and surveyed the area, searching for the agents, and watching for Sheldon's imposing outline to appear out of the crowd.

She'd been such a fool for his distinguished graying hair and his sense of presence. What would Thomas Fitzwater say when he heard that she'd gotten romantically involved with the thief trying to steal the tablet? He'd sent her here, trusting her to keep it safe, and she'd practically led the thief right to it. Would the university hear about her failure? What would it mean for her career?

Emilie sighed. She'd never signed on for all of this. If she could stay alive until the whole thing was done, her days of adventure would be over.

The minutes passed. Where was everyone? It suddenly occurred to her that while she had been busy losing Jack, she might have lost the agents as well!

You're such an idiot. Now what will you do when Sheldon comes? Follow him yourself? She'd have no choice.

Emilie rested her arm across the top of the tablet case where it lay on the bench. Her terrified clutch of the past thirty minutes had tired her arm. *How long am I supposed to wait?*

She scanned the evening tourist crowd milling through the square. The sun was still hot, glaring in her eyes from where it hung in the sky across the city. Would one of the many tourists suddenly materialize into Agent Washko or Zacharia, telling her to give up and go back to the hotel?

She watched a toddler break away from her mother and run toward Emilie. Her blond, bouncing curls and toothy grin brought a smile to Emilie's face. A few feet from Emilie, the little girl's shoes tangled together, and she fell into the gravel at Emilie's feet.

"Mommy!" The child's wail accompanied huge tears.

Emilie glanced up at the mother, whose attention was on snapping pictures of the town square. "Are you okay?"

"Mommy!"

Emilie stood and reached down for the child, still lying in the gravel. "Here, stand up, honey." She glanced back at the black case, still on the bench.

"Mommy!"

Emilie brushed off the girl's knees. "Look, no blood. Just a few dents. You're okay."

"Cecilia!" Mommy had finally noticed and jogged over to Emilie.

Emilie stood. "She's fine. She just tripped and fell."

Cecilia's mother grabbed her hand. "Next time you stay right beside Mommy." She pulled the girl away from Emilie, and melted into the tourist crowd.

Emilie returned to her bench and laid her arm on the case once more. In a sudden surge of paranoia she spun the numbers and opened the case. The tablet still lay in its foam padding. She closed the case again.

The sun continued to dip lower in the sky. Emilie lowered her eyelids to escape the glare, and felt them grow heavy with fatigue. She popped them open again. How could she fall asleep in the middle of playing spy? She searched the square once more, but this time a figure in a baseball cap caught her eye. Was that Agent Washko? She pushed her hair behind her ear and slowly pivoted her head, letting her gaze trail across the distance between them. The man in the hat nodded slightly and touched the brim of the cap.

Emilie exhaled her relief. *They're here.* Now all she needed was to get through this thing with Sheldon. Would he take her with him? They were supposed to go out for the evening, but he wouldn't let her tag along while he sold the tablet, would he?

She didn't have to wonder long. Sheldon appeared with the sun at his back, towering over her.

"Emilie."

She swallowed hard. "Hello, Sheldon." Emilie stood and smiled as he kissed her cheek.

"How are you this evening?"

"Fine, thank you." *Get it over with, you big liar.*

Sheldon motioned to the case. "Did you bring the piece?"

Emilie nodded. In her peripheral vision she saw Agent Washko strolling toward the two of them. She saw his quick nod to his left, a signal to someone she couldn't see.

"Yes, I brought it."

Sheldon looked at his watch. "You know, it's early still. I hate to have the piece any longer than necessary. Why don't I just take it over to my friend right away, then pick you up afterward? You can get it back where it belongs and we'll be done with the whole thing."

Emilie smiled sweetly, but she wanted to scream, "Do you think I'm an idiot? You don't even have the combination! Did you really expect me to just hand it over?" Instead, she handed the case to him and said, "That sounds like a good idea, Sheldon. I'll just wait for you at my hotel?" Did she sound overly casual? Should she have expressed concern over giving it to him? She was pretty new at this spy stuff.

"I'll call you when I'm on my way over to get you," Sheldon said. He leaned over for another quick kiss. "See you soon."

"I can't wait."

Emilie watched Sheldon's back, watched Agent Washko fall into position behind Sheldon, and nodded as Washko appeared to be speaking into his collar. A couple that might have been Sudiwitz and Zacharia wandered along behind the first pair, seemingly out for a casual stroll. Emilie took a deep breath and headed back to the Ashkelon Plaza to wait for their call.

▲ ▲ ▲

The sun was nearly down when Victor Herrigan walked into Yacov's bar. Shabbat was upon the country, but those inside

Yacov's probably didn't care. Certainly Komodo did not. Herrigan searched the bar, squinting to see through the darkness. He didn't see Komodo.

He chose a booth near the front door, where he could watch those who entered. A waitress in a tight, short skirt asked him what he wanted. He ordered a drink and waited. Komodo was late.

His drink came, but he left it untouched. Several minutes later, the Asian man sauntered through the front door, swinging a black case much like the one in the safe in Victor's room.

"You're late." He watched as the other man laid the case on the table and lowered himself into the booth. Komodo flicked his eyes toward the waitress and pointed at Victor's drink. She nodded and held up one finger.

"Let's see it," Victor said.

Komodo shrugged and twirled the numbers on the case. He turned the case toward Victor so he could see the combination. *Seven-eight-two.* Victor stared at the numbers in concentration. He would not give Komodo the satisfaction of seeing him need to write them down, but he prayed he wouldn't forget. *Seven-eight-two.*

He flicked the metal tabs on the case and raised the lid partway.

The waitress came with Komodo's drink. Victor pulled the lid down as she approached.

Komodo tossed back the drink. Victor opened the case again.

It was perfect. He wished he could have brought the original, but there didn't seem to be a way to get it away from Emilie Nazzaro without suspicion. Still, even without the original, he could see that the workmanship was flawless. The orange-red clay looked as though it been molded into a tablet three thousand years ago, and the cuneiform had a weather-worn quality that only thousands of years of exposure could have accomplished. Victor nodded once and closed the lid.

"Rumor has it the real thing is cursed."

Victor waved away the comment. "I started that rumor myself. To keep people away."

Komodo rolled his eyes. "A curse only makes people more intrigued, Herrigan." He leaned back. "So where's the money?"

Victor swallowed. "There's been a slight change of plans. I'll have the money in a few hours."

Komodo's face narrowed and his dark eyes seemed to grow closer, darker. "What do you mean 'in a few hours'?"

"My buyer was delayed."

"You don't have the money?"

"You'll get it."

Komodo shook his head, wrapped his hand around the case and stood. "I don't do business that way, Herrigan," he said. He snorted in disgust. "Should have known better than to deal with a professor."

"I'll get the money! I'm not trying to trick you."

Komodo nodded and pulled the case back into his own possession. "We'll see. Call me when you're ready to do this right."

▲ ▲ ▲

Victor's drive back to the hotel passed in a blur of rage: at himself, at Komodo, at the buyer who had delayed everything. Even Emilie Nazzaro had gotten in his way. He was running in circles. But everything would still work out as long as Komodo didn't disappear on him. He'd go back to his room and retrieve the tablet. If Emilie were still there, he'd kick her out. Then he'd get this deal done and the whole thing would be over.

Victor made it past Margaret's door without being accosted, for which he was grateful. He knocked once on his own door, as a courtesy to Emilie if she were still inside, then opened the door.

"Hello?" he said. There was no answer.

He stepped inside. Emilie was not here. The safe was closed. At least that much was going right.

Victor opened the safe quickly, checking his watch as he twirled the numbers. He needed to hurry to make his eight o'clock meeting with the buyer. He reached in for the case, waving his hand through empty air.

He bent to peer inside. He patted his hand against the bottom and the sides of the safe.

The case was gone.

Victor checked the table where Emilie had worked. He checked the floor, the couch, the entire suite. The case and tablet were not here.

Don't panic. There had to be a reasonable answer. Maybe she'd taken it to her own room to continue working. Stupid, but better than the alternative.

What else? What other explanation besides the one he wouldn't think about? Nothing came to him.

Victor paced the room, his fingers clenched into fists so tight his hands began to ache. *Stupid, stupid, stupid.* He should have trusted his instincts about that girl and never let her near the tablet alone.

Should he call the police? Not yet. Even if Emilie had taken it there was still a chance he could get it back.

Unclenching his fists, Victor pressed his fingertips to his throbbing temples. He would just have to find out what Emilie did with it.

▲ ▲ ▲

Emilie sat alone in her hotel room, tapping her foot against her chair leg like an anxious relative in a hospital waiting room. When would they call? Would they bring the tablet back to her immediately? She stared at the phone, willing it to ring. The minutes passed.

A knock on the door startled her. She jumped to answer it. It must be the IAA returning the tablet already! *Herrigan will never even miss it if I get it back this quickly.*

She swung the door open wide. "Did you get—"

"Where is it, Emilie?" Dr. Herrigan's scowl told her more than his words.

"Come in, sir." She stepped aside and let him enter.

Herrigan turned to face her. "I don't know what your plan is, Emilie, but if you return the tablet immediately, I will not press charges."

"No, Dr. Herrigan, you don't understand—"

"The tablet, Emilie. I want it. Now."

Emilie waved toward the table and chairs beside the window. "Please, sit down. Let me explain."

Emilie chewed her lip as Herrigan walked to a chair and lowered himself to the edge of it. How much could she tell him? The IAA agents had told her not to speak to anyone. But surely Herrigan wasn't involved.

"I don't have the tablet here, Dr. Herrigan."

He jumped to his feet. "You haven't already sold it?"

"Nothing like that." Emilie sat in the chair opposite and waited for him to sit again. "I suppose I need to start at the beginning. I was contacted, you see, by the IAA as soon as I arrived in Israel."

"The IAA has been on to you from the beginning, then?"

Emilie laughed. "Dr. Herrigan, I'm not a thief. Please, just hear me out."

He nodded once, and Emilie resumed. "They wanted me to keep watch for anyone who seemed overly interested in the tablet. They were afraid someone might try to steal it."

Herrigan's brow furrowed, but he said nothing.

"I called them when I realized that someone was trying to use me to get to the tablet. They instructed me to meet with him and give him the tablet—"

"You gave the tablet away!"

"They were all there, Dr. Herrigan. The IAA agents were watching the whole thing. They wanted to follow him to his buyer, and then get them both. They'll bring the tablet back as soon as they make the arrest."

Herrigan sat back against the chair, but still gripped the arms. "And you didn't see any need to inform me of the situation?"

"They told me to keep it quiet. I'm sorry."

"So when will the tablet be returned?"

"I'm just waiting here for the call. They said to wait."

Herrigan shook his head. "No, that's unacceptable. We have a right to know the whereabouts of the tablet at all times." He got to his feet. "I'm calling the IAA."

Emilie shrugged. "They may not know anything yet, but go ahead. I'm anxious to hear if they've got him."

Herrigan crossed the room to the phone. "Who are these agents that contacted you?"

"His business card is right there beside the phone. Amir Sudiwitz is his name."

Herrigan glanced around the bedside table, picked up the phone and set it back down. He shook his head. "I don't see any card."

"Hmm." Emilie walked to the table. "I was sure I left it there. Maybe it's in my purse again." But a search through her purse yielded nothing.

"I don't know," she said. "Just call a general number for the IAA. They'll know how to reach him."

Dr. Herrigan used the hotel's operator to place the call, then sat on the bed while the call connected.

"Agent Amir Sudiwitz, please."

Emilie exhaled. Would Sudiwitz be back already, with the tablet?

Herrigan frowned and glanced up. "You said Amir Sudiwitz, right?" he asked Emilie.

"Yes, that's the agent who did all the talking."

"They don't have any agent by that name."

227

"That's ridiculous. Try Washko."

Herrigan lifted the phone to his mouth again. "How about Washko?" He looked back to Emilie. "First name?"

Emilie shrugged.

"Was it Samuel?" Herrigan asked.

"I don't know."

"Samuel Washko died last year."

"Then I guess it wasn't him!" Emilie tapped a frustrated rhythm on the table.

Herrigan was speaking into the phone again. "I don't know. I need to speak to someone who knows the details of a specific operation. An antiquity being delivered to a black market trader in order to follow him to a buyer. Yes, I'll hold."

Emilie stood. Something felt wrong here. Why would they say there was no Agent Sudiwitz?

"What's that?" Herrigan said into the phone. "Levy? Fine, Mr. Levy. What can you tell me about the sixth century B.C. Babylonian tablet that your people insisted be put in the hands of the black market?"

Herrigan listened for awhile, then shook his head. "No." His gaze flitted toward Emilie, then away. "Emilie Nazzaro. No. Yes, I understand. Yes. All right. The Ashkelon Plaza Hotel. Room 576." He replaced the phone and stood. "They would like us to wait here, so they can give us the rest of the details in person."

"Did they say if they have the tablet back yet?"

"He didn't say. Perhaps he wants to bring it to us himself."

Emilie took a deep breath and resumed her seat. "Are you sure everything's okay?"

Herrigan's face was unreadable. "We should wait."

Twenty awkward minutes later, a fist pounded against the door. Herrigan went to open it. Emilie stood.

A gray-haired man with puckered lips entered the room. He showed an identification badge and then stood across from Emilie, his arms folded. "I am Agent Levy. What is going on here?"

"I'm Emilie Nazzaro. I'm working at the Ashkelon dig—"

"Where is the tablet, Ms. Nazzaro?"

"I gave it—you know about the tablet? Then you know that Agent Sudiwitz—"

"No one from our department was working in conjunction with you on this matter, Ms. Nazzaro."

Emilie's heart lost its normal tempo for a moment. "What are you talking about?"

"Did you remove the artifact from the Ashkelon Plaza Hotel, Ms. Nazzaro?"

"Yes, but only because—"

"And where is it now?"

"I gave it to a man who called himself Sheldon Gold. He was going to sell it—"

Agent Levy nodded. "I will return."

He left as abruptly as he'd entered. Emilie stared at the closed door and sank into her chair, her hand gripping the edge of the polished cherry table.

Seconds later, the door reopened. The gray-haired man entered again, followed by two uniformed policemen. "Emilie Nazzaro, you are being placed under arrest for the theft of property of the State of Israel."

Emilie felt her jaw drop and her fingers loosen their grip on the table. The agent continued to speak, and Emilie watched his lips move, not comprehending the words. She stared at those lips, willing them to make sense. The officers on either side of her lifted her to her feet by her elbows.

"This is crazy," she finally said. "Your agents are the ones who told me to give it to him! They said they were going to follow him to his buyer!"

"You can tell us your story in the local police station, Ms. Nazzaro," Levy said. "We'll be interested in hearing it."

▲ ▲ ▲

Emilie couldn't stop twisting her fingers. She watched her hands perform their nervous cycle, first one hand, then the other. Finger-twisting, hand-wrenching—they belonged to damsels in distress in black and white movies.

The table in front of her was chipped and cracked. She looked up into the officer's eyes once more.

"Ms. Nazzaro, do you realize that the tablet belongs to the State of Israel?"

"Yes, and I—"

"Tell us again whom you passed the artifact to, once you left the hotel."

"I've already told you, these men met me at the airport—"

"Yes, we've heard that story. Unfortunately, it doesn't match any of the facts. We'd like to hear the truth."

"Listen, why would I stick around if I stole the tablet? Why wouldn't I disappear? If I'm some professional thief, does that make sense?" She rifled through her purse for the hundredth time, searching for Agent Sudiwitz's card. "He gave me a card, they were all so intense, seemed so professional. . ." She was rambling, but her thoughts were getting tangled. She dropped the purse and looked up again. "Why would I make up this whole story?"

"Because you're playing some kind of game and you think we will fall for it."

"Game?" Emilie intertwined her fingers.

"Besides Victor Herrigan, you were the only person with unre-stricted access to the artifact. Suspicion would obviously fall on you. You took the piece, as you have already admitted, and passed it on to a colleague. In order to avoid suspicion, you then con-cocted your ridiculous story and presented it to the IAA, believing that they, and we, are fools."

"No! It's true!" Emilie closed her eyes as the truth became

undeniable. "They must have been working for Sheldon Gold. They said that—"

The officer stood. "You will wait here." He swiveled in place and strode from the room.

Emilie placed her hands side by side on the table, palms flat. She raised her eyes to the mirrored wall across from her. Were they watching her from behind that mirror? Evaluating her every breath? She folded her hands in her lap and tried to look innocently distressed, whatever that looked like.

She had to admit, their version of the story sounded more plausible than hers did.

▲ ▲ ▲

Jack stood with his chin resting on one hand, elbow braced on the other arm. He looked through the one-way glass and studied Emilie's hands, flat on the table. He watched her fold them in her lap. She looked—what? Upset, certainly. But was there guilt mixed in?

The door opened behind him. Jack didn't turn around.

"She is not changing her story."

Jack nodded once. "So I heard. Can we hold her on what we've got?"

The officer came to stand beside him at the glass. "The tablet is missing, she was last seen with it, she admits to taking it, and you have established that she has been in contact with a black market collector." He shrugged. "It is not much, but I believe it is enough for now." He gave Jack a half-smile. "The Shabbat has begun. We may choose not to disturb a judge for a bail hearing until after it ends."

Jack looked back at Emilie. Her wide eyes stared back at him, as if she could see through the mirror. Such an innocent face, masking such a deceitful heart.

Emilie Nazzaro would be sorry she'd played him for a fool. Perhaps a night in an Israeli jail cell would loosen her tongue.

▲ ▲ ▲

Emilie watched the door now. How long until someone came back? Would they badger her any longer to change her story? She had nothing more to tell them, no matter how hard they pressed. If the truth couldn't satisfy them, she was out of luck.

She'd never felt more alone in her life. Who did she have that could rescue her? Sheldon Gold wouldn't be swooping in. She'd probably never see him again. Thomas Fitzwater, dying of cancer on the other side of the ocean? Besides, she'd lost his tablet. The realization that she had no one pressed on her like a heavy weight.

Jack Cabot. The name bubbled unbidden to the surface of her mind. Were her earlier suspicions unfounded? If Sheldon Gold had been after the tablet all along, could Jack have been in on it? That didn't seem to make sense. Was he working alone? Or had she once again badly misjudged someone's character? Could Jack be completely innocent?

Emilie stared at the mirror again. Was someone on the other side? Was there any way to get a message to Jack?

▲ ▲ ▲

"Margaret?" Emilie looked over her shoulder at the officer standing guard beside the payphone. "It's Emilie. I'm in trouble." She gave Margaret the abbreviated version.

"Honey, I'll be right down. I'll have you out of there in a minute."

"It's not that easy." Emilie sniffed and forced back the tears that waited behind her eyelids. "The Sabbath has started. They won't give me a bail hearing until tomorrow night or Sunday. I have to stay here."

"Don't worry about anything. You just hang in there, and I'll take care of things on this end."

"Thanks, Margaret." Emilie placed the grimy receiver back into the payphone's cradle and turned back to the guard. He jerked his head down the hall. She followed.

Thirty minutes later she was stationed in what was to be her new home for the next twenty-four hours, a six-by-six cell with a cot and a toilet. Emilie stood at the bars for twenty minutes, refusing to sit or even acknowledge the furnishings behind her. She dropped her backpack to the ground, grateful that the officer had at least allowed her to have a pen and paper. Maybe she could make some sense of all this if she could write down all she remembered.

How had this happened? She'd been trying to please everyone, trying to be the good guy, but she'd ended up here.

The hours passed with Emilie first perching herself on the edge of the cot and later moving back to lean against the wall. The cell had no window. She lost track of time. Her eyes grew heavy.

In spite of the grayness of the pillow and the one scratchy blanket she'd been given, Emilie finally lowered herself onto the cot. She didn't remove her shoes.

Sleep came.

The sun hung low in the sky, a fiery globe skimming heat and light

233

across the desert, across the city of Babylon. Chanters and singers from every house and shop thronged the streets. Soon the sun would be no more, and the night would descend. A night of darkness, for it was the monthly death of the moon god, Sin. The Day of Lying Down prompted a monthly feast, one more excuse for Babylon to enjoy her excesses.

The sun dipped and disappeared beyond the walls of the city. The crowd surged through the streets, and she was carried along with it. A dancing, jingling crowd, with bells sewn to the edges of their robes and torches lofted high above their heads. Around and around the city, until she was dizzy with confusion and ached from dancing.

Her mind was no more at peace than her body. Today she must choose, choose between Marduk Bel-Iddin and Qurdi-Marduk-lamur, one who claimed her religious loyalty and one who claimed her heart. There was nothing but perplexity where her conviction should have been.

Belteshazzar had apparently done nothing to accuse either Marduk or her for their actions the night before. She had heard nothing from the palace, but she knew that things could not remain as they were.

She had sought to control her destiny and had found only frustration. She had been swept along through the course of her life as surely as she was swept along by the crowd tonight.

Qurdi was suddenly there beside her, two of his special slaves trailing behind them. The backs of their hands bore the star of Ishtar, branding them for the goddess.

"You were not at the temple today," Qurdi said. His voice was nearly lost in the chanting of the crowd. She said nothing. "I have heard nothing of Marduk's disgrace. Does this mean you were unsuccessful?"

"He had other things on his mind last night. It was not the right time."

Qurdi grabbed her arm and squeezed hard. "There will never be a right time for you, will there? Your loyalty is not to the goddess."

She yanked her arm away. "Do not question my loyalty. You treat me as if I were one of your slaves. I am the high priestess!"

"A high priestess who refuses to do what is best." Qurdi allowed the crowd to sweep him away in another direction, but she saw his gaze still on her, those empty eyes.

He wanted to use her, just as Marduk claimed the gods were using him. She could trust no one but herself.

Was there no god out there who cared for humanity? Who cared for her? She watched the stars as the crowd carried her on. If there were a different god out there, how could she reach him? How would he speak to her, high priestess of Ishtar?

She broke away from the crowd when they reached the River Euphrates. The crowd continued along the harbor toward the palace. She sought solitude beside the river. The water reeds rustled at the bank. She stood among them, watching the water and running her fingers through the tops of the reeds.

A soft wail behind her caused her to turn. A slave approached, bearing a package. She waited, thinking it must be something for her. But he went to the water's edge some distance from her.

"What do you have?" she asked.

The slave turned and bowed. "A deformity, born minutes ago. An ill omen for the household. It must be discarded."

"Bring it to me."

The slave came nearer and held out his hands. She pulled away the linen to reveal a newborn baby girl, still covered in its mother's blood.

"What is the deformity?"

The slave pointed to the infant's foot, where two toes were fused together.

She nodded, folded the linen around the child again, and took the infant in her arms. "You may return to your duties. I will tend to this problem."

"Yes, High Priestess." He bowed and disappeared into the streets.

The infant's tiny face peeked from the linen. The mouth worked in a silent cry for a moment, then let out a fierce wailing.

"Shh, little one." She touched the child's mouth with her finger.

What was she doing? The gods required that this child be destroyed to preserve the family from the curse associated with it. She knew that. She believed that.

Yet that other, distant part of her argued. It was not right. An innocent child should not be killed.

And then the distant part turned on itself. *All cultures must be respected. We cannot impose our ideologies on the beliefs of another people. We must allow all cultures to exist in the way that they deem right for themselves.*

She shook her head. The voices were too discordant, impossible to reconcile.

The baby squirmed in her arms. She stepped to the water's edge, knowing what she must do. The river rippled past, ready to welcome the child into itself.

But instead, she laid the baby in the weeds at the river's edge and ran into the night, praying to an unknown god that someone would find the child. Someone who was also willing to defy the gods.

As she ran, she grew more frightened. To break out of one's beliefs, to challenge the prevailing thought—it was a dangerous thing to do. If she were to carry on, she would need to stand alone. Could she move against the current of the gods who controlled the people?

"Warad-Sin!" The voice was a harsh whisper, coming from a darkened doorway. "I have been searching for you!"

"Marduk?"

He beckoned. She glanced at the crowds filtering past, absorbed in their own activity, and went into the house.

"Where have you been, Marduk?" She was anxious to know what had happened after she'd left him on Belteshazzar's floor.

"It does not matter now. All that matters is that I am going away."

"Away?"

"I cannot stay here. I no longer serve the gods, Warad-Sin. Qurdi will have me killed when he learns. The king will not allow me to serve."

"Where will you go?"

"I do not know. Perhaps to Israel—to learn of Belteshazzar's One True God. No one will look for me there."

"What will you do with the tablet? Will you destroy it?"

A shadow passed over his face and he lowered his chin. "I am afraid to destroy it. They are so powerful, Warad. I do not dare anger them further. I will take it with me, far from here. To a place where no one will ever use it. I will bury it where no one will find it."

"Qurdi will not let you go so easily. He will send slaves to kill you."

Marduk held her arms. "Come with me, Warad. Leave Babylon. We will find a life free of the gods somewhere."

She watched his eyes, the freedom in them. He asked her to give up her life, to run the course opposite that of the whole world. She pulled away. "I cannot, Marduk. My life is here. I am dedicated to the goddess."

The disappointment marred his handsome face. He squeezed her hands once and kissed her cheek. And then he was gone.

She rejoined the dancers in the streets and lifted her voice in the mindless chant once more. Dancing, swirling through the empty night, through the empty people who were searching, always searching, and never finding. Pretending to be their own masters but giving themselves to powers that controlled and destroyed them.

As the dance went on, her face was wet with tears.

▲ ▲ ▲

Emilie awoke like she'd been jolted by electricity, threw her legs over the side of the cot, and jumped to her feet. Her mind cleared, her memory returned. She fell back onto the prison cot.

The tablet was lost to her. Everyone had betrayed her. Had she truly once believed that she controlled her own destiny? If that were true, she was doing a lousy job of it. But how could she believe she was divine when she was virtually powerless to change the course of events? It was a head-in-the-sand position, and Emilie couldn't believe how she'd closed her eyes and shoved in her head.

"If I were divine, I'd have never let anyone hurt me," she said aloud to the darkness. But Jenn's words replayed. "There is no absolute right or absolute wrong. No one can tell you that you've done anything wrong." So the people who had hurt her in the past, even Sheldon Gold, had not done anything wrong. They'd only done what they felt was best for them.

"Didn't feel like what was best for me." Talking to herself was probably the first step in going crazy, but Emilie didn't care. Her words echoed in the hollow cell, circled her mind, and came back again.

And then she saw it. The complete impossibility of Jenn's position—of her position, though she hadn't ever thought it through.

Two people could not both do what was right for each of them at the expense of the other and still both be right. No more than two people could pass each other on the street and both be walking uphill. It was a logical impossibility that one person could be victimized without the other person committing a wrong. If there were no right or wrong, there could be no victims. Yet she had always believed other cultures had been victimized.

The whole philosophical structure tumbled then. Emilie watched as the arguments she'd so proudly upheld had their foundations swept away in the tide of logic.

If truth were relative, no person, no society, had the right to impose standards on anyone. Judicial government must be abolished. Laws, justice, prisons—all of them must go.

If truth were unknowable and the universe random, humanity could not count on universal laws, either. It was just as Margaret had said—gravity, thermodynamics, everything—it was all one person's opinion.

We're saying one thing but living our lives on the basis of the opposite. We must. To live with no absolute truth would be impossible.

Without truth to rely on, Emilie had turned to other people to become her anchor. Without people who could be trusted, Emilie was without resources—drifting.

Chapter 20

Shabbat in an Israeli jail cell could feel like a week rather than a day. Emilie tried to sleep through the silent hours, but her mind wouldn't rest. When her lunch tray was removed, she reached for the pen and paper.

She intended to outline the answers she had figured out since being set up to take the fall for the tablet's theft, but instead found herself jotting the questions that wouldn't leave her alone—the personal spiritual journey that this trip had become.

Signpost #1: Realizing there is a spiritual side to life. She'd definitely gotten past that point, probably way back in childhood. Emilie Nazzaro was more than a random accident of molecules held together by mere chemistry.

Signpost #2: Seeing the bigger picture of humankind's search for spiritual answers. This concept was the one that had angered Jenn when Margaret had explained it. But Emilie was inclined to agree with Margaret. Jenn had tried to condemn the church of the Middle Ages for controlling people's access to spirituality and insisted that we have broken free from that tyranny.

But Margaret's more complete view of world history told a

different story. Humans have been trying to reach God in various ways since the beginning of time, discarding one theory after another, yet never getting any closer. Even in her cell, she could almost hear the chanting of the Babylonian crowds, surging through the streets in search of their own connection to the gods.

Signpost #3: Understanding that the spiritual part of us longs to connect with its source. Jenn had tried to agree with Margaret on this one, insisting that the universal energy was the source we had all come from. But Margaret insisted that their definitions of "source" were quite different, as were their methods of connecting to it. Emilie knew that Margaret believed in a personal God rather than a universal, anonymous consciousness. But she had never said anything more about how to connect to that God.

Signpost #4: Admit that we're somehow blocked from connecting with God. What had Margaret said? "Too much junk in the way that can't be ignored." What did that mean? What was blocking her from God? She had tried to be a good person most of her life. She'd made mistakes, but hadn't everyone?

Emilie exhaled and clicked her pen shut. Margaret had said there were seven signposts on her journey.

God, if You're really out there, You'd better fill me in on the rest of them.

▲ ▲ ▲

Emilie stirred on her cot at the sound of her name. She lifted her head and blinked at the metal bars that had been her horizon for the past twenty-four hours.

"Margaret?"

"Hi, hon. How you holding up?"

Emilie swallowed and sat up. "I can't believe they let you in here."

"It's after sundown. Shabbat is over."

Margaret reached a hand through the bars, and Emilie walked closer. The older woman squeezed her arm. Emilie was surprised at how much the human contact affected her. Tears threatened to flow, and she tried to blink them back.

"You poor girl," Margaret said. "We'll have you out of here as soon as possible."

"Thanks, Margaret."

"What can I do for you in the meantime?"

Emilie shook her head. "Nothing. I guess I just have to wait it out."

They talked for several more minutes about the unfairness of her situation. Margaret patted her arm once more before she turned to go.

"There is one more thing, Margaret," Emilie said. "It's about your signposts. I've been thinking about them. You told me that there are things in the way of connecting with God and that you tried all kinds of substitutes because of that. I think I've been doing the same thing. But I don't understand why we can't just get that connection we want."

Margaret smiled. "It looks like you're ready for the fifth signpost, then." She wrapped her fingers around the metal bars and leaned close. "You know, God gave us each such an extraordinary ability, Emilie. He could have created us to serve Him unconditionally, without any choices. Instead, He gave us each free will—the privilege of choosing for ourselves whether we would serve Him or not. Unfortunately, with free will comes the possibility of choosing evil. And in our own way, we've each chosen it. We've turned away from Him to serve our own selfishness. That's the thing that blocks us from connecting with God, Emilie. It's our own rebellion against Him. We had a choice, and we chose ourselves."

"So, what then? You can't take back all those choices."

"No, you can't. There's a debt you owe now. And a relationship with God is impossible without that debt being paid."

Emilie nodded. "That's what I thought. We need to live good

lives, make sure that by the end we've balanced the scale and paid back the debt."

Margaret smiled. "Emilie, the debt isn't a pile of the little wrong things you've done, each one balanced by a good deed. The debt is your rejection of the very God who created you. How could you ever repay that?"

Emilie rubbed her toe against the floor, where the metal bars met concrete. She felt a weight pressing on her, as if she were back in that dark, tiny cave from her childhood. But it wasn't claustrophobia that threatened; it was the knowledge of an inescapable debt she could never pay.

Margaret touched Emilie's hand where it lay on the cold metal. "Would you like some good news, hon? You've heard the sentence pronounced, but now it's time to hear what's been done about it." She pulled a small book from her jacket pocket. "Read some of this." She pushed it through the bars. "You'll understand."

Emilie took the book, a Bible not much larger than her hand.

"Start with the Book of John. You'll find it in the table of contents. I think it'll give you a much better idea of where to go from here."

"Thanks, Margaret."

The woman turned again and took a few steps away from the cell. "And Emilie," she said, looking back, "getting connected to God is just the beginning. There's so much more beyond that. Everything you need."

Emilie tried to smile. "I'll read some tonight, Margaret. I promise."

▲ ▲ ▲

Emilie's cell felt cold and damp, and the buzzing fluorescent lights did little to warm the atmosphere. She huddled on her cot and wished for a friend, a cell mate, even a friendly rat or cockroach to talk to.

The hour grew late, but Emilie couldn't sleep. She lay on her cot with her eyes closed, willing even to take another trip to Babylon if it got her out of this place for awhile.

Images of the ancient city danced through her mind. Torches, chanting, blood. Tonight the images frightened her. She felt vulnerable, almost as if she were surrounded by something unseen, something evil. She opened her eyes and pulled herself to a sitting position, but the fear didn't vanish. Instead, the presence transferred itself from her mind to her cell, floating above her head like an angry mist.

Thoughts of Margaret's hopeful words sparked the darkness like tiny flames being lit, but the fear doused them just as quickly with other, darker thoughts.

Are all these questions necessary? Why can't I just go on the way I've been going? What Margaret believes is fine for her, but why should I buy into it?

The oppressive weight was back, and Emilie needed to do something to offset it. She pulled the sheets of paper out once more and sat on the floor, her back to the metal bars. The feeble glow coming from the only light still burning at this hour was barely enough to read by. She looked back over the notes she'd made throughout the day. As she read, she realized she'd raised more questions than answers.

I believe in myself. I can direct my own destiny. But that couldn't be right, because she'd just been faced with utter helplessness as the theft of the tablet spun out of her control. Sitting in this prison cell, she was forced to admit that she was not in charge of everything that happened to her.

There is no objective truth. There is only each person's choice of what to believe. But then Margaret had pointed out that her life's work was based on discovering the truths of the past, so why are there no truths of the present and future? And how can one realistically live in a world where there is no truth, no laws, no absolutes? *It is a logical impossibility. Truth must exist!*

Jenn had said there was no good or evil. There are only choices made by people doing what's best for them. Yet Emilie had seen evil. Seen it in Babylon and, more importantly, in herself. If there were no evil, then nothing anyone had ever done was wrong. Without a basis for laws, no society could condemn anyone's actions.

The bottom line: When a person believes she is part of the divine and then gets to the point where she is left with no control, no recourse, no reserves, no future, no hope, the only logical conclusion is that she would be forced to question her divinity.

Emilie dropped the pages to the cement floor and picked up Margaret's Bible. She was ready for a different answer. But could she swallow that there was one God and that she could somehow find Him?

The contents page took her to the book of John easily. She sat back against the bars, folded her legs, and began to read.

She never got past the first chapter.

▲ ▲ ▲

"In the beginning was the Word, and the Word was with God, and the Word was God."

Emilie reread that first verse of the Book of John, and her heart rate sped up again. *The Word! It's the words that connect.* She had trained herself to understand words from the past, knowing that it was the only way to connect with someone wholly other. The only way for someone beyond our reach to connect with us and share meaning with us. And here was the Word, with God, God Himself. The explanation came in the fourteenth verse.

"The Word became flesh and made his dwelling among us." *God took His message for humanity and transformed it into flesh, born into our world to share the heart of God with us.*

"We have seen his glory, the glory of the One and Only, who came from the Father, full of grace and truth." The Word that became flesh—Jesus—was God Himself. *Love for the human race compelled Him to become the living Word that would connect us back to Himself.*

Emilie had loved and lived for language for so many years, knowing that it was the way that dissimilar people in different times and places could communicate with each other. It was as if John had written these words just for her.

Jesus is the Word. What message does He have for me?

▲ ▲ ▲

"Ms. Nazzaro, before we process you through the system, I'd like to ask you a few more questions." Officer Itkoff crossed his arms where he sat on the other side of the table. Shabbat was over, and Sunday morning had brought more interrogation.

Emilie closed her eyes, still burning after a broken night's sleep. "I've answered everything a hundred times. There is nothing more to tell."

"I will determine that, will I not?" He laced his fingers together and cracked his knuckles like a Mafia thug in the movies.

Emilie took a deep breath. "Go ahead. Ask your questions."

Itkoff stood and snatched a folder from the hands of another officer. "There are a few things in here that might interest you," he said. He flipped through the items in the folder, pulled out several, and tossed them to the table. Three black-and-white photographs skidded to a stop in front of Emilie.

She leaned forward. "Someone's been taking pictures of me!" Emilie's stomach churned.

"As you can see, we had reason to suspect you before you stole the tablet."

"I did not st—"

Itkoff held up a hand. "Yes, yes. I remember."

Emilie studied the photos.

"Who is the man at the table with you, Ms. Nazzaro?"

"There are two men." Emilie pointed. "There. And there." She pointed to the edge of another photo. "You can see that someone else was there with us. Just the edge of his jacket. That's Sheldon Gold. We're eating dinner. Ribs, if you must know."

"Ah, yes. Sheldon Gold. And the other man? The one who is clearly visible beside you?"

"His name is Leon Hightower. He's a friend of Sheldon's."

Itkoff leaned toward her, his forearms against the table, his gaze never leaving her eyes. "You are wise to admit you know Hightower, for of course we know him quite well."

Emilie wrinkled her forehead.

"As you doubtless know, Leon Hightower is one of the biggest black market collectors the Middle East has seen."

"Black market—?"

"Take a look at the pictures again, Ms. Nazzaro. You and Mr. Hightower do not seem to be getting along so well."

Emilie studied the photos. She could tell from her body language that they'd been snapped during her argument with Leon over the provenance of items on the antiquities market. She'd gotten heated, and it showed in the pictures.

Itkoff chuckled. "Does that look like a casual conversation between two strangers?"

"No. But it doesn't look like two friends working together, either, does it? We were arguing about the antiquities market."

"About the price, perhaps? The price of the tablet?"

"No!"

Itkoff returned to his folder, flicking through it, but stopping to peer over the edge at Emilie every few seconds. He threw another item onto the table. "You are planning to leave our country, Ms. Nazzaro?"

"Not until I finish with the tablet, or at the end of the dig season." Emilie leaned over Itkoff's newest show-and-tell. It was a copy of a plane reservation in her name, departing Tel Aviv later that day.

"Then you can explain why you made travel plans?"

"I didn't!"

"The airline faxed us your reservation, Ms. Nazzaro."

"That's not mine! Why would I— Someone must've used my credit card!" Emilie slouched in her chair, a moment of darkness swirling through her mind. When the darkness cleared, she saw the truth. This was not a case of mistaken identity. "Someone is trying to frame me," she whispered.

Itkoff laughed and turned to the younger officer behind him. "Someone is trying to frame her, Girsh." He turned back to Emilie. "Yes, we hear that often."

Emilie straightened. "It's true! Sheldon arranged for me to meet Hightower. He must have known I was being followed. He must have made that reservation."

"And arranged the counterfeit IAA agents to meet you in the airport?"

"Yes!"

"And the other agents, who followed you to Main Square and told you to give the tablet to this Sheldon Gold?"

"Yes."

Itkoff nodded. "A grand conspiracy, eh? Ms. Nazzaro, you must think us fools."

"No." Emilie slouched into her chair. "It's the truth."

Itkoff checked his watch. "It is time for your arraignment. You will come with us."

Ninety minutes later, Emilie had been charged, bail had been set—and paid by Margaret Lovell—and Emilie was on her way back to her hotel with Margaret.

The telephone was ringing when she opened the door to her room.

"I'll see you later, Emilie," Margaret said with a wave.

"Okay, Margaret. Thanks again!" Emilie jogged across the room to answer the phone. "Hello?"

"Emilie? This is Thomas Fitzwater."

"Mr. Fitzwater. I—"

"Emilie, please. I will not ask any questions. You are your father's daughter, and I should have anticipated this. But I must beg you to return the tablet."

"Mr. Fitzwater, I did not steal your tablet!"

"Emilie, it will remain confidential, I assure you. But I must have it. You know what I hoped to find. Will you deny me my last hope?"

"I can't speak with you right now, Mr. Fitzwater. I did not take your tablet." Emilie hung up before the man could plead again.

She fell to the bed and buried her head under her pillow.

▲ ▲ ▲

A knock at the door startled her. A young woman in a hotel uniform stood at the door. She smiled shyly and held out a Federal Express package. "For Emilie Nazzaro," she said. "Just arrived."

"Thank you." Emilie took the package and closed the door. She looked at the return address. *Thomas Fitzwater. It must be my father's journals!*

Emilie took the package to the table and tore into it. Inside, two leather-bound maroon books lay amidst packing material. She emptied the package onto the table. There was no letter, just the journals Fitzwater had pulled from storage. She grabbed the two books and settled into the chair.

The entries began in the 1970s, when Emilie was still a young child. She read of her father's early digs, his first significant finds. The text was youthful and eager, full of the dreams of a young scholar beginning his career. But for Emilie, she did not feel as though she were reading the private thoughts of her father. It was as if it were all familiar, as though she understood each step, each new thrill.

She read on, to the point where Tobias Nazzaro had unearthed his first find of major importance. The collected writings of Marduk Bel-Iddin, sorcerer of Babylon. It was his first introduction to Marduk, before he'd found the tablet.

Emilie felt a strange thrill run along her veins at the name. Although she had spent hours studying Marduk's tablet, it was her dreams that connected her to the man. She felt almost a sadness, a sense of loss, remembering his disappearing through the crowd. Did he ever find peace in Israel?

Her father's journal outlined the progress of the translation work. Emilie laughed at her father's impatient ravings at the epigrapher, whose slow work was a constant source of irritation. She could imagine how the epigrapher felt, with her father feverishly leaning over his shoulder every moment.

The translations of Marduk's other writings were there, also. Not word for word, but her father's paraphrase of Marduk's words. Emilie was awed. Once again the thoughts and passions of someone unreachable could touch her life through the amazing power of the word.

Marduk Bel-Iddin had been a diviner for Nebuchadrezzar, her father's journal explained. Emilie noted with a scholar's pleasure that her father used the correct transliteration for the Babylonian king's name rather than the "Nebuchadnezzar" so often used by those less informed. She was also pleased, in a strangely possessive way, to see that her dream had been accurate about Marduk's position.

The story of Marduk's life was here on these pages; and as she read, Emilie's heart rate continued to accelerate.

Marduk had been in constant war with another priest, Qurdi-Marduk-lamur, vying for the position of chief of magicians, currently held by the Babylonian captive-turned-politician, Belteshazzar—the Old Testament's Daniel. Marduk sought power from the gods to heal in order to unseat Daniel and all other contenders from favored positions. The journal recorded how Marduk received this desired power and was given a healing ritual to recite, which he recorded on a clay tablet, kept secret.

On and on Emilie read, watching detail after detail of her dreams come alive on the page. The high priestess Warad-Sin was there, and even the man with leprosy, healed before the king.

It was all true. It really happened. Emilie stared out the window into darkness. How could this be? She read on.

Her father's journal grew sketchier in its portrayal of Marduk's words, as though her father had no patience for what the sorcerer said in the later portions of his writings. Inserted between his paraphrases of the translation were personal comments. "Will he include the healing recitation in these writings?" and "If they are not here, where is the tablet with the healing recitation?" But between her father's concerns, Emilie could trace the beginning of doubt in Marduk's life—his fear that the gods were really demons seeking to control him.

And then the incident with Daniel. Her father's explanation was brief, but Emilie's mind filled in the missing details. Her imagination went again to that bedroom chamber, where Daniel's prayer over Marduk had stopped everything.

All the questioning in Emilie's mind over the past weeks boiled to the surface. It appeared that she did have a past life in Babylon. How else could her knowledge of Marduk's life be explained?

And then she turned the page.

It was tucked into the crease of her father's journal. A single, browned stem with a tiny blue cornflower still clinging to it. Pressed flat by the years. Emilie touched the flower with one hesitant finger.

Tears filled her eyes and overflowed, and the memories flooded back with them. She was thirteen years old. Still eager to please her father, the only parent she had. A blue cornflower, his favorite, picked from the side of the road. She would press it in a book, then give it to him.

Why not press it in the one book she was certain he would look through? She had sat at his big desk and found his journal in a drawer. She'd placed the flower into the book just before the last entry. A special message of love for her father.

The book had intrigued her, with its gold embossing on the leather and its pages filled with her father's tight scrawl. She had begun to read.

Emilie saw herself curled up in that big desk chair, reading through the fascinating story of Marduk Bel-Iddin, her imagination captured by the far-off time and place.

And then her father had come. Angry that she was reading his journal. "Don't you know the meaning of privacy?" he said and grabbed the book from her. She jumped from his chair and watched him bring a box from the closet and put the journal inside it.

"What are you going to do with it?" she asked.

Her father didn't speak. Instead, he continued to fill the box, carefully selecting books from his shelves and items from his desk. Finally, he looked at her. "I'm going away."

It was the last time she ever saw him.

Emilie's tears came in heaving sobs as she looked at the blue flower. The writing continued for only a few more pages in this book. She checked the date. The last entry was dated only a few days before he died. Had he seen the flower? Kept it there as a memento of her?

She read the last few entries, but there was nothing to indicate that her father had intended to steal the tablet.

Emilie dried her face and realized the other implication of this memory. She had read the journal before! All the details of Marduk's life that she had dreamed—they had all been planted in the fertile imagination of a thirteen year old, then filled in with the knowledge and study of future years. Perhaps the heartbreak of desertion that had followed that reading had made the memory of it fade.

She had no past life in Babylon. Her only past life was the one represented by the blue cornflower, one of hurt and betrayal.

Emilie closed the book and cried herself to sleep.

▲ ▲ ▲

Victor Herrigan was a man without hope. He found himself at the beach on Sunday evening, unaware of even how he got there. He had set out from the hotel to get away from his thoughts, but they had followed him, and here he was.

The moonlight traced a path across the water. The sight should have calmed him but did not. The still-crowded beachfront restaurants and clubs, with their loud music and dancing crowds, should have cheered him, but did not.

Instead, Victor stood in the sand, looking out over the water, wondering what life was even about.

What had brought him to this moment? A series of events outside his control—first his failing health and the resignation from teaching that had to accompany it, then the news that he would be replaced on the dig team by someone younger. Fitzwater had backed out of their understanding, leaving him without the money he'd counted on for retirement. All of it had forced him into this crazy plan to switch the tablet, gain his revenge, and secure the compensation he deserved. Hadn't it? He needed a drink.

He found a club that wasn't too crowded and sank into a corner table. The green tablecloth was sticky with the drinks of those who'd come before him, but he didn't care.

The drinks kept coming, but they didn't dull the memories. Why, when he wanted to forget, did every detail of his life play before his eyes with perfect clarity?

What had he done with his life? He'd studied and dug in the dirt. But what did any of it matter? He'd pushed everyone away who had ever tried to get close to him. No time. Too much to accomplish. And where had it gotten him? Alone, with nothing to do with the rest of his life.

Victor paid the bill and left the club. He headed back to the beach. The moon had risen higher, and the path it had created across the water earlier had disappeared. Victor thought it was a shame. That path had been beautiful. He walked toward the water, tripping a few times in the soft sand and cursing at his feet.

A little boy ran in front of him. Victor stopped just before he would have fallen over the child. The boy bent to pick up a shell from the moonlit beach.

Victor scowled down at the child. "Watch where you're going!"

The boy held the shell up to Victor. "Isn't it swell?" he asked. His voice carried the lilt of a British accent, and his eyes were large and dark.

"It's a stupid shell," Victor said.

The boy's mouth turned downward into a tiny frown.

"Shouldn't you be with your parents?" Victor asked. "Little boys shouldn't be bothering people at this time of night!"

The boy dropped his hand, still clutching the shell, but he didn't move.

"Go away!" Victor didn't care that his voice was loud enough to compete with the breakers. The boy's eyes filled up with tears, and he ran past Victor and left the beach.

Victor watched him go, strangely sad that the boy had given up so easily. Was that all it took to frighten children? He turned back to the water.

So now he was at the end, and he had nothing. Nothing to show for his life's work. Nothing to do with the rest of his years. No one to share anything with.

He heard a child's voice in the distance, thought of the boy's frightened eyes.

The water seemed to invite him. He wished that moon path was still there.

Look at me. What am I? I am some kind of monster, consumed with revenge and hate, with nothing and no one to care about. This is Victor Herrigan. Senile old beast.

And Victor sank to his knees in the sand and he wept.

▲ ▲ ▲

Jack paced his hotel room at the Ashkelon Plaza Hotel, pausing every minute to slam his hand against a wall or tabletop.

Maybe he wasn't Interpol material, after all. Twice in two months he'd let a fascinating woman scam him. He remembered Emilie's serious eyes on him, asking, "Why won't you admit there's a caring person inside there?" *Yeah, right.*

Jack dropped into a chair and stared out the window at the night sky. Emilie had been bailed out. They'd called him when Margaret Lovell had showed up. He was tempted to knock on Emilie's hotel room door and go head-to-head with her.

But that wouldn't do any good. He worked better from the outside. Layna Sardos hadn't stood a chance once Jack was onto her, and Emilie Nazzaro wouldn't, either. He'd find the tablet and take Emilie down at the same time.

Jack pushed a fist into the arm of the chair and stood. It was time to ask a few questions.

A quick cab ride through the darkness to the Crowne Gardens Hotel and a few questions at the front desk confirmed what he'd already suspected. Leon Hightower had checked out, no forwarding address. Jack sat in the lobby and used his cell phone to check other hotels, asking for Hightower or Sheldon Gold. Neither name showed up on anyone's computers.

There had to be a way to find that tablet.

Chapter 21

Emilie groaned before she even opened her eyes on Monday morning. The previous day's events flooded into her consciousness.

"You finally awake?" Jenn's cheerful voice barely penetrated the fog.

Emilie sat up in bed. "What time did you get in last night?"

Jenn stood near the bathroom, rubbing a white towel against her wet hair. "I don't know. Late. You were out cold."

"You wouldn't believe the weekend I had."

"Margaret told me some of it so I wouldn't worry about your being gone all weekend. But she didn't give details."

Emilie told her story.

"No way!" Jenn said, her eyes wide. "Now what?"

"Now, nothing. I wait for a trial, I guess. Try to prove my innocence."

"That's some bad karma, Emilie. I'm sorry."

Emilie flopped back onto her pillow. "Yeah. I guess I should just get back to work for now."

Jenn tossed the towel onto the bed and opened a dresser

drawer. "No work today, remember? The volunteer team has the day off so the staff can do some photos and cleaning and stuff."

"I forgot. What are you going to do?"

"I don't know. See what everyone else is doing, I guess. Maybe head into Tel Aviv."

"Tel Aviv." Emilie closed her eyes and remembered her evening with Sheldon. It seemed like a lifetime ago. "Wait a minute!" Emilie bolted upright in the bed.

Jenn jumped. "What's wrong?"

"Nothing's wrong. Something may be right, finally!" She swung her legs over the side and stood. "When I was in Tel Aviv with Sheldon, they took those surveillance photos of me with Hightower, but there was another picture!"

Jenn's eyes narrowed. "What do you mean?"

"A photographer. You know—one of those guys who takes pictures of tourists and tries to sell them. Sheldon didn't want him to, but the kid took a picture of the two of us."

Jenn turned toward the mirror above the dresser and picked up a hairbrush. "I don't see what good that's going to do."

Emilie grabbed a pair of shorts from the chair where she'd thrown them last night. "Don't you see? If I can get that picture, I'll have something to show the IAA. Maybe they'll believe me about Sheldon."

Jenn shrugged. "Seems like a long shot to me."

"It's the only shot I've got."

Emilie skipped the shower, skipped the makeup. She forced her hair into a quick ponytail and was ready to walk out the door five minutes later. Jenn was sitting cross-legged on the bed.

"Come with me, Jenn. I could use some support."

Jenn tilted her head and studied Emilie. "I don't see why you're bothering. A picture isn't going to prove anything. I don't think you should go."

"I'm going, with or without you." Emilie grabbed a small back-pack and threw her wallet inside.

"Okay, okay. I'll come. But I still say this is a long shot."

The two left the room and stepped into the elevator. The doors slid open at the main floor, and Emilie took a step forward.

"Wait a second," Jenn said. She pulled Emilie backward.

"What's wrong?"

Jenn nodded her head toward the lobby. "Check out that guy."

Emilie leaned forward to follow Jenn's gaze. A suited man loitered in the lobby, his eyes scanning the room. Emilie pulled back. "I'm being watched."

Jenn nodded. "Maybe they think you'll lead them to the tablet."

"Yeah, that and I'm not supposed to go anywhere 'til this whole thing's cleared up." Emilie punched a button, and the elevator doors closed again. "We'll find a service elevator and get out of the hotel through a back door."

Jenn raised her eyebrows. "You sure you're not an international thief?"

"Ha, ha." Emilie tightened her ponytail. "Maybe I'm just sick of being used."

They found another elevator beside the Coke machine in the vending room at the end of their hallway on the fifth floor. It opened to a maintenance room on the bottom floor.

"Come on," Emilie said, leading the way.

The back hallway led in one direction toward the main lobby. Emilie headed the other direction. They padded through carpeted halls, past unmarked rooms and supply closets. At the end of one hall, they turned a corner and saw an exit at the end of the next hall.

"There we go." Emilie broke into a jog.

Outside, they found themselves at the back of the hotel.

Jenn turned to Emilie. "Now what?"

"We walk downtown until we're well away from the hotel. Then we catch a cab."

Emilie took a deep breath. The morning was already sticky with the promise of crushing heat, but Emilie felt as though she were breaking out of a cocoon, a web of self-protection that had been insulating her from the world for so long. It was time to stop letting things happen to her and start making things happen for herself.

They stayed away from the streets for more than ten minutes, until Emilie felt comfortable merging into the downtown crowds.

Before they could find a cab, Jenn moaned. "I must have dropped it."

Emilie turned to her. "What?"

"My bracelet. I know I had it on when we left the hotel." She furrowed her brow and looked back down the street. "I think I know where it must have fallen off. Why don't you go to Main Square—that's the easiest place to grab a taxi. I'll meet you there."

"Jenn, I—"

"I know, I'm slowing you down. But the bracelet's special. It'll only take me a minute."

Emilie shrugged. "I'll meet you there."

She had barely reached the square when Jenn jogged up behind her. She held out her wrist, and the silver bracelet caught the sunlight. "Found it."

Emilie hailed one of the waiting cabs and the two jumped in. "Tel Aviv," she said to the driver. "Hayarkon Street."

"That will cost much money, lady," the driver said.

Emilie nodded and sat back. "Tel Aviv."

▲ ▲ ▲

"I'm tracking down all her contacts now, Levy—"

The IAA officer held up a hand against Jack's explanations. "We've placed our own team on the problem now. You know Interpol is supposed to turn things over to local law enforcement at this time. We won't be needing your assistance any longer."

259

Jack leaned farther across the agent's desk. The little man looked up at him from his seated position, apparently unimpressed by Jack's height. Jack could feel the heat rising in his neck. "Look, I've been on this case from the beginning. I know the players. You need me in there."

Yoval Levy pressed his fingertips together. "You've done nothing to keep the tablet safe thus far." The telephone on the desk rang. He picked it up midring.

"Yes?" His glance flicked toward Jack. "What were the informant's exact words? I understand. Thank you." He replaced the phone.

"It seems you are one step behind again," he said. He leaned his head back and returned Jack's gaze. "We have just received an anonymous phone call informing us that Emilie Nazzaro is attempting to flee the country. She is headed for Tel Aviv as we speak."

▲ ▲ ▲

Emilie's bare legs stuck to the hot vinyl in the backseat of the ancient cab. She leaned forward and called to the driver over the drone of the gravelly street. "How much longer?"

He shrugged. "Can I wave my hand and make traffic be gone? We will get there when we get there."

Emilie dropped against the seat beside Jenn, who checked her watch once more. "Don't sweat it, Emilie. We'll get there."

"I just wish I knew if I'd be able to find that photographer. And if he keeps photos this long."

"I already told you I think it's a waste of time." Jenn studied the sea flowing past on their left as they headed up the coast.

Emilie closed her eyes against the gritty wind filtering through the half-open window. "What choice do I have? I have to do something to prove this guy exists." She sighed. "I'm such an idiot.

Everything he said was just a ploy to get his hands on the artifact. And I fell right into it. He could be anywhere by now."

"The police will get him somewhere."

Emilie snorted. "They don't even believe he exists. They think I did it. They're not going to be looking for him. Besides, where would they look?"

The cab slowed, snarled in heavier traffic as they approached Tel Aviv's outer limits.

Emilie opened her eyes. "Where should they look? If he were going to take it out of the country, where would he go, Jenn?"

Jenn shrugged and sat straighter, looking through the front windshield. "I think we're getting close, aren't we?"

Emilie ignored her. A thought twitched at the edge of her memory, a scrap of conversation. *Thomas Fitzwater.* She and Sheldon had been discussing how Fitzwater might intend to smuggle the tablet out of the country for himself.

The cab driver interrupted her memory search. "What street are you wanting, miss?"

"Hayarkon."

What was it Sheldon had said? If Fitzwater wanted to take the tablet out, he could get it out of—

"Haifa!"

Jenn turned her head sharply. "What?"

Emilie sat forward again, her heart pounding. "Haifa! That's where he's taking it out of the country!"

"We're almost to the restaurant, Em."

Emilie grabbed Jenn's arm. "Listen to me. I know he's in Haifa. If I can find him before he ships out, I can prove he took it!"

"You're jumping all over Israel with these ideas, Emilie. First Tel Aviv, now Haifa. Let's stick with one plan at a time." Jenn surveyed the scene ahead as the cab made a slow turn onto Hayarkon Street.

Emilie followed her gaze. A police car roared past them and joined three others in the middle of the street, just past the Shle'ykes Restaurant.

"There is some excitement here, miss," the driver said. "You want me to continue on?"

"I want to go to Haifa."

"Emilie." Jenn shook her head. "This is crazy. We're right here. Let's at least go in and see if we can find the photographer. You can tell the police about Haifa."

"The police won't believe me, Jenn. They'll find a way to turn it around on me. But if I can find Sheldon in Haifa, I can stop him. Or at least call the police to stop him."

The cab driver was slowing, nearly parallel with the knot of police cars. "What to do, miss?"

Emilie studied the cars absently for a moment, watching as the officers jumped out and formed a tight group.

Jenn leaned forward. "Stop here."

"No," Emilie said.

One of the officers glanced their direction, but then all of them jogged toward the restaurant.

"Take us to the next bus pickup." She turned to Jenn. "You can bail on me here if you want, Jenn. I'll understand. But I have to do this."

Jenn growled in exasperation and flopped against the back of the seat. Emilie smiled, a taut smile that took effort.

▲ ▲ ▲

Sheldon checked his watch for the hundredth time that morning. He studied the Haifa harbor, watching the *Windward* bring its nose into port. A Greek flag whipped in the sea breeze above the black-and-white cargo ship. The horns and machinery of the port echoed across the terraced city to where he stood watching the sunlit sea.

Captain Thardolis would disembark soon, and Sheldon would meet him as planned. The captain was an old acquaintance, one

Sheldon had cultivated over the years to their mutual benefit. This evening's trip would be more profitable than most.

It had been a simple matter to pick up the tablet from those he'd hired to pose as IAA agents for Emilie Nazzaro. He'd rewarded them well and handed them plane tickets. They were on their way out of the country already.

Now for him to get out of the country with his precious cargo.

Customs regulations prevented Sheldon from merely checking his baggage and sailing out of Israel with the tablet. But that could be circumvented if one knew the right people. And Captain Thardolis was one of the right people.

The ship completed its entry into port. Sheldon watched as harbor officials boarded and were met by a lanky, uniformed crewman. He squinted, trying to recognize Captain Thardolis's wide shoulders and bushy hair. The man was not Thardolis, though he seemed to be in charge. An uneasy feeling found its way to Sheldon's gut. He continued to watch.

The harbor officials stepped off the ship and returned down the walkway that ran along the dock. Sheldon patted his jacket pocket. He had the documents he needed in case he was questioned. The tablet was locked in the trunk of his car. He detested leaving it there, but it was better than carrying it around. It would be safe soon.

Sheldon descended the wide steps toward the water. The crewman he had seen had returned inside the boat. He needed to find Thardolis.

No one stopped him from boarding the ship. Sheldon went to the bridge of the ship and stopped the first seaman he saw. "I'm looking for Captain Thardolis. Where would I find him?"

The man laughed. "If I could tell you that, I'd be in a bit of trouble, wouldn't I, mate?" He continued past Sheldon.

The man he'd seen talking to the harbor officials appeared. "Can I help you, sir?"

Sheldon nodded. "I'm here to see Captain Thardolis." Sheldon didn't miss the captain's uniform the man wore.

He frowned. "I'm afraid I can't tell you where he is. Seems Interpol is looking for him as well. Apparently he's suspected of illegal exportation. I'm running the *Windward* now." The new captain furrowed his brows and studied Sheldon. "What business did you have with him?"

Sheldon pulled his documents from his pocket. "No business, really. I had arranged to pull out with the ship this evening. Headed back to Greece." He handed the documents to the captain. "I trust there won't be a problem with that?"

The captain scanned the paper. "No, I suppose not. We don't usually take passengers onboard, but it looks like everything's in order." He gave Sheldon a searching glance again. "That's all there is to it, then?"

Sheldon smiled. "That's all." He waved and backed away. "I'll see you later this evening."

"Ten o'clock," the captain said. "We set sail at ten o'clock."

"Right."

Sheldon forced himself into a casual walk as he left the ship, but his mind was screaming with frustration. *Now what?* He didn't stop walking until he sat in an open-air café with a Perrier in front of him.

Could he find another ship, one whose captain would close his eyes when Sheldon brought a package on board that had not been cleared through customs? No, his contacts weren't that good. Captain Thardolis had been his only plan.

Another way out of the country, then? Across into Egypt, perhaps? Some way past the checkpoints?

No, it had to be this ship. He had the documents ready. He checked the time again. Noon. Only ten hours until the *Windward* sailed.

It had to be that ship. All that was left now was to find a way to get that case on board without it being seen. He'd come this far. He'd do whatever was necessary to finish this.

▲ ▲ ▲

Jack fumed at the traffic that held him in check just outside Tel Aviv. He'd jumped in his own car when he'd heard that Emilie was headed for the city. Now he wished he'd waited for a car with a siren that could plow through the hard-packed city streets.

When he reached Hayarkon Street, four officers milled around outside the Shle'ykes Restaurant. He pushed his car up against the curb, jumped out, and flashed his badge. "She here?"

One officer turned a disinterested look toward him. "Nothing here."

Jack pounded the hood of the car.

The anonymous phone tip had said she was headed out of the country but had to make contact with someone at the restaurant first. If Emilie wasn't here, maybe her contact still was. He trotted toward the entrance.

"Where are you going?" the officer asked.

"Just doing my job." The officer looked like he was considering getting in the way. Jack kept going.

Inside, the restaurant was nearly empty. Jack checked his watch. It was still only 11 A.M. Tel Aviv nightlife left most of its residents and visitors in bed until at least noon.

A woman brushed past him on her way to the main dining room.

"Excuse me," he said. "Do you speak English?"

She slowed to a stop and studied him through narrowed eyes. "What can I do for you?"

"I'm looking for a woman. She's about this tall." He held a flat hand to his chin. "Long, black hair—"

"She was not here five minutes ago when the police asked, sir, and she is still not here."

Jack nodded. "She was supposed to meet someone here. Maybe someone who works here. Do you know who that might be?"

The woman pursed her lips. "I do not keep track of the social

265

lives of my employees. I cannot help you."

Jack exhaled and waved her away. She took a step backward, then turned away, contempt in her eyes. Jack returned to the blinding heat of Hayarkon Street. The police officers were loading up to leave.

Where had she gone? Had the police arrived too soon and tipped her off? Would she have skipped her appointment at the restaurant and gone directly to the airport?

For once, the screwup hadn't happened on his watch. But still, he had burned to face Emilie once more, to tell her what he thought of her phony smiles and the way she'd made him think she was vulnerable, damaged. He'd wanted to protect her, he realized. The way Emilie had played him made it look like he was the one who had needed protection.

Chapter 22

Jack arrived back at IAA headquarters by one o'clock. The afternoon sun did its best to fry the top of his head as he locked his car and walked toward the building. One of the agents he'd worked with earlier, Heilman, appeared in the door and passed Jack on his way out.

"Anything new?" Jack said.

Heilman shook his head. "Don't think so. I'm out for today."

"I'd better get in there, see what I can do."

Heilman laughed. "I don't think they're waiting anxiously for you."

Jack scowled and pushed through the door. He'd find Levy and see what his next step should be.

Yoval Levy still hunkered behind his desk where Jack had left him that morning. "I've been talking with Vitelli."

Jack slumped to a chair. He hadn't talked to his boss at Interpol since he'd informed him about the tablet going missing. "And what have you two been chatting about?"

"I'd suggest you rid yourself of the attitude, Mr.—Cabot? Is that the name you're using?"

267

Jack lifted one shoulder in a half-shrug.

"I've informed Mr. Vitelli of your failure to protect the tablet. He agrees that it would be best if our agents here took over the problem."

Jack closed his eyes, trying to block out the rest.

"You can contact him for further instructions, I suppose." There was amusement in the little man's voice. "If he has any further instructions for you."

▲ ▲ ▲

Jack had no destination in mind when he got behind the wheel of his car, but it barely surprised him when he turned a corner and found himself in Main Square. He parked and slouched out to a bench to stare at the crowds.

So it was over. The danger, the intrigue, all the comic book stuff he'd lived for since he was a kid and found in his job with Interpol. It was over. They didn't need him on this case; and after Turkey, he'd messed up one too many times. He knew what came next.

Nearby, the two preserved sarcophagi were attracting visitors with their carved depictions of Greek and barbarian battle scenes. He never had gone there with Emilie.

He'd always imagined himself giving up this life someday, settling down into a comfortable home-and-family life. Figured he'd meet some amazing woman along the way who would make it worth it to give it all up. But here he was, thirty-six, soon-to-be unemployed, and most definitely alone. Not the way he'd envisioned it at all.

And what was left for him? He was an adrenaline junkie; he knew it. The job pumped through his veins like oxygen in his blood. Without it, he'd shrivel into a has-been, gloating over old assignments like an aging veteran, hauling out the battle stories to remind his friends once again that he'd seen action.

What friends? The job had left him alone in that department, too.

He was too young to retire, too old to start over. Just old enough to be looking at stretched-out years of some stupid desk job.

Because of Emilie Nazzaro. Emilie, who had played him and then vanished, free to move on to her next target.

Jack stood. He'd find a way to stop her—make her pay.

Back at the hotel, in her room. It was a place to start. There had to be a lead somewhere.

▲ ▲ ▲

"How long will it take to get to the bus?" Emilie asked the cab driver.

"Again you ask me how long. Can I know the future, miss? You must learn to enjoy the journey, not only the destination."

Is everyone in this country a philosopher?

Jenn tapped a fingernail against the door handle. "I don't like this. Why don't we stop and call the police?"

Emilie sat with her back against the seat, her gaze fixed on the road ahead. She didn't answer.

"At least let's stop to get something to eat and drink and use the rest room before we get a bus to Haifa."

The cab pulled up to the bus pickup. Emilie paid the agreed-upon amount and stepped out. The bus pulled up a moment later. The two boarded, but Emilie turned toward Jenn with a smile. "You know, I feel bad about dragging you into this whole thing. I don't want you to get in any trouble. You should go back to the hotel."

Jenn shook her head. "No, I'm with you all the way, Emilie. I just want to be sure you don't do anything stupid. Or dangerous. You're way too impulsive for your own good."

"Aren't you the one who keeps telling me to be spontaneous?"

The two stepped onto the bus and sat near the middle. Emilie studied the road as the miles passed, but her memory flashed a fragment of the past few days across the screen of her mind. Jenn, telling her to be spontaneous and surprise Sheldon at his hotel. Sheldon had shown up in the lobby just as she was asking for his room number. Except he wasn't really staying there. How did he know she'd be looking for him? And Jenn, suspicious of Sheldon and dropping suggestions that he might not be honest. At the time, it seemed like she was being a good friend. But it turned out that Emilie's suspicions of Sheldon were all part of the plan, intended to send her to the fake IAA agents with the tablet.

The police on Hayarkon Street. Were they there for her?

Now, Jenn's objections to Haifa.

Emilie kept silent until they pulled into Herzliyya. The bus slowed to a stop, and she turned to Jenn. "You know, Jenn, this whole thing is crazy."

Jenn nodded. "That's what I've been telling you."

"And you were right. What am I expecting to do in Haifa? Roar into the port in my Batmobile and capture Sheldon?" She stood. "I'm going back to the hotel."

Jenn slapped her hands on the seatback in front of her and jumped to her feet beside Emilie. "Finally, you're making sense."

Jenn led the way down the aisle. Emilie paused to let an elderly woman with a scarf wrapped around her head into the aisle in front of her. Jenn turned her head and watched the woman for a moment. Her glance flicked over the woman's head to Emilie. Emilie smiled what she hoped was a tired, defeated smile.

A mother with a small child waited patiently for the line of disembarking passengers to clear. Emilie paused again and motioned with her hand for them to step in front of her.

And then she waited for a young man with a backpack, who looked like he could be a Hebrew University student. And a stooped-shouldered man in a black shawl.

Emilie risked a glance toward the front of the bus. Jenn turned the corner to step down. Her eyes locked onto Emilie's. She paused, and a flicker of uncertainty crossed her face. The man behind her called out something in Yiddish, and Jenn stepped forward. Her head disappeared from view.

Emilie sidestepped into the seat to her left. When the last passenger getting off the bus had passed, she turned and fled to the back and sat in the last available space, crowding onto the seat beside a portly, middle-aged man with a massive camera slung across his Hawaiian-print shirt. He smiled and nodded to her as she sat.

Emilie kept her chin lowered but raised her eyes to watch the driver. He glanced into his mirror, then reached for the lever to close the bus door. Emilie squeezed her eyes shut in relief.

The squeaking of the closing door was interrupted. Emilie opened her eyes and leaned forward. The door continued its close, and Jenn's head reappeared, bobbing back up the bus steps. She stood at the head of the bus for a moment, taking in the passengers like an angry first-grade teacher with an errant student. Emilie tried to slide lower in her seat, but her new friend beside her didn't leave much space for escape.

Jenn spotted her and marched toward the back of the bus. She stopped in the aisle beside Emilie. The bus started forward with a lurch, nearly knocking Jenn off her feet. She grabbed the seatback in front of Emilie. "I thought you were getting off here."

"I changed my mind."

Jenn's lips tightened until they were nearly white. "Why don't we sit closer to the front?"

"I'm fine here." Emilie glanced at her seatmate, who looked ready to capture the incident on film if it got ugly enough.

"What's going on, Emilie?" Jenn seemed to glue a pleasant smile back onto her face.

"I just think it's time I handled things on my own, that's all."

"Have I done something to upset you?"

Emilie paused. "I don't know, Jenn. Why don't you tell me?"

Jenn's eyes went cold. She leaned forward until her mouth was inches from Emilie's ear. "You need to come with me to the front of the bus. We have some things to discuss."

"No."

Jenn's voice was a hiss now. "Trust me, Emilie. You don't want to mess with me. I'll have you back in a jail cell faster than you could scream 'frame-up.' "

The tourist beside her finally spoke up. "Is everything all right, miss?"

Jenn straightened and glared down at Emilie.

"I'm fine, thanks." Emilie stood and followed Jenn to an empty seat toward the front. Jenn stopped and motioned Emilie into the seat first. Jenn squeezed in beside her, trapping her against the dusty window.

"You've been part of this all along, Jenn?" Emilie asked. The realization swept over with more sadness than anger. Another so-called "friend" had proved to be false. "I thought better of you."

"Shut up, Emilie." Jenn watched the front of the bus. "You don't know anything about me."

"I know you're trying to be a good person."

Jenn laughed, a bitterly cold sound. "How many times do I have to tell you—there is no 'good' or 'bad.' The choices I make are the right ones for me."

"No matter how they hurt others?"

"If others are hurt, that is what is right for them. That's their karma. Perhaps the universe is trying to teach you something."

Herzliyya faded into the distance behind them. Emilie leaned her head against her window, watching the Mediterranean Sea sparkle in the midafternoon sun as they traveled along the beach-front. "What are you going to do with me?"

"Nothing's going to happen to you if you cooperate, Emilie. We're getting off at the next stop. But trust me, if you try anything, I'll have the closest soldiers on top of you in seconds. They take security very seriously in this country."

"I'm no threat to security."

"You're a criminal fleeing the country." She patted her jeans pocket. "I have the documents right here that show you're leaving Haifa this evening."

Emilie sat up. "So I was right! He is leaving from Haifa."

"Shut up, Emilie," Jenn said. "It's time to stop playing detective."

The bus slowed in Netanya a few minutes later, and Jenn grabbed Emilie's arm and hauled her to her feet. "We get off here."

The town was as crowded as every other beachfront town, with sun-worshippers headed to and from the sparkling blue sea and shoppers milling the promenade that ran along the beach. Jenn pulled Emilie toward a group waiting for another bus.

Emilie made Jenn work to get her there. "Where are we going?"

Jenn stood close behind her. "You couldn't just sit quietly until we left the country, could you? Well, you're going to do it now. Don't worry. Someone will find you, eventually. But by that time, we'll be gone."

"You and Sheldon? Do you do whatever he tells you?" A group of children tromped past, herded by several women. Emilie turned to face Jenn. "Is that how it works?"

Jenn's eyes narrowed. "I'm his partner, not his employee."

Suddenly Emilie understood the tension in their hotel room when she returned from time spent with Sheldon. Jenn had romantic feelings for him. Emilie couldn't help a little dig. "Does he feel the same about you? Or are you just a means to an end, like I was?"

Jenn tightened her grip on Emilie's arm and looked away.

The southbound bus pulled to a stop in front of the group, and Jenn urged her onto it with the others. She kept a grip on Emilie's arm until the two were seated, again with Emilie fenced in between Jenn and the window. Jenn didn't answer her question, and Emilie kept silent during the bumpy ride, wondering where Jenn was taking her and trying to formulate a plan.

Emilie watched as the bus neared Ashkelon again. Jenn jerked her head toward the front of the bus and stood.

The sweaty ride from Netanya had given Emilie time enough

to realize she was being a cowardly idiot. She and Jenn were probably equal in size and muscle. Jenn had no weapon other than her
threat to accuse Emilie of fleeing Israel. But back here in Ashkelon,
how convincing would that be? Maybe Jenn had the documents she
talked about and maybe she didn't. And maybe Emilie could get
them somehow and tear them up. Emilie's resolve strengthened.
Once they were off the bus, she intended to take off.

They stepped off the bus into the blinding afternoon sun.
Emilie took a step away. A group of Israeli soldiers, armed and
serious, stood nearby. Emilie glanced at Jenn. She had noticed
them, too.

There was a second of indecision as Emilie weighed the risk.
She would wait.

"Walk quietly past them," Jenn said in a casual tone.

"To where?"

"We're going to the national park."

"The dig site?"

"Yes, now shut up."

Emilie headed in that direction, assuming they'd be taking a
cab the rest of the way. It was too far to walk. She already regretted her hesitation a few moments before. "What are you going to
do, bury me in one of the grids?" She laughed through her question, but the laugh caught in her throat at the end.

"Not quite. You're going to wait it out with the supplies."

Emilie's heart dropped. "In the Conex container?" The large
metal box was like a cave inside. It was always padlocked from the
outside.

Jenn shrugged. "By now they're done over there for the day.
They'll find you in the morning."

"It's locked."

Jenn laughed. "Even you must have noticed that Dr. Herrigan's
not all there sometimes. Getting a copy of the key was like a scene
from *The Absent-Minded Professor*."

Emilie swallowed hard at the thought of spending the night in a metal box. Images of that tiny cave when she was eight years old surged. "What about the heat? I'll be cooked in there."

"Look at it this way," Jenn said. "Maybe when they find you in there, they'll finally believe your story."

That was almost a tempting thought, but there was no way Emilie was going to submit to being locked in that box. She walked two steps ahead of Jenn and a fraction to the right, keeping Jenn in her peripheral vision. She would wait for the perfect opportunity.

It came several minutes later. A swarm of children selling trinkets and souvenirs buzzed toward Emilie. She smiled broadly and pointed to Jenn. "She wants to buy everything you've got!"

The children squealed and mobbed Jenn. Emilie ran.

She heard Jenn's shout behind her, heard her curse at the children to scatter them. Emilie ran harder.

Shops and tourists flew by in a blur of reds and yellows and blacks. Emilie leaped to the left to avoid a cart of oranges and nearly tripped over a small boy. She righted herself and him and darted down an alley between two shops.

She could hear Jenn's shouts somewhere behind her. Another alley opened to her right. She took it. With every zig and every zag, she felt like she were in a child's maze searching for the finish. Where was the finish? Where was she going?

She stopped to breathe. A cramp in her side doubled her over, hands on her knees as she panted. Jenn did not appear. Had she lost her?

She ran on, determined to put more distance between them. When she could run no longer, she collapsed against the back of a shop and sank to the ground.

Now where? The police? She had nothing new to offer them except yet another accusation with no proof to back it up. She could tell them about the photograph taken of her and Sheldon in

Tel Aviv. Or Sheldon's comment about Haifa. Would they believe any of it? Or would they think she was merely adding to her list of false information?

There was still only one way to clear her name: Find Sheldon in Haifa, find him with the tablet.

Jenn had said that she had documents to show Emilie leaving Haifa tonight. Was that a bluff? How could Jenn have gotten them when Emilie's plan to head to Haifa was a last-minute decision? But what if they were Jenn's documents? Did she intend to leave Haifa with Sheldon? If so, Emilie had until evening to find them.

It was too risky to head back to Haifa now. She would find a place to wait for a couple of hours.

Where?

It had to be behind a locked door somewhere. Her hotel room was out since Jenn had a key. But another hotel room would be safe.

Emilie swiped at the sweat running down her temple and stood again. If she could make it into the hotel, Margaret would hide her, she knew. And if she couldn't find Margaret, she'd settle for Jack.

▲ ▲ ▲

Emilie watched the faces of strangers as the cab wound its way through Ashkelon toward the hotel. It seemed as if every tourist and local turned a suspicious eye on her as she passed.

When they neared the hotel, she instructed the driver to go around to the back. She'd go in the same way she'd gone out earlier in the day. Less chance of being seen.

Emilie paid the driver and launched out of the cab as though the devil himself were behind her. The back door seemed a hundred miles away, and her legs were still shaking from her escape from Jenn. She heard the cab pull away just as she reached the door and yanked on it.

Locked. *Stupid!* She should have known it could only be opened from the inside. She had no choice now but to enter through the front doors.

The back of the hotel was deserted. She crept around the side, staying close to the wall. *As though I'm not about to stroll through the front lobby in plain view in a minute.* She wasn't cut out for this kind of thing.

In the front of the building, Emilie peered through the glass into the lobby. The dark suit who had scared her out the back door earlier was gone. That made sense if she'd been reported outside the building already. *Besides, I'm going in, not coming out. Who's going to have a problem with that?* She pulled the door open and held her chin up as she walked toward the elevator. She stepped in and exhaled in relief as the doors slid closed. She was safe for the next fifteen seconds at least.

When the doors opened on the third floor, Emilie leaned her head into the hall. All clear. She trotted to 315 and knocked once.

Margaret opened the door immediately.

Emilie burst into tears.

Chapter 23

Margaret pulled Emilie into the room and closed the door. "What in the world?" was all she said before wrapping her arms around a sobbing Emilie.

"I'm sorry, Margaret," Emilie said. "I didn't know where else to go." She stepped away from the comfort of Margaret's arms and went to the door, looking through the peephole. She turned the deadbolt and slid the chain into place.

Margaret touched her arm. "Honey, what's going on?"

Emilie turned back to her. "It's a long story."

"Come, sit down." Margaret propelled her to a chair by the window and took the other seat herself. "Tell your story."

The sun sank lower in the sky as Emilie filled in the details she hadn't given Margaret from the police station earlier. She sniffed a few times and wiped at her eyes at the mention of Sheldon's betrayal. Through clenched teeth, she explained how Jenn had been deceiving her all along.

Margaret shook her head. "You've had a rough time, honey. I'm sorry. What are you going to do next?"

"I just need to wait somewhere safe for a little while, until I think Jenn's gone. Then I'm going to Haifa."

A frown creased Margaret's forehead. "And what are you going to do there?"

"Stop Sheldon."

"Honey, you need to bring in the police on this one."

"I can't. They won't believe me."

Margaret sighed. "Then at least get some help. What about Jack Cabot? I've seen the way he looks at you. He'd help."

Emilie felt herself flush. She laughed in spite of the situation. "What do you mean?"

"He'd help you find Sheldon."

"You know what I meant. About the way he looks at me."

"Come on, Emilie. You must have noticed. He's stuck closer to you than skin on a banana. That boy likes you, and you know it."

Emilie sat back. She'd convinced herself that Jack Cabot was after the tablet. But was that the only source of his interest in her? With Sheldon and Jenn suddenly revealed as thieves, did it make it less likely that Jack was also? Could he be working with them, too?

She shook her head. "I don't trust him, Margaret."

Margaret nodded, pursing her lips. "That seems to be an issue with you, doesn't it?"

"What?"

"Trust." Margaret folded her hands on her lap. "I hear it running through everything you say. People you trusted who betrayed you. People you don't trust. People you never should have trusted in the first place."

Emilie pushed her hair back and crossed her arms. "Yeah, I guess it is. But life seems to keep teaching me the same lesson: Don't trust anyone."

"I'm glad you've made an exception for me."

Emilie smiled. "You're different."

"Thank you."

"I mean that. I don't know what it is, but you seem—together—somehow. I know I can trust you."

Margaret's gaze drifted toward the window. She was silent a moment, then turned back to Emilie. "Who's made you so fearful, Emilie?"

Emilie squirmed in her seat. "Fearful?"

"Who's hurt you so badly that you decided not to trust anyone again?"

It was Emilie's turn to stare out the window. She wondered what it was about this woman that engendered not only trust, but confession.

"My father."

"Ah." Margaret nodded, as if those two words explained everything.

"He was an archaeologist. That artifact I'm working on—he discovered it years and years ago. It became his obsession." Emilie let the memories flow back again. "When I was thirteen, he heard about a dig in Israel where the tablet might be. He packed up and left me." She turned to Margaret. "Usually he took me with him on his digs. But that summer it was as if he didn't want me around to distract him."

Margaret frowned in sympathy and nodded, but didn't interrupt.

"They found the artifact that summer, and he worked with an epigrapher for months deciphering it. From the two or three letters I got, I think he truly believed that the tablet had power." Emilie stopped. She had probably revealed too much. But at this point, what difference did it make?

"Eventually, he sent for me. But at the end of the season, when the find should have been turned over to the local antiquities department, my father disappeared. The tablet disappeared with him." She swallowed and wiped at her eyes. "They found his body weeks later in Gaza. The cause of death was drowning. That's all anyone ever knew."

"And the tablet?"

"Gone. Until Thomas Fitzwater located it a month ago on the black market."

"Emilie, I'm so sorry for your loss."

"It wasn't just his death, you know? It was the fact that he left me behind. For the dig season, but then at the end as well. He was more interested in that precious tablet than his own daughter."

"Where did you go after that summer?"

Emilie smiled. "My mother passed away when I was very young. Her parents took me in when my father died. They were good to me, became like parents, you know? But it wasn't the same."

"They weren't your mother and father."

"My grandparents are both gone now." She smiled tightly. "So, I'm all I've got. No parents, no siblings. Just me."

Margaret patted her hand. "You're not alone, and I think you know it. There's someone who's been trying to get your attention for some time."

"Do you really believe that, Margaret?"

"I think He's trying to get everyone's attention in one way or another."

"That first chapter of John really got me thinking. I believe in the power of the word, you know? The idea that Jesus was God's Word to us—it kind of blew me away."

"Is it so hard for you to believe that God wants a relationship with you?"

Emilie frowned. "I think I turned my back on the possibility years ago because I'd been hurt and He wasn't there to rescue me. I decided that I was the only one I could count on, that I'd rescue myself."

"Are you so sure He wasn't there?"

"What do you mean?"

"Perhaps He's been protecting you, leading you to this point all along. Perhaps He's built this understanding of the word into your heart to prepare you for His Word."

Emilie sighed. "If He has been there, I've never seen it."

"Or maybe you've been ignoring it?" Margaret questioned.

"Maybe," Emilie said. "I guess maybe I've just been doing things my way all this time."

"And now?"

"And now I'm seeing that it's a lonely job. I've tried to overcome the loneliness by connecting with other people, but I keep getting hurt by relationships."

Margaret nodded. "There's only one relationship that will never disappoint you, Emilie. But you have to be willing to do the one thing that seems to be hardest for you."

"What's that?"

"You have to trust."

▲ ▲ ▲

Jenn reached her room panting and sweating. Would Emilie be inside? Doubtful. She pushed the keycard in and out of the door lock and swung the door open. The room was empty.

It took her only ten minutes to pack her suitcase. Inside it, she buried her travel documents for leaving Haifa tonight. It had been a bluff, telling Emilie she had the documents with her on the bus. They had still been here, waiting in her dresser drawer under her jeans and T-shirts.

Jenn zipped her bag closed and stood. It was almost four o'clock. She still had time to search for Emilie. She feared that if Emilie didn't end up in custody, Sheldon wouldn't care if Jenn made it to Haifa or not. He was counting on her to get the job done. But where to start? Where would Emilie go? Whom did Emilie trust to help her? Jenn could think of only one person. She left the suitcase on the floor and slipped out of the room again.

▲ ▲ ▲

The sun was low in the sky behind him when Sheldon strolled into the warehouse area of the Haifa port, swinging the black case in his left hand. Should port authorities stop him, he had a few "stupid American tourist" questions ready.

It had taken several hours, but Sheldon had called in some favors and found out where the *Windward*'s future cargo was stored. Now if he could find a suitable place to hide the tablet, the unexpected problem of Captain Thardolis's disappearance would be overcome. He'd come back later, go through customs, and board the ship as planned; no one would ever know that he'd left a little package for himself in a wooden crate somewhere on the ship. If Jenn caught up, great. If not, too bad.

The long walk across the asphalt finally ended at a warehouse door. Sheldon slipped into the warehouse and surveyed the area. He'd already seen several dock workers outside taking the dinner break. He was counting on that.

The warehouse was filled with crates. Sheldon checked the slip of paper in his hand and began his search. Several minutes later he spotted the stenciled numbers on the side of one crate. Sheldon grabbed a nearby crowbar.

Five sweaty minutes later, he still hadn't opened the crate. But he had made progress. He could feel the lid give a fraction of an inch each time he applied pressure. But he feared he was running out of time. He leaned on the crowbar with every ounce of strength he had in him, feeling the burn of blisters forming on his hands.

The lid gave way with a creak and a bang and flew open to reveal itself to Sheldon. It was packed with what looked like computer processors. Sheldon lifted the tablet case into the wooden box and set it on top. From ancient to modern. He reached for the lid.

"What are you doing there?"

Sheldon pushed and the lid thumped shut. He turned to face a dockworker, probably about thirty years old. The man's upper body stretched the seams of his T-shirt, muscles upon muscles no doubt born of tossing ropes and cargo for years.

"I say, what are you doing there? Who are you?" The man's accent was British, just as the captain's. It didn't seem to fit the hulking figure.

Sheldon smiled. "Just touring around a bit, friend. I've got a ride with this cargo tonight—just wanted to make sure everything was in good order."

The crewman scowled. "That doesn't sound a bit right to me. What's your name?"

Sheldon reached for his documents. "It's all right here. You'll see everything's in order." He stepped closer to the laborer and smiled. "No need for concern."

The man ignored the outstretched hand and the documents. "I think I'd better take a look at what's in this box." He pushed past Sheldon, leaned over the box, and yanked it open.

Sheldon noticed the crowbar on the floor where he had dropped it. He picked it up and held it behind his back.

"What's this?" the dockworker asked, pulling the black case from the crate. His face registered concern. "Did you put a bomb here?"

Sheldon laughed. "A bomb? Of course not. Why would I bomb a ship I'm supposed to sail on? But you have caught me, I confess. It's just a few, shall we say, souvenirs that I didn't want to have to check through customs. You understand?"

"What kind of souvenirs?"

Sheldon smiled and leaned in for a conspiratorial whisper. "Just a few recreational chemical substances, if you know what I mean."

"Drugs?"

Sheldon shrugged and reached his free hand into his jacket pocket. "Listen, I'm certain you could use a little extra cash today, am I right? Something above and beyond the paycheck? We can keep this between us, right?"

The man hesitated, watching Sheldon pull out several large bills. "I don't think so, chap," he said. "I'm afraid I'll need to report this to the port authority."

He stepped past Sheldon, the tablet case in his hand.

Sheldon felt his hand tighten around the crowbar, felt the blood surge to his head. He knew that this guy was the only thing standing between him and the payoff this job would bring. And knew that he could never go back to being poor.

His arm whizzed through the air before he had time to think it through. The crowbar landed on the man's neck with a nauseating *thwump*. He fell like a marionette whose strings had been tossed down by a tired child.

Sheldon heard the crowbar clang to the ground, but he could only stare at the man. He'd never done anything so violent—never believed that he could. He waited for the revulsion, for the self-loathing.

It didn't come. Instead, his survival instinct kicked in, and he started to run through possible solutions to this new problem. He knelt beside the body. The man's head was turned at an unnatural angle, as if it didn't belong to his body. Sheldon felt for a pulse. There was none.

In the end, the solution was so simple. Sheldon reopened the wooden crate, then spent a panicked two minutes dragging the body across the floor and up into the box. He laid the tablet case gently on top of the body, closed the lid, replaced the crowbar in the toolbox, straightened his jacket, dusted off his pants, and casually returned to the sun-baked port.

▲ ▲ ▲

Emilie searched the horizon outside Margaret's hotel window for answers. "What kind of trust does it take, Margaret? What does God want from me?"

285

"It's not what He wants from you, Emilie, but what He wants to give you. We've talked about the debt we all owe God. You can't pay it back, can't balance it out. God knew that. The message He sent when Jesus became man was a message of love. One that said, 'I'll do whatever it takes to have a relationship with you, Emilie Nazzaro. Even die.' "

"How does that work?"

"Jesus' death was for you, Emilie. He died in your place, paid the debt you owe, so that you can have a relationship with God, both now and forever."

"But if that's true, it would mean I don't have to do anything."

Margaret smiled. "It takes most people much longer to understand that, Emilie. You're an insightful girl. That's the point. There's nothing you can do. You can only gratefully accept the payment made on your behalf and trust that Jesus' death was enough to connect you with God."

Emilie leaned her head back against the chair and closed her eyes.

"He wants you for a daughter, Emilie. And He's a Father who will never fail you."

Emilie exhaled and tried to get her mind around that one, but a knock at the door sent her to her feet.

Margaret stood and nodded silently to Emilie, who stepped to the head of the double bed, out of sight. Margaret crossed the room and looked through the peephole in the door.

"Who is it?" Margaret said.

"It's Jenn."

Emilie bit her lip and listened. She heard the door open slightly.

"What can I do for you, Jenn?"

"I'm looking for Emilie. Is she here?"

"I saw Emilie awhile ago. She's been through so much. I should think she would go to her room."

"I was just there. She wasn't."

"I see. Could she have come back while you've been gone?"

"Do me a favor, Margaret. If you see her, give me a call."

"Take care, Jenn."

The door clicked shut.

▲ ▲ ▲

It was nearly five o'clock when Jack left the town's main square. He zoomed over to the Ashkelon Plaza Hotel, strode through the lobby like he was late for a meeting, and mashed the elevator button with his thumb. The elevator seemed to take an hour to descend. He jumped in and crossed his arms as it rose to the fifth floor.

He knocked twice on Emilie's door. Satisfied that there was no one inside, he used his special card to open the door.

"Hello?" he called into the room. The bathroom door was open, the light off. Everything looked clear. Jack slipped in and let the door shut behind him. He would have to work fast.

What was he looking for? He scanned the room for anything unusual, but it was just a standard room, with the beds neat and girl stuff lined up on the dresser. He picked up bottles of lotions and things, not knowing what he hoped to find.

He would start with the dresser. The first drawers contained various articles of clothing. Jack tried not to think about Emilie as he rooted through her undergarments. The first three drawers held nothing but clothes. The last three were empty.

Strange. Don't women usually have more clothes than they know what to do with?

Jack went to the closet and searched the pockets of clothes hanging there. Again, the closet was only half full. He found nothing.

He checked his watch. He'd been in here for ten minutes. His luck could run out at any time. He went to the beds and checked under them. He pulled back the spreads and swiped an arm under each mattress. The nightstand drawers were empty. He crossed over to the other side of the far bed to check behind the drapes.

A suitcase lay flat on the floor between the bed and the window. Jack looked at it for a moment, then kicked it with his toe, oddly hoping to find it empty. It wasn't.

He dropped to his knees, unzipped the blue canvas case, and pulled the flap away. It was jammed with clothes, hastily packed.

So Emilie was leaving. That explained the empty drawers and half-full closet. She would jump bail, probably leave the country, and that would be the last they'd see of her and the tablet. Jack rocked back on his heels, surprised at the disappointment he felt once again at evidence of Emilie's dishonesty.

He allowed himself only a moment of self-pity, then dug his hands into the clothes and felt for anything that would give him a clue as to her destination.

Aha. His fingers closed around an envelope. He pulled it out, slid the papers from it, and scanned them with a practiced eye.

Haifa. Tonight. A fake name, no surprise. He memorized the ship, the time, the pier, and pushed the papers back into the envelope. The package slipped back into its original spot. Jack reached for the zipper.

The door handle creaked and the door opened. Jack zipped the suitcase and rose on his knees. Jenn entered.

Shock and anger played across her face. "What are you doing?"

Jack stood and laughed self-consciously. "You caught me. Just being a little nosy, I guess."

"How did you get in here? What are you doing with my suitcase?"

"I was just—your suitcase?"

Jenn seemed to realize her mistake. "I'm calling security." She headed for the phone between the two beds.

Jack leaped over the bed and met her there. He grabbed her wrist as she reached for the phone. "I don't think you want to do that."

"You broke into my room!"

"And what did I find?" Jack watched the fear creep into her expression. "Evidence of someone planning to leave the country via Haifa tonight."

"You're no spoiled rich boy." Jenn wrenched her arm free of Jack's grasp. "Who are you really?"

He pulled a wallet from his pocket and flipped it open. "Interpol. I've been working with the IAA to protect the tablet."

Jenn sat on the bed. "So what? It's not illegal to leave the country. And how do I even know that thing's real?" She jutted her chin toward his ID.

Jack took a step closer until he towered over her. "You're going to tell me exactly what you've done to Emilie Nazzaro."

Chapter 24

hanks for covering for me with Jenn," Emilie said to Margaret.

"Well, it wasn't a lie. Not technically, I don't think."

"She must be back at the room by now." Emilie peered through the peephole. "But she won't stay there long when she doesn't find me. I've got to get out now."

"I'm right behind you." The older woman snatched her purse from the bed.

"Where are you going?"

"I'm going with you." Margaret pushed past Emilie and opened the door a crack.

"No, you're not." Emilie pushed a hand against the door.

Margaret perched her hands on her hips. "Do you want to stand here and argue? She could be back any minute."

"Margaret, I don't want—"

"Listen, Emilie, I'm going and that's that. You need someone to watch your back, and if I'm the only one you trust, then so be it. Besides, I haven't finished telling you the rest of the story yet."

Emilie sighed in exasperation and pulled the door open farther. The hall was empty. "Follow me."

The back route out of the hotel was easy this time, down the service elevator, through a few hallways, and out into the arid late afternoon. Emilie didn't stop when they hit the street. If Margaret couldn't keep up, then she'd leave her behind. It was a bad idea anyway, taking her along. But Margaret was right about one thing: She didn't have time to argue.

"Where are you running to?" Margaret called from behind her, the words coming between huffs.

"To get a bus."

"Honey, forget the bus."

Emilie slowed and Margaret caught up.

"We'll rent a car."

Emilie shook her head. "I don't have the—"

Margaret patted her purse. "I've got everything we need right here. A car will be safer and faster."

Emilie nodded. "Thanks, Margaret."

They turned toward the downtown district. One cab and twenty minutes later, they were turning the key in an older Nissan. Not that pretty, but it would do the job. Margaret insisted on driving so Emilie could rest.

Emilie sank into the seat, buckled herself in, and locked her door. "I don't think I can rest. This whole thing is too crazy."

Margaret backed out of the rental lot's parking space and turned the car into the northbound road. "It'll take over an hour to get to Haifa. At least close your eyes."

▲ ▲ ▲

Jennifer Reddington wasn't giving up information as easily as Jack had hoped. She sat on the bed with her arms folded, daring Jack to force her. He debated calling in other agents immediately; but whatever information she had on Emilie, he wanted it first.

"Where is she?" he asked.

Jenn shrugged. "How should I know?"

"Are the two of you working together?"

"I thought you were the cop. Don't you already know everything?" She stared at him through darkened eyes.

"I know you're taking the tablet out of Haifa tonight."

Jenn's gaze faltered, then steeled itself again. "Your girlfriend's already there," she said, "getting ready to ship out."

He could have strangled her, he really could have. She was taunting him, waiting to see how much he would fall for. Two could play at that.

"You're full of it. We already know Emilie had nothing to do with it. You set the whole thing up, you and your partner."

"Partner?"

Jack hesitated, then decided to go for it. If Emilie really was innocent, he might as well swallow everything she'd told them.

"Sheldon Gold. Whatever his real name is."

Jenn shook her head, a nasty smile on her face. "Never heard of him."

"Whose plan was it to frame Emilie? Yours? Or are you just a nobody in this game, somebody to do the little jobs no one else wants?"

Jenn's face darkened. "You don't know anything."

"Ah, hit a sore spot, did I? What's the matter, Mr. Gold doesn't appreciate all you do for him?"

"He appreciates me more than anyone else ever has!"

Jack congratulated himself silently. He'd gotten her started. "I don't know. You're sitting here with me, and he's in Haifa ready to ship out. Seems to me if he cared about you, he'd make sure you were safe before he said good-bye to Israel."

"He won't leave without me."

"And what about Emilie? Maybe he's decided she's a better partner than you ever were."

Anger flashed in Jenn's eyes. "Emilie Nazzaro's a stupid fool. She never had a clue what was going on. Sheldon has no interest in her."

"So then, where is she?"

"I told you, she's a fool. She thinks she can stop him. Save the tablet, be a hero. But he'll disappear. And then he'll find me. And you'll never know what happened to either of us."

Jack nodded. *That's all I need, sweetheart.* "Come on," he said and pulled her to her feet. "Let's go for a walk."

The way Jack saw it, he had two options. Number one, take Jenn to headquarters, get a statement, go through the red tape, report her confession to his superiors. Number two, pawn her off on someone else and head for Haifa, where Emilie planned to confront Sheldon. It wasn't even a toss-up. He called the police and headed for the hallway, Jenn in tow.

He didn't have to wait too long in the lobby for the local cops to arrive. He handed Jenn over to the two and explained briefly. He stopped on his way to his car and pulled his phone out to call Yoval Levy. His thumb hovered over the numbers as he debated with himself. Levy was convinced of Emilie's guilt, and if Jack called in the IAA, everyone would be out to protect the tablet. Nobody was concerned about protecting Emilie.

It might be better to get this job done alone. Besides, it was one sure way to redeem himself after fouling up again. If he could pull it off.

As he drove through Ashkelon, Jack allowed himself a moment to adjust to the new situation. Emilie was not the thief, after all. Everything she'd said about the mysterious Sheldon Gold had been true. She hadn't been playing him! She was just an epigrapher trying to do her job, deciphering the tablet—and deciphering him at the same time. Jack swallowed, the memory of her piercing smile threatening to distract him from what he had to do.

All the anger he'd felt pouring toward Emilie Nazzaro over the past few days had run its course, and now another feeling was rushing in behind the anger, washing it away. Jack didn't know what to call this new emotion.

But it scared him.

Chapter 25

The car trip to Haifa seemed uneventful compared to the past few hours. Emilie fought the drowsiness, wanting to stay alert. "Are you ever going to tell me about your last two signposts, Margaret?"

Margaret nodded and smiled. "I'll tell you. But I'm not sure you'll really understand them yet. There's a point you need to cross before you're ready to fully grasp the next two."

"It's that trust thing, isn't it?"

"You've got it." Margaret turned a corner and accelerated. "Once I decided to trust what God had provided for me and I established a real, living relationship with my Creator, I wanted to know what to do next. I'd gained so much by doing nothing but trusting, I wanted to know what I could do in return. That started a real period of growth on my part—one that hasn't ended yet—of learning how God wants me to live through studying His written message to me. And I'm understanding more each day about the power He gives me to live that life."

"That's the sixth signpost?"

"Yes. Learning His instructions on how to live life fully and realizing He's given the power to do it."

"And the seventh?"

Margaret sighed. "The best for last, Emilie. The best for last. Eternity with God. Reward for serving Him. Reigning with Jesus. A new earth to replace the one we've corrupted. God's Word says that 'No eye has seen, no ear has heard, no mind has conceived what God has prepared for those who love him.' "

▲ ▲ ▲

It was nearly seven-thirty when they reached the port city of Haifa, situated between the Mediterranean Sea and Mount Carmel. The terraced landscape of the city provided a breathtaking view of the sea, with the port at the base of the city. To the northeast, across the harbor, the medieval fortress city of Acre could be seen, along with the snowcapped peak of Mount Hermon. Margaret drove downward toward the sea and parked near the industrial warehouse area that surrounded the port. The evening sun hung just above the watery horizon, reflecting like a million diamonds across the surface of the sea.

More ships jammed the harbor than Emilie had ever imagined. How would she find Sheldon among all this confusion? She had nothing to go on, no known destination for Sheldon, except away from Israel. She and Margaret left the car on the side of a street near the water and wandered down to the docks.

"What now?" Margaret asked.

"I have no idea." Emilie shielded her eyes from the glare of the sun going down over the sea. "I don't know where to start."

A voice penetrated the buzz of boats and conversation around her. Someone calling her name.

"Emilie!"

She turned toward the voice, scanning the crowds. A blond head stood out against the dark skin and dark hair of most of the people.

"Jack!" Emilie glanced at Margaret, who raised her eyebrows.

Should she run? Was he working with Sheldon? Her feet seemed rooted to the ground.

"Emilie!" Jack jogged to her side. "I can't believe I found you so quickly."

"What do you want, Jack?"

"I came to help you."

"With what?" Emilie watched as Jack's gaze lifted above her head and scanned the boats in the water.

"Is he here?"

"Who?"

Jack dropped his head to look at her once more. "Sheldon Gold."

Emilie took a step toward Margaret. "What do you know about all this, Jack?"

Jack touched her arm. "Emilie, listen to me. I know you're innocent. I know Gold framed you and that Jenn's been helping him. I know you're here to stop him, but it's a stupid thing to do alone. You're not trained for this kind of thing."

Margaret leaned forward. "Are you?"

Jack sighed impatiently. "Yes." He turned to Emilie. "I'm working with the IAA."

Emilie shook her head and backed up. "Oh no. I've heard that one before. Do you think I'm stupid?"

"Emilie, it's true!" He pulled out his ID. "I'm an Interpol agent. I was assigned to keep track of the tablet."

Emilie studied his wallet. The ID looked real. *But what do I know? I've been fooled too many times already.* "If you were supposed to keep it safe, it looks like you messed up."

Jack scowled. "Believe me, I know. I thought you were going to steal it."

"Me!" Emilie's mind whirled. "You've been suspecting me all this time? Did you know I was arrested?"

"Yes, I was on the other side of the glass when you were interrogated."

"What!" Emilie pounded his chest with her fist. "You left me in that cell! Do you know how scared I was?"

Jack grabbed her wrist and pulled her toward him. "I'm sorry, Emilie. I'm so sorry. I was wrong."

Margaret took a step toward them. "Is there anything I can do to help, Jack?"

Jack shook his head. "No, thank you, Margaret. It would be best if you went back to the hotel until this is over."

Margaret winked at him. "I'm happy to leave her in your capable hands."

Emilie pulled away from Jack. "That's it?" she said to Margaret. "You're going to leave me here with him? What if he's really working for Sheldon Gold?"

Margaret smiled, a small, patient smile. "Emilie, it's time to learn to trust." She walked away.

Jack held her other arm now, and Emilie wasn't sure if he was comforting her or holding her hostage.

"She's right, Emilie. You've got to trust me. We need each other."

Emilie swallowed. "We do?" She watched Jack's eyes, unsure of what she saw there. If he were for real, had he been feeling everything she'd been resisting since they'd met?

"We each have information the other wants," Jack said.

"Oh." Emilie pulled away. "And what is that?"

"I know what ship Gold is sailing on. You know what he looks like. Together we can get him."

Emilie turned her back on him for a moment and studied the water. Should she believe him? Was he just after the tablet? If so, she'd be leading him right to it. But if he was who he said he was, he might be her only shot at getting the tablet back.

A horn sounded from the harbor. Emilie watched the crowd moving along the water. And then she ran.

Jack wasn't expecting her to run. He'd been convincing, even charming. At the very least, sincerely apologetic. Why would she run?

He chased her into the crowd away from the water. She wouldn't know where to go. It was useless for her to run. Was she that frightened of him? He'd seen the softening in her eyes when he said they needed each other. Why had he followed that up with talk about finding Gold, when all he really wanted to do was to tell her he needed to see her every day for the rest of his life?

Jack lost sight of her for a few moments, then spotted her again on the level above the harbor. She ran up another set of steps to a market street above the port. It took Jack only a minute to catch up with her and follow her inside a tiny shop.

The darkness left him blind for a moment. He swept his gaze around the shop, noting colorful scarves and jewelry; but the faces were still indistinct to his sunstruck eyes. He stayed near the door, knowing he would at least block her exit.

When his eyes had adjusted, Jack saw her in the back of the store. She had covered her head with one of the scarves in the traditional Arab style, but her Caucasian features were unmistakable. He cornered her between racks of jewelry.

"Emilie!"

She turned away from him.

A smooth voice behind him startled Jack.

"I'm surprised you're still in town, Jack."

He whirled to find the double-crossing Tawny smiling across a rack of scarves. He edged to the right to block Tawny's view of Emilie. He could practically feel Emilie's eyes watching from behind.

"Didn't expect to see you, either," he said. "Why don't we take our business outside?"

Tawny chuckled. "I think I'll stay here, if you don't mind. You might decide to kidnap me or something."

Jack took a step closer to Tawny and lowered his voice. "It would serve you right after your stunt at Layna's hotel."

"You know how the game is played, Jack. Every woman for herself."

Jack lifted an eyebrow. "Guess you didn't play the game well enough, though, did you?"

Tawny's sarcastic smile turned ugly. "Paulos made it clear who had taken the statue. But you'll be glad to know I didn't tell Layna who you were."

"Of course not. You'd have to admit your part in the whole thing."

Tawny shrugged. "So you're the winner, after all." Her gaze flicked to a spot over his left shoulder. "Who's this, Jack? Your next mark?"

Jack saw Emilie beside him. He wrapped a hand around Tawny's upper arm. He'd left his gun in the car to avoid problems with customs, but it would have done little good here anyway. "Excuse us," he said to Emilie and then dragged Tawny into the street.

She twisted away from him. "Always on the job, I see."

"Listen, Tawny, I'll make you a deal. That statue's on its way to the buyer now. I've gotten my money; I'm out of it. But I'll tell you where it's headed."

Her eyes narrowed. "If I do what for you?"

Jack pointed a thumb back toward the shop. "Leave me alone here with this girl. Don't say another word to her about our—past business relationship."

"Ah, you have found something new to pursue. Or is it just someone?"

"Do we have a deal?"

A minute later, Jack reentered the shop. Tawny was gone, and it would take days before she realized he'd sent her chasing the wind. *It's the least I could do.*

He barreled toward Emilie, still waiting in the back of the shop. She turned toward him, searching his eyes, and he slowed to a stop. "Emilie, you have to believe me. I wouldn't hurt you."

Her eyes held fear. "Let me go, Jack."

"Emilie." He took two more steps toward her, until their faces were inches apart. Jack lowered his voice to a whisper. "You know how I feel."

Emilie pushed against his chest with both of her hands. "I don't know anything. Everything you've ever said to me has been a lie. How am I supposed to suddenly trust you now? That woman who was just here—I saw you with her at the restaurant. How do I know you didn't just tell her, 'You know how I feel, baby'?"

"Not everything has been a lie, Em." He touched her hair and swept the scarf away. "Not everything."

▲ ▲ ▲

Emilie wanted to believe him. She really did. His eyes were honest. She'd resisted those honest eyes all along, not wanting to trust that he was real, that the feelings they seemed to share were real. She'd turned to Sheldon's easy, transparent affection instead. *Look where that got me.*

Jack's hand lingered against her hair and then touched her face. "When I watched you in that interrogation room, answering those questions and twisting your hands together like a scared kid, all I wanted to do was rush in there and save you."

Emilie closed her eyes. "Why didn't you?"

"I was so angry. I thought you'd tricked me—that you weren't real. I didn't want to believe it, but the evidence seemed so obvious."

A couple browsing through the shop's inventory stopped to look at Emilie and Jack. Emilie lowered her face. Jack dropped his hand.

"I'm sorry, Emilie. I'm so sorry. I should have followed my instincts instead of my head." He nudged her chin up with his fingers. "Can you forgive me?"

Emilie smiled. She felt the distrust fall away. She might be sorry later; but for now, she couldn't keep her heart locked up any longer. "I forgive you."

Jack leaned toward her then, and she closed her eyes and felt his gentle kiss fall on her lips. She reached for him, but he pulled away.

"We have to go, Emilie. We have to stop Sheldon Gold."

Chapter 26

It had been a gradual awakening, this change that was taking place in Victor Herrigan. When he awoke on Monday, he felt different somehow. As if last night's complete breakdown on the beach had been a cleansing of his soul.

He had taken his time getting showered and dressed. There would be no digging today, although he did need to meet with some photographers and experts later in the morning.

What had changed? He couldn't say. But the burning, the consuming nature of his previous thoughts was gone. In his mind's eye, he saw only that little boy on the beach holding up his shell, his eyes filling with tears.

During breakfast, he searched for Margaret but didn't see her. He met with the photographers, kept his appointments, and went to lunch.

It was as if Komodo and the fake tablet had never existed. It was not a memory lapse; he just didn't care anymore. In the back of his mind, he wondered what Komodo would do when Victor didn't contact him again, but the thought barely registered.

After lunch, Victor strolled through the lobby. A student

stopped him to ask a question, and he took his time in answering, giving the student his full attention. When he saw a little boy struggling to tie his shoe while his mother talked with the desk clerk, Victor bent to help him. He realized it was almost cliché, this Scrooge-like transformation, but he didn't care. Somehow, he had released the anxiety that had plagued him. If only he could cure his physical problems so easily.

He returned to the third floor and almost knocked on Margaret's door. He was anxious to see her. Was that possible? What did he plan to say? *I'm a new man, Margaret. Let's start over.*

He decided that losing that tablet was the best thing that had ever happened to him. He went to his room and took a nap.

A knock at the door roused him from his place on the couch. He jumped to his feet and took a moment to clear his head. He opened the door to a smiling Margaret. She wore a yellow-and-red flowered dress and a straw sunhat with one yellow flower stuck in its band.

"Hello, Victor."

"Margaret!" He opened the door wider to allow her to enter.

She seemed surprised at the invitation. "I came to give you some news."

"I wanted to talk to you, too. Please, sit down." He waved a hand at the couch and chair in the sitting area.

Margaret hesitated, and a flicker of confusion crossed her face. "You want me to sit down?"

"Yes. There are things I want to say. That is, I think some things have changed."

Margaret sat on the edge of a chair and folded her hands in her lap. Victor sat across from her on the couch. "I have things to tell you, too." She smoothed her dress over her knees.

Victor waved a hand toward her. "Go ahead. You first."

She smiled. "It's about the tablet."

Victor's heart stopped and then restarted. "What do you know about the tablet?"

303

She laughed. "Probably more than you, at this point."

Victor felt the tension build in his jaw. He forced himself to unclench his teeth.

"Victor, you know Emilie and I have gotten to be friends. . . ."

"She stole the tablet."

"No! She didn't. She has proof now. And she is helping the IAA find the man who did steal it. They may have already recovered it by now!"

"Margaret, what are you talking about?"

Victor sat perfectly still as Margaret told him the story. When she ended with Jack's arrival at Haifa, he breathed again. "And you say that this Sheldon Gold has the tablet on a ship, ready to take it out of the country?"

"Yes, isn't it exciting? Jack and Emilie will stop him, though."

Victor swallowed. The tablet was back within reach. The whole thing was still workable. If the tablet were recovered, he could still connect with his buyer, make the switch. He'd be back where he started, with everything he wanted.

"Victor?" Margaret asked. "What's going on in that head?"

"Hmm?"

"Are you having one of your spells again?"

"No! No. I'm just thinking."

"What was it you wanted to tell me?"

He stood and stretched the tension from his neck. "Nothing. I mean, something, but we can talk later. There's something I need to do right now." Margaret stood, and Victor guided her to the door. "Thanks for updating me on the situation," he said. "I'll talk to you later."

"Victor, are you sure you're all right? You look—strange."

"I'm fine. Fine." He opened the door and nearly pushed her out. "I'll see you later." He closed the door on her confusion.

He would change. He really would. But later.

▲ ▲ ▲

A twilight sun glimmered across the Mediterranean Sea. The Haifa Bay was like a crescent moon, with the shoreline spreading in an arc in both directions. Far across the azure blue water, the hazy skyline of Lebanon could be seen. The port jutted into the bay like a finger pointing to the sea, with terminals and warehouses clinging to it. Half a dozen cargo ships floated in the harbor, waiting for the huge cranes to deliver their containers or relieve them of those they'd brought from distant ports.

Emilie followed Jack out of the tiny shop, down the market street, toward the harbor. They descended the steps from the street above the port and scanned the water for the *Windward*.

"Can I see the ticket again?" Emilie asked.

Jack handed her the document he'd found in Jenn's suitcase. The *Windward* was scheduled to leave the port at 10 P.M. Emilie checked her watch. It was just after eight. They had only two hours. Somewhere on that ship they'd find Sheldon Gold and the tablet. Right now, they couldn't even find the ship.

"There it is!" Jack said. He pointed toward a black-and-white cargo ship secured parallel to the dock. An enormous crane on the quay swung a wooden crate toward the deck of the ship, where dozens of other crates stood in solid rows. Jack grabbed her hand. "Let's go."

Emilie stuffed Jenn's ticket into the back pocket of her shorts. The two jogged toward the water, then followed the shoreline up to the customs terminal.

They slowed to a walk as they approached the terminal. Jack pulled out his wallet. "I'll request that customs officials take Sheldon's cargo off the ship and inspect it," Jack said. "But I have to assume he's traveling under a name we won't recognize. I'll need you to ID him for me, and then you can go."

Emilie pulled up short on the sidewalk. "Go? Where?"

"Emilie, I'd rather not have you in the area when I move in. I don't know what this guy's capable of doing."

"Forget it!" Emilie marched toward the building. "You're not getting rid of me. I'm in this until it's over!"

She heard Jack huff behind her, but he didn't argue.

Inside, Jack approached the customs desk and flipped his ID open. "I need to speak with the person in charge."

Emilie could see the dock through the glass doors. She wandered in that direction, hoping to catch a glimpse of Sheldon. Would she give it to him straight if she saw him? She'd had so many years of practice cutting herself off from people rather than solving problems. Had anything changed? Was she still the same injured little girl she once was?

The conversation behind her rose a level in volume and intensity. Emilie turned around to catch Jack's last phrase.

"You're going to be responsible for letting a national treasure be stolen from your shores!"

The customs official shook his head. "You don't even know what container we are supposed to look for. Do you know how long it takes to load all that cargo?"

"Fine," Jack said and pulled out his phone. "I'll call the IAA down here. But if they don't get here in time, we'll know who to blame." He punched in a few numbers and scowled at the unconcerned expression on the clerk's face.

Emilie returned to Jack's side. "What's going on?"

He held up one finger. "Levy. It's Jack. Yeah, I'm up here at the Haifa port, and I think I have a lead on the artifact, but they're refusing to unload any containers from a ship without the whole red-tape paperwork thing." He listened for a moment, and his expression grew darker. "Fine. Don't expect me to feel bad when that ship pulls out with the artifact on board."

He disconnected and shoved the phone back into his pocket. Jack looked at the customs official. "Your paperwork will be here as soon as possible." He turned away. "Come on, Emilie."

Emilie followed him toward the exit. "What's wrong, Jack?"

He exhaled loudly. "I'm not supposed to be here. I haven't exactly been following protocol lately. The higher-ups want me to hang around 'til they arrive to take over."

Emilie grabbed his arm. "You think they won't get here in time?"

"Probably not. But they're not willing to use me to push this thing through."

The sky was nearly dark, but on the quay and in the water, hundreds of lights illuminated ships and cranes. Even in the darkness, ships continued to be loaded and unloaded of their cargo. Jack and Emilie walked toward the *Windward*.

"What are we going to do?" Emilie asked.

"I'll have to find a way to do this myself," Jack said.

"You need my help. I know what he looks like."

"I changed my mind. I don't know how this thing will go down. You're just going to have to describe him for me."

Emilie stopped walking and put her hands on her hips. "But—"

"I'm not risking your safety, Emilie. I want you to go back to the hotel." He kept walking.

Emilie ran to catch up with him.

"Besides," he said, "you're out on bail. If you're spotted here, you'll just have more explaining to do." He turned to face her. "I'm serious, Emilie."

Emilie couldn't argue with the concern on his face. It was too nice to have someone looking out for her. She sighed. "Sheldon's in his forties, with dark hair just starting to gray. Handsome. You've seen him from a distance a couple of times."

"Yeah. That'll have to do."

"Will you call me as soon as you know anything?"

He kissed her on the cheek. "The minute the tablet's in my hands I'll let you know."

"Okay." She smiled and lifted her hand in a small wave. "See ya later."

Emilie moved toward the steps that led back to the street above.

She glanced over her shoulder. *He's still watching. Keep walking.*

Finally he quit watching. Emilie turned back toward him. From the street level, she had to squint into the fading light to follow Jack's blond hair moving through the crowd. She watched him walk past the ship. She had no idea what he'd do next. But she knew her next step.

Emilie pulled Jenn's ticket from her back pocket. Jack had probably forgotten she still had it. As soon as he was out of sight, she would put it to good use.

Jack continued up the quay away from the customs terminal. Emilie hurried back down the steps and into the building. She chose a different counter than the one where Jack had demanded service. It took only a few minutes to move through the paperwork. She carried nothing but her backpack.

Outside, Emilie headed for the ship. She kept her head down and her eyes up, hoping to avoid Jack. The crowd in the darkening harbor was easy to fade into.

The *Windward*'s white paint was flaking in spots, and the dark and choppy water splashed up at the crusty red and black stripes painted just above the waterline. The ship was longer than a football field, with rigging flying high above.

Emilie climbed a ramp and stepped onto the deck. The salty wind whipped her hair around her face and took her breath away. She hadn't been prepared for how large the ship would be. How would she find Sheldon aboard it? She walked past a three-story-high stack of red, orange, and blue shipping containers.

"Emilie!"

She turned toward the voice to find Sheldon staring at her from across the deck. His eyes widened and he took a step backward. "What are you doing here?"

"It's okay, Sheldon. I'm alone."

He angled his head and sniffed the air nonchalantly. "There's nothing you can do here, Emilie."

"I know." Emilie stepped to the rail. "I need to talk with you."

Sheldon glanced around the ship and onto the dock. Emilie followed his gaze. From the well-lighted ship it was difficult to see much on the dark quay. "Come on, where's the police?"

"No police, Sheldon. Really. I'm alone."

He shrugged and followed her to the rail.

Emilie breathed in the salty evening air and wrapped her fingers around the metal pole. "You really played me, didn't you, Sheldon?"

"It was nothing personal, Emilie. Just a job."

"I know." She lifted one shoulder and dropped it. "I was angry at first, but I understand now. I think I might have done the same thing."

Sheldon scanned the port once more. "You're nothing like me, Emilie."

"Oh, I know. I don't have the connections to pull off something like this. But there were times I was wishing I could just take that tablet myself, you know? I hate to see it in some museum."

Sheldon laughed. "Is that what you think? That I care about that old piece of clay? It's about the money, Emilie. Pure and simple."

Emilie nodded. "Yeah, I kinda figured that." She looked up into his eyes. "But listen, Sheldon. I want to help anyway." His eyes narrowed and she hurried on. "I know Jenn was helping you. But she's run into trouble. I thought—"

"What kind of trouble?"

"The IAA is on to her. They're holding her, I think."

Sheldon clenched a fist and hit it once against the rail.

"That's why I want to help you, Sheldon. I can take her place for awhile. I know it's not the same; I don't really know what I'm doing. But I'll do whatever you tell me. Just let me stay with that tablet."

Sheldon's forehead furrowed. "What help could you possibly give me?"

"I don't know. But you must need a second set of eyes or something. I'll do anything."

Sheldon clutched Emilie's elbow and pulled her around to face him. "Walk with me."

Emilie squirmed out of his grasp. "You're hurting me." She followed him into a small room filled with ropes and small machinery.

Sheldon closed the door and stood against it, trapping Emilie inside the room. "What's going on, Emilie?"

"Nothing. I just—"

"Forget it. I heard you argue too eloquently with Leon Hightower about the sanctity of every artifact to fall for this 'I want to help you' story. What are you doing here?"

Emilie sighed and closed her eyes. "They should have believed me."

"Who? Believed what?"

Emilie shook her head, eyes downcast. "The IAA. They made me do this. I told them you'd never fall for it. But they said they needed you occupied."

Sheldon's eyes were like beams of heat in the dark room. "Why?"

Emilie didn't answer.

Sheldon took a step closer. "Why?"

"They're starting a search of the boat. They got Jenn's ticket. That's how we knew where to find you. Plus, I was the only one who could tell them who you were. They forced me to play this game with you, even though I warned them it wouldn't work."

Sheldon took two steps forward and grabbed her arms again, this time squeezing harder. "Where are they now?"

"They're probably just boarding. I was supposed to get you out of the way while they searched."

Sheldon shoved her away.

Emilie rubbed her arms where his fingers had gripped her. "What are you going to do?"

"Get out of here," he said.

"What should I tell them—?"

"I don't care what you tell them! Tell them I jumped over the side. Just get out of here before I regret letting you go!"

Emilie stepped around him and opened the door. She turned back for one more look. "They're going to get you, Sheldon. And the tablet. And you deserve everything that's coming to you."

With that, she slammed the door behind her and ran across the deck. She spent a few wild seconds searching for the perfect spot and then chose a narrow opening between two ten-foot-high stacks of crates. She slipped into the crack.

She heard the door open. She counted to three, then peeked out. Sheldon had gone the other direction. She sent up a quick prayer that Sheldon wouldn't turn around and wondered if that sort of prayer was okay or not. *I'll take whatever help I can get.*

Just as she had predicted, Sheldon seemed to be heading for the cargo area here on the ship. *He must have stashed the tablet in a crate before it got loaded on board.* Emilie followed, ducking behind every crate and into every doorway she passed. He stopped once, just as she was turning a corner. She froze, held her breath, and waited; but he didn't come back for her.

By the time she caught up with Sheldon, he had a crowbar in his hand and was prying the top from a large wooden crate. She slipped around a corner and heard the splintering of wood. Footsteps thudded past. She leaned around the corner and saw Sheldon's back. He was headed her direction with a black case in one hand. Emilie followed again, but this time let a greater distance fall between them. *He's getting off the boat.*

She'd only have one shot at this. There was no way she could overpower Sheldon for the tablet. He'd outmaneuver her and be gone. She needed Jack.

The sun had long since dipped below the horizon, and the port lay in massive shadows created by the ceaseless cranes and the hulking ships they loaded. Sheldon headed for the terminal, head down. Emilie followed, searching the crowd for Jack.

Sheldon entered the terminal. Emilie watched through the glass as he pulled papers from his jacket, no doubt offering proof that he wasn't entering the country, but only temporarily disembarking. He stalked away from the desk and toward the exit.

It had to be now! Where was Jack? Emilie dashed into the terminal, determined to do it alone if she had to.

There! Jack had returned to the uncooperative clerk and was arguing his case again. Emilie ran to his side and grabbed his arm.

"Hey!" Jack pulled back. "What are you doing here?"

Emilie put her finger across her lips to shush him. "Sheldon," she whispered and pointed toward the exit. Sheldon disappeared into the darkness outside the bright terminal.

Jack's eyebrows lifted. "And the item?"

"He's carrying it."

Jack took off after Sheldon. Emilie followed.

▲ ▲ ▲

Sheldon had disappeared.

A ship's horn blared in the night air. Emilie wondered if the *Windward* was already leaving. It wouldn't matter now. She ran after Jack. Did he see Sheldon? Did he somehow sense where the man would have run?

The street level above them hummed with nighttime activity. Emilie expected Jack to take the steps, but he ran along the quay instead. There were many bright lights in the loading areas, but here overhanging ledges formed pockets of deep darkness.

And then suddenly Sheldon was in front of them, walking away. He hadn't seen them. Jack turned to search Emilie's face. She nodded and pointed.

Jack ran five steps and leaped onto Sheldon's back. The two careened into a recess.

Emilie's feet seemed to weigh hundreds of pounds. She took in the large crane lifting a container across the dock and the dockworker in a red baseball cap strapping cables to a nearby crate. The worker hadn't noticed Jack's flying tackle only thirty feet from him. The sounds of the struggle silenced abruptly.

"Emilie!" Jack's voice called her back into the darkness.

"What?"

"Come here!"

She stepped forward, biting her lip. Her eyes adjusted to the darkness, and she saw Sheldon, his arms pinned behind him.

"Emilie," Sheldon said through clenched teeth. "You have talents I didn't expect."

Jack loomed over Sheldon's shoulder and pointed to the ground with his chin. "Check the case. Make sure the tablet's okay." He twisted Sheldon's arms. "And it had better be."

Emilie watched Sheldon's eyes on her. Surprisingly, the anger there didn't bother her. She laughed. "I'm sure it's safe and sound, Jack. Sheldon was running for his life, trying to avoid the hordes of port authorities that were combing the ship for the tablet."

Jack frowned. "What port authorities?"

Emilie laughed again. "Exactly." She bent to the ground and reached for the dial lock on the case's edge. She gave Sheldon a sly smile as she spun the numbers. "Looks like I learned a thing or two from you, Sheldon. I knew you'd never believe I wanted to join you. So I faked it until you forced that confession from me. I knew if you thought you were about to get caught you'd lead me right to the tablet."

Emilie lifted the lid and spun the case toward Jack. Even in the semidarkness, the clay's edges stood out against the black foam surrounding it. "Perfect." She snapped the lid closed again, stood, and wiped the dirt off the knees of her jeans. "Now what?"

"Now this con man is going to tell us who he's working for." Jack spun Sheldon around and shoved him to the ground. Sheldon slid backward a foot until his back was against a stone wall. Jack stood in front of him, arms crossed.

Sheldon sneered at him. "I'm not saying anything. Emilie's

told me about you. You're nothing but a spoiled rich kid who never grew up. You've no idea who you're dealing with."

Jack sniffed and reached for his ID. "Little surprise info for you, Gold." He flipped his wallet open and flashed it in front of Sheldon. "Interpol, working with the IAA."

Sheldon's eyes reflected panic, then hardened into indifference. Emilie nearly laughed again.

Jack pocketed his ID. "So you can talk to me here, or you can talk to me there. Makes no difference to me."

Sheldon stood and dusted himself off. "Your backup's a little slow, then, isn't it, Cabot?"

"They'll be here."

"Not soon enough." Sheldon bent at the waist and drove forward. His head slammed Jack's chest.

"Jack!" Emilie rushed in and danced around the two. She reached for Jack but was knocked backward by an arm that shot out of the tangle. There was nothing she could do.

Jack landed a punch on Sheldon's jaw, but Sheldon bounced back and swung at Jack. His fist thumped into Jack's stomach, and Emilie heard the air whoosh from Jack's lungs. He stood quickly, ready for the next swing. Sheldon's arm shot forward, but the fist never connected. Jack grabbed Sheldon's forearm and shoved it upward. He got in another blow near Sheldon's eye. Sheldon went down.

Emilie stood only a few feet from Sheldon now. She leaned forward instinctively, searching for a way to help.

She never expected the knife. Sheldon pulled it from somewhere, his pant leg, maybe. "Jack! He's got a knife!"

She thought Sheldon would lunge upward into Jack's chest. Instead, he slid toward her, jumped to his feet, grabbed her around the waist, and pulled her back against his chest. Emilie felt the cold edge of the knife on her throat.

Jack was at least five feet away. He stood with his hands extended at his sides. "Come on now, Sheldon," Jack said. "Don't be a moron. You're looking at nothing more than attempted smuggling here. Don't turn it into something more."

Sheldon's arm tightened around Emilie's stomach. She felt her heart pounding and wondered if he could feel it, too. Jack didn't move. *Doesn't he have a gun or something? What kind of secret agent is this guy?*

"It doesn't have to turn into anything," Sheldon said. He nodded toward the black case on the ground at Jack's feet. "Slide that thing over and I'm out of here."

Jack bent and picked up the case. "Let her go and come get it."

"Yeah, right."

Emilie felt a prick at her throat. "Jack!"

"Don't move, Emilie," Jack said. "You'll be okay." He laid the case on the ground again. "Take it, Sheldon. Let her go." He nudged it with his toe and slid it across the space between them.

"Pick it up, Emilie," Sheldon said.

Emilie leaned over, waiting for the knife to pierce her skin. Her fingers scrabbled for the handle of the case and finally closed around it. She stood.

Sheldon eased his arm away from her waist but kept the knife at her throat. "Hand it to me."

She put the handle near his hand. He snatched the case from her.

Now he had them both.

Chapter 27

Thomas Fitzwater never expected to see Fadim Al-Mirabi, his contact from the clandestine alliance, in Israel. Then again, Thomas never expected to be in Israel himself. When Al-Mirabi opened the back door of Thomas's car in the dark street of Haifa, Thomas nearly choked on his cigarette.

"Mr. Al-Mirabi, what are you doing here?"

Al-Mirabi slid into the backseat beside Thomas. "We keep a careful watch on all that concerns us, Mr. Fitzwater."

"The tablet is almost safely out of the country."

"So it would seem." Al-Mirabi nodded, but kept his eyes focused through the front windshield. "However, it has come to our attention that such pieces are a particular hobby of yours."

"I have an abiding interest in ancient power, as you and the rest of our—friends—do, Mr. Al-Mirabi."

Al-Mirabi nodded again, the movement barely perceptible in the dim light of the street. "There is some concern that this piece may be too interesting for you to part with."

Thomas clenched his teeth. He lowered the car window and tossed the cigarette through it. "I don't know where you are getting your information, Al-Mirabi, but my commitment to our cause is as strong as your own. There is no collector's piece so valuable that acquiring it would be more important than the peace of the world. I have seen too much killing to sit idly by while the world is destroyed."

"You know the destruction of war." Al-Mirabi's comment was a statement, as if he had been fully briefed on Thomas's family history.

"My father, my brother, my sister. All victims of those who would enslave others."

"And so you are dedicated to our new kingdom."

It was another statement, but Thomas felt obliged to back it up. "I will do whatever it takes to see our new leader installed in his rightful place in the new kingdom of Babylon. I know as well as anyone that it is a seat of ancient power and will be once again."

"You will do whatever it takes?" Al-Mirabi repeated.

Thomas narrowed his eyes. "There is no cost too great and nothing I will not do."

Al-Mirabi nodded, then got out of the car and vanished into the night.

▲ ▲ ▲

Victor Herrigan screeched to a stop in a street above the market district in Haifa. He backed into a curbside parking spot and fumed at his incomplete information. Back in his hotel room, Margaret had only said that the tablet was on a ship in the port, nothing more.

It had taken far too long for him to get here. He had expected resistance from Komodo, even refusal. But in the end, Komodo had agreed that Victor would be a simple target if he didn't get his money. Victor convinced him that the only way he'd ever get paid was if Victor could take the forgery now.

317

Victor jumped from the car and pocketed the keys. He'd leave the fake tablet in the trunk for now. That was the safest place for it. First, he had to find the real thing.

He didn't have a plan, didn't even know what he hoped to accomplish here. He only knew that if that tablet sailed out of Haifa, he'd never have his revenge, never get the money he deserved. Thoughts of his recent revelations, his glimpse of a fresh start with Margaret, troubled the back of his mind. He ignored them.

Victor descended to the level of the markets and fought through the evening crowds. He could see several ships bobbing in the dark waters of the Mediterranean below him. He had no idea where to start.

He took the steps two at a time until he stood on the quay, watching the cranes load their cargo onto ships. From cut diamonds to high-tech equipment, to fruits and vegetables, the ships would be loaded with Israel's top exports. But where would a twenty-six-hundred-year-old clay tablet be? It suddenly seemed like a hopeless task.

Victor walked along the quay, searching for a familiar face. If he could find Emilie Nazzaro or Jack Cabot, the tablet would certainly be close. But the familiar face he saw was not the one he expected.

Above him, peering down at the harbor, stood a small, wrinkled man with chalky skin. Victor hadn't seen him in a year, but he'd know him anywhere.

Thomas Fitzwater.

Victor hurried in the opposite direction. He'd worry about Fitzwater later. A scream from the darkness jolted him. He ran toward the sound.

He recognized Emilie's profile when he neared. The man who held the knife to her throat was a stranger. But the black case in his hand was all too familiar.

Victor did the first thing that occurred to him. He yelled.

▲ ▲ ▲

Emilie heard the yell behind her but couldn't move. Not with the knife aimed at her jugular. Sheldon half turned, though. She felt his body pull away from hers. She leaned away from the knife and him. A blur of white leaped in front of her eyes and she was on the ground. Jack slammed a forearm into Sheldon's arm. The knife did a slow-motion arc through the air and clattered at Emilie's feet. She grabbed it.

Jack had backed up, but now he charged Sheldon like a bull, driving him backward, out of the darkness. Sheldon didn't drop the case. Fighting one-armed put him at a disadvantage, which he compensated for by swinging the case at Jack's head.

Emilie cringed. She feared for Jack, but she also didn't want that tablet damaged. Sheldon swung again but didn't connect.

Emilie scrambled to her feet. She realized for the first time that the distracting shout had come from Victor Herrigan. He stood off to the side, as if unwilling to risk himself in the middle of the fray. *What's he doing here?*

Jack made another run at Sheldon. Sheldon swung the case once more. This time the handle slipped from his fingers and the case sailed into the night sky.

"Jack! The tablet!" Emilie took a hesitant step forward. Jack's attention was on his struggle with Sheldon.

With a thunk, the tablet landed on top of the wooden crate suspended by a heavy cable and soaring across the quay. The red-capped crane operator didn't notice. Emilie watched, openmouthed, as the crane arm swiveled across the water, carrying its double cargo to the *Windward.*

At least it's safe from Sheldon. She glanced at Dr. Herrigan. He turned toward her, and she guessed the surprise in his eyes mirrored her own.

The brawl on the quay had drawn attention now, and Emilie

was surprised to hear sirens wailing. Emilie watched in relief as uniformed men ran from both directions toward the foursome. Jack had Sheldon pinned on the ground by the time they arrived.

Jack glanced up at Emilie and saw Dr. Herrigan. His eyebrows lifted. "Herrigan, get Emilie out of here. She doesn't need to be in the middle of this right now." Jack pulled his ID from his back pocket once more and flipped it open for the port authorities. "Relax, guys. I'm on your team."

Emilie felt Herrigan's hand close over her elbow. "Come on, Emilie."

She pulled away. "But Jack, the case is on that crate headed over to the ship! You've got to get it off!"

Jack looked at the load dangling from the crane's arm. "Right, Emilie, thanks. I'll get it. You go on."

"No, I want to stay."

Jack shook his head in her direction. "Go, Em." He caught her gaze and nodded. "I'll catch up with you after I finish here and get the tablet. It's best you go. Now."

Emilie exhaled. She hated to miss anything, but Jack was right. Questions from the police right now would only complicate things. Jack would straighten everything out; if she were lucky, she'd never see the inside of an Israeli jail again. She followed Herrigan toward the steps.

▲ ▲ ▲

"What are you doing down here, Dr. Herrigan?"

He cleared his throat. "Margaret told me what was going on. I was concerned."

"You showed up at the right time."

"Lucky break, I guess." They reached the bottom of the steps and Herrigan pointed upward. "The boss is here."

Emilie stopped, her hand on the rail. "What boss?"

"Fitzwater."

Emilie's jaw dropped. "He's here, in Israel? What's the deal? Did everybody show up to save the tablet?"

Herrigan shrugged. "I guess he came when he heard you'd been arrested."

Emilie snorted. "Probably thinking 'like father, like daughter.' "

"I never knew your father was arrested. He always seemed like a man with integrity." Dr. Herrigan leaned against the rail.

"You knew my father? I thought you'd only heard of him as the one who'd discovered the tablet."

"No, I knew him. We worked together the summer he— passed away."

Emilie continued up the stairs. "Then you know the kind of thief he was. Why shouldn't his daughter follow in his footsteps, right?"

Herrigan touched her arm. "I don't know where you've gotten your information, Emilie, but your father was no thief."

Emilie stopped, one foot on the step above her.

"That summer, he and Fitzwater argued furiously over the tablet. Fitzwater wanted to keep the find a secret, wanted to add it to his collection. Your father wouldn't allow it. When the tablet and your father disappeared at the end of the season, we all assumed he'd taken it to the government. Fitzwater was furious. I didn't hear about his death until much later."

Emilie shook her head in confusion. "But I always thought— Fitzwater said—"

"I wouldn't pay much attention to what he told you, Emilie. You can't believe that the words he says are always altogether true."

They continued up the stairs, but Emilie's head was spinning. If Herrigan were right, it threw everything she'd thought about her father into a different light.

He stopped at the top of the stairs. "Will you be okay from here, Emilie? I have something to attend to."

"Yeah. Fine. Thanks." Emilie wandered away, lost in thought.

Her father had been trying to protect the tablet? He'd felt strongly that it shouldn't be kept private, that it should have been documented properly and put into the right hands? How did that fit with what she knew?

But then, what did she know? Only the version of the truth that Fitzwater had put forth all those years ago when her father's body had been found: Tobias Nazzaro had stolen the tablet because he was obsessed with it and wanted no one else to have it. His drowning had been ruled accidental.

So what had happened to the tablet if her father had tried to save it from Fitzwater? Herrigan had said that Fitzwater was angry. Had he engineered her father's death in an attempt to get the tablet back only to lose it to the black market anyway? Was he capable of murder? If Fitzwater were responsible for her father's death and for the lie Emilie had believed all these years. . .

There was only one way to find out.

She didn't have to search far. Fitzwater's rented car stood out on the lamp-lit street like a hulking black monster compared to the shriveled man who leaned against it. His cigarette tip glowed orange in the darkness.

Cancer, my foot.

Emilie felt all the years of anger toward her father distilling into one single point of hatred for the man who casually observed her from across the street. She stalked toward the car, heedless of the traffic crossing in front of her.

"Ms. Nazzaro, nice to see you." Fitzwater nodded once and puffed his cigarette. "How do you like Israel?"

"We need to get a few things cleared up, Fitzwater."

He raised his eyebrows. "The little cat has her claws out tonight. What's wrong, Emilie? Find out you're not half the crook your father was? Didn't plan to get caught, did you?"

"Shut up, Fitzwater. I don't want to hear anything but the truth from you. You've been lying for too many years." She stepped closer, until they were inches apart.

"Lying? Why would I lie?" He lowered the cigarette and angled his head.

"You blamed my father for stealing the tablet, when he was only trying to protect it—from you. And then you had him killed!"

Fitzwater chuckled. "You're proving to be more of a problem than I'd anticipated, little Emilie." He reached into his jacket.

Emilie saw the tiny pistol in his hand. It looked like a toy, like something that would pop a flag out of its barrel.

Fitzwater's voice was low. "I assure you, Emilie, this little marvel will do plenty of damage."

"You can't shoot me in the middle of the port."

"Can't I? Look around. Who in this crowd is going to know what happened? I'll be long gone. Get in the car, Emilie."

Emilie looked around, hoping to spot Jack or even Dr. Herrigan. She was alone.

She got into the car.

▲ ▲ ▲

From his vantage point on the quay below, Jack could see Emilie approach Thomas Fitzwater and speak to him. Jack had never met Fitzwater, only seen a picture when he'd been briefed, but the guy was hard to forget.

The port authorities were doing their part in restraining Sheldon. Jack watched in satisfaction as Emilie got in Fitzwater's car. Probably best if she got out of the area completely.

A horn blared from the ship behind them. The *Windward.* It would be leaving port in just a few minutes. Jack needed to get up there and retrieve the tablet. The wooden crate had since been lowered to the ship's deck, and the crane operator was loading what appeared to be the last crate. Jack realized with a jolt that the last crate would be stacked on top of the previous one on the deck, sandwiching the tablet between them.

He turned to the officials handcuffing Sheldon, who eyed him with disgust. "You guys got this covered?"

"Yeah, we got it," one of the officials said. "Hey, is this the guy that left the body in the crate?"

"Body?"

"Yeah, that's what all the excitement's about. Crewman found a crate pried open and a body inside."

Jack shook his head. "We'll sort it out later." He checked his watch: 9:45. It had been more than an hour since Levy had promised to be there with the paperwork for customs. "Just hold onto him for now. IAA will be down to arrange custody and file formal charges."

"You'll never hold me on anything," Sheldon said. "I was just doing my job."

Jack glanced at the last wooden crate, hanging from the crane. He had maybe three minutes. "Your job? I knew you couldn't be the brains in this operation."

Sheldon laughed. "You still have no idea what's going on."

"Why don't you enlighten me?"

Sheldon lifted his chin to the street above him. "Ask him."

"Fitzwater? What's he got to do with this?"

"You expect me to do your job for you?"

"You're going down for smuggling, Gold. I'd suggest you cooperate all you can."

Sheldon's eyes narrowed. "I'm not going down without him, though."

The ship's horn blasted across the port again, a final warning before sailing. The crane operator was nearing the deck with his last piece of cargo, ready to bury the tablet. The crane operator was farther away than the tablet itself—no way to stop him in time. Jack searched the street again. Fitzwater's car was gone with Emilie inside. Time to make a choice.

▲ ▲ ▲

Emilie edged toward the door in the backseat of Fitzwater's car. The driver had already eased the car into the quiet warehouse area that lay at sea level. She had no idea where he would take them.

Fitzwater touched her arm and shook his head. "Don't do anything stupid."

"What are you going to do?"

"Where is the tablet, Emilie?"

Emilie pressed her lips together and stared at him.

He tightened his fingers around her arm. "Where is it? I know you came here to get it. I saw Sheldon Gold in custody. I want to know where it is. Does your boyfriend have it? Is that it?"

"Why are you doing this?"

"I've told you, Emilie. The tablet has healing power."

"If you're in such need of healing, why do you keep smoking? Tell me the truth, Fitzwater: You're not sick at all, are you?"

"Only sick of hearing you jabber, girl."

She shook her head. *Wrong about another one, Emilie. Way to go.* She sighed. "But I don't get it. You had access to the tablet until the end of the dig season. You didn't have to steal it."

Fitzwater half smiled and released her arm. "You have no idea of the tablet's potential, do you? Did you suppose I could be content with one healing? I must have it permanently, and I must have it deciphered."

"What then? You want to heal the world?"

"Only certain parts of the world."

Emilie frowned.

"You are naïve, little Emilie. You still believe that America is always right and its enemies are always wrong. But America is only a wayward child when compared with the ancient wisdom that still exists at the center of the world."

"Center?"

"Babylon." Fitzwater's eyes gleamed. "She is still there, you know. In the heart of Iraq, waiting. Waiting for the right person to resurrect her and make her the glorious world capital she once was."

"And you think the tablet will do this?"

"The tablet, yes. And the people it will empower."

"Empower to do what?"

He only smiled.

"Whatever it is, it will never work, Fitzwater."

"We'll see." He leaned forward toward the driver. "That's far enough, I believe. We don't want anyone stopping us to check for the little lady."

The car pulled to the side of a deserted warehouse. Emilie searched the darkness and didn't see much.

"Time to get out, Emilie."

"What are you going to do?"

Fitzwater shook his head. "I'm finding you have become as much trouble as your father was. I'll have to deal with you in the same tediously inconvenient way I dealt with him."

Emilie slapped him across the face.

Fitzwater put a wrinkled hand to his cheek and smiled. "Still the foolish child." He opened the door and tossed his cigarette onto the pavement. "Get out."

Emilie grabbed at the door handle and kicked the door open. She was outside in a heartbeat and never stopped moving. Behind her, she heard Fitzwater shout to his driver.

She pumped her arms and legs in a full-tilt sprint away from the darkened warehouse area and toward the harbor. She waited for a gunshot to end her escape.

Instead, a freight train hit her in the back. She slammed into the pavement hands first, and then her forehead hit. Through the haze she felt Fitzwater's driver climb off and jerk her back to her feet. Her head pounded, but when she put a hand to her hairline, she felt no blood. Probably a concussion.

The driver half walked, half dragged her back to the car. Fitzwater stood at the back of it, beside the open trunk. He made eye contact with his driver and twitched his head toward the trunk.

Emilie stared into the tiny, coffinlike space. "Please, Mr. Fitzwater. Please, I'll duck down inside the car. Don't make me get in there." She felt the familiar heaviness in her chest already and took a deep breath to relieve it.

"Oh, it's 'Mr. Fitzwater' now, is it? Not the face-slapping witch of just a few moments ago?"

"Please. I'm sorry. But I can't get in there. I won't be able to breathe."

"You won't be able to breathe with a bullet in your chest, either, Emilie." He nodded to the driver. "Put her in."

Emilie felt tears welling and blinked them away. She would not cry in front of this monster. She took one last deep breath. The man gripped her around the waist and tossed her in like a piece of luggage. As she lowered herself to her knees, a blinding panic gripped her. A wave of dizziness and nausea threatened. She closed her eyes, tried to think of wide-open spaces, and lay on her side.

Fitzwater slowly let the trunk lid close. The last thing Emilie saw was a pair of headlights growing brighter behind them.

▲ ▲ ▲

Victor had followed Fitzwater's car at a discreet distance; but when he saw the black vehicle ahead of him pull behind the warehouse, he slowed his own car and debated.

This is crazy. All I've got to do is wait for my chance at the tablet again and I can revive my original plan.

But then there was Emilie. He'd seen Fitzwater take her. She didn't look willing when she'd gotten into his car. And Victor was almost sure Fitzwater had been holding a gun.

Nothing was worth that sacrifice. Not even his own revenge. *There's hope for me yet. But this is my test.*

He sped up and around the corner, until his headlights illuminated Thomas Fitzwater, standing behind his car, alone. Fitzwater shielded his eyes and peered toward Victor's car.

Victor pulled over and put the car in "park" but left it running. He opened the door and stood behind it, glad for his superior position behind the lights.

"What's going on, Fitzwater? Where's Emilie Nazzaro?"

Fitzwater lowered his hand from his eyes. "Herrigan? This is no concern of yours. Get back to your dig site, doddering fool."

"I think it is my concern, Thomas. You've got Emilie Nazzaro. And I've got the tablet." Victor enjoyed the shock on the old man's face.

"You have it?"

"You know I don't care about it, not the way you do. Give me Emilie and you can do what you want with it."

Fitzwater's expression wavered, then cleared. "Bring it to me, Herrigan. You can have her."

Victor retreated behind his car, opened the trunk, and pulled the black case from inside. When he circled back, he saw Fitzwater put his hand on the trunk lid, but he couldn't stifle the pounding that reverberated from inside.

"Dr. Herrigan!" Emilie's muffled voice sounded panicked.

"You put her in the trunk, Fitzwater? What kind of animal are you? Let her out!"

"When I'm certain I have what I need." He pointed to the case. "You sure that's the tablet, Herrigan? How do I know it's not empty?"

Victor spun the dial lock—seven-eight-two—and opened the case. He turned it and lowered it to the headlight beams. "It's all there, Thomas."

Fitzwater nodded and held out his hand.

Victor closed the case and handed it across the space between them. "Now let her out of there."

Fitzwater's fingers closed around the handle of the case. "Sorry, Victor. There's too much at stake for loose ends. And I'm afraid you're just one more loose end."

The tiny gun made a surprisingly loud sound when fired.

▲ ▲ ▲

The sound of Herrigan's voice had brought Emilie to her knees in a crouch. She wedged her back against the trunk lid and pushed. It didn't move. She shifted to her back and flailed at it with her fists and feet.

Panic was taking over again. *Breathe, breathe, breathe.*

Was Dr. Herrigan giving Fitzwater the tablet? How did he get it off the ship? She breathed again. The heaviness in her chest dissipated slightly. *Let me out, let me out, let me out.* She bit her lip to keep from screaming. It was almost over. Herrigan was trading her for the tablet.

And then Emilie heard the pop of Fitzwater's gun. The trunk lid opened, the black case flew in, and the lid slammed again. It happened so fast, she only had time to begin to sit up before the lid knocked her back down. She lay on her back and put her hand over her mouth.

She was buried alive, with the cursed tablet beside her. And was Dr. Herrigan all right?

You're not buried yet. Keep your head, Em. There's plenty of air. Think of wide-open spaces.

It wasn't working. Her breath came in short, shallow gasps. Waves of dizziness rushed from her head to her feet.

She took a deeper breath, willing her brain to be steady. *Think, think, think. Forget the trunk, forget yourself. Think about what will happen if you don't do something.*

In spite of her efforts and Jack's, somehow Thomas Fitzwater had the tablet. If she didn't stop him, he'd use it to empower some crazy attempt to rule the world from Babylon. It probably wouldn't work, but people would surely die in the process.

The car was moving again. Emilie felt for the case. She would never be able to dial the right combination in the blackness of the trunk. She pushed on the clasp, just in case. It popped open.

She lay on her side and ran one hand over the tablet, remembering the first time she had touched it. So much had happened since then. Did she still believe in its power? She had so many questions that remained unanswered.

But what should she do? The only thing standing between Fitzwater and his plan was a hyperventilating graduate student locked in the trunk of a Mercedes.

What would her father have done? He had died protecting the tablet. If he were here, would he continue to protect the tablet at any cost? Or would he hear a higher calling and destroy the tablet for the sake of others?

Emilie groped around the inside of the trunk, searching for anything else that might be there. Her hand closed around something cold. She brought the object to her other hand and examined it with her fingertips. It was metal, heavy, and long. A tire iron, maybe? It didn't matter. It would serve her purpose.

She noticed vaguely that her breathing had evened out while she concentrated on the tablet. Claustrophobia was a mental thing, after all. There was no actual danger of suffocating for quite awhile. The heaviness started to return. She forced her mind back to the tablet.

It was difficult to heft the tire iron while lying on her side. She gently rested the end of it on the face of the tablet.

Can I do it?

The tablet had come to symbolize another life to her, but one she no longer believed was real. There was no supernatural connection here, only the fragments of childhood memories. Could the tablet have healing power? She was beginning to understand that no object could hold power within itself.

Still, it was precious. Filled with ancient words. *Our connection to the past. Our connection to someone unknown.*

And what would Fitzwater do when he opened the trunk and found her with the tablet in crumbled fragments?

Emilie, do you trust Me?

The words came from somewhere inside her mind, but they might as well have been audible. *This is it, isn't it, God? The big question. Can I trust You with my life? Can I trust You with my eternity?*

And then something broke within her. Something she'd been holding onto for so many years. The illusion of self-sufficiency. Just an illusion. She needed God. And she needed Jesus' death in her place to make it possible.

I believe, God. It's time to trust.

Emilie lifted the iron awkwardly with both hands. She felt tears spring to her eyes in the darkness. She smashed the iron downward onto the tablet and heard the first heartbreaking crack.

▲ ▲ ▲

Car tires squealed on the level above the dock. Yoval Levy jumped out of the driver's seat.

Jack ran for the steps, took them three at a time, and ignored Levy's stunned expression as he wrenched the car keys from his hand and jumped into the man's car. "I might need backup," he yelled as he pulled the car door closed. "Send your men after me!"

Behind and below them, the *Windward*'s horn sounded for what Jack assumed was its final call. Jack didn't look back. By now the tablet would be hidden between two huge wooden crates.

Hopefully protected, not flattened. There was nothing that could be done about it now. Somewhere ahead of him Thomas Fitzwater was speeding into the night with Emilie.

Jack accelerated through the port toward the warehouse area. He was flying blind, hoping to catch a break and spot Fitzwater's car.

He swerved around one warehouse, slammed the brakes, and barely avoided rear-ending a parked car. His headlights shone on the license plate, and he recognized it. He jerked his door open and jumped out.

"Dr. Herrigan?"

Herrigan's car was still running. Where was he?

"Victor? Can you hear me?" Jack circled to the front of the car. "Dr. Herrigan!"

The older man lay on the pavement. He groaned and moved his arm toward his head.

Jack knelt and examined the wound. "You're going to be okay, Victor. You've been shot in the side." He pulled off the denim shirt he wore over his T-shirt and pressed it against the blood. "Can you hold this here?"

"Jack," Herrigan said, his voice a harsh whisper, "Fitzwater— has Emilie. And tablet."

"The tablet's shipping out, Victor."

Herrigan shook his head. "Other one. Forgery. I—switched."

A police car swerved in behind them, its headlights flashing across them. Jack waved the officer down, pointed to Herrigan, and jumped back into Levy's car. He zoomed around Herrigan's car and began his search again.

Up ahead, taillights headed away behind another darkened warehouse. Jack floored the gas pedal and willed the car to rip through the night faster. He switched off his own headlights and watched the red taillights grow larger and larger ahead.

The driver wasn't expecting company. Jack roared past the car, swerved, and braked. The black Mercedes' tires screamed and the back end fishtailed before it came to a stop.

Jack leaped from the car. The driver's door opened on the Mercedes, too, and the guy who lumbered out looked twice Jack's size. *More bodyguard than chauffeur, I'll bet.*

In spite of the darkness behind the warehouse, Jack could see the driver was unarmed; but a moment later, he ducked back into the car from his protected position behind the open door.

Jack hurtled across the space between the two cars and threw his body against the car door. The blow shoved the driver headfirst into the car and pinned his legs. Jack rammed the door again, until the driver screamed in pain. Jack saw his hands fumbling for the glove compartment.

Jack flung the door aside. He reached in, grabbed the back of the guy's collar, and dragged him out onto the black pavement, face down. He checked the driver's hands. Still empty. He put a foot on the back of his neck, leaned into the car, and opened the glove compartment himself. A gun lay inside. He grabbed it. Thomas Fitzwater cowered in the backseat, alone.

"Don't move," Jack said to him. To the driver, he said, "Stand up. Put your hands on top of your head." He moved Fitzwater's goon toward his own car with the barrel of the gun. "Lean over the car," he said and reached into his backseat. "Put your hands behind your head."

Jack had him cuffed and in the back of his car a moment later. He returned to the Mercedes. He threw the back door open and lowered the gun toward Fitzwater's chest.

"Where's Emilie?"

Chapter 28

Emilie brushed the clay dust from her fingers. The car had stopped abruptly, and it was time to face Thomas Fitzwater with the crumbled tablet beside her. She knew he'd kill her when he saw what she'd done.

Emilie debated her best position while she waited and finally rolled to her back with the tire iron gripped in both hands. From there, she could try to jump out of the trunk as soon as it opened. If she were lucky, she'd knock someone off-balance, whack him on the head, and have a chance to run. No more fragile damsel in distress. If she died here, at least she'd go down swinging.

The minutes passed, and Emilie began to wonder if she'd been abandoned. She took a few deep breaths at that thought.

She heard the key in the lock. They were coming to execute her and drop her body into the Mediterranean. She held the tire iron ready. The trunk popped and lifted upward.

Emilie shoved it open, jumped to her feet, and raised the iron like a baseball bat.

She stood looking down on Jack's amused expression.

"Please don't."

She dropped the tire iron and grabbed his shoulder. "Get out of my way and let me out."

Jack put one hand around her waist and lifted her out. She turned and saw Thomas Fitzwater waiting beside the car. They had driven to an upper lot overlooking the port area below and bordered by a knee-high brick wall.

She smirked at Fitzwater. "Guess it's over for you in more ways than one."

Fitzwater's eyes narrowed. "They will find a way to get the tablet. With or without me, they will use its power to achieve our goals."

Emilie ran her hand along the edge of the trunk. "Afraid not, mister." She pointed into the trunk.

Fitzwater moved toward her with a wary glance at the gun in Jack's hand. He peered into the trunk, lit from within by a small bulb. Fragments of the tablet lay scattered across the gray carpet.

"What have you done, you—" Fitzwater's lips pulled back in a snarl. He took a step toward Emilie.

"Whoa, there, old man." Jack pushed a hand against Fitzwater's shoulder. Emilie glanced at Jack, who stared into the trunk, a puzzled expression on his face.

Fitzwater's snarl morphed into a hiss. "You will be punished for this."

Emilie watched as he raised his hands to the sky and threw back his head, eyes closed. A chill shook her. It was a posture familiar to her from her dreams of Babylon.

"Great gods of the night, hear my cry," he called into the night air. "Do you see what those ignorant of you have done? Do not let them go unpunished for their deeds!"

Emilie edged closer to Jack. The wind seemed to pick up, swirling in a damp chill from the water. Jack put an arm around her waist, but her unease only grew.

"Great gods, hear my cry!" Fitzwater screamed again. His eyes popped open and he jerked his chin downward to level a hateful stare at Emilie. She nearly turned away, until she saw his glance dart to someplace behind her, beside her, above her.

"Destroy them! Destroy them!" He seemed to speak to the night, but Emilie knew otherwise. Did she imagine the air grow colder around her? Fitzwater's lips worked silently. White foam flecked the corners of his mouth.

Jack lowered the gun and stepped toward him. "Let's calm down, now, buddy."

Fitzwater's right arm shot out. Bony fingers wrapped around the handle of the gun. His left arm swung upward and connected with Jack's jaw.

Emilie stepped back in shock. The superhuman blow knocked Jack off his feet. The gun was in Thomas Fitzwater's hand.

Fitzwater panted with the effort, but an evil light glinted in his eyes. He swung the gun up to point at Emilie. "Back!" he said. "Move back!"

She took a hesitant step backward, then another. Fitzwater came at her with the gun. Jack still lay on the pavement.

She checked the space behind her. Only ten feet remained between her and the edge of the knee-high wall. She couldn't be sure how far the drop to the dock below might be, but it was farther than she wanted to take a chance with.

"Keep moving!" Fitzwater waved the gun wildly.

Emilie moved backward until she stood at the edge. The eighteen-inch ledge wouldn't do much to stop her if he kept pushing. She glanced over the side. The main level of the port was at least thirty feet down.

Jack, come on. Get up!

Fitzwater jerked his chin toward her as if he expected her to just step out over the edge. He bared his teeth. "I told you there would be punishment."

Emilie didn't move.

Fitzwater lifted his free arm and clutched at her neck with cold fingers.

She clawed at his grasp. He shoved her backward.

She flailed her arms to hold her balance and in that second saw Jack get to his feet.

"Hey!"

Jack's yell startled Fitzwater. The older man pushed Emilie backward again and spun toward the shout. Emilie's calves scraped the wall. Her body leaned over the edge until her feet slipped. She heard the gun fire repeatedly. The sky rotated above her as she fell.

Oh, God, don't let him kill Jack.

Somehow her hands found the edge of the wall. Her legs dangled in thin air. She braced one arm over the edge, clutched at the bricks with the fingers of the other hand, and waited for the shooting to stop.

Her arm ached. She couldn't hang on to the edge for too long, but she didn't want to get shot climbing back up there. "Emilie!" Jack's voice filtered down. "Can you climb up?"

Fitzwater cut her off before she had a chance to answer. "I will shoot you, Ms. Nazzaro. Have no doubt. I've already wounded your boyfriend."

"Jack, I can't hold on!"

"Climb up, Em—" Jack's command was interrupted by Fitzwater's howl. The sound of scuffling feet and a groan drifted to where she hung.

Her arm cramped. If she didn't pull herself up soon, she'd drop. "Jack!"

"Trust me, Emilie!" She could hear the sound of struggle between the two men. Were they fighting over the gun?

It only took a moment of decision to trust. She heaved the other arm over the wall. Her leg came next, after a failed attempt. Then the other leg, and she was straddling the wall. She rolled off, dropped safely to the pavement, and waited for Fitzwater to start shooting.

Instead, she heard an empty click.

"Emilie," Jack said, "come over here."

She jumped to her feet and raced past Fitzwater, who stood

open-mouthed with the gun dangling from limp fingers. Another unearthly howl sounded from the man's lips, and he rushed at the two of them, the gun raised above his head.

Jack raised an arm to fend off the blow, but Fitzwater seemed to have the strength of three men. He slammed Jack's arm with the empty gun and chopped Jack's neck with his other hand. Jack crumpled to the ground.

Fitzwater studied him for a moment, then raised his eyes to stare at Emilie.

She had seen that vacant look before, in a Babylonian bed-chamber where a diviner obsessed with power had tried to kill a good man.

Fitzwater dropped the gun and took a step toward her. His fingers reached across the empty space, fluttering slightly as if to draw her in. Emilie swallowed and took a step backward. She glanced at Jack. He wasn't moving.

"I will destroy you, Emilie," Fitzwater said. His gaze never left her face.

It was all so strange and yet so familiar. The look in his eyes, the dark oppression she felt like a heavy blanket of evil. Emilie heard a word come from her mouth, but as though it were spoken from a distant place.

"No."

The word had power, power like what she'd seen in Belteshazzar's bedchamber in her vision.

Fitzwater slowed. A flicker of confusion crossed his face.

Again Emilie heard herself speaking words of power. "By the Most High God, I demand that you stop."

Fitzwater's face contorted. "You have no connection with—"

"But I do. Through Jesus."

At the name, Fitzwater stepped back as though slapped. "Do not speak that name to me."

His fear gave Emilie confidence. "You have no power over me because of Jesus Christ, Fitzwater. Leave me alone."

Fitzwater leaned toward her, his teeth bared. His rage seemed to boil just below the surface. "You have no idea what you've done, what they'll do to me."

At his feet, Jack stirred and then stood. "No one's going to do anything to you, Fitzwater," Jack said. "Except put you in prison for antiquities theft."

Fitzwater's gaze drifted back to the stars. He shook his head once, as if disagreeing with what he heard there. "No. No."

The simple word made Emilie shiver again. She got the feeling that the old man actually spoke to someone present. She looked around the deserted warehouse lot. Only the three of them stood in the darkness.

Fitzwater grabbed the sides of his head. "No! There is still time! I can find something else! Do more. . ." His steps led him away from them, though with his back to the edge of the wall, he couldn't know how close he was.

"Be careful!" Emilie reached forward.

Fitzwater seemed lost in the inaudible conversation, his lips moving, his eyes fixed on the sky. He screamed and fell to the ground. "Stop—stop—stop!" He rolled back and forth, his hands over his ears.

And then he stopped moving. Slowly, he regained his feet and raised his head to Jack and Emilie. He was so near the edge, Emilie almost reached for him, but Jack held her back.

The light in Fitzwater's eyes seemed to die, and he threw himself backward over the wall.

"No!" Emilie lunged for him, but it was too late.

The wail of a siren pierced the night air as if on cue. Flashing lights and screeching tires flooded the upper lot where Jack and Emilie still stared at the edge of the wall.

Several car doors slammed. Emilie shielded her eyes against the glare of headlights.

Levy ran forward. "Everything under control here, Jack?"

Jack released his grip on Emilie and ran a hand through his

hair. "One in there." He nodded toward Fitzwater's driver, still locked in the backseat of his car. "And one down there."

Levy cursed. "Sorry, ma'am," he said to Emilie. "Are you hurt at all?"

"I'll live."

"What's the story on Herrigan?" Jack asked.

"He'll live, too. A lady friend showed up, says she's a nurse. Bossing everybody around."

Emilie gave a half smile. "That would be Margaret. She'll take good care of him."

Jack looked toward the port. "The *Windward* sail yet?" he asked Levy.

"Yes, it's away. Why? Were you planning to leave the country?"

"You gotta pull it back in. The tablet's on it."

Emilie turned to Jack. "Jack, that's not right. I just—"

"The one you smashed was a fake," Jack said. "I think Victor Herrigan had it made. He must have planned to switch them."

Levy interjected. "Jack, that's a Greek ship. Do you know the red tape required to bring it back to port? By the time we got it authorized, the ship would be out of our jurisdiction. We'll put you and some of my men on a smaller boat and you can go out and retrieve the tablet."

Jack shook his head. "It's inaccessible without a crane, Levy. It has to be back in port where they can pull a container off of it."

Levy sighed and rolled his eyes. "Wonderful, Jack. Then it looks as though you will be baby-sitting a container ship until it pulls into its next port."

Jack grinned. "Never been on a cruise to Greece."

Levy snorted. "Get down to the dock. We'll get you out to the ship immediately." He whistled for other officers to join him in rounding up the driver. Another crew headed down to retrieve Thomas Fitzwater's body.

Emilie watched Jack's face, but he seemed to be avoiding looking at her.

"I'm sorry about everything." He leaned over and kissed her quickly on the cheek. "I wish things could be different. But you have to understand—"

Emilie nodded. "I understand."

"I don't know what will happen when this job's done—"

"Don't worry about it, Jack. I'll be fine."

And then he was gone. Emilie stood alone, in the middle of the flashing lights and shouting officers, a million miles from the private university life she'd once envisioned for her future.

Chapter 29

Five months later

A bright December sun did its best to warm Emilie's back where she stood in the Parkerwood Cemetery. The holly and poinsettia wreath in her hand poked her skin with its shiny tips of green. She laid it at the foot of the grave marker. "Merry Christmas, Dad."

The stone said nothing but "Tobias Nazzaro" and the dates of his life. She regretted not having had something more etched into the stone all those years ago. But she had been angry then. And still a child.

Things were different now. The last few months had proved that no matter how damaging one's past has been, there could be healing. As Emilie learned more about her new Father, memories of Tobias Nazzaro became more precious as well. Israel had been the beginning of truth for Emilie. Truth about her father and about God. With a foundation of truth to stand on, Emilie's life had begun to change.

Emilie looked at her watch and groaned. *One-thirty. Late again.*

With a farewell smile at her father's stone, she trotted across the cemetery to where her car was parked along the winding asphalt path.

She drove as quickly as she dared, chiding herself for the time. *Some things never change.*

It took twenty minutes to get there. She threw the car into "park," jumped out, and raced across the parking lot and into the T. G. I. Friday's.

"There she is!" A lively group waved at her from a large table across the room.

Emilie smiled and waved back. The hostess approached, but she pointed to her friends and crossed the restaurant, pulling off gloves and coat as she walked. "Sorry I'm late, guys."

"You're not late," Margo said. "We told you a half hour earlier than everyone else!"

Emilie made a face at Margo and everyone laughed. Brett Martens pulled an empty chair from another table and squeezed it in beside his own. "Join us," he said, smiling.

She slid into the chair and picked up a menu to avoid the raised eyebrows and knowing smiles from the rest of the group. "Thanks, Brett."

Rebecca Engle raised her water glass in a toast. "To four weeks of no classes."

"Here, here." The group clinked water glasses all around.

Margo leaned forward over her menu. "So who's got great holiday plans?"

Rachel Rabin pointed to Emilie. "I'll bet you've got some new adventure planned."

Emilie laughed. "Adventure? Me? Does that sound like me?"

Margo waved a finger at Emilie. "We don't know what sounds like you anymore, Em. Ever since your summer playing tomb raider—"

"I wasn't—"

"Whatever. But does everyone agree?"

Heads nodded all around.

"See? You've already decided to change your program to focus on fieldwork. What happened to teaching in some quiet New England town?"

Emilie buried her nose in her menu again. "Sometimes you have to take some chances."

The chatter around the table grew quiet, and Emilie glanced around, wondering what she'd said to shut them all up. But their eyes were focused above her head. She turned.

"Jack!"

He looked as incredible as ever, blond and tan like the Ken Doll she remembered; but the insincere smile she'd tried to break through since the first day she met him was gone.

"Hi, Emilie."

"How did you find me here?"

He grinned. "We have ways."

Margo spoke up from the other side of the table. "You going to introduce your friend, Emilie?"

Emilie pushed her chair away from the table. "I'm sorry," she said and stood beside Jack. "This is Jack—" She stumbled over "Cabot."

"Jack Cardello."

Emilie raised her eyebrows. "Really?"

"Really."

Brett Martens stood to shake Jack's hand. "Nice to meet you, Jack. You a grad student, too?"

Jack laughed. "I'd be a little out of my element in a classroom, I think."

Emilie turned to the group. "I met Jack this summer."

"Ah." The sigh of understanding seemed to come from all around the table, and suddenly all eyes were studying menus.

Jack touched her arm. "Can I speak with you, Emilie?"

She followed him silently until they stood outside in the crisp winter air.

Jack stared across the parking lot to the shopping mall across the highway. "It's been a long time."

"Hmm. How've you been?"

"Busy. They gave me another assignment right after I got to Greece. I figured after all the screwups, I'd better take it."

"I heard the tablet had been delivered safely to the Tel Aviv Museum. Did you have any trouble getting it?"

Jack shook his head, still not looking at her. "The hardest part was leaving you."

Emilie inhaled and followed his gaze. She leaned back against the cold stone pillar beside her. "I didn't think you minded."

Jack's hand found hers, and he turned her face toward his. "Emilie, I haven't been able to stop thinking about you. I wanted to call—"

Emilie smiled. "So you're between assignments now?"

Jack dropped his hand away from her face. "Vacation, actually. Long overdue. Headed for a beach in the south of France. That's why I'm here."

Emilie tilted her head and waited.

"Wanna come?" he said.

"To France?"

"It's beautiful."

"And then what?"

Jack shrugged. "I don't know." He smiled. "Trust me?"

Emilie reached her arms inside his jacket and lifted her face to meet his kiss. "Haven't I always?"

About the Author

With a rich background in drama writing, T. L. Higley released her first novel in 2002. She is a fan of fantasy and historical genres and loves to write about the unfamiliar times and places that have captivated her since childhood. Tracy makes her home in the greater Philadelphia area with her husband, a pastor of education and family ministries, and her four children. She can be found online at www.tlhigley.com.

Would you like to offer feedback on this novel?

Interested in starting a book discussion group?

Check out www.barbourpublishing.com
for a Reader Survey and Book Club Questions.